KILLER'S DOZEN

Killer's Dozen

Richard A. Lupoff

Wildside Press

2010

CONTENTS

INTRODUCTION

ED GORMAN

I. DICK LUPOFF: SCIENCE FICTION WRITER

I was one of the lucky ones. I received each issue of the legendary fanzine *Xero* as it appeared. All too soon copies became difficult to find. Today they're just about impossible to come by.

If there was such a thing as royalty in the science fiction fandom of the early 1960s then Pat and Dick Lupoff embodied it. Not only did they publish the finest fanzine of the time—and one of three or four best of all time—they were true inspirations for teenage boys and girls who wanted to publish zines of their own.

I was one of those teenagers. *Xero* was the benchmark. I had never read a zine as sophisticated and fresh as the Lupoffs were publishing. Looking back I think what made it work so well was that it acknowledged there was a world outside fandom. Bob Stewart's artwork often spoofed fandom and most of the articles were written without an undue use of fanspeak. Non-fans could enjoy the zine, too, especially some of the blistering reviews.

This was my introduction to Dick Lupoff. He published fanzines.

In 1965 he became a published and formidable author with his lengthy biography of Edgar Rice Burroughs. To me it's still the most informative and readable of all the ERB biographies. Dick's work helped bring attention back to Tarzan's creator. Thanks to Ballantine and Ace Books ERB was back big time.

I still remember the day in 1967 when I bought Dick's first novel, *One Million Centuries*. Nothing was cooler to me back then than to than to buy a novel by somebody I'd known during my fannish days. Didn't even have to be a good book. The fact that it got published was enough for me. But *One Million Centuries* was a great read and fine piece of work.

Since then I've followed Dick's writing through his science fiction and fantasy years—from Ova Hamlet through *Sacred Locomotive Flies* through *Circumpolar* and *Countersolar*—and then damned if he didn't have to go and start working my side of the street—mystery novels.

And he's done all this while remaining a genuinely nice guy. I know that kind of statement is mandatory in pieces like these. Somebody probably said the same thing about Stalin back in the day. But with Dick Lupoff it's true. He's been helping people with advice and counsel for fifty years now.

II. DICK LUPOFF: MYSTERY WRITER

The Hobart Lindsey and Marvia Plum mystery novels

"Let's take Marvia Plum first. She is an amalgam of three women whom I knew and admired at different times in my life. I drew character traits from each of them: intelligence, warmth, generosity and dedication. When I first introduced Marvia in an early draft of *The Comic Book Killer*, my agent exclaimed that she was the best thing I had ever written. She had only a small role in the novel at that point, and he demanded that I give her more to do as I revised the book. She has proven immensely popular with readers ever since, and I credit her three prototypes for her success.

"As for Hobart Lindsey—a good many people have suggested that he is Dick Lupoff. I don't see it that way and certainly didn't create him as a surrogate for myself. Hey, if I wanted to put myself into a story I'd be a baseball player or a boxer or an astronaut, not an insurance adjuster!

"But in fact I had done work similar to Lindsey's at one time in my life, and readers may indeed see something of me in him (or vice versa). Readers often see things that authors didn't realize were there, that they surely didn't consciously put there. Readers are entitled to interpret the stories using their own insights. They sometimes detect things that emerge from the author's subconscious, experience moments of revelation that are perfectly valid and may be very profound, that the author himself was quite unaware of."

Ω

The above is from an interview Dick did with the *Infinity Plus* website about his masterful mystery series featuring the quiet claims adjuster (Hobart) and his lover and fellow sleuth Marvia (making this one of the earliest series featuring an interracial romance). The books are a major contribution to the field of crime fiction.

Strange and wondrous are the worlds the two discover as they find themselves searching for killers among the fascinating but eccentric people whose passion (hell: obsession) is collecting items that can range from comic books to 1928 Duesenbergs.

If you think I'm exaggerating the "strange and wondrous" worlds Hobart and Marvia have to travel to find the culprit or culprits consider this enthusiastic review for *The Comic Book Killer*: "We meet an eccentric club that pretends it's 1929; Lindsey's mother, who has mentally blocked out all years since 1953, when her husband died; and unrepentant Nazis who decorate their outwardly normal homes with WWII memorabilia. During a '1929 gala,' a 1928 SJ Duesenberg convertible Phaeton valued at $425,000 vanishes from Oakland, California's Kleiner mansion. Lindsey rushes to the scene to question the revelers; the only witness was too drunk to accurately determine when the car drove off. Soon, rumors that the Kleiner mansion's bankrupt former owner has a fortune stashed away are linked to the car's theft; the stakes go up when the unlovable Kleiner heir is found dead, homicide detectives join the fracas and Lindsey is hit by a bullet."

Not exactly the type of people you meet at Starbuck's every morning, which is part of the charm of the series. While the books bear no obvious relationship to Rex Stout's Nero Wolfe they do effect the reader in the same way. They create worlds you want to escape into. Their worlds are a lot more fun than the one on TV every night.

Here is a list of the Lindsey and Plum books:

> *The Comic Book Killer*
> *The Classic Car Killer*
> *The Bessie Blue Killer*
> *The Sepia Siren Killer*
> *The Cover Girl Killer*
> *The Silver Chariot Killer*
> *The Radio Red Killer*
> *The Emerald Cat Killer*
> *One Murder at a Time: The Casebook of Lindsey and Plum*

III. DICK LUPOFF: WRITER

If there's one thing Dick Lupoff understands (with perverse glee) it's the sorry state of the human condition. In this collection with Lindsey and Plum as well one of Dick's other fine creations, investigator Nick Train, you'll find a wide variety of humans whose conditions leave much to be desired. (Another team of Lupoff detectives, Chase-and-Delacroix, recently had their own collection, too.)

A pit bull owner who's just as nasty as his dog.

A thief who believes his father-in-law was a real Nazi.

A dead-end boxer who has come back in a boxing movie.

A detective named Caligula Foxx who might be Nero Wolfe in drag.

A crooked corporal whose payoff is death.

Not only are the storylines original, the writing is indelibly stamped with Dick's vision and voice.

> "*The place was cool inside and it wasn't as crowded as the restaurants and saloons that pulled in tourists in the French Quarter. There was a single big room in the place, with a little office to one side and a couple of doors that must lead to the kitchen at the back. If King Arthur had a roundtable, it might have been any one of twenty or thirty tables that filled the big room. There was a bar running along the wall opposite the office, in the back half of the place. The ceiling was high, covered with patterned metal squares. Big wooden fans turned slowly above the customers' heads.*"

That's from "*You Don't Know Me, Charlie.*" I like the idea of an Arthurian roundtable in a bar.

Or how about defining a character by what he eats. This from "*Cinquefoil.*"

> "*Reuter had served the meal and Foxx and I had consumed our fill. For me, that meant a small salad, a medium-rare lamb chop with Reuter's brilliant sauce of apricot and half a dozen herbs, a roll and butter, and a cup of coffee. For Foxx, you can just multiply each item by a number anywhere from two to five, add a couple of chicken croquettes and several large ears of yellow corn, baked in the husk, liberally salted and dripping sweet butter, then top it off with three large slices of Reuter's freshly baked peach cobbler served hot and topped with raw vanilla ice cream.*"

I have to admit I have an unquenchable need for screwball comedy and farce, both of which are among the most difficult of forms to work in. Dick's story "*Triptych*" is one of the most successful blendings of the two I've ever read by anybody. And it has a Hitchcockian stinger you'll never forget. Here's a sample of miserable man and miserable wife "communicating."

He would have to prompt her, he knew. She wouldn't just come out with the story, but there would be no peace until she'd told it, so he forced himself to feign curiosity. "What did she do this time?"

"I don't suppose you've listened to the tape, Arthur, have you?"

"How could I? I just got home." He slipped out of his warm coat and hung it in the closet. He loosened his tie.

"Maybe you should hear it," Linda said, "but I was so mad, I erased it."

"Oh," Arthur grunted. What was he supposed to say to that? If he said he was pleased not to hear the tape he'd contradict her and a tirade would follow. If he agreed with her—was this a verbal trap? He decided to chance it. "That's too bad, I'd have liked to hear it."

"I'll bet you would! You just love everything about that slut, including her voice, don't you?"

Wrong!

Perfect. Dick takes two essentially comic characters and turns them into serious human beings with serious human being problems.

I could go on quoting passages from this book for many more pages to come. But that would just keep you from reading the stories yourself. And even I'm not cruel enough to do that.

So let me finish by saying that Dick's writing talents really can't be defined by the usual means. Yes, he writes science fiction. Yes, he writes fantasy. Yes, he writes mystery. But what he really writes are Lupoffs. Long, short, hilarious, whimsical, dark, mysterious—they're all Lupoffs.

In Dick's interview with *Infinity Plus* that I quoted earlier, Dick also talked about the creative process. The truth and eloquence of his explanation are typical of everything he writes.

"I've heard of something called the creative trance, and to me that's a state in which the artist becomes not a creator but a conduit for essences that exist all around us, all the time, but that are not often visible or tangible to us because they are so subtle, so elusive and evanescent.

"They're—what, ethereal forces, maybe even supernatural powers— that, if we have the strength and the courage and will to surrender ourselves to them, can take over our minds and our hands and create symphonies or sonnets."

Ω

An eleven-year-old bugler was blowing Reveille while a couple of eight-year-olds, selected for the honor of raising Old Glory, were earnestly tugging at the ropes. The rest of the camp community stood in line for the daily flag-raising ceremony, hands raised in pseudo-military salute. Counselors stood at each end of the line of city kids enjoying their annual dose of fresh air and wholesome athletics at Camp Orinsekwa for Boys, Niverville, New York.

That was when Harry Mendelssohn came charging up the long dirt track that led from the lake to the grassy mound where the flagpole stood. Not that many years past his days as an Olympic water polo star, Mendelssohn grabbed me by the elbow and dragged me away from the hundred-and-fifty or so kids and their not-much-older counselors. Harry was an exception, a muscular forty-something. I was another, almost as ancient as he was, back from the war and happy to dress in blue jeans and a tee shirt. If I never struggled into another uniform again, it would be too soon for me.

We drew up behind the headquarters cabin and Harry shook his head as if he couldn't believe what he was about to tell me. He had muscles like iron beneath a tanned skin. He was balding and wore a heavy gray moustache. He wore his customary swim trunks, lightweight jacket and moccasins.

"Nick," Harry began, "you're a cop—"

"Ex-cop," I interrupted.

"Okay. You've gotta come with me."

I started to ask why but Harry didn't wait and he didn't say another word. He hustled me back down the track he'd just climbed. When we got to the lake he pointed to a picnic table that campers used for cookouts. Someone was lying on the table. It didn't take me any time to realize that he was dead.

The male body was clad in pajamas. They were soaking wet. The feet were bare. At first I couldn't recognize the man because his forehead and in fact the whole upper half of his face was crushed in. He looked like some of the corpses I'd seen in Europe during the war.

I've seen a lot, had seen a lot as a member of New York's Finest before Pearl Harbor and as a CID—Criminal Investigation Division—military cop for next three and half years. I'd seen a lot, but I still recoiled from his one. But there was no gainsaying Harry Mendelssohn. He had me by the elbow and he dragged me over to the picnic table.

1

"Look at that, Nick." He pointed to the corpse. "I found him floating in the reeds near the canoe dock. He was face down. I pulled him out and brought him up here before I even saw—" He paused, then started again. "I'm going to get Bloom." He started back up the track. He still had the powerful lungs of an Olympic swimmer.

He didn't have to tell me what he saw.

The lower half of the face was intact. I recognized a nasty scar that I'd seen on this guy before, a scar that ran along the side of his jaw. He'd told me that he got it from a Nazi bayonet during the Battle of the Bulge. He was the counselor from Van Buren Cabin, Camp Orinsekwa's holding pen for thirteen-year-olds. Every cabin was named for a former President of the United States, starting with Washington Cabin for the youngest kids, the six-year-old innocents, and running through Taylor Cabin, for the seventeen-year-old junior criminals.

His name was Eric MacTodd, known as Scotty for his Scots origins and his rolling burr. He'd been a boxer before the war, he claimed, a tough club fighter in Edinburgh and Glasgow. After the war he'd come to America to make a new start. He was working at Camp Orinsekwa this summer, like me, one of the two token *goyim* in a summer camp for Jewish kids.

MacTodd was—had been—a talented guy. He gave boxing lessons to those kids who were interested and he doubled with Ira Rosen, the camp's theatrical producer, director, and amateur impresario, teaching comedy and music. Halfway through the summer the camp held its annual Parents' Day, and Rosen and MacTodd pulled together a wildly successful camper-and-counselor talent show. MacTodd did a Harry Lauder impression complete with sporran, kilt, and Tam o' Shanter that brought down the house.

It was cold up here at this hour of the morning. Most of the kids wore sweaters and long pants for the morning ceremony, then switched to tee shirts and shorts after breakfast. I had to show how tough I was, and I shivered, in part because a chilling breeze came off the lake and in part because of what was lying on the rough wooden table.

I made myself study MacTodd's ruined face. There was no question of who he was. We'd sat together the night before, sharing a beer and shooting the breeze with a handful of other counselors after Taps had sounded and the campers were all in bed.

Terry Aronsky was there. A journalism student from Columbia, he was the editor of the *Orinsaga*, Camp Orinsekwa's more-or-less daily mimeographed newspaper. The *Orinsaga's* single page was normally dominated by news relating to the kids—casting calls for stage productions, results of swimming tests, baseball games, tennis tournaments, track and field competitions. Some of the kids could run like the wind. Others were really strong. The *Orinsaga* kept all-time Camp Orinsekwa records for the hundred-yard dash, broad jump, javelin throw, shot put. One of this year's kids had broken the camp record for tossing that sixteen-pound iron ball.

Last night Terry had passed out advance copies of this morning's *Orinsaga*. Among the usual camp news he'd inserted a brief reminder that today, August 15, would be the first anniversary of VJ Day, the day that Japan had surrendered, ending World War Two. That meant that Morris Bloom, Camp Orinsekwa's head counselor, would be making a little speech after the flag-raising ceremony and before the kids headed to the dining hall for breakfast. And that meant that Harry Mendelssohn would find the Camp Orinsekwa community still assembled around the flagpole.

I shook my head. What had happened to MacTodd? There were some pale yellow smudges around the crushed area in his face. It looked like an impact wound. His forehead was smashed in and the bone splinters, all too visible, had punched into his brain. Whatever had struck him had clearly killed him instantly, but there was no sign of what it was.

After a few minutes I turned away from the body, gazing out over the tranquil scene of the swimming area, the diving float and the roped-off crib where pre-swimmers played and took their swimming lessons. I turned around and saw Harry Mendelsson striding down the track. Morris Bloom was puffing along, trying to keep up with Mendelssohn. Shirley Levine, the petite, businesslike camp nurse, was with them. I muttered under my breath, "Fat lot of good you can do the poor bastard, Shirley."

They halted and stared at the body. Bloom turned away, a sickened expression on his face. Levine leaned over the picnic table. She touched MacTodd's face with her fingertips, something I hadn't been able to do. "Cold," she whispered. She held up her fingers. They were smudged with yellow. She sniffed them. "Huh, paint."

Morris Bloom faced us again. He had recovered a little of his usual hearty manner. "Everyone is eating breakfast now. We'd better get up to the dining hall and put everybody on a rainy day schedule. The kids have to make their beds and clean their cabins after breakfast anyway. That'll keep them there reading comic books and writing letters home while we figure out what to do."

He started to move toward the dirt track.

3

Shirley Levine said, "I think I'd better stay here."

"There's nothing you can do," I told her. "MacTodd is way beyond anything anybody can do for him."

She nodded. "Even so," she said.

Before anyone else could move, Harry Mendelssohn said, "I'm going to stay with Shirley. Whoever did this—" He tilted his head toward the picnic table.

Bloom grunted. He started back up the track. I stuck with him. By the time we reached the dining hall the kids were well into their meal of hot oatmeal, scrambled eggs, English muffins, toast, marmalade and orange juice. There were pitchers of milk on the tables and coffee for the counselors.

There were more counselors than there were cabins, specialists in arts and crafts and theatrics who filled in supervising the kids when their regular counselors had their occasional days off. Terry Aronsky spent full-time supervising a staff of ambitious junior journalists and turning out the daily *Orinsaga* and Harry Mendelssohn's waterfront duties were expected to occupy all of his time and energy. Morris Bloom leaned over Terry Aronsky and whispered a few words. Aronsky looked astonished, then pushed his chair away from his table and left the dining hall.

Morris Bloom stationed himself on the platform in front of the tables and blew a whistle that had hung on a lanyard around his neck. The rumble and buzz of conversation and the clatter of silverware and china stopped.

I wondered what he was going to say about MacTodd but all he did was announce that the camp was on a rainy day schedule until further notice. There were some exclamations of surprise at that, not unexpected as the August sun was bright and the day had already started to warm, but Bloom refused to answer questions. Instead he strode from the platform.

A hundred fifty pre-adolescents and adolescents and college-age counselors have a monstrous cumulative appetite. The buzz of conversation resumed and they went back to their scrambled eggs and English muffins.

Morris Bloom left the platform. He headed for the back of the dining hall, took me by the elbow and steered me from the building.

Outside, the colors seemed super-intense. The green grass, deep blue sky, puffy white clouds and brilliant sun were like something out of a Technicolor movie. A couple of robins swooped overhead, circling each other in something that must have been a mating dance.

"Scotty had Van Buren," Morris Bloom said. "I had Larry Chernov from arts and crafts sit with Scotty's kids for breakfast but they're going to need somebody stronger than Chernov to get them through this. I want you to herd them back to Van Buren and settle them down."

I nodded. "You want me to tell them about Scotty?"

Bloom pursed his lips. "Maybe not."

"They're going to ask."

"Tell them he was called away."

"Won't work. These aren't little kids. They're thirteen. Isn't that a coming-of-age point for them?"

Bloom nodded. "They've all been *bar mitzvah*. They're citizens of the House of Israel."

"They'll have to know eventually, Morris. Their counselor can't just disappear. They're going to find out. Best if I tell them."

Morris Bloom studied the toes of his shoes, took a couple of steps toward the headquarters cabin, then stopped and looked back at me. "You're right, Nick. You're a cop, you understand this kind of thing."

"Ex-cop," I corrected him. I strode back into the dining hall. Some of the kids had started a song and it spread through the room as if nothing unusual had happened.

Two more weeks of vacation /
Then we go to the station /
Back to civilization /
And then we go to school!

They drew out that final *school* as if it had a dozen O's in it instead of two. Table by table as the kids finished their meal they pushed their chairs back and left the dining hall in clusters. They would head for their cabins grumbling. I hoped that Harry Mendelssohn and Shirley Levine had shown enough presence of mind to erect some kind of barrier at the head of the dirt track and close off the waterfront area. And to find something to throw over MacTodd.

I signaled Larry Chernov and he kept the thirteen-year-old Van Buren kids at their table while I pulled up a newly-vacated chair from the Jackson table and plumped myself onto it. In the rest of the room the waiters were clearing the tables. I signaled a waiter and said, "I think these kids are still hungry. Bring us another platter of eggs and muffins."

The waiter looked puzzled but he obviously knew that something strange was going on and he said Okay and disappeared into the kitchen.

Kids are kids. When they realized that I wasn't going to tell them anything, at least not yet, and Larry Chernov didn't know anything that he could tell them, they went back to their previous topic.

Baseball.

After six weeks of an eight-week camp season, I knew every one of the hundred-and-fifty kids at Camp Orinsekwa. Of the Van Buren kids, Hy Goldberg was a rabid Yankee fan and Stanley Cohen lived and died with the Dodgers. They were arguing about which team had a better outfield. The Yankees had King Kong Keller in left, Joltin' Joe DiMaggio in center, and Tommy Henrich in right. The Dodgers had Pistol Pete Reiser in left, Carl Furillo in center and Dixie Walker in right.

Benny Goodman, the Van Burens' forlorn Giants fan, tried to put in something about his favorite team but Goldberg and Cohen hooted him down. "Go play your clarinet, you goof!"

"That's just a coincidence and you know it. I'm not even related." Goodman's voice was just cracking, it alternated between a rumble and a squeal.

At that point the new round of food arrived and the kids forgot their argument and pitched into the eggs and muffins.

When we headed back across the rolling hillside to Van Buren, Larry Chernov went with us. There would be no business in the arts and crafts shed today and he needed somewhere to go. I was glad to have an ally who was old enough to shave.

I half-expected either an outbreak of roughhousing or an organized rebellion once we reached Van Buren and the spring-loaded screen door swung shut behind us, but nothing like that happened. The place looked like the basic training barracks where I'd learned to soldier back in Georgia.

All the cabins at Camp Orinsekwa were built on the same pattern. There was a small porch, a single room filled with cots and wooden cubbyholes, a partitioned-off area designed to give the counselor a slight degree of privacy, and a common bathroom. The bathroom held sinks and toilets. There was a common shower house attached to the headquarters cabin, but with twice-daily swim sessions the kids didn't need to shower often.

Construction was simple wood frame raised a few feet on a cinder block half-foundation. Overhead rafters braced the structure and the peaked roof was covered with tar-paper. The rafters, I knew, gave Morris Bloom fits. They were as tempting to campers as local women had been to GI's during the war. The little kids—say, Washington through Jefferson—couldn't climb them. And the older teenagers—Tyler through Taylor—were too sophisticated to be tempted. But from age nine through fourteen or so—Madison to Harrison—they swarmed up and played overhead like

Tarzan on jungle vines. Climbing in the rafters was strictly against Camp Orinsekwa's rules, of course, but that only made the sport more attractive.

To my surprise the kids took off their sweaters and folded them neatly, made their beds in teams of two, checked a duty roster posted outside the counselor's area, swept out the cabin and dumped the trash in a barrel on the porch.

Larry Chernov and I stared at each other. Eric MacTodd must have been a hypnotist to get a dozen thirteen-year-olds to function the way these kids did. A hypnotist, I thought, or maybe a tyrant. They had done their jobs with precision and energy, but they weren't a happy bunch, and when they were done they quieted down more than I thought was natural.

Each kid had a personal shelf above his cot, and they all had pieces of fruit that the kitchen staff distributed every day or so. Every kid but one, Mikey Nadel.

Mikey was a giant by thirteen-year-old standards. He already stood over six feet tall and must have weighed a good two-twenty. He moved slowly but I'd seen him hit a baseball past the outfield so it was lost in a field of wild grasses and never found. He held the Camp Orinsekwa shot put record, and in inter-cabin football games he protected the quarterback, his best friend Noel Epstein, from all comers.

He was sitting on his bed staring at a copy of *Green Lantern Quarterly*. I watched him for a long time. He didn't seem very interested in the story, didn't turn a page, just sat there with a blank look on his face.

I said, "Mikey, how come no grapefruit?"

He didn't respond.

"Mikey?"

He laid the copy of *Green Lantern Quarterly* on his neatly made bed and looked up at me.

"No grapefruit?" I asked.

He shook his head as if I'd asked the question in classical Greek. "Everybody has a grapefruit over his bed except you. Where's your grapefruit?"

He didn't seem to understand me. He shook his head, looking bewildered.

Larry Chernov had been watching the exchange. He joined Mikey Nadel and me. "Are you all right, Mikey?" He turned toward me. "Mikey comes into the arts and crafts shop sometimes. He's a nice boy." Then, turning back, "Do you want me to take you to the infirmary?"

I nudged Chernov and shook my head, but it was too late to stop him. And it wasn't his fault, he didn't know that Shirley Levine was at the lake with Harry Mendelssohn and the cold remains of Eric MacTodd.

Mikey seemed to understand what Chernov had asked him. "No." He shook his head. "I'm all right. I don't need to—want to—I'm just—I was just thinking, that's all. There's nothing wrong with me."

The other kids were showing some life now. Goldberg and Cohen had resumed their debate, switching their focus from outfielders to pitchers. Now Goldberg was going on about the virtues of Spud Chandler, the Yankees' great right-hander, who had won twenty games in his last pre-war season and seemed headed to another twenty-win record in this, his first full year back from the war.

Cohen conceded that Chandler was a great pitcher but he preferred Kirby Higbe of the Dodgers. "He won fifty-one games in his last three years before the war and he's better than ever now."

Poor Benny Goodman tried to get in a word for the Giants' George Bernard Koslo, a tricky left-hander, but as usual he only succeeded in getting Goldberg and Cohen to drop their differences and gang up on him.

Larry Chernov gave me a look that seemed to say that things were threatening to get out of hand, and he expected me to take charge and do something about it because he had no intention of doing it.

"Men," I said. Everybody stopped talking, dropped comic books, and looked at me. I'd used my old policeman's command voice. I hated calling on my old cop skills, I was trying to start a new life just as Eric MacTodd had been, but I kept slipping back into my old cop ways.

"Look," I said, "men," addressing this gang of thirteen-year-olds as if they were adults, "I have some bad news for you."

They shifted and rustled and waited for me to go on.

"Some really bad news."

How the hell was I going to do this? I'd told parents that their sons had been arrested, that their daughters had been raped and murdered, that their families had been wiped out in automobile crashes, but I'd never told a cabin full of kids that their counselor was dead.

There was no other way.

"Eric MacTodd is dead."

No tears, no gasps. One kid, Gerald Gold, must have been more advanced than his cabin-mates. He had outgrown comic books and moved on to pulp magazines. He picked up his copy of *Phantom Detective* and opened to his story. Another kid, Paul Abelson, reached up and took his grapefruit from its place. He started methodically peeling it.

I exchanged looks with Larry Chernov. He looked as surprised as I felt at the kids' reaction to the news that their counselor was dead. Or rather, at the lack of reaction. I could have told them that the Italian government had fallen for the third time this week and they would have shown more interest.

What the hell was wrong with them? Goldberg and Cohen had gone back to debating baseball performances with poor Benny Goodman hovering behind them. Mikey Nodel re-immersed himself in *Green Lantern Quarterly* and Gold buried his nose in *Phantom Detective*. Three or four kids were peeling and eating grapefruit.

Young Sid Metzler, a stringbean of a kid with bushy red hair and freckles, wanted to know if the scheduled volleyball game with the fourteen-year-olds from Harrison Cabin was still on. I didn't know and told him he'd just have to wait and see.

Something . . . something . . . something was tickling at the back of my brain. I came close to climbing the rafters myself, then realized that would be a bad idea. Instead I crooked a finger at Larry Chernov. We exited through the screen door.

Outside on the porch I asked Chernov if he could find a ladder and bring it back to Van Buren. He said sure and scampered away. I'd almost forgot that most of the counselors at Camp Orinsekwa weren't much older than the oldest campers. The seventeen-year-old sophisticates of Taylor Cabin.

From the end of the porch I could see the track that led down to the lake. It had been a couple of hours since Harry Mendelssohn found Eric MacTodd's body. I didn't know how he and Shirley Levine were going to deal with the cadaver, but I could see at least that they had managed to set up a token blockade consisting of a row of folding chairs from the social hall, closing off the track to the lake.

I could see a vehicle parked just outside the blockade. As I watched, Mendelssohn came swarming up the track, dragged the chairs aside, and signaled the vehicle through the opening. The vehicle was the Orinsekwa camp car, a Chevy station wagon painted in the camp colors, the metal parts of its body a forest green, the camp logo, a stylized *C-O* painted on the door in simulated gray wood. The actual wood body of the Chevy, along with the green-and-gray painted metal, was coated with yellowish dust

Okay. Somebody was acting with a modicum of intelligence. When Morris Bloom had sent Terry Aronsky scurrying from the dining hall he had told him to take the camp car into Niverville and notify the authorities of MacTodd's death. Camp Orinsekwa had no telephone connection with the outside world. Half the kids and counselors were upset at being cut off from their parents or girlfriends, the other half were relieved.

A figure in khakis and a broad-brimmed drill sergeant's style hat climbed out of the Chevy. I wondered if Aronsky had found the lawman in Niverville or if he'd had to drive on to the next bigger town, Valatie. He and Aronsky headed down the dirt track. Mendelssohn set the chair-barrier back in place. I figured that the lawman—he had to be a county sheriff's deputy in that outfit—would ask some questions and make some notes. Then they would load MacTodd into the Chevy and head for the nearest mortuary. They certainly couldn't leave a corpse in the sun, and storing MacTodd in the big refrigerator behind the dining hall was too gruesome an idea to contemplate.

Besides, where would they keep the makings for a hundred fifty campers' next few meals?

Larry Chernov came pacing over the grass, an aluminum ladder over his shoulder. I helped him muscle it through the screen door and into Van Buren Cabin. I had him help me set it up so I could climb almost to the roof. From there I would be able to look down at the upper surface of the rafters.

With Chernov steadying the ladder, I scrambled up. As I'd expected, the dust was disturbed by the passage of shorts, blue jeans and sneakers. In one corner somebody had left a stash of magazines—*Esquire, Laff, Pic, Beauty Parade.* Thirteen-year-olds are wonderful. I leaned over the partition to peer down into the counselor's cubicle like a dive-bomber pilot looking at a potential target.

There was Eric MacTodd's bed. If he'd slept in it last night, it had been carefully remade. The blanket was as taut as the one on an officer-candidate's cot, a white sheet folded down with military precision and the pillow looking as if it had never felt the weight of a head. I could see MacTodd's cubbyhole, his neatly folded changes of clothing and his toilet articles arranged in perfect order.

Nothing surprising about that. But there was a surprise for me on the rafter itself. Just over MacTodd's pillow there were some small stains on the heavy wooden surface. Little more than smudges, they would have been invisible if there had been an accumulation of dust covering them, but they were very recent and there was no dust on them yet. I touched one and looked at my fingertip. Yellow paint.

I called on Larry Chernov to run another errand for me. While he was gone I tried to make small talk with the Van Buren kids but they were reluctant to participate. I'd seen this before. In France an unpopular West Point grad had been blown up by a hand grenade somebody had booby-trapped his field pack with. I was sent in to investigate and suddenly nobody in his platoon knew anything. It was amazing.

The Van Buren kids were acting just the way that lieutenant's soldiers had acted. Gosh, nobody knew anything, they were all busy doing other things when the loot bought the farm. And none of the Van Buren kids knew anything about Eric MacTodd except he was a swell guy and he always made them toe the line on neatness and cleanliness and it was too bad he was dead but they were really looking forward to their volleyball match with the Harrison Cabin kids.

Larry Chernov stood in the screen doorway and gestured. I went outside with him and we put our heads together. What he told me was no surprise, but now I knew for sure how Eric MacTodd had been killed. And I was almost sure that I knew who had done it. Who was the only person who could have done it.

I had Chernov stand in the doorway to make sure that no one left the cabin, not that there was anywhere they could have run to here in Camp Orinsekwa's rural isolation. I went over to Mikey Nadel and put my hand on his shoulder. I tilted my head toward the counselor's cubicle and led Mikey to it. There wasn't much privacy there, but at least we weren't surrounded by the rest of the campers in the cabin.

How the hell do you start a conversation like this one?

"Why?" I asked him.

At first Mikey tried playing dumb, but I pointed up at the rafter and down at the pillow on Eric MacTodd's neatly made cot. "Did he bleed?" I asked.

No response.

"Probably not."

No response.

"Your aim must have been terrific. Either that or it was a lucky shot. No, you're too good for that. It must have been aimed."

No response.

"Mikey, don't drag this out. I know what happened and I know how you did it. Larry Chernov told me that the sixteen-pound shot is missing from the track-and-field equipment shed. And he told me that you'd been in the arts and crafts shed a few days ago working on some mysterious project involving yellow paint."

Michael Nadel looked at the floor and muttered something under his breath. I asked him to repeat it. He looked up at me and repeated what he'd said, using words and phrases that I hadn't heard outside of a foxhole in the Black Forest.

"Why, Mikey?"

The screen door slammed and I heard Larry Chernov protesting feebly. I heard footsteps crossing the bare wooden floor of the cabin. Michael Nadel startled me by picking me up and setting me aside. Man, that kid was powerful. Of course he'd been the only one strong enough to pick up a sixteen-pound iron shot and carry it up onto the rafters in the cabin. He'd painted it yellow, kept it on his shelf where it looked like a grapefruit, climbed the rafters last night after everyone including MacTodd was asleep and dropped it onto MacTodd's forehead.

Had MacTodd awakened at the last moment? Had he seen that yellow ball falling? Had he tried to dodge, to jerk his head sideways too late to avoid the sixteen-pound weight that was about to kill him? Or did he sleep peacefully, dreaming perhaps of his childhood home in Scotland, during that fraction of a second it took the shot to drop from Mikey Nadel's hand to MacTodd's skull?

Nadel rushed out of the counselor's cubicle, back toward the door of the cabin. I was fast behind him.

He skidded to a halt, facing a newcomer.

A heavy-set woman stood in the middle of the cabin, surrounded by campers, Larry Chernov hovering uncertainly behind her. She wore her gray hair in a short, severe style. Her features bore a strong resemblance to those of Mikey Nadel. She wore no makeup. Her eyebrows were heavy, wirey and gray. Her mouth was set in what looked like a perpetual frown. A flat gray hat covered the top of her head. She wore a shapeless gray dress. An ugly gray handbag hung from one arm. Her shoes were square, heavy, and graceless.

"Mama," Michael Nadel cried, "he knows I did it. Nick Train knows I killed him."

Mrs. Nadel—she had to be Mrs. Nadel—started to say something but Noel Epstein got there first. "No he didn't, Nick, I did it. I killed him."

"No!" Hy Goldberg, the Yankee fan, jumped off his cot. "He didn't. I did it."

Stanley Cohen, the Dodger fan, jumped up. "No, he didn't. I did it."

"I killed him." Benny Goodman, the Giants fan.

"I did it." Sid Metzler, the volleyball player.

"I did it."

"I did it."

In a minute there were a dozen confessed killers in the cabin.

"Mr. Train," the mother said. She reached past her son and shook my hand. "Mr. Train. Mikey wrote to me about you. I saw you, too. I saw you at the talent show on Parents' Day." She spoke with a heavy accent, a combination of German and Yiddish. I'd heard that accent before. It was common among the few German Jews who had survived Hitler's filthy work.

"You're a policeman, Mr. Train."

"Ex-policeman," I corrected.

"None of these boys killed the monster, Mr. Train. None of them. These are innocent boys, Mr. Train. My Mikey is innocent. His friend Stanley is innocent. Every one of them is innocent. I am the killer."

I shook my head. "I don't know what you're talking about, Mrs. Nadel. Besides, it's impossible. You just got here. MacTodd was murdered last night or very early this morning."

"I killed him," she insisted.

I took a step past her and looked outside. Through the screen door, past the porch of Van Buren Cabin, I could see her car. It was an old Studebaker, something out of the early 1930's, its paint job as dull and tarnished and gray as Mrs. Nadel. She had driven it across the campus, bumping up and down hills, and parked outside the cabin where her son awaited.

"Look, I'm not a police officer. That was all a long time ago. I'm just a camp counselor. I think you'd better come with me."

Larry Chernov stayed in the cabin with the dozen self-confessed murderers. I led Mrs. Nadel past a dozen kids and a young arts and crafts teacher. We crossed the wooden porch. The screen door slammed behind us. We headed toward the dirt track that slanted down to the lake. I could see that the green station wagon was gone. My guess was that somebody had been drafted to drive to Niverville, or Valatie, or Albany if need be, to deliver MacTodd's cadaver where it would receive proper care.

Shirley Levine was sitting at the picnic table. A cool one. I don't think I could have done it. The sheriff's deputy in the drill sergeant's hat was questioning Harry Mendelssohn and busily jotting notes in a flip-up pad. He was using one of those new "ball-point" pens that are supposed to write upside-down and under water. Under the brim of his hat I could see grizzled, iron-colored hair and skin that had been out in the sun for a lot of summers. The deputy was no kid. I wondered if he had been a doughboy in the war against the Kaiser.

Mrs. Nadel touched the deputy on the wrist. Harry Mendelssohn stopped talking and the deputy stopped writing.

"You can stop with the Sherlock Holmes, mister. I killed him."

The deputy looked startled. "Who are you?"

"My name is Shulamith Nadel, Mikey's mother, and I am your killer."

Still looking startled, the deputy shifted his focus to look at me. "And you, sir?"

"Train. Nicholas Train, deputy."

Something clicked. "Oh, yeah. I've heard of you. Cop, aren't you?"

"Ex-cop."

"Okay, good enough. You know the drill, Train. What's the story with this lady? What's she talking about?"

"I don't know, deputy. Maybe we'd better let her tell her story."

The deputy considered that, then agreed. "You say you killed Mister . . . uh"—he consulted his flip-up pad, "Mr. Eric MacTodd."

"Not Eric MacTodd," Mrs. Nadel said. "Erich von Todt." The way she said it, even through her mixed German-Yiddish accent, made the difference in spelling obvious.

"Not Eric MacTodd?" the deputy repeated.

"No!"

"How do you know this, Missus . . . uh"—he consulted his flip-up pad—"Mrs. Nadel?"

"I knew him in the camp. He was a captain. Hauptmann von Todt. He liked me, you know." She raised a hand and the deputy flinched. I knew the reaction. But she was only raising her hand to indicate her face. The deputy relaxed.

"I didn't always look like this," she said. A peculiar smile came and went on her face, bitter and wistful at the same time. "I was very pretty. It wasn't so long ago, only a few years ago. We change. He liked me. It was against the rules but they all did it. He had me brought to his office. He wanted me to—do things."

She paused as if she wanted someone else to speak, but no one did, not Harry Mendelssohn, nor Shirley Levine, nor I. Finally she resumed.

"I went along for a while. I hated it, I hated him, but I went along. My husband and me, we had a baby. When he was born—it was the same year the Nazis took over—we sent him to my sister in Brookline, Massachusetts. My Michael, yes. My husband was in the camp, and I was there, too. I thought, *If I go along with Herr Hauptmann von Todt he might do something for my husband.* I thought, *We can survive this, we'll do what we have to do, and the war will end, and we'll go to America.* So I went along."

She stopped and spat on the dusty earth, as if clearing her mouth of something filthy.

"Finally he asked for too much. Too much, the Herr Hauptmann. Too much. I grabbed for something. He wore a bayonet on his uniform belt. The Nazis, you know, they loved toys and trinkets and shiny things, like evil birds, like black crows. He wore a bayonet in a scabbard attached to his belt. I grabbed it. I went for him. I got him."

She stopped and gestured, drawing a blunt-tipped finger along the ridge of her jaw.

"I tried to cut his throat but I missed. I got him here. Here." She drew her fingertip along her jaw again and again. "I got him but he got me back. He had my husband brought to his office in chains, and chained to a chair. He made him watch while he did things to me. When he was finished he took the bayonet and he cut my husband. He cut him here."

She showed us where Herr Hauptmann von Todt had cut her husband.

"He made my husband watch him do things to me, and then he made me watch while he cut my husband, and while my husband died."

She smiled again, her expression a weird, humorless grimace.

"Did I tell you, I knew him before the war? Before he was Hauptmann von Todt. When he was Erich der Narr, Erich the Fool. He was a music hall entertainer. He was really quite good. He played the music halls in Berlin and München during the Weimar days. He was very funny. He knew many languages and he could do accents. *Ach*, his French, his English, his Italian. He was so funny. But then the Nazis came and he was no more Erich the Fool. And when the war came, he served his *Führer*. Oh, did he serve his *Führer*."

Shirley Levine had come over from the picnic table. She put her arms around Mrs. Nadel's shoulders and guided her back to the table. She made her slide onto a wooden bench. Mrs. Nadel couldn't have known what had lain on the table until a little while before.

The deputy heaved a sigh. He lowered himself onto the bench opposite Mrs. Nadel and laid his pad on the table. "Are you saying, ma'am, that this man, this man who died, this, ah, Eric MacTodd, was really a Nazi war criminal? That he was really Erich von Todt?"

He managed to say the German words with a fair degree of accuracy.

"Yes. He was the man. That's why I killed him. For what he did to me and what he did to my husband, and to how many others? How many others, Mr. Policeman?"

"But—everyone knows he was Scottish."

"No. He wasn't Scottish." She exhaled heavily. "He was a Nazi. He was a beast. What he got was kinder than he deserved, but it's better than

15

nothing."

"But—how do you know?"

"I saw. I was in the audience. I saw him doing his Harry Lauder act, his funny Scottish songs and jokes. It was the same act I saw him do in Berlin when he was Erich der Narr. I caught his eye when he came out to take his bow. He caught mine, too. Nobody saw, everybody was watching the stage, but he saw me. He saw me go like this."

She drew her finger along her jaw again.

"Nobody else saw. But he saw. After the show, I talked to my Michael. I told him who his Eric MacTodd really was. I told him what to do. I planned everything. I told him when to act. Today. Today. The day the war ended. This was the day to act. I wrote him letters about it, told him everything to do. You can see. I know he saves my letters. You look in his cubbyhole. You'll find my letters."

"I don't know. I don't know. It's too fantastic for me." The deputy closed his flip-pad and slipped it into his uniform shirt pocket. He screwed the cap back on his fancy "ball-point" pen. "If he was a Nazi officer how did he get to England and then to America? It doesn't make sense."

"You are such a *Narr*, Mr. Policeman. Such chaos there was in the camps, when the Allies arrived to free us. So many were dead. Such chaos there was. I know what he did. He took the clothes from a dead Jew, that's what he did. He told the soldiers he was a German Jew. They let him go. Then he got other clothes and said he was Scottish. He was a soldier, he was a prisoner of war. Now he was free and he wanted to go home. Oh, it was so easy. You don't know, you can't know, Mr. Policeman, it was so easy."

She stopped and breathed the clean air there beside the clean lake.

"I told my Michael how to make a shot look like a grapefruit. I told him how to kill the monster. I told him to throw the body in the lake. He's a big, strong boy, my Michael. And his friend, I knew his friend Noel would help him. They did it in the night. Then they went back to bed. You look in the lake, Mr. Policeman, look where the monster was thrown in. You dig around a little, you'll find a grapefruit. A sixteen-pound grapefruit."

Then I said, "But, Mrs. Nadel, I don't understand."

She turned toward me. For the first time I saw her eyes. I looked away. I said, "Everybody confessed. Everybody in Michael's cabin, I was there, they all said they had done it."

"Of course. Of course, young man." She put her hand on my wrist and smiled up at me. I looked at her again. Somewhere inside that tired, aged, tormented face I could almost see the beauty that had been there not so many years ago. Almost, but not quite.

"Of course they all did it. What happened to Michael's father, it happened to Noel's parents and his sister. It happened to Hyman Goldberg's grandparents. It happened to Benny Goodman's cousins. It happened to all of them. It happened in Auschwitz. It happened in Birkenau. It happened in Bergen-Belsen. It happened in Ukraine. It happened in Czechoslovakia. It happened to everybody. So they killed him. They all killed him. None of them killed him. None of those boys. None of them. They were all innocent tools. They were my tools. The gun does not know who it shoots. The knife does not know who it cuts. They are innocent. I killed him."

She stood up and held her hands in front of her. She knew how to hold her hands to be cuffed.

The deputy stood up. "No," he said. "No. You didn't do it. You didn't do it and those boys didn't do it. I can tell a lie when I hear it, lady. I've been a deputy far too long. I know what happened, and the truth is going into my report."

He unbuttoned the flap on his uniform shirt and took the flip-up pad from his pocket. He unscrewed the cap from his "ball-point" pen and made a note, then put the pad and pen away and buttoned the flap on his shirt.

He took Mrs. Nadel's hands in his hands and pushed them down so they hung at her sides.

"You're a liar, Mrs. Nadel, and you know that's a serious offense. It's a serious offense to lie to an officer of the law in his official capacity, but I'll overlook it this time because you're obviously upset. But I know what really happened to this fellow Scotty MacTodd."

He looked at Harry Mendelssohn and at me and at Shirley Levine, the camp nurse.

"Scotty liked a drink, didn't he?"

We looked at one another, then Shirley said, "He used to come over to the infirmary and we'd have a nightcap a couple of times a week."

"And he liked a beer or a shot of scotch sometimes at a counselors' poker game," Mendelssohn said.

I couldn't say anything, I just nodded and grunted my agreement.

"I thought so. All right, here's what happened," the deputy said. "He had a snootfull last night. That's right, isn't it, Train?"

"Yes."

"He went to bed but he couldn't sleep. Something was bothering him. So he decided to treat himself to a little midnight swim. He must have been pretty drunk to try it in his pajamas, that proves he wasn't right. He swam out to the diving float and climbed the ladder to the high board and lost his way. He turned around and dived in the wrong direction. Hit his head on the corner of the float. Poor bastard. Knocked his brains out. A fall like that will do it. Knocked his brains out and fell in the water. He didn't drown. He was dead before he ever hit the water."

He took his notebook out and looked at it for a little while and put it away again.

"Anybody have any problem with that?"

Nobody said a word.

"Okay, then. Okay. That's that. That's what my report is going to say. It was a tragic accident. Proves you shouldn't drink and dive."

He stopped and laughed at his own joke but nobody else laughed.

"All right then. That's my report, and that's what the official finding will be, or my name isn't Deputy Dougal MacDougald."

Ω

"Hey, Sarge, feel like buying a girl a drink?" He felt a soft touch on his shoulder and turned on his barstool.

He'd been nursing an Abita Wheat beer, studying himself in the backbar mirror, his image broken into vertical fragments by the fifths of whiskey and gin and cordials ranged behind the bartender in his classic white shirt and bow tie.

The soldier peering back at him between the bottles looked a lot more than four years older than he'd looked before the war, but war does that to you. He was still in his khakis, and they were still clean and pressed. The brass insignia on his shirt collar was still brightly polished, *US* on one gleaming disk, the crossed pistols of the Military Police on the other.

She had hoisted herself onto the stool next to him even though it was mid-afternoon and the Decatur Street saloon was mostly empty. She looked good. She was the first American girl he'd been close to since he'd shipped out in '42. After that it had been English birds and French mam'zels and finally German fräuleins. Of course fraternization with German civilians was forbidden, but as a college-boy buddy of his liked to say, "*Quis custodiet ipso who-gives-a-damn,* we're the cops, who's going to bust us?" But now he was back in the States at last.

She had frizzy hair, so black it was almost blue like the sexy babes in comic books, big dark eyes and bright red lipstick. She wore a satin blouse and a short skirt and she was the finest sight he'd seen in forty-eight months.

"You don't know me, do you?" she asked.

He studied her face, his own head tilted like a puzzled Airedale's. Now that she challenged him, he could have sworn that he did know her after all, but for the life of him he couldn't figure out how.

"Wait a minute." He frowned, then broke into a huge grin. "You're that WAC lieutenant. Jesus, you wouldn't give me the time of day in the ETO. What the fuck, pardon my French, loot, what the fuck are you doing here? And how did you get so . . . so . . ." he made a hopeless gesture with both hands, barely avoiding knocking over his tall beer glass.

She laughed, and he thought he'd never heard anybody laugh like that before, or maybe it was just that this was his first day back in the States and everything was new and wonderful and slightly frightening.

"Sure," he managed. "Bartender, give the lady whatever she wants."

She asked for a hurricane and the bartender set to work making it.

She said, "I'm from this town. They demob you in your home town, don't they? I thought you were from New York, Sergeant . . . Train, isn't it?"

"Nicholas Train, US14562078, except it's plain Nick now." He looked at his Elgin wristwatch. "For the past fourteen hours, fifty-three minutes and thirty seconds."

"But why New Orleans, Nick? You don't mind if I call you Nick?"

"No, no, course not." He looked into her face. Her eyes were as dark as her hair. Her skin looked like something he'd dreamed about for four years. Christ, he was feeling like a teenaged kid, something stirring in his belly or wherever.

She must have copped to what was going on inside him. "I've been home for a couple of weeks now. But you were going to tell me why you're in New Orleans."

"Typical demob SNAFU. Some hick clerk must have switched a couple of sets of orders, some other GI who was supposed to demob in New Orleans got sent to New York instead and he's probably trying to figure out where the fuck all those tall buildings came from."

"Right. And why everybody talks funny."

Had any woman ever smiled like that before?

The doors of the saloon swung open and a couple of sailors lurched into the establishment. They stood leaning on each other while their eyes adjusted to the dim lighting. Then they started toward Train and the ex-WAC.

One of them leaned over Train, "Hey, dogface, guess what, the war's over."

Train said, "I know it."

The second sailor put his hand on Train's companion's shoulder. He leaned in close to her and said something that Train couldn't make out.

The woman said, "Fuck off, swabbie."

The sailor grinned. His pal turned away from Train so the two sailors held the woman hemmed in.

Faster than Train could follow she swung a foot upward and caught one of the sailors in the crotch with a sharply-pointed pump. As he doubled over she poked two fingers at his face. Train hadn't noticed her fingernails before, bright red and long and tapered.

The sailor staggered back and tumbled over a chair, holding his crotch with one hand and his face with the other. Blood ran from his eyes.

At the same time the bartender came across the bar with a shortened baseball bat and slammed the other sailor on the skull. The sailor's white cap flew across the room and rolled to a halt.

"Okay, fellers, take it outside. We don't go for that stuff."

The second sailor staggered in a circle, then stumbled toward the bar.

Nick Train was off his stool and standing between the sailor and the woman.

"Go on," the bartender said, "out of here and take your pal with you before I call the cops."

The sailor helped his pal to his feet and they lurched out of the saloon.

"You folks all right?" the bartender asked. "Good. Sorry about that. Tell you what, next round on the house."

The woman sipped at her hurricane. Train asked her what was in it and she told him. "Light rum, dark rum, passion fruit and lime juice."

"Is it good?"

"Why do you think I'm drinking it?"

Train said, "I guess I'll stick with beer for now."

She laughed. "So here you are out of the army and in New Orleans. What are you going to do now, Nick?"

He shook his head. "Don't really know."

"You were an MP."

"Right."

"And before that?"

"Cop. I was a cop. I was a cop in New York. In Brooklyn."

"You can get the job back, can't you?"

"Yeah. Fuck. I don't think I want it."

"You could probably get a job on the force here."

"Not interested."

"You going to keep your uniform on?"

"No. I don't even have any civvies." He shook his head, took in a deep breath and let it out. "Everything I have is in here."

He tilted his head, indicating a duffel bag on the floor next to his stool.

"We better get you something more suitable to wear." She laid a coin on the bar and slid off her stool.

Train said, "You don't have to do that."

"Why not? You bought me a drink, our genial host bought me the second, least I can do is make a contribution. Besides, I still have most of my mustering-out pay."

"Yeah. Me too."

"Then come on. We'll find a department store on Canal Street and get you into something different."

They left the bar, Train carrying his duffel bag, the woman's heels clicking on the sidewalk. The late afternoon sun was still bright. The sidewalk was shaded by a wooden overhang but even so it took Train's eyes a few minutes to adjust.

The streets were getting more crowded as evening approached. Men and women, GI's and swabbies and civilians mixed. Music floated from some of the drinking and dining establishments. Kids sang and danced, upturned hats on the sidewalk for coins that passers-by tossed.

They passed a middle-aged army major walking with an overdressed woman wearing a picture hat. Train spotted the artillery insignia on the major's uniform blouse. He grinned and tossed the major a salute. The major returned it. His wife clung to his free arm, a proud look on her face.

"You didn't have to do that," Train's companion said.

"Felt like it. Probably made the bozo's day. Maybe get him laid tonight."

The woman laughed.

They found a store on Canal Street and Train bought a set of ready-to-wear civvies. He left the store wearing them. He'd packed his uniform carefully in his duffel bag in the dressing room. He made sure that nothing showed, that anybody who accidentally brushed against the duffel bag would feel nothing in it but clothing.

Outside the store, the woman said, "What now, Nick?"

"You know, you don't act the way you did in Europe. I remember we used to sit around the day room or the NCO club and talk about you WACs."

"I can guess what you had to say."

"Well, to be honest, you looked different. Hair pulled back. No make-up. And those uniforms weren't exactly designed to show off your, ah . . ."

"No, they weren't, were they? And of course army regs—I was an officer and a lady, you know. Couldn't consort with enlisted men except in the line of duty."

"But you could consort with officers."

"Per regs."

"Per regs."

"Where are you headed now?" she asked again. "You staying at a hotel?"

"I don't know where I'm staying."

"Come on and have dinner, then."

"With you?"

"Yes, with me. With me and my roomies."

"Oh."

"A whole detachment of us girls were demobbed here. Four of us decided to take a house together."

"I thought this was your home town."

"It is. But my folks are retired now. They moved to Florida, can you believe that?"

"I can believe anything."

"Marie Swanson, Cheryl Rossi, Babs Dundee, we were all together in Europe."

"I remember. We used to call you the Four—uh, I'd better not say."

"That's okay. We all knew."

"I'm sorry."

"Jesus, don't be sorry. What's the matter with you, Nick? We just came through a war. How many Germans did you kill?"

"Me? Kill Germans? Fuck, I was an MP."

"I thought everybody was infantry first, whatever else he was, second. That's what they told us."

He walked for a while, flashing on images and wiping them aside. "Yeah. I killed a few. Jesus, especially at the end. I killed a couple of krauts. They were in a foxhole and I threw an HE grenade in and got them both. Jesus, it was winter, they were hugging each other. I got a look at their faces. The grenade blew out their torsos. Their faces, they looked the same. They looked like an old man and a kid. They looked like they might be a grandpa and a grandson."

He stopped walking and dropped his duffel bag. He leaned against a concrete pilaster on the front of a building. He pressed his face against his sleeve. He felt her hand on his shoulder for the second time.

She said, "I'm sorry."

"Don't ask me again, okay? Don't the fuck ask me again, okay?"

"I won't."

"Please."

"I won't."

He picked up his duffel bag. They reached the corner of Canal Street and St. Charles Avenue.

She said, "We'll take the streetcar."

"Why?"

"It's where I live. Out past the big Jewish synagogue. It's a nice neighborhood. We rented a house, Marie and Cheryl and Babs and me. It's really nice. Cheap, too. We can afford it."

The streetcar arrived and they climbed aboard. They found seats together. Nobody looked at them. Train was relieved.

The house looked like something out of a Hollywood movie. A slanting roof and white pillars and big trees and flowers growing outside. They went inside and Train looked around. For a moment he thought it was like being in America again, and then he realized that he really was. He dropped his duffel bag and stood there crying and feeling like an idiot.

When he got control of himself he sat down on a comfortable sofa. The woman asked if he'd like a cup of tea and he said, "Yes, please," and waited while she went into the kitchen and brewed it.

He said, "What are you going to do now?"

She said, "I'm going back to college. To Tulane. I can walk there from here. Or take the streetcar. Cheryl owns a little Nash, we use that for shopping."

He said, "Did the war bother you?"

She didn't answer.

He said, "Fuck, I'm sorry, I told you not to ask me about that and I asked you. I'm sorry."

She said, "It wasn't so bad. I felt sorry for the nurses. They saw boys wounded, boys losing eyes and limbs, boys dying. Shit, Train, I just worked in an office. The worst thing I had to put up with was sex-crazed GI's."

He managed a smile. "If you knew how many guys fucked you in their dreams."

"Nick, I knew. We all knew. We used to laugh about it."

"The only one I really hated was Hamburger."

"Speak no ill of the dead."

"No?"

"No. Wait a minute. Yes. Yes, God damn the bastard, yes. Speak plenty of ill of that slob. What did he do he before the war?"

"You don't know?

"No."

The front door opened and two more women came in. They were carrying paper bags.

"Babs, Marie, this is Nick Train."

They stood in the middle of the room. "Cheryl is putting the car away. She'll be right in."

Train pushed himself to his feet. "Can I help?" He reached toward the paper sacks, saw that they were filled with food. He realized that he'd slipped back into his prewar persona, offering to help ladies with their groceries.

Babs and Marie disappeared into the kitchen, then returned empty-handed. By this time the fourth housemate, Cheryl, had entered the room.

"I remember you," Babs said. "You were an MP, right?"

Train nodded.

His companion said, "We were just talking about Captain Joseph Saint Francis Xavier Hamburger."

"Rotten bastard."

"What kind of MP were you, Nick?"

"CID."

"Criminal Investigation."

"Right."

"You ever figure out what happened to Hamburger?"

"Nope."

"You sure?"

"My boss, Lieutenant Lester —you know him?"

"I knew him."

"Figured some Nazi infiltrator got him. Why Hamburger, why the Germans wanted him, beats me. But the way he was carved up. Looked like somebody got him good and drunk and went to work on him with a carving knife. All those puncture wounds in his belly, he must have had a hard death."

"You feel sorry for him?"

The women seemed to be taking turns carrying on the conversation with Train.

"Not a bit."

"Why not?"

"Fucker. He was going to seminary before the war. Quit to join the army. Hell on wheels to the enlisted men and even to junior officers. Total fucking lickspittle to anybody higher up."

"Liked girls, did he?"

"He used to brag. Not to EM's, of course. He wouldn't give an enlisted man the time of day. But he used to drop these little snide comments, which WAC's had the nicest tits, which ones had the cutest ass, always asking, 'Wouldn't you like to sink it into that one, hey?' and he'd snicker as if he'd been fucking the whole damned WAC detachment. He . . ."

Train stopped. "Fuck, I'm sorry, it's just—you get used to—I mean, I'm sorry, I shouldn't talk like that, I'm sorry."

"It's all right." That was Marie. Or maybe Cheryl.

"He was a rapist." That was Cheryl. Or maybe Babs.

"He used to get the WACs alone and make them go down on him, or he'd fuck them. He was a big bruiser."

"I know."

"He raped me." That was Train's friend. He'd known her for a couple of hours, the others just for minutes.

25

"You bring home any war souvenirs, Nick?"

"No."

Her expression said she didn't believe him.

"Yes. I've got a Walther P38 in my duffel bag."

"Nice souvenir. We brought something."

Train's dark-haired friend crossed the room. There was a fireplace with a broad mantelpiece above it. On the wall above the mantelpiece a weapon was displayed. Train eyed it carefully. He recognized it immediately. It was a carbine, an M1, .30 caliber. It looked like a miniature version of the standard infantry rifle, the M1 Garand. The carbine even had a bayonet stud and was issued with a junior sized bayonet. Some officers carried .45 automatics, others used carbines.

"This was ours." Train's dark-haired friend pointed.

"We compared notes," Babs said. Or maybe Marie.

"We invited Captain Hamburger to a party."

"We had a bottle of whiskey there and we got him good and drunk."

"He thought it was going to be a quintet. Can you believe that? Four WAC whores and Captain Hamburger. Can you believe that?"

"You killed him," Train said.

They laughed. Four college girls. Four roommates. Four girls sharing a house just off St. Charles Avenue. Laughing and laughing.

"We have plenty of groceries," one of them said. Cheryl or Babs or Marie or Train's friend from Decatur Street, his friend from the friendly, dark bar.

"Won't you stay for dinner?"

"And after that—do you need a place to stay? We have a whole house. We have an extra bedroom."

"It'll be nice to have a man around the house."

Four girls giggled.

Ω

Private Nicholas Train was sitting on his bunk polishing his combat boots, wondering if he hadn't made a mistake when he passed up the chance for an exemption. They considered cops essential, the Selective Service Board did, and he could have filed papers and stayed out of the draft, stayed safely at home. Pounding a beat in Brooklyn wasn't exactly cherry duty, but it beat the hell out of getting shot at by the krauts or the nips and maybe coming home with some pieces missing, or maybe in a box.

But, what the hell, he hadn't liked Hitler from the start, and when his Chinese girlfriend asked him to take her to Mott Street for roast duck lo mein and he'd got an earful from her about what was going on in China he decided that the nips were no better than the Nazis.

Pearl Harbor was the last straw. He was ready to sign up the next morning but there would have been nobody to take care of his mother so he kept pounding his beat, mooning around the house when he was off duty, and taking his Chinese girlfriend to Mott Street whenever she asked him to.

Then, almost a year after Pearl Harbor, Mom died. The day after the funeral Train had dressed in civvies, put in his papers at the precinct and signed up for the United States Army.

And here he was halfway through Basic, sitting on his bed polishing his boots. Somebody had brought a portable radio into the barracks and they were playing Christmas music. A couple of guys were writing letters home. There was a lazy poker game going on, the cards smacking down and coins rattling on a foot locker. And Private Aaron Hirsch was sitting on his bunk crying.

"What's the matter with you, Jewboy?" That was Private Joseph Francis Xavier Schulte, former altar boy, former star fullback of St. Aloysius's Academy, designated barracks anti-Semite. "You got no right to cry at Christmas carols, you Christ-killer."

Hirsch jumped up. His face turned the same color as his crinkled red hair. "Shut the hell up, Saint. What I do is my business."

"Oh, listen to the little kike. Ain't you tough, Hirsch? You want some of what I gave that Jewboy halfback from Maimonides? I put that bastard in the hospital, in case you don't remember."

"*Cut it out!*"

Ah, the voice of authority. The soldier standing in the doorway wore two chevrons on his winter OD's. His olive drab uniform was neatly pressed. In it he looked like a military fashion plate compared to the trainees in their baggy fatigues. He wore a brassard around one sleeve, designating him as the corporal of the guard.

"Hey, Pops!" He pointed a finger at Train. "Grab your piece and report to the company office. Captain Coughlin wants to see you."

"Me?"

"Yeah, you."

"Captain Coffin?"

"Very funny. Don't let him hear you call him that."

"What's he want me for?" This had to be something serious. If it wasn't, Corporal Bowden would have handled it himself, or at most Sergeant Dillard. The company first sergeant was as close to God as they ever saw, most days. Officers were some kind of exotic creatures who kept to themselves and spoke to the GI's only through sergeants and corporals.

"Christ, Pops, how the hell do I know?" Bowden took a few steps and clicked the portable radio into silence. "Hey, it's Saturday morning. You guys get a few hours off to polish your gear and get your letters written. What's this?"

He picked up the playing cards and the cash that was laid out on a foot locker between two cots. "You guys know there's no gambling allowed in the barracks. And it's payday. How do you have any mazuma left to play for? Now I have to confiscate this evidence." He stuffed the cards in one pocket and the money in another. "I don't know, I don't know, how are we ever going to make soldiers out of you sad sacks?"

Nick Train had shoved his feet into his boots and tucked his fatigue jacket into his trousers. "Coughlin really wants to see me, Bowden?"

"No, I'm just trying to ruin your Saturday. Of course he wants to see you."

"No idea why?"

"Nope."

Train smoothed out the blankets on his bunk, took his Garand rifle down from the rack near the barracks door and headed out into the wintry Georgia air. For a December morning the day wasn't too cold, certainly no colder than Train was used to in Brooklyn. The sky was clear and sparkling and the sun was a brilliant disk. There were a few patches of snow still on the ground. The last snowfall had been three days ago. Train held his rifle at port arms and quick-timed across the company area toward the office.

The building behind him was new construction, whitewashed wooden walls under a green tar-paper roof. It would probably be hot as blazes in the summer but he wouldn't know that. It was definitely freezing cold in the winter.

First Sergeant Dillard was working at his desk in the company office. He looked up when Train arrived, then back at his paperwork. He didn't say anything, didn't indicate why Train had been summoned.

Train stood at attention facing the First Sergeant's desk.

After a while, Dillard looked up again and grunted. "Go back to the door and knock the snow off your boots. What kind of pigsty do you think this is?"

Train complied. Then he returned to stand in front of Dillard, his Garand at his side, butt on the linoleum floor beside his polished boot.

"Captain Coughlin wants to see you, Train."

"Corporal Bowden told me. What's it's about, Sarge?"

"Sergeant."

"Sorry. Sergeant."

"I don't know." First Sergeant Martin Dillard shook his head. "I don't know, but it's something big. He's got Lieutenant McWilliams in there with him. And I heard some walloping a while ago." He shook his head again. "Just go knock on the door, Train, and maybe say a prayer while you're at it."

Lieutenant Phillips McWilliams opened the door to the captain's office when Train knocked. McWilliams was gussied up in officer's dark greens, the silver bars shining on his shoulder straps like miniature neon bulbs, the US insignia and crossed rifles of the infantry on his lapels polished to a sheen. He even affected the Sam Browne belt that every other officer Train knew had abandoned.

Train almost expected him to be wearing a parade ground saber with his uniform, but he wasn't. Instead, there was a holster hooked to his uniform belt, the regulation holster issued to officers along with their .45 caliber Colt automatics.

The lieutenant jerked his head toward Captain Samuel Coughlin's desk.

Train crossed the room, halted, thumped his rifle butt on the floor and executed a sharp rifle salute, the way he'd been taught a few weeks ago.

Captain Coughlin bounced his forefinger off his right eyebrow, then folded his hands in front of him on his desk. Even in December he sat in his shirtsleeves, his uniform jacket with the railroad tracks on the shoulders on a nearby hanger. Train had never been in the captain's office before. He kept his posture but even so he was able to see the pictures on the freshly whitewashed wall behind the captain. There was a standard shot of President Roosevelt, one of old General Pershing and one of

General Marshall, and a blow-up that must have been made in France during the First World War. It showed a very young Samuel Coughlin standing rigidly while an officer who had to be Douglas MacArthur himself pinned a medal on his khaki tunic.

There was a fire axe on Captain Coughlin's desk. Behind him, Train saw another doorway. The door-frame and the door had been damaged, Train guessed, by the fire-axe.

"They call you Pops, don't they?" Captain Coughlin asked.

Train said, "Yes, sir."

"Why is that?"

"They're mostly kids, sir. All of them, in fact. Seventeen, eighteen, nineteen years old. I guess Hirsch is a little older, maybe twenty. They think I'm an old man."

"How old are you, Train?"

"I'm twenty-four, sir."

"Used to be a police officer, did you?"

Captain Coughlin knew damned well that Train used to be a police office. He knew how old he was, knew everything else that was in Train's 201 file, the personnel folder that every man Jack in the Army had. Still, he answered.

"Yes, sir."

"Twenty-four." The Captain smiled sadly. "Twenty-four and they call you Pops. Well, I guess we did the same thing in '18." The Captain's face was leathery and etched with lines, his hair graying at the temples.

Captain Coughlin jerked his thumb in the direction of the damaged doorway. "Do you know what's in there, Train?"

"No, sir."

"It's the company safe room. We keep classified information locked up in there. What passes for classified information in this kindergarten. We also put the payroll in there the night before payday."

Captain Coughlin pushed himself back from his desk and stood up. He moved toward the damaged doorway. "Take a look, soldier. Go ahead in there."

It was only a few steps. Once inside the safe room Train stopped. The safe door hung open. Train couldn't tell what if anything was inside. A coffee mug stood on top of the safe. Corporal Miller, the company pay clerk, sat beside it in a battered wicker chair. His arms hung over the arms of the chair, almost but not quite dragging on the linoleum. His head was canted to one side. His hair was matted with blood. He wasn't moving, and Train had seen enough bodies in the line of duty as a cop to know that he was dead.

Even so, he flashed an inquiry to the Captain, got a suggestion of a nod in return, then felt the side of Miller's neck, searching for a pulse. There was no pulse. The body was cold. There were no windows in the room. Most of the light came from a shaded fixture hanging by a long cord from the ceiling, casting macabre shadows on Miller's face. A little more light filtered through the open doorway from the Captain's office.

Train turned around. Captain Coughlin was standing with his fists balled and balanced on his hips. "Poor fellow," Coughlin murmured. "He was one of our good boys, you know. Religious as all get-out. Chapel every Sunday. Rosary in his pocket, Missal in his foot-locker. Poor bastard."

Coughlin didn't use strong language very often.

Lieutenant McWilliams stood in the doorway, looking like a photographer's model.

Turning back to Corporal Miller, Train observed that Miller, too, had been issued a forty-five. The holster hung from Miller's belt, the butt of the automatic visible from where Train stood.

"I should probably call the Provost Marshal right now," Captain Coughlin announced. "It's his business eventually, in any case. But they're looking to put me out to pasture. I shouldn't tell you this, Train, I wouldn't tell it to any of the kids in this outfit, but I'm going to rely on your maturity. If I turn up with a dead payroll clerk and an empty safe, they'll decide I can't cut it any more and I'm out of here on a pension. Not for me, Sunny Jim! Not with a big war going on."

He walked around the safe and the wicker chair with its motionless occupant. "No, sir, not for Samuel Coughlin, USA. If we can solve this thing and present a solution to the Provost Marshal instead of a mystery, I just might get out of this kindergarten and got a chance to do some fighting before I'm through."

"I don't know if that's wise, Captain."

Lieutenant McWilliams had a cultured voice. He was the opposite of the Captain.

Train knew—everybody in the unit knew—that Coughlin was a mustang. He'd been an enlisted man in the First World War, earned a commission and spent the Roaring Twenties and the Depression years soldiering at backwoods Army posts. Now he was overage in grade and hanging on by his fingernails.

But McWilliams was the scion of a high society family. Barracks rumors claimed that his mother had wanted him to live out her own thwarted ambitions, to become a great and famous botanist. Either that, or enter the priesthood. Or both, like old Gregor Mendel. Instead, Old Man McWilliams was delighted when Junior opted for the United States Military Academy. All it took was a couple of phone calls and a generous campaign contribution to a United States Senator, and young McWilliams was in. And he'd done his daddy proud. Cadet Captain, top ten per cent in his class, starting quarterback on the Army football team until a knee injury sidelined him for his senior season. And that might have been a blessing in disguise. The team had played badly and wound up the season losing the Army-Navy game for the third year in a row. At least Phillips McWilliams wouldn't be tarred with that loss. And the 1942 football season hadn't been much better, ending with another loss to Navy, a disgraceful fourteen-nothing shellacking.

But now Phillips McWilliams was a First Lieutenant in the United States Army, executive officer of a training company at the Infantry School with a glittering future before him and only a careworn middle-aged Captain to climb over—at least for the moment. As an officer his duties weren't too rigorous. Train knew that. The ordinary GI's knew more about the lives of officers than the other way around. The people on the bottom always knew more about the people on top. That was one of life's constants. The trainees knew that Lieutenant McWilliams drove a shiny new Packard convertible, one of the last to roll off the line before the factory switched to war production, and he used it to cruise down broad Lumpkin Boulevard to Columbus or across the Chattahoochee River into Phenix City, Alabama, for a night of drinking and gambling and whoring pretty much whenever he felt like it.

McWilliams's Packard was just one car that all the trainees recognized. All the officers and NCO's in the permanent party had cars: Captain Coughlin's gray Plymouth, Sergeant Dillard's battered Ford station wagon, Corporal Miller's little green Nash. They all bore Fort Benning tags, blue for the officers, red for the NCO's, all carefully logged in or out every time they passed through the post gatehouse.

Captain Coughlin was talking again. Train snapped back to the moment. To the—he grinned inwardly—crime scene. "The First Sergeant called me this morning," he said. "Told me that he couldn't get a rise out of Miller. Corporal had spent the night in the safe room, same as every month the night before payday."

The Captain paused. The room was silent. A platoon of officer candidates passed by outside. Train could hear their boots crashing on the frozen Georgia soil, hear them singing the unofficial Fort Benning Infantry School song.

High above the Chattahoochee/
Near the Upatois/
Stands our dear old alma mater/
Benning's School for Boys.

They were past the company office now, their voices growing fainter. But Train knew the song, as well.

Forward ever, backward never/
Follow me and die/
To the ports of embarkation/
Kiss your ass good-bye!

"Safe room door is secured with a hasp and padlock inside and out," Captain Coughlin resumed. "Not exactly Fort Knox, is it, but it's the best Uncle gives us to work with. Miller locked his side, I personally locked the outside. Sergeant Dillard, Lieutenant McWilliams and I all have keys to the outside lock, but that wouldn't get us in if Miller didn't open his. You see?"

Train grunted, then remembered himself and replied, "Yes, sir."

"That's why we had to use the fire-axe." Lieutenant McWilliams sounded as if he disapproved of the whole proceeding.

Train knew the type. It was all beneath him. All beneath Mister Phillips Anderson McWilliams of the Newport and Palm Beach McWilliamses.

Captain Coughlin grasped Train's bicep. The touch came as a shock. Officers didn't touch enlisted men. They might become contaminated. Coughlin's grasp was remarkably powerful. His fingertips dug into Train's arm.

"What are you doing in this outfit anyway, Train?" He released Train's arm, stood eye-to-eye with him. Train was taller by four inches easily but he felt no advantage in facing this older man. "Why are you here? Why didn't you apply for a commission? You ought to be in CID."

"Criminal Investigation Division? Me, Captain?"

"I said that, didn't I?"

"Yes, sir. I . . . I just have to get through Basic first, don't I?"

"Course you do. All right. Look, I'm calling on your skills, soldier. You know how to deal with a crime scene. You know how to conduct an investigation."

"Sir." Lieutenant McWilliams interrupted. "Sir, you're risking big trouble, sir. This is against regulations. Don't you want me to call the Provost Marshal? I really think that would be best, sir."

Captain Coughlin said, "Train, I want you to get to work on this. I'm relieving you of your other duties. You don't need the training anyway, you know everything a soldier needs to know."

After another silence Coughlin asked, "What do you need, Train?"

"I don't suppose you could get me an evidence kit, sir?"

"I'd have to get it from the Provost Marshal. The jig would be up."

Train pursed his lips. He crossed the room, stood near one wall. He touched his fingers gingerly to the thin structure, then examined them. Fresh whitewash. He laid his rifle carefully on the floor, bolt lever upward. He went back to the doorway and examined the splintered wood.

"Who did this?" he asked.

"Sergeant Dillard."

"Did you see him do it?"

"McWilliams and I were both witnesses."

"What time was that?"

"McWilliams and I had breakfast together at the mess hall. Sergeant Dillard came pounding in there to get us." He looked at Lieutenant McWilliams.

The younger officer said, "We ate at 0530 hours, Train. We were finishing our meal at approximately 0555 hours when Sergeant Dillard arrived. He was out of breath, seemed upset."

Captain Coughlin grunted. "Go on, McWilliams."

The Lieutenant looked annoyed. For a moment Train was puzzled as to the reason, then he realized that Captain Coughlin had called him McWilliams, not Lieutenant McWilliams. Train held back a smile.

"We came through the day room, saw the lock was open from the outside. We tried to raise Miller but we couldn't. So the Captain had Sergeant Dillard used the fire axe."

"And this room—?" Train inquired.

"What about this room?"

"Did you touch anything? Move anything? Sir?"

McWilliams said, "Nothing."

Train stationed himself just inside the doorway, studying the damaged wood and the area around it. The walls themselves were made of thin plasterboard. They had been recently whitewashed. Train bent closer to the door-jamb. He studied the wood and the adjacent plasterboard. He didn't say anything.

Behind him, Lieutenant McWilliams said, "Aren't you even going to look at the corpse, Private?"

Train turned back, made what might have been an almost imperceptible bow to McWilliams, then addressed Captain Coughlin. "I'd like to be alone at the crime scene, sir. If that's possible, please. I know, well, normally in police work there are a lot of professionals present. Photographers, fingerprint men, coroner's people, detectives. I'm not a detective myself, sir, but I've been at a lot of crime scenes and I was hoping for a promotion to detective. But we don't have those professionals here, so if I might, sir, I'd like to be alone in this room."

"Not possible!" McWilliams sounded furious. "This . . . this buck private, this plain GI . . . just because he used to be a flatfoot pounding a beat, wants to act like a big shot and order us around, Captain? Who does he think he is? He belongs back in his barracks, the Provost Marshal should be in charge."

Captain Coughlin let out a sigh. "Just go and—I tell you what, Lieutenant, scamper over to the mess hall and get us some coffee, will you?"

"I'll have Sergeant Dillard send a man."

"No, McWilliams, you go yourself."

This time Train couldn't restrain his grin. The Lieutenant looked as if Captain Coughlin had asked him to march around the parade ground in his skivvies. The air in the room was so full of tension you could have picked it up on a Zenith radio. But at last the Lieutenant took his leave.

Captain Coughlin said, "Train, I'll be in my office. You call me if you need anything, otherwise just come on out when you finish in here."

Captain Coughlin winked at Private Train. Yes, he did, he actually winked at the buck private. Then he left the safe room. He stopped and drew the damaged door shut behind him, the hole that the fire axe had gouged out admitting light from the outer room.

Train took one more, confirming look at the splintered wood and the adjacent plasterboard. The whitewash was recent enough to show traces of fingers dragging vertically on the door-jamb, then sliding horizontally onto the plasterboard.

Returning to the corpse, Train knelt and examined the two cold hands, first one and then the other. As he'd already noted, the fingertips were white. He lifted them and sniffed. There was whitewash on them.

He studied the wound on the side of Miller's head, feeling through the bloodied hair to try and determine whether the skull was damaged. It didn't seem to be. He scuttled across the linoleum and returned with his rifle. He stood over the body, holding the weapon so that its butt-plate was adjacent to the wound. He walked around the body and tried again, from behind.

It didn't fit. Miller had been hit with something smaller than a rifle butt.

Train studied the safe. He wasn't an expert safe man, he didn't know very much about locks, but there was no evidence that the safe had been forced or blown open. If it had been, there would surely have been some reaction to the blast. Who had the combination of the safe? He'd have to find out.

In any case, Sergeant Dillard had tried to rouse Miller shortly before 0555 hours and failed to do so. He had a key to the outer lock and presumably used it—something else to check on—only to be stymied by the fact that the inner lock was dogged.

Captain Coughlin, Lieutenant McWilliams, and Sergeant Dillard all had keys to the outer lock. Only Miller had a key to the inner lock. Where was it? The lock itself was in Captain Coughlin's office, still attached to its hasp and the splintered wood that the hasp had been screwed to. But where was the key? Train searched Miller's pockets but failed to find it. The room was not brightly lighted, but Train searched anyway, going to his hands and knees and covering every square inch of floor.

The key turned up in the last place he looked—of course—a darkened corner of the room five or six feet away from the door.

Train stood up, squeezing the padlock key as if it could tell him what had happened. It couldn't, but he was convinced that the contents of the room could, if only he asked them the right questions.

Once again he studied the damage to Miller's head. He was convinced that was not the cause of death. Eventually the Provost Marshal's people or the Quartermaster's people would come and take away the body, and the Medics would perform an autopsy and pronounce cause of death, and Miller's parents would get a telegram from the Secretary of War and they would go out and buy a service flag with a gold star to hang in their window in place of the one with the blue star that Train was sure hung there now.

But he didn't want to wait.

He knelt in front of the corpse and studied its face. He leaned forward and smelled Miller's nostrils and his mouth but detected no odor. The features were relaxed in death. There was no rictus. He stood up and placed himself behind the wicker chair and tried to imagine Miller's last minutes.

Someone had struck Miller high on the skull on his left side. The blow didn't look serious enough to cause unconsciousness no less death. Who had struck Miller? Who could get into the safe room once it was locked from both inside and out? Only Captain Coughlin, Lieutenant McWilliams, or First Sergeant Dillard, and then only if Miller let them in by opening the inside lock.

He heard voices from the outer office and a moment later Captain Coughlin invited him to join him.

Lieutenant McWilliams was standing in front of Captain Coughlin's desk. There was a tray on the desk, with a steaming pot and three cups. First Sergeant Dillard stood nearby looking uncomfortable.

Captain Coughlin addressed Train. "Come in, soldier. Pour yourself a cup of java."

McWilliams, uniform pressed and buttons polished, was red-faced, his jaw clenched. With an obvious effort he said, "Sir, I must protest. This soldier—there are only three cups . . . it's a violation of protocol . . ."

Coughlin waved his hand. "We'll make do somehow, Lieutenant."

McWilliams drew himself up, suddenly taller than he'd been. "If the Captain will excuse me, sir, I have to return to my duties."

Coughlin signaled Sergeant Dillard to approach. "What's today's schedule, Sergeant?"

"We've been pushing the trainees pretty hard, sir. They have the morning off, then grenade drill this afternoon."

"Good."

"And, Captain—it's payday, sir. The men expect to be paid today."

"All right." Captain Coughlin swung around in his chair and raised his eyes. It was impossible to tell whose picture he was consulting: President Roosevelt's, General Pershing's, General Marshall's, or Douglas MacArthur's. Or possibly, Nick Train thought, he was communing with his own younger self, the bright young soldier who went to France to whip the Kaiser.

Coughlin swung back to face the others. "McWilliams, Dillard, here's what I want. Lieutenant, find yourself a swagger stick."

"I have one, sir."

"I expected as much. All right. And, Sergeant, grab a clipboard. I want the two of you to inspect the trainees' barracks. I want you to find at least a dozen gigs. I don't care how hard you have to poke around to find 'em. If they're not there, make some up."

Lieutenant McWilliams's anger was clearly turning to pleasure. Sergeant Dillard kept a straight face. Nick Train made a supreme effort to become invisible.

Captain Coughlin leaned back in his chair and drew in his breath audibly. "Go slow. Keep those trainees braced. When you finish, you get out of there, McWilliams. Sergeant, you tell those trainees they're confined to barracks except for meals and training exercises. They'll have a GI party tonight. The works. Swamp out the barracks, polish the plumbing, climb up in the rafters and get the dust out. They have a barracks leader, do they?"

Sergeant Dillard said, "Schulte, sir. Saint Schulte, they call him."

"All right. You tell him that he's responsible for supervising the party. When the barracks is ready for reinspection, he's to notify you. You'll bring Lieutenant McWilliams back in and reinspect."

"Yes, sir," Dillard grinned.

"And tell 'em that we're holding onto their pay for them, they'll be paid as soon as they pass reinspection." He made a sound somewhere between a snort and a guffaw. "That's all. Lieutenant, Sergeant."

They saluted and left.

"Well, Private Train, what do you think?" the Captain asked.

"I think I have an idea, sir."

"All right, soldier, what is it?"

"May I take this with me?" He filled one of the cups on the tray Lieutenant McWilliams had brought back, then held it up.

"All right."

Train took the cup with him, back into the safe room. He placed it carefully on top of the safe, beside the cup that had been there when he first entered the room. He studied the cups. They were identical. Of course that didn't prove much. But there was a small Infantry School crest on each of them. That meant that they came from either the Officers Club or the NCO Club, not the mess hall, despite the instructions that Coughlin had given McWilliams.

He sniffed the coffee in the cup he'd brought, then bent over the other cup. Being careful not to touch the cup or its contents, he tried to detect an odor coming from it, but without success. Even so, he thought, even so, he was making progress.

He'd been attempting to recreate Corporal Miller's actions when Lieutenant McWilliams had arrived. Now he resumed that effort. He squatted beside Miller's wicker chair and reached for his coffee cup, the cup that was resting on top of the safe. He lifted the cup, sipped at the coffee, lowered the cup once more and pushed himself erect.

He crossed the room to the door and extracted the padlock key from his pocket.

So far, so good. But Miller had not opened the lock. Instead he had struck the wood and plasterboard repeatedly with his hands, as if he was trying to grasp the lock and insert the key. The key had tumbled from his fingers and clattered across the room.

Why would it do that? Why did that happen?

If Miller was dizzy, losing consciousness, trying to leave the room, he would have done that. He would have opened the lock, trying to get out of the safe room. Of course he would have failed, the outer padlock would have stopped him. But if he was confused, struggling, he might not have thought that through.

With the key lost, lying in a dark corner of the room, his vision and equilibrium failing, Miller would have staggered backwards.

Train duplicated the act.

Two, three, four steps and—Miller would have collapsed into the wicker armchair. Train collapsed, found himself sitting in the lap of a cold cadaver, leaped to his feet.

No, the blow to Miller's head had not caused his death. It was a red herring, designed to direct the investigation of Miller's death—the inevitable investigation of Miller's death—away from what had really happened. He'd have to have Miller's coffee tested, but in all likelihood that was the means by which a lethal dose had been administered.

Train peered into the corpse's face again. If it hadn't been for the blow to Miller's head, any investigation would have found that he'd died of natural causes. Even young men have heart attacks, and the rigors of military life on a man whose former lifestyle had been sedentary could bring on a sudden deadly embolism.

But who had administered the blow to Miller's head, and why, and when?

Nick Train retraced his route from the door to the wicker chair, to the safe, back to the door, back to the chair. Then he stopped, staring down at the remains of Corporal Fred Miller, company pay clerk.

He wasn't an expert on poisons but he'd learned a little bit about them, first in high school and then at the police academy. Miller had apparently realized there was something seriously wrong with him, tried to get help, then staggered backwards and collapsed into his wicker armchair to die. The only mark on his body was the obviously superficial head wound.

What would cause a death like Miller's?

Based on Train's police training, the likely suspect was digoxin, an easily soluble form of digitalis. That would come from a common plant called purple foxglove, also known as bloody fingers or dead men's bells. The victim might well drink it, for instance in a cup of coffee, and not notice anything for as long as several hours. Then his heart action would slow, he would become dizzy and disoriented, lose consciousness and die quietly.

Just as Corporal Fred Miller had died.

Train made his way to Captain Coughlin's office and told the captain his conclusions. He described his reconstruction of Miller's movements from the wicker chair to the padlock, the struggle with the key, and Miller's collapse and death.

"I don't know what an autopsy will show, Captain. I'm not sure what signs that poison would leave in the body. Maybe none. I'm not a trained toxicologist, sir. But I'd bet my month's pay that a chemical test will show digoxin in Miller's coffee."

Captain Coughlin grunted. "Sounds very plausible, Train. And we'll get the right people in to check those things damned soon. I don't think I can hold out on this thing more than another hour or two." He put his face in his hands and rubbed, as if that would stimulate the blood flow and help his brain to work.

"Great job so far," he resumed. "But if that's how Miller was killed, you still haven't told me how the money was removed from the safe. Not to mention—what do you call it in the detective business, Train—*Who Dunnit?*"

"Sir, I'm not a detective. But I have an idea of how the money was removed. I think that Miller was working with his killer. Whoever was his partner double-crossed him."

Coughlin picked up his cup of coffee and raised it to his lips. An odd expression crossed his face. He lowered the cup without taking any coffee.

"What would you call that, Train—an inside job, right?"

"Yes, sir."

Train paused for a few seconds to gather his thoughts. The silence was punctuated by a booming sound. An artillery unit was practicing coordination with an infantry brigade on the other side of the post. The sound was that of a .155 millimeter howitzer.

"Captain, here's the way I think it happened. Miller's partner opened the outer padlock, Miller opened the inner one. The partner brought a cup of coffee with him. Miller thought that was nice. He left it on top of the safe. Miller's partner opened the safe."

He stopped, then asked, "Who knows the combination to the safe, Captain?"

"Same people who have keys to the padlock. Lieutenant McWilliams, Sergeant Dillard, and myself."

"Yes, sir. Well, Miller's partner opened the safe and removed the cash. Then he hit Miller. The wound looked to me as if it could have been inflicted with the butt of a forty-five. Miller was still conscious. His partner left, taking the money with him. Miller relocked the door from the inside and his partner relocked it from the outside. The idea was that

Miller would claim he'd been attacked by an unknown assailant, maybe a masked safecracker who managed to open the safe and get away with the payroll. That would send the CID off on the trail of an imaginary crook from outside, someone who had managed to get copies of the keys to both padlocks, while in fact Miller and his partner had the money."

"And what would they do with the payroll?"

Train shrugged. "I don't know, sir. But I have a suggestion."

There was another boom, another howitzer round fired.

"The first thing to do is check Miller's belongings. No telling what we'll find there."

Captain Coughlin summoned the Sergeant of the Guard and had a corporal and a private stationed outside the company office. They had strict orders not to step inside, not even to look inside, on pain of court martial. Then the captain told Nick Train to come with him.

Train was feeling less like a soldier and more like a cop by the minute.

Permanent party had better housing than transients at Benning. Corporal Miller had lived in a tiny room, partitioned in an NCO barracks. Train used a pair of bolt-cutters to open the padlock on Miller's door and then to remove a second padlock from Miller's foot locker.

The locker contained clean uniforms, underwear, toilet articles, all in inspection-ready order. Boots and shoes lined up beneath Miller's bunk. Civvies on wire hangers on a wall-mounted rod.

The only non-regulation items in Miller's foot locker were his religious paraphernalia. Rosary, Douay Bible, religious pictures, a couple of saint's medals.

Train was kneeling in front of the foot locker, carefully examining its contents. He sensed Captain Coughlin standing behind him and turned to look at him. Captain Coughlin was studying the contents of the locker, as well.

"I don't see anything here," Train said.

"I do." Captain Coughlin frowned.

"Sir?"

"You know Miller was a very religious man, don't you?"

"Yes, sir."

"His most precious belonging was his Missal. He always carried it around with him. But it wasn't in the safe room, was it, Train?"

"No, I'd have seen it."

"Then it should be in his foot locker. Not here, is it?"

Train shook his head.

"Where is it?"

41

"Don't know, sir."

"How's this, Train? Maybe the old man can play detective, too. It was just a little book, you know. He could have put it in a uniform pocket. Could have had it with him in the safe room. Probably did. It's a long night in there, no companions, no entertainment, another man might ask permission to bring in a radio, or might smuggle in some comic books or magazines. But a man like Miller would bring either a Bible or a Missal and spend his time communing with the Almighty."

Train struggled to his feet. He was pushing a quarter century and his knees weren't as flexible as they'd been ten years ago.

"You think Miller's partner took the Missal?"

"Yep."

"But why, Captain?"

Coughlin shrugged. "Who do you think Miller's partner was, Train?"

"It had to be someone who had the key to the outer lock."

"Yes."

Another distant howitzer boom.

"Who, Train? Don't be afraid. Who was Miller's partner?"

"It had to be Lieutenant McWilliams or Sergeant Dillard, sir."

"Or—who else?"

"You, sir."

"That's right. We have three suspects now, Train. That's progress. That's real progress. It has to be McWilliams or Dillard or Captain Coffin. Oh, I know what they call me. Don't be naïve." He paused. "Three suspects. Don't be afraid to say it."

He walked to the window. At least Miller had had a window in his room. He peered outside for a long moment. Looking past the captain, Train could see the patches of snow covering the red west Georgia clay.

"Where do you think the money is, Train?"

"I don't know. Sir."

"Try. If you were the killer, Train, if you were McWilliams or Dillard or Old Man Coughlin, Captain Coffin, and you had just robbed the company safe, what would you do with the money?"

"I think I'd try and get it off the post, Captain."

"I think so, too. All right, come on back to the company office, soldier."

The two soldiers posted outside the company office rendered smart rifle salutes to Captain Coughlin as he and Private Train returned. The captain motioned Train to sit opposite him, then picked up a telephone and placed a call. He picked up a pencil and scribbled a few notes, then grunted into the receiver and hung it up.

"McWilliams and Dillard both drove off post last night. McWilliams left around 2300 hours. Returned at 0400 this morning. Dillard left at 2346 hours and returned shortly after 0500. There's no record of my leaving the post, and in fact I did not. What do you make of it, Train?"

"I don't know, sir."

Train followed Coughlin's glance to a wall-mounted clock. It was well into the afternoon. He and Captain Coughlin had missed the noon meal. Train's barracks-mates would be on the practice range, throwing dummy hand grenades at cardboard targets.

From outside the building, Train heard a familiar voice. It was Lieutenant McWilliams, dressing down the two soldiers for what Train knew would be some petty offense. A moment later, McWilliams strode into the office and halted before Captain Coughlin's desk. He snapped a sharp salute and all but clicked his heels, Gestapo-fashion.

"Sit down, Lieutenant," Coughlin instructed. "Good. Make yourself comfortable. Don't worry about sitting next to an enlisted man, you won't catch a disease."

McWilliams sent a filthy glare are Train.

"Where were you last night, Lieutenant?"

"I was here, sir. In the company office. Catching up on paperwork, looking over training schedules."

"Right. And then?"

"Then, sir?"

"Then, Lieutenant. You didn't spend the night here, did you?"

"No, sir."

"Well, where did you go?"

"I went to my quarters, sir. I got a good night's sleep, then I went to the mess hall and met you there for breakfast."

"Right."

Coughlin picked a sheet of paper off his desk, fingered it briefly, then dropped it again.

"Gate guards indicate that you left the post at 2300 hours last night and returned at 0400."

"Oh. Yes, sir. That's true."

"That's all right, Lieutenant. You're an officer and a gentleman. You don't have to stand bed check. So long as you're present for all duties, you can come and go as you please. That's per regulations."

"Yes, sir."

"Where were you, though?"

"Am I required to answer that, sir?"

"I am directing you to answer, yes, Lieutenant."

McWilliams had removed his visored cap and was holding it in his lap. "Sir, I met some friends and enjoyed a social visit."

"Right. And where was that?"

"Columbus, sir."

"Broad Street?"

"Yes, sir."

"You get laid, McWilliams?"

"Sir!"

"Jesus Christ, man, you have a pair of gonads, don't you? What did you do, pick up a woman in a bar? Do you have a steady girl-friend? Go to a whorehouse? This isn't a Sunday School class, Lieutenant, we've had a murder and robbery here. Where were you last night?"

"The, ah, that one, Captain."

There was another boom. It was louder than the howitzer booms, but in fact it seemed to be a smaller explosion, sharper, closer to the company area.

"Which one?"

"Ah, the last one, sir."

"Please, McWilliams, let's have it in plain English."

"All right, sir. I was at the Cardinal Hotel."

"Okay. We all know what that place is. I just hope you were careful, Lieutenant."

"I was, sir."

The young officer's face was crimson.

"All right. One more thing. I want to inspect your vehicle."

"Yes, sir."

"Right now, McWilliams." The captain turned to Nick Train. "Did your police training include checking out vehicles for contraband, Private?"

"It did, sir."

Train wound up inspecting Lieutenant McWilliams's 1942 Packard Darrin One-Eighty. The convertible came up spotlessly clean and innocent, inside and out. McWilliams stood by fuming, Captain Coughlin watched noncommittally. Nothing under the hood but a perfectly maintained straight-eight engine. Nothing in the trunk but a jack, a tire-iron, a tool kit, and a spare tire. At the end, Train crawled out from under the car, dusted himself off and presented himself to Coughlin.

"Nothing, sir."

"All right, Train. Lieutenant McWilliams, you hurry out to the grenade range and have a look-see. That was a nasty pop a little while ago. I hope somebody didn't set off a real grenade. Train, you come with me. We're going to have a look at Corporal Miller's vehicle. McWilliams, you don't mind if we borrow your tire iron, do you? Just in case we need it to pry open Miller's car?"

But Miller's little '36 Nash 400 had been left unlocked. The True Believer in All Things Holy had trusted his fellow man to that extent. Or maybe he had nothing worth stealing. There was no trunk lid in the odd little car. Train scrambled over the seat to get into the trunk. The car wasn't as well maintained mechanically as McWilliams's Packard, nor was the interior quite as clean and innocent.

Train emerged with a half-empty bottle of Bourbon in one hand and a stack of ratty publications in the other. "Girly books," he grinned, offering the loot to Captain Coughlin.

The captain grinned and shook his head. "So little Miller had a pair of gonads, too." He brushed his hand across his forehead. "Well, we'll just toss that stuff. No need to upset his family, they've got grief enough coming. No Missal, though?"

"No, sir."

"Okay, soldier. On to Sergeant Dillard's wagon."

But before they got to that vehicle, a soldier in olive fatigues came panting up, perspiring profusely despite the winter chill. Train recognized the ruddy complexion and the curly rust-colored hair sticking out from under the man's fatigue cap. It was Aaron Hirsch. He wasn't crying, just sweating.

He managed to pull himself together and salute the captain.

"Sir, Lieutenant McWilliams sends his respects and a message for the captain."

"Yes, yes." Coughlin returned the salute. "What is it, Hirsch?"

"It's Sergeant Dillard, sir."

"What happened?"

"He was demonstrating grenade technique, sir. He had a practice grenade. It was painted the way they are, to show they're not armed. He pulled the pin and counted down to show us how long it took for the fuse to burn. It went off, sir. It wasn't a practice grenade. It was a live grenade. He—it went off, sir. It blew him to bits, sir."

"Jesus, Jesus, Jesus, Joseph and Mary. Jesus. The poor bastard. He must have known the jig was up. All right, here comes McWilliams now."

And Lieutenant McWilliams arrived, polished shoes covered with red Georgia dust even in winter, uniform spotless and pressed, every brass button glittering in the December sunlight. Even before McWilliams got off his salute, Captain Coughlin barked at him.

"You've sent for the medics, of course."

"Yes, sir."

"Cancelled the rest of the session and sent the men to barracks."

"Under command of Private Schulte, sir. A fine soldier, I can see that already."

"I'm sure of it. All right, McWilliams. Let's have a look in Sergeant Dillard's vehicle."

They found it concealed inside the spare tire in Dillard's Ford. Miller's missing Missal. The annotations were in a simple code; the Provost Marshal's men and the CID investigators would have no problem cracking it. Poor innocent Miller, the payroll clerk had made notes to himself in the Missal, notes that gave the key to his carefully maintained records. It was obvious that he never thought anyone would see the contents of the Missal except himself and his God.

Everything was there. The identities of the gamblers, the amounts they owed. The monthly payroll would have got a lot of military men out of debt with whoever held their IOU's. A lot of military men including Sergeant Dillard and Corporal Miller. And Lieutenant McWilliams.

"You, Lieutenant? That's hard to believe. You drive that Packard, you wear custom-tailored uniforms, you're from old money, McWilliams. How could you get in so deep? Why didn't you just ask your family to bail you out?"

"You wouldn't understand, Captain. With due respect to your rank, sir, you really wouldn't understand. I couldn't go to my family. I had to work this out myself."

Captain Coughlin moaned, as if he and not Lieutenant McWilliams had been caught. "It was the Army-Navy game that did it, wasn't it? Loyal to the old school, you went double-or-nothing on everything you owed, and Navy whipped Army again, didn't they? You poor sap, McWilliams. You poor, poor sap."

The captain drew in a deep breath. Then he said, "I take it you and Sergeant Dillard and Corporal Miller were all in this together? Who was your bookie, that's not in Miller's book. Was it Jackalee Jennings in Columbus? Or somebody in Phenix City? Big Mike Norris? Larry Sunday? You know, those fellows don't keep their operations very secret, they're pals with the sheriffs on both sides of the river. Who was it, son?"

McWilliams looked angry for a moment when he heard Captain Coughlin use that last word. Then he shook his head. "I don't think I should say anything, Captain. Under the Uniform Code of Military Justice I have the right to a civilian attorney and I will ask my family to provide one. That much, I will accept from them."

"Did you kill him, McWilliams? Tell me that much. Was it you or was it Dillard? Which one of you killed Miller?"

"I'm not going to answer any questions, sir."

"Dillard is dead now. Very convenient, McWilliams. You can lay it all on his grave. I suppose that's what your lawyer will do, isn't it?" He looked up, looked over McWilliams's cap with its glittering eagle ornament and its polished leather visor. Train wondered what Captain Coughlin saw. He couldn't guess. Coughlin said, "All right, Lieutenant. Report to the Provost Marshal and tell him to place you under arrest pending investigation."

Nick Train watched Lieutenant McWilliams salute, execute a smart about face, and march off like a good little soldier.

"Where did they get the poison?" Captain Coughlin asked. He didn't direct the question to anyone in particular, but Private Train and Private Hirsch were both within earshot.

"Foxglove is common," Train said, "it grows in every ditch in the State of Georgia."

"Lot of it in Spain, too," Hirsch volunteered. "I was there with the Lincolns, you know. Saw plenty of Foxglove."

Captain Coughlin said, "All right, boys, you go back to your barracks and polish your boots."

Ω

THE SQUARE ROOT OF DEAD

WITH MICHAEL KURLAND

Professor Harker lay in the grotesque, unembarrassed posture of death, his arms sprawled out, his right leg doubled under him, his eyes staring up unblinkingly at the final unknown. He looked mildly surprised, as though this was not the answer he expected.

Lieutenant Loman stood to one side, his ungloved hands thrust under his arms for warmth, and looked at the body while his partner, Sergeant Stametti, and the lab men finished the methodical detail work that had to be completed before the corpse could be moved. They photographed it from all the necessary, undignified angles, dusted all the plausible surfaces for fingerprints—not likely out here in the middle of the snow-covered quadrangle—and conducted a painstaking search of the immediate area, bagging whatever they found, no matter how mundane or meaningless: cigarette butts, soda bottles, all the detritus with which the human race clutters up the surface of this planet.

Loman had ruled out anything clearly dropped before the snow started that evening, for which the lab crew was properly grateful. It was evident that, when Professor James Conrad Harker had met his rendezvous with that greater calculus in the sky, the snow had just about stopped falling.

A thin man joined Loman, carefully skirting the yellow rope the lab crew had put up to circle and define the death scene. "You're Lieutenant Loman," the thin man said, extending a gloved hand. "I'm Professor Pyne. If there's any way in which I can help . . . I mean, I don't know what I could do but—this is startling, you know. I mean . . ."

"You knew Professor Harker?" Loman asked, looking into Pyne's slightly bulging eyes while he took the offered hand.

"We've been colleagues for over twenty years," Professor Pyne said, shifting his gaze to stare down at the body. "I'm head of the department now. Can't they cover up the body? I mean . . ."

"What department, Professor?"

"What? Oh—mathematics. James Conrad Harker was one of the leading algebraic topologists in the country—in the world. Can you tell me what happened to him?"

"That's what we're trying to find out. He appears to have been stabbed, but we don't know as yet with what, by whom or why. Who told *you* about it, Professor, and why did you come down here?"

Pyne bristled. "You don't think—"

"It's my job, Professor," Loman interrupted, "asking questions. I very seldom know the answers in advance or I wouldn't bother asking the question."

"A student—one of Harker's graduate students, actually—called me up and told me about it. I came down because I felt I should. As head of the department, I mean, and his friend. To see if there was anything I could do."

Loman nodded. "Tell me about Professor Harker," he said. "What sort of man was he?"

"Brilliant," Pyne said. "Can we . . . ah . . . talk somewhere else?"

"In a minute, Professor." The ambulance had just arrived, and Sergeant Stametti looked over to Loman with a mute question. Loman nodded, and the body was carefully picked up and placed on the stretcher. Now the area under the body would be examined, and Harker's clothing would be cursorily searched, pending the complete examination at the morgue.

"It's Professor Harker's personality I'm interested in," Loman said, leading Pyne away from the scene. "Was he gregarious and friendly, or surly and private? Did he have a temper? Was he the sort of nit-picking pedant who provokes fits of temper in others?"

They walked together toward Euclid Avenue, which bordered the near side of the quadrangle, while Professor Pyne thought that over. It was just after eleven at night, and most of the shops were closed. Two coffee houses were still open, and Loman and Pyne headed into the nearer.

"Professor Harker was a friendly, easygoing man," Pyne said. "He had a variety of interests outside his field, like glass collecting, Go, science fiction and heuristic programming techniques."

"Go?" Loman asked. "Isn't that a game?"

"Right, Lieutenant. Something like chess, only not."

"And what's this 'heuristic programming'? You mean, computers?"

"That's right. A heuristic program is one which, so to speak, allows the computer to learn from experience. Not to make the same mistake twice, I mean."

"I didn't know they could do that," Loman said. "I thought all a computer could do was add and subtract, only incredibly fast."

"That's basically right," Professor Pyne agreed. "That's what makes heuristic programming such a challenge. It's like teaching an adding machine to think."

Sergeant Stametti pushed through the door of the coffee shop and hurried over to Loman's table, his feet distributing snow over the hardwood floor as he stamped down the aisle. "Something for you,

Lieutenant," he said, setting a small plastic box gently on the table. "Found it under the body. It's one of them hand computers."

"Calculators," Professor Pyne corrected absently, staring with interest at the little mechanism. "It's his—Professor Harker's, I mean. We gave it to him as sort of a joke for his last birthday. He was fifty-five."

"It's lit up," Loman said, looking at the bright, ruby-red number 3, which shone up at him.

"That's why I brought it in to you," Stametti explained. "I doubt if even a math professor would walk about carrying the number three all lit up. I thought it might be a last message, or something."

"A dying message, eh? Why not? I've been on the Homicide Detail for eight years—I deserve a dying message. Tell me, Professor Pyne, does the number three mean anything to you?"

Pyne smiled. "I could probably give you a two-hour lecture on the number three," he said. "But if you mean in specific relation to Professor Harker, no."

"Nothing at *all*, Professor? He wasn't a member of a three-man committee, or holding a three-student class, or maybe on some list where the members are always put in the same order. You know: one, two, three . . ."

"Not anything meaningful," Pyne said. "Not that I can think of—I mean. Harker does—did—have three graduate student research assistants in this office."

"Were they listed in any order?"

"If so, it would be alphabetical. Let's see: it's Mr. Bliss, Miss Bohle, and Mr. Quipper. And, of course, there's the faculty list for the department. But I believe Harker himself is number three. *Was.*"

"*Great!*" Lieutenant Loman said.

Pyne stared down at the calculator. "Wait a second!" he said. "It might be . . . may I?" He reached for the machine.

Loman pushed it over and watched Professor Pyne as he carefully pushed down the button-switch in the lower right hand corner marked (=). As he did, a whole row of numbers lit up in front of the 3.

"It's as I remembered," Pyne said. "The device automatically suppresses all but the last digit after thirty seconds."

"What for, Professor?" Sergeant Stametti asked, staring curiously at the plastic box.

"To save the battery," Pyne explained. "The thing that draws most of the current in these devices is the lighting display, so many of them are made to suppress the display after thirty seconds except for the last digit

50

to remind you that you're holding a number."

Lieutenant Loman pulled absently at the corners of his trim moustache and examined the number now glowing up at him. It was 2 1 9 8 . 2 1 1 3.

"Could this be part of some problem that Professor Harker was working on?" he asked.

"I wouldn't think so," Pyne said. "Topologists don't work with numbers, actually."

"Then why did you get him the calculator?" Loman asked.

"It was sort of a joke," Pyne said. "Professor Harker had an absolute eidetic memory for numbers. He never had to write down addresses or phone numbers. Each number had a separate personality for him. I mean, that's the way he described it. But he absolutely couldn't add or subtract. We got him the calculator to balance his checkbook."

"Phone number, eh?" Loman said. "Maybe . . . no, it's too long."

"Say," Stametti said, "maybe it spelled out something, like the name of the guy who attacked him. We didn't find a pen or a pencil on him. Maybe this was the professor's only way to name his killer."

"Right," Loman agreed. "Now all we have to do is go up to old two-one-nine-eight and tell him the game's up."

"No, Lieutenant, really. My kid showed me. You can turn the thing upside-down and get words. Here, I'll show you."

"Wait a second," Loman said. He copied the number off the display into his notebook, and then handed the calculator to Stametti.

"Here, look," Stametti said. He cleared the instrument and tapped in 3-2-0-0-8. "There!" He handed the calculator back to Lieutenant Loman.

"So?" Loman asked. He frowned.

"Turn it upside down," Stametti instructed. "Read the dial upside down."

Loman obeyed instructions and read B-O-O-Z-E in the amber lights. "Well!" he said. "Clever. The eight is a 'B' and so forth. Let's see what it says with Professor Harker's number." He reentered the number that had been on the machine and then turned it upside down and stared at the result. "It doesn't mean anything to me," he said finally. "And I really thought we had something for a minute. What do you think, Professor Pyne?"

Pyne examined the upside down display. "E-I-I-Z-point-B-could be an R maybe—I-Z. No, I can't say it means anything to me. Sorry. Frankly, I doubt if it would have occurred to Professor Harker to play that sort of game with his calculator. I mean, he didn't think that way."

Loman stood up and stuck the little calculator in his pocket. "Thanks for your help, Professor," he said. "Would you please give the full names and addresses of Professor Harker's three research assistants to Sergeant Stametti so he can question them in the morning? I'm going home to bed now so I can dream about numbers."

Ω

Lieutenant Loman didn't see Stametti again until eleven the next morning, when the sergeant slammed into the office in his usual enthusiastic way. "Busy morning," Stametti said. "Got a lot for you. Don't know what good it is, any of it. What're you doing?"

"I borrowed an instruction manual from the store that sells these calculators," Loman said. "I figure that if I know how to work it right, I'll have a better chance of figuring out what in hell Harker was trying to tell us."

"I been thinking about that, Lieutenant," Stametti said. He paused.

"And?" Loman prompted as Stametti stared morosely down at the instruction book in his hand.

"It don't mean anything, Lieutenant. You'd better give it up and just read my reports when I get them typed up."

Loman and Stametti had a long-established system of working together—Stametti dug up the information and Loman analyzed and interpreted it. Each was particularly good at what he did, and each admired the other for his particular ability. They worked well together.

Lieutenant Loman put the booklet down and leaned back in his wooden swivel chair. "Let's hear it Stametti—why should I give it up?"

"I've been questioning the three grad students and assembling information on their backgrounds," Stametti said, "and it's odds on that one of them did it. All three of them have possible motives, and as far as I can tell they're the only ones. Harker didn't have any money, he didn't have a job anyone else wanted, his wife died three years ago and he hasn't been seeing anyone since, and everyone at the university respected him."

"Good work," Loman said. "Get it typed up and I'll stare at it. Why does that mean that the number on the calculator isn't a dying message? The professor didn't have anything to write with on him when he died."

"He wouldn't be obscure," Stametti said. "He'd have no reason to leave a number with four places on each side of the decimal point. No reason at all."

"Explain."

"Sure. The three research assistants are named Robert Quipper, Jan Bliss, and Susan Bohle." Stametti paused expectantly, staring at Loman.

"Go on," Loman said, a trace of annoyance showing in his voice.

"Sure. I thought you'd see it. You can write all three names upside down, like I showed you, on the calculator. Here. Look." Stametti picked the calculator up from Loman's desk and tapped 808 into it. Upside down it became BOB. Then he demonstrated how 55178 became BLISS and 37408 reversed to BOHLE.

"I see," Loman said thoughtfully. "So if Harker could name his attacker that easily . . ."

"Right," Stametti agreed. "He had no reason to leave two-one-nine-eight -point-two-one-one-three as a clue if he could leave an easily understandable eight-o-eight."

"Perhaps Mister eight-o-eight isn't the killer," Loman suggested. "Or Bliss or Bohle either. Perhaps it's more complex than that. Or even if you're right about no one else having a reason to eliminate Harker, maybe it was a nut killer."

"If it was a nut killer," Sergeant Stametti said, "then that number is a nut clue, and you'll never figure what it means." He put the calculator back down on the desk.

Loman shook his head in disgust. "You're probably right," he said. "Go type up those reports and get them to me, so I can get the feel of these three students."

Sergeant Stametti went off to his own desk, leaving Loman staring down at the calculator. He punched BOB and squared it. Then he took the square root of BLISS and the reciprocal of BOHLE, and no matter how long he stared at the results they were merely numbers, nothing more.

About an hour later, slightly after noon, Stametti returned to Loman's desk and flopped a set of typed forms on the battered wood surface in front of the Lieutenant.

"Thanks, Stametti," Loman said. "I'll look at them after lunch. I'm trying to make up the duty roster for the next month."

"How'd you get stuck with *that* job?" Stametti asked him. "You'd better look over the reports now."

"It's the Captain's new policy," Loman said. "He believes, all of a sudden, in delegating authority. Why had I better look over the reports now?"

"Because they're all going to be here at one-thirty to talk to you. I thought I told you."

Loman stiff-armed the work-sheet to the back of the desk with his right palm. "No, Sergeant," he said, "you didn't mention that."

"I arranged it," Stametti said. "We don't want this case to drag on, so I figured you'd wrap it up this afternoon after you read my reports."

Loman stared at Stametti, but could make nothing out of his bland expression. "Well then," Loman said, "I guess I'd better get at those reports. All three graduate students are coming at one-thirty?"

"Right. And the professor, too."

"Professor Pyne?"

"Right. *Him.*"

"Why?"

"He's a possible. Not a probable, but a possible."

"What's *his* motive?"

"Try professional jealousy. Harker was more highly regarded as a mathematician. I have it from the rest of the department. Pyne's been jealous of Harker for twenty years. A thing like that can build up. It sounds like a slim motive for murder, but people have been killed for a lot less. Pyne might be slightly batty on the subject."

"Any sign of that?"

"No. Apparently they were good friends. Anything else you want, let me know."

"Ham and Swiss on rye toast, light coffee, no sugar—and don't forget the pickle."

"You eating lunch at your desk? I thought we'd go to Pronzini's and have a steak."

"You're the one made the one-thirty appointment. Now let me read these reports and see if I get any bright ideas."

"Right. One ham and Swiss on rye." Stametti gave a gesture vaguely reminiscent of a salute and left.

On top of Stametti's stack of papers was the Medical Examiner's preliminary report. The ME confirmed what had been apparent last night. Professor Harker had been killed by a single thrust from a narrow, sharp instrument, which penetrated between the third and fourth ribs, severing the thoracic and carotid arteries, and causing almost immediate death by cutting off the blood supply to the brain. The professor was conscious for no more than a minute or two.

$$\Omega$$

Just long enough, Loman thought, *to tap out that dying message on his calculator before he fell over. And I have to be smart enough to figure out what he meant. And he was a genius.*

Lieutenant Loman put the Medical Examiner's report aside. Below it were Stametti's reports on the four suspects, based on questioning each of them, and other, unverified data gathered that morning in the university's Math Department. He put the four reports side by side on the desk and read them alternately, line by line.

The vital statistics first: name, address, age, sex, phone number, occupation, police record (none admitted to having any—that was being checked), physical description. Then came the statements, which were put into narrative form in the style Loman called "third person police impersonal."

* *** *

NAME Quipper, Robert L.
AGE 26 SEX M
ADDRESS 3132 Percy Street
PHONE 483-2132

Robert Quipper, the oldest of the three graduate students, had been a sergeant in the army, serving in Southeast Asia, before getting out and letting the government put him through school. He was in the midst of writing his doctoral thesis, and expected to have his degree by the end of the year.

It was known that he felt Professor Harker had walked off with an original idea of his and developed it without giving Quipper sufficient credit. The consensus in the Math Department was that what Harker had done was proper, and that the mention of Quipper in Harker's published paper was sufficient. But Quipper had a quick temper and had previously had several loud arguments with Harker on the subject.

* *** *

NAME Bliss, Jan (nmi)
AGE 21 SEX M
ADDRESS 661 ½ Yeath Drive
PHONE 484-8947

Jan Bliss had never known any life except the world of science. A shy, introverted boy, he had turned to the study of the logical, invariable laws of the universe when he found himself unable to understand the whimsical, inconsistent customs of humanity. Normally Jan was quiet to the point of invisibility, although distantly polite if approached. The other students' opinions were that he would like to make friends if he knew how.

On very rare occasions, for no outward reason that anyone could tell,

Jan falls into what psychologists call a fugue state, and would walk around as if in a dream, or perhaps visiting some other plane of existence. During these periods he tends to be destructive; at one party he methodically destroyed every salad plate in the house, leaving dinner plates, soup plates, cups, and glasses untouched.

He was never known to have harmed anyone or even attempted to while in this state. He was seeing a psychiatrist once every two weeks, all he could afford. The psychiatrist would not discuss his patient, but would say that he considered it extremely unlikely Jan could have stuck a knife into Professor James Conrad Harker.

* *** *

NAME Bohle, Susan S.
AGE 23 SEX F
Address Rm D-12, 181 Tetra Street
PHONE 480-4896
Susan Bohle was an intelligent, articulate 23-year-old from a well-to-do family, who didn't encourage her choice of careers. Women were supposed to settle down and have children, according to Susan's mother. That being so, Susan's father felt, graduate school was surely a waste of money. College, of course—everybody went to college. But why fool around getting a higher degree when you should be out getting a husband?

It was known that Professor Harker espoused similar views. Women belonged in the home, not the graduate school. Certainly no woman could ever hope to be a really top-flight mathematician. Competent, yes, but not genius. As a result of this prejudice, Harker was much harder on women students than on men. He was known to resent the pressure that had been brought to bear to make him take Susan Bohle as a research assistant. Common gossip had it that he was going to ease Susan out as quickly and as gracefully as possible with a Master's degree that, in this university, meant you weren't quite good enough to make your PhD.

Susan, who was really a brilliant student with an original mind, would have no trouble getting her doctorate from whichever professor took Harker's place as her major professor. She was also very stubborn and tough-minded. She would have to be to buck her parents and her major professor. Was she tough-minded enough to stick a knife in Harker?

* *** *

Stametti delivered the sandwich, and Lieutenant Loman paused long enough to eat half before turning the reports over and reading the suspects' statements as to where they had been when Professor Harker was murdered.

None of them had what you'd call an alibi. Robert Quipper had been home brushing up for the calculus course. He was a teaching assistant, half-expecting Professor Harker to call and make arrangements to talk over a paper they were preparing. The professor had never called.

Jan Bliss had been out at a meeting of the Society of the Round Table, a group dedicated to bringing back the social graces and customs of the early Middle Ages. They dressed in period costumes, and Jan seemed more at home in the garb of an earlier time.

Twenty-five people were ready to swear he attended, but the hall they met in was only a few blocks from the park where Harker was killed. He could have slipped out long enough to make the round trip before he was missed. And he had been wearing a three-foot sword.

Susan Bohle claimed that she was visiting a boyfriend for the night. But, in a curious reversal of traditional morality, she refused to give his name, saying he wouldn't want to get involved. It was Susan who had called Professor Pyne, having herself been called by a friend and told of Harker's death.

So the identity of her boyfriend must be common knowledge on campus if someone had known to call her there. It could be obtained, if necessary. Of course, there was the possibility that she knew of the killing because she had participated in it, and no one had called her at all. In which case there was probably no boyfriend.

Professor Pyne, Stametti's fourth suspect, was at home all evening until he received the phone call from Susan Bohle. His wife would swear to that. But the testimony of wives in regard to their husbands was always suspect.

Lieutenant Loman stacked the reports together and weighed them in both hands. One of these four? Which one? If only the professor had been carrying a portable typewriter with him instead of a calculator. He could have just tapped out the name.

The name? Loman turned the reports over and stared at the headings, with the typed-in names and addresses. *Perhaps he did,* Loman thought. *Perhaps that's just what the professor did.*

A half hour later Stametti came into the office to find Loman leaning back in his chair, folding a paper airplane. Several others were distributed about the office.

"They're here," Stametti said, ignoring the aerodynamic experiment. "Which one do you want to see fist?"

"I'll see them all," Loman told him. "Come on!"

"You've *got it!*" Stametti said, doing his best to keep up with Loman's long strides without breaking into a trot. "I can tell. You've pegged the killer."

"I have," Loman admitted, doing his best not to sound smug.

"Are you sure?"

"Sure enough to have obtained a warrant. The killer's rooms are being searched even as we stand here waiting for the elevator."

"Something I gave you?" Stametti demanded.

"Right—something you gave me. And something Professor Harker gave us."

"The number on the calculator?"

"Right."

"Then it means something?"

"It does—and it doesn't. Come along. The elevator's stalled again."

They went down the wide stairs in the old precinct building in the second floor, then down a long corridor, past the Juvenile Division, past Safe and Loft, to the large interrogation room Stametti had left the suspects in. "What do you mean, 'It does—and it doesn't'?" Stametti asked.

"We were looking at it wrong."

"Upside down?"

"No, backward. You'll see."

They entered a room. The four suspects were sitting around the conference table with a litter of plastic cups of coffee and cigarette butt-filled ashtrays in front of them.

Lieutenant Loman looked them over, sorting them out in his mind. Professor Pyne was farthest away, facing the door. The girl was, of course, Susan Bohle. She was very pretty, with long blonde hair and piercing hazel eyes. Somehow Loman hadn't thought she'd be pretty. The slender young man with the aquiline nose who kept his left hand in front of his mouth must be Jan Bliss. The stocky man with the aggressive chin who kept his chair teetering precariously back would then be Robert Quipper.

"Good afternoon," Loman said. "I'm Lieutenant Loman. And you are"—he named them, left to right—"Mr. Bliss, Miss Bohle, Professor Pyne, Mr. Quipper."

Three of them nodded. Quipper straightened his chair with a crash and leaned forward across the table. "Look here," he said. "What's all this about? Why are we here?"

"I apologize for the inconvenience," Loman said. "At least to three of you, I apologize. You see, some new information has come to light."

"New . . . ah . . . information?" Professor Pyne asked, frowning.

"Yes." Loman turned to Robert Quipper. "You told my investigator that you stayed home that night and waited for Professor Harker to call."

"That's right," Quipper said.

"The telephone company records show that you received that call," Loman said. He nodded to Stametti, who circled around to stand behind Quipper's chair.

"That's ridiculous," Quipper said, trying to keep an eye on Stametti and stare belligerently at Loman.

"How is it ridiculous?" Loman asked. "Because he called you from a pay phone? But there is a record of the call, and which pay phone it was from. It was the last call from that phone, and Professor Harker's prints are all over the handset."

"You have the right to remain silent," Stametti intoned, reading from the little card in his hand.

Quipper listened impassively as his rights were read to him. "I'm not saying anything," he said, when Stametti put the card back in his pocket.

"That's your right," Loman told him.

Quipper shook his head. "The god damn phone," he said.

"We have more," Loman said. "We have a witness that places you at the scene of the crime—that names you directly. I'm telling you this with the others present so you won't think I'm playing some kind of cat-and-mouse game and taking each of you aside to accuse you of the murder. You killed James Harker, Mr. Quipper, and I know it."

"What witness?" Professor Pyne asked. "Who?"

"Not 'who,' Professor," Loman said, pulling the little calculator from his pocket. "This is my witness. Professor Harker did name his killer, and it was Robert Quipper he named."

"How?" Pyne asked.

"Why didn't he just write 808?" Stametti asked.

"As Professor Pyne told us last night," Loman said, "Professor Harker didn't play games like that. Let's look at what he did. We found this number in the machine—2 1 9 8 . 2 1 1 3.

"Now there are three possibilities. One, that the number was there by some sort of cosmic accident, having nothing to do with the professor or his murder. I rejected that on the grounds that the professor wouldn't have left the calculator turned on as if he wasn't using it. The battery would have died in a few hours. As a matter of fact, the full charge on the battery when we found the device shows that it wasn't turned on much before Professor Harker's death.

"Two, that Professor Harker put the number 2198.2113 in the calculator as a dying message, hoping it would tell us who killed him."

Professor Pyne leaned forward. "And you say it did? That number somehow implicates Quipper as Professor Harker's assassin?" He pulled out a pen and a notebook, wrote the number down, and stared at it.

A uniformed officer came in behind Lieutenant Loman and handed him a note. He read it, and then put it in his pocket and went on. "Not directly," he said. "For that we get to the third possibility—that Professor Harker actually put some other number down in the calculator, but that the number was somehow altered before we saw it.

"For example, as the professor fell he might have inadvertently pressed one of the buttons, or it might have knocked against the pavement. A button that would alter the number that the calculator was holding. Say, the square button, or the square root button.

"Let's test that out. Now, if we square the number we're working with, we get" —he pressed the x^2 button on the calculator and read out, '4 8 3 2 1 3 2 . 9.'

"Which brings nothing immediately to mind as the identity of the murderer. If we, on the other hand, press the square root function"—and Lieutenant Loman put the original number back in the machine and pushed the button marked $\sqrt{x}$, getting 4 6 . 8 8 5 0 8 6."

Professor Pyne stared at the number, trying to read its mystical significance. "So?"

"So we were doing it backward. The professor *did* punch a number into his calculator. Then as he fell he hit the square root button.

"The number he punched in was Robert Quipper's phone number—4 8 3 2 1 3 3."

"But the number you get when you square our number is 4832132.9," Sergeant Stametti objected. "I admit it's uncomfortably close, but why the difference? How did the 3 change to a 2.9?"

"Try it," Loman invited, handing Stametti the calculator. "Put in the phone number first, then hit the square root button."

Sergeant Stametti did as instructed. He tapped Quipper's phone number into the machine, then took the square root. He stared down at the familiar number they had found on the machine.

"But when we reverse it," Loman said, leaning over the table and hitting the square button, "it ends in 2.9."

"Of course!" Professor Pyne said. "The calculator rounds off the last figure on numbers that exceed capacity. This causes the error when the process is reversed."

"And we didn't look for a phone number," Lieutenant Loman said, "because the results had eight digits. But we were doing it backwards."

"It'll never stand up in court," Quipper said.

Loman took the note he had just received and flipped it in front of Quipper. "We got a warrant," he said, "and searched your apartment. Found an old hunting knife in a leather sheaf. If that fresh stain on the blade is human blood, you're in trouble. Along with what we got from the phone company I think we'll be able to put your away."

"You don't understand," Quipper said.

"I never do," Lieutenant Loman said. "Sergeant, take this gentleman downstairs."

Ω

"You have to get rid of her!" Linda screamed. "I can't take any more of this, Arthur! You have to do something about her!"

Arthur Pym put down his heavy briefcase, took one look at his wife, and decided that she would not respond favorably to a husbandly kiss. Not even a token peck on the cheek. "What now?"

"Arthur, I work hard at my job. I know it doesn't pay a lot, but I make my contribution to this family. And you know this house is mine. And that shiny car you love so much! If it hadn't been for Daddy's money, we'd be living in a dingy apartment and driving an old clunker."

"Yes, yes, you're right." He longed for a martini. Something icy cold and sparkling clear, with a tiny green olive in it and just a whisper of vermouth. He wished that he'd stopped on the way home and had one, instead of planning to sip it at home, but it was too late now.

"I work a long day, too. I just got home a few minutes before you did," Linda said.

He would have to prompt her, he knew. She wouldn't just come out with the story, but there would be no peace until she'd told it, so he forced himself to feign curiosity. "What did she do this time?"

"I don't suppose you've listened to the tape, Arthur, have you?"

"How could I? I just got home." He slipped out of his warm coat and hung it in the closet. He loosened his tie.

"Maybe you should hear it," Linda said, "but I was so mad, I erased it."

"Oh," Arthur grunted. What was he supposed to say to that? If he said he was pleased not to hear the tape he'd contradict her and a tirade would follow. If he agreed with her—was this a verbal trap? He decided to chance it. "That's too bad, I'd have liked to hear it."

"I'll bet you would! You just love everything about that slut, including her voice, don't you?"

Wrong!

Arthur managed to edge past Linda and make his way to the liquor cabinet. He got out the cocktail shaker and the ingredients. He'd have been quite willing to forgo the olive, but he had to get to the kitchen anyhow for ice, so he might as well have both. An oliveless martini was no great sacrifice, but a warm one was unthinkable.

Linda kept her shoulder behind Arthur's, chivvying him as he carried the silver shaker and the gin and vermouth bottles into the kitchen. She managed to make her proximity a hostile act, keeping inside his personal space, making him uncomfortable.

As Arthur broke ice cubes from their tray, Linda kept up a verbal barrage. Arthur wrapped the ice cubes in a dishtowel and pulverized them with a hammer. The cocktail shaker was cleverly designed. It had a double skin, and Arthur sifted the pulverized ice into the space between the layers. Thus the contents of the shaker itself could be chilled but not diluted.

"There were five calls," Linda was saying. "Five, can you believe it?"

Arthur grunted and held the gin bottle over the open shaker. He had an accurate eye and a fairly steady hand. "Martini?" he asked.

"Don't change the subject! The first one was supposed to sound like a business call. "This is Miss Morgan at Acme and Jones,'" she mimicked Mae Anne Morgan's voice, "'calling for Mr. Pym. I have an urgent message.' Urgent message my foot! That strumpet! As if you were going to take business calls at home in the middle of the day!"

"I won't take her calls at work, Linda. You know, I told her not to call me either there or here."

"Then the second one, 'Is Arthur there, please?' Butter would melt in that bitch's mouth! 'Is Arthur there, please?'"

Arthur had to admit that Linda was a good mimic. If he closed his eyes, blotting out Linda's dark hair and eyes, her sharp features and slim figure, he could almost *see* Mae Anne Morgan. Mae Anne was the antithesis of Linda. Blonde, round-faced, buxom.

"Then the other three calls," Linda went on. "She just let the tape run and hung up. Just to annoy me. Just to make herself felt!"

Arthur tried to ask his question once more, this time using only his eyes and a little body language, but Linda refused to respond. So Arthur poured enough gin for them both, added a drop of oily liquid from the green bottle, and swirled the concoction gently. He didn't want to bruise the vermouth. He put the shaker on a tray with two glasses and edged around Linda to the doorway. In the living room he put the tray on the low table and poured two martinis. If Linda didn't drink hers, Arthur would.

"She isn't really doing any harm," Arthur offered tentatively. "If we just ignore her, maybe she'll get tired and stop pestering us."

"Don't be a fool! She'll never do that. She's after you, and she won't stop until she has you. Sometimes I think I'd be better off if I just let her have you. Good riddance to bad rubbish!"

"No, no. I'll do something about her."

"You rutting goat! Are all men like you? They think with their gonads? Or is Mae Anne that much better than I am?"

Arthur resisted the temptation to make some wisecrack of an answer. Like, *Wait while I try and remember, it's been so long, Linda.* He thought better of that. "How may times do I have to apologize?" he asked instead. "I was wrong. I'm sorry I did it. You said you forgave me, that you wanted us to stay together. Can't we forget the whole thing?"

"Not with Mae Anne chasing around after you with her claws out. First she was sending you those coy little invitations. Then the time she showed up on our doorstep—to drop off a parts catalog, of all the feeble excuses!"

"She *is* in the business," Arthur offered.

"I'll bet she is!"

"She really is, Linda. I wish she weren't. If she hadn't been in Chicago for the convention, this would all never have happened. I wish I'd never laid eyes on her!"

"Too bad that wasn't all you laid on her!"

His hand holding the tall-stemmed glass shook and drops of gin-and-vermouth spattered onto the table-top. He managed to put the glass down without spilling any more, pulled a bandanna from his pocket and wiped the liquid away.

"You are such an easy mark, Arthur. If you were a woman you would have been pregnant by the age of twelve. The boys would have lined up at your door like dogs after a bitch in heat. Do you really think you met Mae Anne by accident?"

Arthur leaned forward and sipped from the rim of his glass. The martini was cold, clear, delicious. Maybe he should have been a bartender instead of a plumbing contractor. No, there was just so much plumbing he could put in his own house—Linda's house—and he had installed the latest of everything. But a bartender who becomes fond of his own wares is in dire peril.

"Arthur! Stop swimming in that booze and answer me!"

He looked at her blankly.

"You don't really believe that Mae Anne was in that saloon by accident, do you?"

"Of course she was. Well, you know, the convention was going on, and everybody heads for the local taverns and restaurants when the proceedings end each day. I just wanted to have a drink or two. I'd been sitting in seminars all day and I wanted a drink, that's all."

"And Miss Blonde Bombshell just happened to be there, too."

"Yes."

"And she just happened to notice your convention badge, and you just happened to notice hers. If she'd been wearing it on her elbow I bet you wouldn't have seen it. My god, what is so goddamned wonderful about big tits, I have never understood that and I never will, not if I live to a thousand."

"Please, Linda, we've been over this a hundred times. Why do we need to drag it all out again?"

"What did you do, ask her about the latest twist in copper plumbing? Or did you offer to buy her a drink? What did she drink, Arthur? Did she have a martini with you?"

"Linda, for god's sake!"

"What did she drink? A Shirley Temple?"

"She drank gin-and-bitters. That's all she ever drinks. We took a bottle back to the hotel with us, to her room. We were going to look at some new product specs. She *was* there on business, you know."

"Sure, Arthur."

"I was wrong. I'm sorry. I was lonely, it was a strange city, I had a couple of drinks too many. I can't undo what's done, Linda, nobody can do that."

"And Miss Superbosom just happened to be transferred to Vernon City the next month."

"Yes."

"All a coincidence."

"As far as I know, that's all it was."

"And she started coming after you again."

"Yes."

"You can't tell me you're not flattered. Miss Big Boobs coming to see you, calling you all the time, trying to get you back into her bed all the time."

Arthur had finished his martini. Seeing that Linda hadn't touched hers, he switched glasses with her and started the second.

"Well?"

"Linda, I swear to you, I don't want to have an affair with this woman. It was supposed to be a one night stand, that's all she ever meant to me. It isn't right, I won't try to justify it, but it does happen all the time, and once it's over that's the end of it. Those are the rules. Everybody knows that. I was just unlucky. I ran into somebody who won't play by the rules. I'd be the happiest man in the world if I could get rid of her."

There was a long pause. Then Linda said, "There is a way."

Arthur looked at her.

"There is a way," she repeated.

"You don't mean . . ."

"Yes, I do."

"I don't know," Arthur said. "In all the books and movies, you can just hire a hit-man, but I don't know any hit-men. They're not in the yellow pages. I wouldn't know how to find one."

"Don't they always ask bartenders about that kind of thing?" Linda asked.

"I don't really *know* any bartenders. I mean, I have a drink now and then at lunchtime or after work, but I don't really know any bartenders. I wouldn't know what to say. What if I asked one and he reported me to the police? Even if nothing happened, isn't that conspiracy or something? I'd be afraid. I don't think I could do that. Besides, it must be awfully expensive."

Arthur wrung his hands. "I guess I could go down to the Commerce Square project. We're doing the plumbing contract on that, and I know some of the fellows working there. They're demolishing that old hotel, the old Commerce Inn. Then we're going to work on the new structure. I could ask if they have any poisonous chemicals there. They have to do the demolition just so, you know, just to take down the old building they want to get rid of, and not damage the others. Some of the chemicals they use, the explosives and the fusing chemicals and dampers—maybe I could borrow something. I know George Smycowski, the foreman there. I don't know what I could say, but I could try."

Linda said, "Never mind George Smycwhatsis, it's all right." She stood up and started from the room.

Arthur looked after her. "All right? It's all right?" Was that all? he wondered. Was she willing to let it go at that?

"No hit-man," Linda said.

"No hit-man."

"No chemicals," Linda said.

"No chemicals."

"You'll just have to do it yourself." She walked out of the room. Five minutes later she was back. She held a small white envelope toward him.

"What's this?"

"Rat poison."

"What?"

"You heard me. She won't leave town, she won't leave you alone, and you won't hire a man to get rid of her for you. So you'll just have to do it yourself."

He held the envelope, staring. "But—how?"

"How did I get it? Don't be stupid. I just took the bus to the Lakeview District and bought it in a hardware store. It was miles from here. The clerk filled out a sales slip and I gave him a false name and address. They'll never connect some woman on the other side of the town with the murder of a plumbing parts saleswoman downtown."

Feeling as stupid as Linda seemed to think he was, Arthur turned the envelope around and around. "But—how do I get her to take it?"

"I'll spell it out, Arthur. Miss Sexpot is so eager to see you again, you call her up and tell her you're willing."

"I guess I could say I want to place an order for some porcelain goods or something."

"Believe me, Arthur, you won't need an excuse."

"But her office—I mean, Acme and Jones is a big outfit."

"Trust me, Arthur, she'll tell you she left the catalog at home."

Ω

As usual, Linda was correct. A phone call the next morning, from Arthur's office to Mae Anne's, brought an invitation to Mae Anne's apartment that very night.

Arthur left the office at six o'clock, stopped for two martinis, and patted the pocket containing the rat poison after every sip. By the time he reached Mae Anne's apartment, the effect of the alcohol had reduced his nervousness from a violent shaking to a gentle tremor and a cold sweat.

Mae Anne answered the door wearing a thin blouse and tight jeans. Arthur was reminded of the lushness he had experienced in Chicago. He started to stammer a clumsy hello and Mae Anne pulled him across her threshold, reaching past him to slam the door. She reached up to kiss him and he could smell her perfume. Arthur was not a tall man, and he looked down and saw that Mae Anne was barefoot. That was why she had had to stand on her toes to give him a kiss.

"Uh—about that plumbing order—" Arthur began.

"Who cares?" Mae Anne said. She pulled him toward the couch and pushed him down. She sat beside him and held his hands. A tray of snacks stood on the table, and a bottle of gin peered from an ice bucket. Beside it stood two smaller bottles: vermouth for him, bitters for Mae Anne.

"I couldn't forget your favorite drink," Mae Anne purred. "I think it's perfect that we like the same brand of gin. Martini for you, gee-'n'-bee for me." She built them each a drink. Arthur sipped his martini. It could have been better, but he had no complaints. The two—or was it three—that he'd had before coming to Mae Anne's apartment were making themselves felt in the form of a noticeable pressure, but he held his ground.

They finished a round.

Mae Anne snuggled a little closer to Arthur. She rubbed her bare foot against his ankle, picked an hors d'oeuvre from the tray, put a kiss on it and popped it into Arthur's mouth. "You're sweating, Arthur. Why don't you take off your jacket and tie?"

"No!" He wiped his brow. "I mean it is a little bit warm. But I think I'll keep it on."

"Whatever you want." She leaned across him to the bottles, to make them each another drink.

The pressure on Arthur's bladder was becoming a distraction.

"To us." Mae Anne said.

She hoisted her gin-and-bitters, waited for Arthur to lift his martini, then hooked her elbow through his to sip from her glass.

"T-to us," Arthur echoed.

Mae Anne put down her glass. "I think I'll go and put on something more comfortable," she said.

"Sure. Uh, while you do, maybe, ha-ha, I'll take a look at the plumbing." He managed a feeble smile.

"Right over there," Mae Anne pointed. Then she disappeared through a doorway.

Frantically, Arthur pulled the envelope from his pocket, tore open a corner, poured the white powder into Mae Anne's drink, and looked around for a swizzle stick. He couldn't find one and he didn't have time to waste, so he stirred the gin-and-bitters with his finger until the powder was dissolved. Then he ran to the bathroom.

He turned on the water and scrubbed his finger with soap, resisting a crazy impulse to taste the poison mixture before he washed it away. When he was sure he had removed all the poison he dried his hands, relieved himself, then washed his hands again, then dried them thoroughly. He patted his jacket pocket and located the potentially incriminating envelope. He held it over the toilet, found a match and lit a corner of the paper. As the paper burned, the ashes sifted into the bowl. When only the tiniest corner remained, Arthur dropped it into the toilet, flushed it, washed his hands still again, and returned to the living room.

Mae Anne was seated on the couch. She had indeed changed into something more comfortable—a transparent peignoir that left even less to the imagination than her former costume had. "My, you were gone an awfully long time, Arthur. Are you sure you're all right"

He perched nervously on the edge of the couch. "T-to us," he said again. They hooked their elbows and emptied their glasses. The act of drinking the poison brought them very close together, and Arthur could feel the softness of Mae Anne's body against him.

As soon as the glasses were empty, Arthur felt suddenly relaxed. He said, "I guess you were right, Mae Anne. It is a little close in here." He took off his jacket and tie, and laid them across the end of the couch.

"You look tired, Arthur. If you had as long a day as I did," Mae Anne said, "well, come on, let's take a little nap." She looked up at him mischievously.

Could he? Arthur asked himself. Should he? Now that Mae Anne had drunk up all the poison, how long would it take to act? If he left suddenly, might she get suspicious? When the symptoms began, would she call the paramedics? Or the police? How long did rat poison take to act? Had Linda furnished the proper dose?

Assailed by a mob of questions, Arthur Pym decided that his only course of action was to stay with Mae Anne and make sure that the poison had done its job. If she showed any sign of suspicion, he would talk her out of it. If necessary, restrain her until she was—was—until it was no longer necessary.

He let her lead him to into the bedroom.

"Here, Arthur, put your feet up. That's right. You look so tired. Let me take your shoes off for you."

He put his head on the pillow. The room was pleasant, Mae Anne's voice was soothing, he *was* tired. And he'd had four martinis, or was it five—or six?—and only a couple of canapés for dinner.

He closed his eyes.

In the morning he wakened to a throbbing, pounding hangover. He felt as if elf carpenters were driving brass screws through his eardrums, hoping to meet in the middle of his brain. He sat up suddenly despite the renewed jolt of pain it caused him and looked at the other side of the bed.

Mae Anne was gone!

Was she dead? Had she wakened in the middle of the night and staggered from the bedroom ad died on the carpet? Had she gone to the hospital, and if so, were the police even now on their way to her apartment to arrest him, Arthur?

No! There was a note on the other pillow.

Arthur, it read, *I have to leave for work now. Phone me at Acme and Jones, without fail—or you'll be sorry! And don't forget to lock up behind you.* It was signed, *Love, Mae Anne.*

Oh my god, Arthur thought, what now? Maybe the dose wasn't enough. Or maybe it's slow-acting rat poison. Or—he reached for the telephone, dialed Acme and Jones, and asked for Ms. Morgan.

"You fool," Mae Anne's voice came over the wire. "What do you think you're trying to do?"

Arthur was unable to frame a coherent reply.

"That drink smelled funny. I decided to risk one tiny drop of it on the tip of my tongue, I know that was risky, but it tasted so weird I poured it in a jar in the kitchen and took a fresh drink while you were making potty."

How could she speak so freely on the telephone? She must have a private office, a private phone line.

"D-did you—" he started to ask.

"Don't look for it, Arthur. I took it with me this morning. Had it analyzed. What a dummy you are!"

"Are you going to call the police? Did you drug me? I can hardly remember—"

"No, I'm not going to call the police. And I didn't drug you either. You just got drunk and passed out, you wimp."

"Then, w-what—?"

"You'd better get to work, Arthur. Meet me at quitting time." She named a pub centrally located between their two offices. She hung up before he could reply, but he knew that he would be there. In the meanwhile, he knew that he had to call Linda at *her* job. He didn't know what to tell her.

Ω

Arthur peered into the dimly-lighted saloon, hoping that he was there before Mae Anne. It was an establishment he'd never been in before. There was a long mahogany bar backed by a mirror. Black leather barstools lined the brass rail. Small wooden tables with red-glass candle-holders on them filled most of the room, and a few curtained booths separated by wooden partitions flanked the open floor.

An old Rock-Ola jukebox glowed in muted colors. From hidden speakers a vaguely remembered Ray Anthony trumpet solo flowed softly into the room.

It took Arthur a moment to get his bearings, as his eyes adjusted from the late afternoon brightness of the sidewalk to the perpetual twilight atmosphere of the saloon. As soon as he had his dim-vision operating, he saw that he had failed to arrive ahead of Mae Anne. She was sitting alone at the end of the bar.

Although the saloon was nearly filled with white collar types stopping for a quick cocktail on their way home from work, Mae Anne had kept the stool next to her vacant. She signaled to Arthur and he slid onto the leather. Even through the woolen thickness of his winter suit the smooth surface felt cool.

"What a disappointment you are," Mae Anne opened the conversation.

Arthur said, "Are you all right?"

Mae Anne shook her head slowly. "Do I look like a dead woman? My friend, I am not even sick. Although I'll admit, I felt pretty silly after I'd tasted that drink. If you'd picked a better poison, one drop should have done me in. Oh well, we live and learn, don't we?"

Arthur said, "What are you going to do?"

Mae Anne had a gin-and-bitters in front of her. She picked it up and sipped at it before answering his question. When she did, it was with a question of her own. "You want a drink, Arthur? Guaranteed non-toxic. Except over the long run, if the doctors are right. What's the old saw? *Name your poison.*"

"I—I don't think I want a drink. Thanks."

Mae Anne said to the bartender, "Bobby, a martini for my friend. And build me another of these, eh? This one is nearly gone."

Arthur was astonished. The bartender hadn't been anywhere near them a moment ago, yet when Mae Anne wanted to order a drink , he was suddenly there. Some people are like that, he thought. Bartenders, doormen, taxi-drivers. Arthur would have sat for ten minutes, trying to get the bartender's attention, embarrassed to make himself conspicuous, getting more and more impatient.

"I, uh, didn't really feel much like . . ." He let his voice trail away.

"Hair of the dog, Arthur. You don't look too great. Hard day at the office?"

The drink was in front of him and he plucked the toothpick from its rim, pulled the olive from it, chewed it slowly. It tasted of salt, vinegar, gin and vermouth. "You look all right," he said nervously to Mae Anne. "I mean," he leaned over and sipped cold martini from the rim of the tall glass, "I mean, uh, after last night. I'm sorry about last night. I mean, ah, what I did last night wasn't very nice. What I tried to do last night, that is."

"You're sorry?"

He nodded.

"You're sorry?" she said again. "You tried to kill me, to poison me, and you're *sorry?* You're *apologizing?* I don't believe this."

"She made me do it. Linda did. She knew all about us, she found out, and she wanted me to kill you. She—" He looked up suddenly. The bartender—it was amazing how one person could serve all the customers at the bar, but he was doing it—the bartender was at the other end of the long mahogany bar, taking orders, pouring drinks, ringing up sales, making change. "Should we be talking about this?" Arthur asked Mae Anne. "I mean somebody . . ." he dropped his voice still farther ". . . somebody might hear us."

"I don't have anything to hide," Mae Anne said. She tossed off the last of her gin-and-bitters. As if by magic, the bartender was in front of her, asking if she wanted another. She nodded. He turned away, made the drink, placed it in front of her with one hand while removing her empty with the other.

"On your tab, Miss Morgan," he said.

Arthur had downed most of his martini and waved his hands, trying to get the bartender's attention so he could ask for a refill. The bartender had started toward a heavyset man in a pinstripe suit with a folded twenty between his fingers, but Mae Anne said, "Refill," while tilting her head microscopically toward Arthur.

The bartender addressed the man in the pinstripe suit. "Right with you, sir." He swooped back toward Arthur and Mae Anne, mixed gin and vermouth, poured, stuck a toothpick through an olive, placed the concoction before Arthur and was gone again.

"Aren't—aren't you even worried?" Arthur asked Mae Anne. "I mean, ah, one of us might say something we'd be sorry for if somebody overheard."

"Nobody pays attention to two people talking in a saloon, Arthur. Don't raise your voice, don't make yourself conspicuous, and we could give each other the formula for the neutron bomb in this joint and nobody would know and nobody would care if they did."

Arthur said, "Okay." He looked around for a bar snack, located a wooden bowl, pulled it toward them, shoved a pretzel into his mouth and munched on it. "Okay. I guess. Mae Anne, why did you tell me to meet you here? What do you want? It has to be about last night, I know that. I'm right about that, aren't I?"

"You are." She put her glass down and gave him a hard, piercing look. "You know what kind of poison that was, Arthur?"

He nodded and made some kind of noise in his throat; he wasn't sure himself what it was.

"Rat poison," Mae Anne said. "You tried to dose me with rat poison."

"It was Linda's idea," he murmured.

"I believe you. But Linda didn't put it in my drink, Arthur. *You* put it in my drink."

"Are you going to call the police?" he asked.

She shook her head. There was a blue neon advertising sign against the wall. From where Arthur sat, Mae Anne was silhouetted against the sign. The blue glow, coming through her blonde hair, created a peculiar and morbid halo-effect.

"You're angry, though, Mae Anne, I can tell." Arthur nodded emphatically, agreeing with his own inference. "You're mad at me because of what happened. I'm glad it didn't work," Arthur said, "I didn't want to kill you. Linda made me do it."

"You already said that."

"You're mad at me."

"No I'm not. I don't believe in getting mad. I believe in getting even."

Arthur felt a chill sweep through him and he put his glass down hard.

"Don't worry, Arthur. I didn't put anything in your drink. Neither did Bobby." She indicated the bartender, once again busy at the far end of the assemblage. "No, Arthur. I'm not mad at you, and I'm not out to get even with you. I don't know what made me pick you up at that convention, but now that I've got you, I'm going to hang onto you. In the right hands, you could be useful. But wifey, now—wifey's another matter."

"Linda?"

"You've got more than one? Of course, Linda. I wouldn't mind so much if she'd tried some other kind of poison, but *rat* poison. *Yuch!* Warfarin! Nasty, rotten stuff! Arsenic, mercury, strychnine, she could have used almost anything. But *rat poison!*"

"What do you want me to do, Mae Anne?"

She stared at him. "If you were single . . ." she said, letting the end of the sentence hang in the air.

"I could divorce her."

"No good."

"The house. The car."

"You'd lose them."

"This is a community property state."

Her eyebrow raised a fraction of an inch. "You bought them? With your joint earnings since marriage?"

"Uh . . . actually, Linda inherited the house from her dad. And the money we bought the car with."

"Didn't you know they're exempt from community property, then? Anything that comes from a family inheritance is exempt from community property."

"I didn't know that," Arthur said.

"Now you do," Mae Anne said.

They sat in silence for what seemed like hours. Arthur looked at the clock set in a vodka sign above the bar mirror. He'd been in the saloon with Mae Anne for less than thirty minutes.

"Wh-what are we going to do, then?"

"What *we*, white man?" Mae Anne asked.

Arthur gave her a baffled look.

"Never mind, Arthur," she sighed. "I'll spell it out for you in words of one syllable. Your little wifey tried to kill me and I am pissed off about it and you— not *we*, *you*—are going to turn the tables on her. You are going to kill her. You inherit her estate, and then you'll settle up with me. Will you ever, Arthur!"

Arthur covered his eyes with his fingers. "Oh, my god." He slid his hands down onto his cheeks, looked wearily at Mae Anne. He said, "You can't mean that. You don't know what you are saying."

"I know exactly what I'm saying," she hissed at him.

"But—to *kill* someone—"

"Keep your voice down, Arthur."

"To kill someone—someone you hardly know, someone you barely met one time—someone who's never done anything to you—"

"She tried to kill me, you moron."

The Ray Anthony record ended on the jukebox and out of the corner of his eye Arthur watched the aged mechanism lift the black disk from the turntable, place it back among the other old singles, lift another and lower it to the turntable. Seconds later the sounds of Glen Gray and the Casa Loma Orchestra drifted from the concealed speakers.

"It was your own fault, Mae Anne," Arthur murmured.

"What?" she exclaimed.

"Well, not exactly your fault, or not all your fault anyhow. I mean—"

"I heard what you said." She smiled faintly. "This is really intriguing. Go on, Arthur."

"Well, only that you wouldn't leave me alone. I mean, Chicago was just one time. You were from another city and everything. I didn't expect ever to see you again." There was a silence. "Well, maybe at the convention again next year."

"And instead I wound up living here, and looking you up," Mae Anne supplied. "Hey? You figured you didn't owe me anything, I didn't owe you anything, just a brief encounter between strangers. Is that it?"

Arthur stared into his drink. "Something like that."

"This is the modern world. I didn't lose my honor or anything like that. No more scarlet letter. You know what, Arthur? I think you're right."

"Then we can forget the whole thing?"

"Too late for that."

"But why?"

"Rat poison, Arthur. Rat poison. Hell hath no fury like a woman who's had rat poison dumped in her highball."

"What are you going to do then? Are you going to call the police after all? You said you weren't going to call the police."

"And I wouldn't do a thing like breaking my word. Arthur, if you weren't so fucked up you'd be funny. I still have the poison, you know. I sent it to a chemist I know to be analyzed, but it only took a little bit to test. The rest of it's still there in the lab, along with the test results. Did you wipe your fingerprints off everything when you left my place?"

Arthur pressed his thumb and forefinger against his eyelids and tried to remember. The glasses, the table top, the plumbing fixtures . . .

"You didn't, did you?"

"I guess not."

"Arthur, Arthur. You really were a mistake, you know it? I'll admit you're pretty good in bed, but anywhere else you're a real dud, you know that?"

He didn't say anything.

"And as for that little cupcake of yours—did she provide the rat poison or did she make you get it yourself? Don't tell me, you wouldn't have had the balls to make up a story and walk into a store and buy poison."

She shook her head sadly.

"I'll tell you, Arthur. I kind of admire little wifey, at least she has some spunk, some backbone. But I'm really pissed off at her. Rat poison! So here's what you're going to do for me. You're going to kill her. She tried to kill me, using you as her errand boy—I'm going to return the favor. Only this time it's going to work."

"What? I mean—how?"

"With a knife, Arthur, with an ordinary carving knife. You do have cutlery in the house, don't you?"

He nodded.

"You won't have to buy anything, you won't have to make up a story. Nothing. Just pick up the knife and kill her."

"I can't!"

"Sure you can. You could put poison in my drink, you can put a knife in Linda."

"But—the blood. I mean—and what if she screams? What if she fights? She won't let me do it. She'll fight with me and then she'll call the police."

"Then don't let her, Arthur."

"What—what do you mean?"

Mae Anne looked away from him. "Bobby, thanks." The bartender was refreshing their drinks. "Snack, Arthur?" Mae Anne shoved the fresh bowl of salted nuts and pretzels toward him. "I mean," she said, "that this is really your problem, Arthur, not mine. But if you don't want Linda to fight or scream, you just make sure that you get in one good fast fatal shot before she can do anything about it. Like, sneak up behind her, reach around, and cut the bitch's throat."

Arthur's skin had turned clammy and he could feel himself shaking.

"Or—here's something even better. Wait until she's sound asleep and get her in the heart. Okay, Arthur?"

He heard himself moan, softly. The record on the Rock-Ola jukebox had changed again, to something by Frank Sinatra accompanied by the Nelson Riddle Orchestra.

"If you think you might not be able to handle that, Arthur, you could hold a pillow over her face with one hand and use the other to hold the knife, to stab her. Then if it takes a little while for her to die, you can muffle her screams."

There was a ringing in Arthur's ears.

"Don't pass out on me, Arthur," Mae Anne slapped him hard across the cheek. Arthur heard the blow more than he felt it, but at once the ringing disappeared. He could feel the blood rushing into his face and he knew that he wasn't going to faint after all. He did feel nauseous, though.

Several customers whirled at the sound of Mae Anne's slap, but they saw her rubbing Arthur's wrists and turned away again, resuming their separate conversations. Bobby the bartender hurried over, said, "Everything okay, Miss Morgan?"

Mae Anne said, "It's okay. My friend was just feeling a little queasy."

"Want me to cut him off, Miss Morgan?"

"It's okay. Thanks, Bobby."

Arthur said, "I couldn't, Mae Anne. I can't. I mean—a knife. All the blood. Screams."

"You'll do it, Arthur."

"But then what? I'll have to call—I don't know. The doctor? The undertaker?"

"Call the police, Arthur."

"But it's murder! They'll arrest me!"

"Arthur, you'll fake a burglary."

"But—but—"

"You can do it, Arthur."

"But it's *murder!*"

"You can do it."

"I won't."

"You will. If you don't, I warn you, I'm going to blow the whistle on you for last night. On you and Linda both. You'll both wind up in jail. You do it my way and you'll almost certainly get off. That kind of thing happens every day. Read the paper. You can do it, Arthur!"

He put his head in his hands, elbows on the polished mahogany, turned sideways to look at Mae Anne. She was perfectly composed, the blue advertising sign halo still shining through her blonde hair.

"When do I . . ." he gulped— "when do I have to do it?"

"Tonight, Arthur."

"T-Tonight?"

"Yes."

"B-but, can't I have a little time? I mean, a few days, maybe a week?"

"Arthur, get your nerve up and do it tonight. The longer you wait the worse it's going to be. You'll lose your nerve, you'll say something, do something, Linda will cop to it, that you're up to no good. It won't work. Tonight, Arthur."

She turned on her stool, took both his hands in hers. For a moment Arthur couldn't help thinking that Mae Anne was beautiful, she was voluptuous, and he knew she was stronger than he was and he had to do what she said.

"Does Linda know what happened last night, Arthur?"

"I—I don't know."

"You didn't call her today?"

"I didn't call her at work. I mean, at her work. I called home from the office, I left a message on the tape."

"What did you say, Arthur?"

"I just said that things hadn't worked out last night, and I'd explain everything when I got home tonight."

"See if you can wipe that tape, Arthur. Get something over it."

"I could wipe the tape, or even throw it away."

"That would be even more suspicious. Try and get something harmless over it. The weather report, anything. But if you can't, then you'd better have a story ready to use. It'll be easy. Work out some yarn about tickets for a show or reservations at a restaurant or anything. But have your story ready."

Arthur nodded. The jukebox was sending the sounds of a Benny Goodman song through the concealed speakers.

"Tonight, Arthur." Mae dropped her hand into his lap and ran her fingernails up the inside of his thigh. It felt like fire-ants stinging. "Tonight, Arthur. Tonight."

II

Arthur had to try three times to get his key into the lock, but he finally managed to work the mechanism. The night had turned chilly and he stood in the foyer blowing on his hands to warm them after closing the door. He checked his wristwatch and found that it wasn't nearly as late as he'd expected.

He peered into the dining room and saw that Linda had spread a white linen cloth and set the table with her good china. He could smell a beef roast all the way from the kitchen. What a stroke of luck! That meant that the carving knife would be on the dining room sideboard. He found the knife and stood, studying its edge. There was a pleasant scent in the house, even in addition to the cooking odors, and Linda had turned the radio to a classical station so the house was filled with sounds of strings and reeds.

Arthur halted. He'd got an idea. He lowered his briefcase silently to the carpet, removed his jacket and his hat and placed them carefully on the briefcase. He knelt, untied his shoelaces, and slipped out of his shoes.

He'd once read in a cheap novel that a proper killer held his knife low and struck upward with it, under the rib cage, rather than holding the blade high and striking downward. That way the blade was less likely to bounce off a bone. He would stand behind Linda, call her name. She would turn and he would bring the carving knife up under her ribs and that would be the end of it. No waking in the middle of the night, no pillow over her face, no faked burglary.

He would do the deed, then call the police. Make sure the knife blade was smeared, but if they found his fingerprints on it, so what— it was his knife, he used it every time they had a roast for dinner. He'd got home late, he'd stopped after work for a business discussion over drinks with a plumbing supplies sales rep, and when he got home he found Linda dead. Who could have done it? No signs of a break-in, no signs of a violent quarrel. It must have been someone known to the victim. Was the Pyms' marriage in trouble? Had she taken a paramour? She might have entertained him while Arthur was at his meeting, the illicit lovers quarreled, then the man picked up the knife and . . .

The music on the radio ended and an announcer identified it as Mozart's symphony number 40, the *Jupiter*. A commercial began for an expensive brand of imported luxury cars.

Arthur advanced through the kitchen doorway, his stockinged feet utterly silent.

He stood behind Linda, gathering his nerve to call her name. She was standing at the electric cooktop, sautéing onions.

He said, "Li—"

She whirled, swinging the heavy iron pan. Arthur stood paralyzed as the black pan described an arc, rising from the cooktop, slices of onions and drops of melted butter flying through the air. The frying pan came down edge-first against his skull. He heard more than felt the sickening thud of impact. He didn't even feel the carving knife as it tumbled from his suddenly nerveless fingers, described a perfect flip in mid-air and embedded itself point-first in his stocking-clad foot.

III

"Talk about incompetence!"

"I know, I know. I mean, you give a guy a simple assignment and he can't do *anything*."

"Well, he put the poison in my drink. He did that okay. Maybe the flaw was in the plan, not the execution."

"Are you saying it was *my* fault, Anne Mae?"

"Mae Anne."

"Oh, yeah. I always think of it as Anne Mae—Anne may, and if you give her a chance she will!"

"Not funny, Linda."

"I'm sorry. I didn't mean to hurt you."

"You didn't."

"I mean, he doesn't amount to much, but he's mine."

"Uh-huh."

"And along you come with your blonde hair and your big boobs and—" Linda reached into her purse and pulled out a handkerchief and wept into it.

"Don't cry, honey." Mae Anne put her hands on the back of Linda's shoulder comfortingly. Bobby poked his head inside their booth and asked if they were ready for a refill. Mae Anne said they were and he disappeared to make their drinks. It was an off hour, the late lunch crowd had finally dragged their tails back to their offices and the quitting-time rush hadn't started yet. In fact, Mae Anne and Linda were the only customers in the place. That wouldn't last, but it was the situation for the moment, and they both had settled into a the seclusion of a quiet, curtained booth.

Mae Anne had fed a fistful of coins into the Rock-Ola jukebox, and Billie Holiday's voice was coming from the speakers.

"You've got the son of a bitch. I had him for one night—"

"Two."

"The second one doesn't count. He passed out on me. After trying to kill me. If he'd had any sense, he would have held back on the juice and tried to get *me* snookered before he dumped the powder in my glass. That's why I think your plan was the pits, Linda."

"I thought he could bring it off. I guess I counted on him having too many brains."

"Besides, you know, you can talk about big boobs and all, but in fact I really envy you. You've got the kind of figure I always wanted, and I haven't had since I was twelve. What size dresses do you wear anyhow?"

"Five."

"Oh, Jesus! Size fucking five!" Mae Anne stuck her head out of the booth. "Bobby! A double! In fact, make me a pitcher and bring it, will you?"

"You know, that was pretty bitchy of you to send him after me with a knife. Right there in my own kitchen! I mean, I work hard all day, and then I come home and set the table and put a roast in the oven and slice up all those onions. You know, I was crying before I even cut into one, and then when I got started I couldn't stop."

"I'm sorry, Linda. I'm really sorry. He was supposed to do it in the night, when you were sound asleep. Pillow on the face, blade between the ribs, you'd never know what hit you."

"Thanks a million, Mae Anne."

"Well, you tried to kill me first, Linda!"

"Okay, I guess you had a right. We're even now?"

"Even."

They shook hands.

Bobby brought them two pitchers, one of martinis, one of gin-and-bitters.

"I don't see how you can stand the taste of bitters."

"I hate vermouth worse."

There was a long silence, punctuated only by the voice of Billie Holiday, pain in its every note.

"Linda, what are we going to do with the fucker?"

"I don't know." She shook her head.

"I do."

"What?"

"Kill the fucker."

"Oh, no! How could we do such a thing? That would be *murder!*"

"You bitch! It wasn't murder to try and poison *me?*"

"Well, but you were—"

"The other woman, right. Trying to steal your man. The crime of passion. The unwritten law."

"Well, you tried to make him stab me."

"Let's not go around this again, all right?"

Linda bit her lip. "All right, Mae Anne." She toyed with her glass, letting the sound of Billie Holiday flow around her. She smiled at her companion. "You know, it *is* an idea."

"It's a god damned *good* idea, sister!"

"But how can we do it?"

"Where is he now? I thought he was supposed to meet us here after work."

"Well, his foot, you know. And his head. He isn't moving so well right now."

Mae Anne laughed. "Serves the bastard right! I can't wait to see him!"

"He was out of the office when I called him the first time. I think he was over at that Commerce Square project talking about their plumbing. He has a friend there, George Something-or-other."

"Big deal."

"But he called me back. He's really very contrite, you know."

"He ought to be. Okay, look here, Linda, I don't know what you saw in the guy."

Linda blushed. Staring into her martini glass she said, "We were classmates in school. It was just a date but we got carried away and, well, one thing led to another, and—and I missed my next period and I panicked and—"

"Say no more."

"I wasn't even pregnant, it turned out. But there we were, married and—"

"Say no more."

"What did *you* see in him, Mae Anne?"

Mae Anne laughed. "In a funny way, it was almost the same thing. There I was in Chicago, all alone at this ridiculous plumbing convention. I mean, can you imagine what it's like to be locked in hotel with 4,000 fucking *plumbers*, honey, and you tell yourself that this is it, baby, this is your life, Mae Anne Morgan? So I picked up the first male that didn't look like a garbage dump or smell like a Hell's Angel." She laughed bitterly.

The curtain was pulled back and Arthur stood there. He had a thick white bandage on his head and his foot was wrapped and packed and he was leaning on a crutch on that side, his battered briefcase in his other hand.

"I —I'm sorry I'm late," he said. "C-can I sit here?"

Linda started to slide over to make room for him in the booth.

"I don't think we quite finished our last topic," Mae Anne said. "Maybe you should take a little hike, Arthur, and then come back."

Arthur hesitated, balancing on his one good foot and his crutch. He'd lowered his briefcase to the floor. "Ah, I guess, ah, but my foot is kind of painful. And my head."

"Come on, Mae Anne." Linda slid from the booth to her feet. "I have to visit the powder room anyway. We can talk there."

"Okay," Mae Anne assented. "I could stand a little trip to the can myself."

They brushed past Arthur, one on either side.

He stood watching until the curtain that covered the alcove concealing both restrooms swung back into place. Then he picked up his battered briefcase and limped painfully toward the street.

IV

The explosion ripped out the plumbing in both restrooms, demolished the entire rear half of the saloon, and totally destroyed a magnificent Rock-Ola jukebox. It would also undoubtedly have caused many casualties if it had come at a time when the establishment was busier.

As it was, only two female customers who had the misfortune of being in the ladies' room were killed. The explosive device had apparently been placed beneath the toilet there, and when the handle was depressed to flush the toilet—*ka-boom!*

Bobby the bartender, busy setting up for the late afternoon rush, suffered a broken arm and multiple cuts and bruises.

Arthur Pym, hobbling painfully on the sidewalk just outside the front door, was thrown to the ground. He was not seriously injured, although he bled spectacularly from a number of shallow cuts caused by flying glass.

Even so, as he lay on the sidewalk a few feet from his crutch and his briefcase, Arthur murmured, "Thank you, George." But none of the passers-by who came running, their attention captured by the explosion and their curiosity by the sight of the demolished saloon and the injured man, made out the words—or would have understood them anyway.

OLD FOLKS AT HOME

MARVIA PLUM

The squeal came in sideways. The reporting person called nine-one-one, Dispatch sent the paramedics, the 'medics reported the subject DOA under dubious circumstances, and the case got bucked to Homicide.

Enter Sergeant Plum.

Marvia was working swing shift, cruising Berkeley in a black-and-white, when she caught the call. She monitored the traffic, phoned in to McKinley Avenue and told the watch officer that she was responding to the scene.

She arrived a microsecond behind the patrol unit. She spotted the maroon and white Paramedic ambulance in the courtyard of Autumn House, the converted Victorian mansion on North Jordan Boulevard that now served as a retirement home for three dozen still-ambulatory seniors.

She tipped her hand to Jeff Felton, pleased to see one of the department's sharpest and most experienced patrol officers, and wondered for the hundredth time why Felton had never put in for sergeant. He could have had the promotion in a walk, she was certain.

The Victorian had been retrofitted with automatic doors; they hissed open for Marvia and Felton. The lobby was filled with heavy, dark, old-fashioned furniture. The walls were covered with red flocked wallpaper that could have served as well in a turn-of-the-century bordello as in the home of a onetime president of the University of California.

Old people shuffled through the lobby—once the vestibule of the Victorian—like ghosts. They stopped and stared at Marvia, residents of another world peering back to hers and viewing her dimly through the gray fog of time, then tottered away to their separate destinations.

A buxom red-haired woman in a tight-fitting white uniform crossed the lobby to meet them. At first she appeared very young, then Marvia realized that she was closer to fifty than forty; the deception was the product of contrast with the old folks.

"I'm Anise MacDougald." She held out a pale hand. Marvia took it, introduced herself, asked Ms. MacDougald if she was in charge of the home. "I'm the manager."

The doors opened behind Marvia. She turned her head and saw the crime scene technicians coming through. The coroner's bureau would be the last to arrive, she knew. Their work required the least urgency. The chief crime scene tech nodded to Marvia, then stood a few feet away, awaiting instructions.

More gray-haired ghosts, their skins transparent and their thin bones visible—or was that Marvia's imagination at play?—gathered around them, drawn by the uniforms, the youth, the living warmth of the newcomers.

"You'd better show us what happened," Marvia told MacDougald. "The paramedics are still there, right?"

MacDougald nodded. "Upstairs." She led Marvia and Felton to a linoleum-floored elevator. Marvia jerked her thumb at the evidence techs, summoning them to follow. In the elevator she asked MacDougald for a quick rundown on the incident.

"Mr. Collins pulled the panic cord. All our rooms have little panic cords, really bead chains. If somebody feels ill or falls down and can't get up, all he has to do is get to the nearest cord and pull it and we send somebody up to see what's wrong."

Marvia nodded.

The elevator stopped and the doors slid open. As they stepped into the hall, MacDougald added, "Mr. Collins pulled the cord. I ran upstairs myself. The old stairs are actually quicker than the elevator. He just pointed to Mr. Smithton. His roommate. We encourage our residents to double up. It keeps their charges down, you see. And the companionship is good for morale. Loneliness is such a problem for old people."

The door was open and Marvia stepped inside ahead of MacDougald. One of the paramedics had stayed beside the man lying on the floor. MacDougald nodded to the still form as if they were exchanging a friendly greeting. "That's Mr. Smithton."

Marvia turned back toward the doorway. She gestured Felton forward. "You're in charge of the scene, Jeff."

Felton moved forward and stretched a yellow crime-scene tape across the doorway. He knelt beside the body, looked up at the paramedic and started asking questions.

Marvia stood with MacDougald, observing. The body was that of a man in his eighties. It was clad in gray trousers, slip-on shoes and a long-sleeved plaid shirt. The hands looked like claws. The sparse hair was a dull yellowish-white except where blood stained it and ran—had run—onto the nondescript carpet.

At the sight of the blood Marvia knelt beside Jeff Felton and peered at the wound without touching Smithton. The surface wound was small but an ugly indentation in Smithton's skull indicated that it had been crushed by the impact. A heavy cut-glass ashtray lay a foot or so from Smithton's head, one corner splashed with blood. A pair of figures in silhouette had been etched into the glass, along with a few words, none of them in English or even in Latin script.

Almost involuntarily Marvia laid her fingers against Smithton's throat, searching for a pulse she knew she would not find. She stood up and came face-to-face with the paramedic.

The paramedic said, "Only thing I touched was the body, Sarge. Soon as I saw he was dead and saw the blood I figured it was for Homicide, not for us."

Marvia nodded. "You did right." She addressed MacDougald. "You said his roommate pulled the cord."

"Mr. Collins."

"Where is he?"

"The nurse took him to the medical room. We have an RN on duty at all times. She saw there was nothing she could do for Mr. Smithton so she took Mr. Collins to the med room. He was very upset, I was worried about him and I asked her to take him to the med room. If he calms down we'll have to put him somewhere, I don't know where we'll put him, I'll have to figure something out."

"Did he say what happened?"

"He just said that Mr. Smithton needed help."

"I want to talk to him right now."

MacDougald looked worried. "I don't know. We'll ask the nurse. I think we may have to send him to the hospital."

Ω

HOBART LINDSEY

American Financial Resources and International Surety Incorporated had been business partners longer than Hobart Lindsey had been alive; their billions spoke with authority. It was a long-standing policy at International Surety, not put in writing in so many words but clearly understood: when AFR whistled the tune, I.S. danced a jig.

So the claim hit Lindsey's desk in a bright red folder that meant *immediate attention, top priority.* Lindsey opened it and read a few lines, then reached for the phone. Somebody had been running up bills on a stolen AFR emerald card. That was a common enough problem, all-out identity theft had become a widespread crime, but this stolen card belonged to AFR's regional VP. The card had no limit and the bills had piled up high and fast before the theft was noticed, and the VP was steaming.

AFR had a fraud policy with I.S. and AFR wanted its money. Lindsey's job was to soothe ruffled feathers at AFR, first, and to recover as much as he could of the loot—the merchandise purchased with the stolen card.

The card itself had been canceled, of course, as soon as the VP realized that it had been stolen, but that had taken fully 48 hours and the purchases were absolutely frightening by then.

Lindsey punched in the number for the regional AFR office and fought his way through the vice president's receptionist, her executive assistant, and her personal secretary. Finally he heard an angry growl and said, "Ms. Whelan?"

"Speak!"

"This is Hobart Lindsey at International Surety. About your emerald card."

"Of course about my emerald card. What are you doing about the fraud claim?"

"Ms. Whelan, that's an awful lot of money. It's an awful lot of money in any case, but retail purchases in 48 hours, it's almost as if the thief was trying to run up bills."

"S.O.P., Lindsey, you ought to know that. Amateurs use stolen cardss to buy things for their own use. Professionals buy fencible items. We're dealing with a consummate pro here."

"Even so, Ms. Whelan. Two Mercedes, from two different dealers no less, and an Acura, jewelry, a Benny Buffano sculpture from a prestigious gallery, well, where else would you get one, half a dozen computers, top-of-the-line home electronics including a couple of flat-screen HDTV's, it's an impressive haul."

"There's more than that."

"I see there is." Lindsey fingered the list in the folder. "What did he buy from Patriot War Goods and Weapons?"

Whelan said, "I have no idea, except it cost a bundle."

"Ms. Whelan," Lindsey continued, "do you have any idea how the thief got your card? Have you made a police report? I don't see a copy of one in the case folder."

"I made a report," Whelan said. Her voice was raspy, as if she were an unreformed chain smoker or as if she'd been cheering at a football game for hours on end. "If you want to know about it I suggest you hustle your little tail over to my office and I'll tell you what you need to know. I don't want copies floating around and I don't feel like describing this criminal's M.O. on the telephone."

Lindsey agreed and reached for his jacket.

AFR's regional HQ was at 101 California Street. Ever since a disgruntled investor had showed up there with a personal arsenal and gunned down an office full of people before blowing himself to kingdom come, the guards in the building had been both more numerous and more diligent than ever before.

Lindsey felt like an astronaut when he climbed off the express elevator. The executive assistant he'd spoken to—his voice was unmistakable—shook his hand. "Garrison," he announced. "Come with me."

Garrison—Lindsey didn't know whether that was his first name or his last—had the dimpled chin and glittering eye of the MBA on the make. His suit couldn't have been more than three days old, straight from Wilkes-Bashford, and Lindsey knew that it would be discarded in favor of a newer model long before it showed the first sign of wear.

Executive assistant Garrison escorted Lindsey into Ms. Whelan's sublime presence and faded into the scenery.

Whelan's official digs resembled a plush hotel suite more than they did a business office. "Jeannette Whelan," the VP grunted. Lindsey responded with his name. She pointed to a chair and he sank into it obediently. Before he could say a word she said, "I talked to your boss, Richelieu. He vouched for you. Good. What was your question again, Lindsey?"

Flustered, he opened his attaché case and pulled out the red manila folder. "Uh, the total amount of this claim—"

He looked up and she locked eyes with him. It was like looking into the face of a great white shark.

"It's, ah, a great deal of money." He dropped the folder; fortunately it landed back in the attaché case.

She nodded but didn't say anything.

"Ms. Whelan, you were going to tell me why it took you two days to report the loss of your card. And the circumstances of the loss."

"Yes."

"Well." He blinked. Seen through a tall window behind Whelan, the sky over San Francisco was crystalline blue and the sun was brilliant. "Ah, how did—?"

"Brilliant racket. I wish whoever did it had come to me for a job instead. We can use that kind of brains in this business. Too many dullards and too many slackers today. Dullards. Slackers."

Lindsey nodded. "Yes. And—"

Whelan worked at a table, not a desk. The only break in the smooth surface was a plasma-screen computer monitor. She folded the monitor down into the desk, pushed her chair back and stood up. She removed her jacket and hung it on the back of her chair. She was wearing a white sleeveless blouse.

She raised her fists and flexed her arms, showing long, graceful muscles. "What do you think, Lindsey?"

Lindsey blinked. "Ah, ah, very impressive," he stammered.

"Think I got these for Christmas?"

"No."

"Hard work. Two hours at the gym every night. The rest of this organization heads for the corner saloon for their liquid tranquilizers but I head for Starwest Fitness Center and my favorite torture chamber. They think they have the good life but thirty years from now I'll dance on their graves, Lindsey, and then go out and run the Bay to Breakers."

She pulled her jacket back on and slid into her chair.

"Very impressive," Lindsey repeated. "Very admirable. But about the credit card."

"Right." Whelan grinned in a manner that Lindsey was unable to fathom. "Last Thursday I left work at the usual time and headed for Starwest. I went through my usual routine."

"Please walk me through that."

Whelan heaved a long-suffering sigh. "Checked in, picked up a couple of towels, went down to the locker room and changed to my gym outfit."

"Did you carry a gym bag with you?" Lindsey asked.

Whelan shook her head. "I keep a couple of outfits at Starwest. They run everything through the laundry for me, it's part of their service."

Lindsey jotted a note.

"Back up to cardiovascular for my warm-up on the stationary bike. Did a few miles on the bike, then to the weight room. Pumped iron for forty minutes, then back to the bike for a cool-off. Then some stretches and mat exercises. Then a steam bath, sauna, shower, and back to the locker room."

"This takes two hours?" Lindsey asked.

"Just about."

An amber light flashed beneath the tinted glass cover of Whelan's desk. She tapped her fingertip on the glass and the light went into a polychrome dance, then winked out.

Whelan said, "That's when it got funny." She did not laugh when she said *funny*, and Lindsey didn't think she meant *amused* at all.

"Couldn't open my padlock," Whelan said.

"Combination or key?"

"Combination."

"You sure you had the right numbers?"

Whelan's eyes widened. "You must be joking. Of course I had the right numbers. It's a perfectly standard rotary padlock and it had always been perfectly reliable. I tried the combination multiple times, finally picked up the phone and summoned the manager. When I told her what had happened she asked the combination and I told her. Of course that meant I'd have to replace the lock, but that wasn't my concern at the moment."

"No, of course not."

Behind her, Lindsey could see into the windows of the office building across California Street. Someone was gazing down at the plaza below as if contemplating a swan dive. But in the sealed environment of these buildings that was no longer an option.

"Once she'd tried the combination herself a few times she conceded that I was right. She had to summon a handywoman with bolt-cutters to sever the U-ring. She couldn't figure out what had happened. Neither could I. I suspected that something odd was going on, so I checked all my valuables."

"Including your AFR card?"

She looked offended that he even needed to ask that, but she replied, "Of course."

"And it was there?"

"In my card case. Everything looked normal."

"But it wasn't."

"Far from it."

"All right. When did you first realize that something was definitely wrong, and how did you know?"

"Saturday night. Friday I went to the gym after work, picked up a new lock at the desk and had my workout. Saturday I slept in, as usual, spent the day with my succulents, and met a friend at the Iron Horse for dinner."

Behind her, sunlight glinted off a huge jet coming in from the Pacific for a landing at SFO. Lindsey nodded and waited for her to resume.

"Melanie Price. She's my oldest friend. We grew up together in Belmont, went to prep school together, roomed together at Stanford. She's in line for city editor at the *Examiner* in another year. If the *Examiner* is still around. We meet for drinks and dinner once a week and we go to the Iron Horse at least once a month."

This time the blinking light in her desktop was green. She tapped once and a message appeared in the glass. Lindsey couldn't read it upside down. Whelan scanned it, muttered, and tapped a reply on the glass. The desk went dark.

"Where was I?"

"The Iron Horse."

"We never split a bill. We just take turns picking it up. I gave the waiter my emerald card and he came back and said it was a canceled number. I couldn't figure that out. It wasn't as if I'd maxed out the card. Couldn't do that anyhow. My emerald is no-limit-no-question. One of the little perks of my job. The waiter said they'd gladly put it on a tab, heaven knows they know Mel and me at the Horse. But I said, never mind, I'll pay cash, and I did. Then I studied the card. It was my signature all right, or a damned good forgery. But it wasn't my number.'

Lindsey shook his head. "I don't understand."

"Neither did I. Until I put two and two together. Mel helped me. I used to be a systems analyst and Mel was on the crime beat at the *Ex* so we both know how to solve problems. We traced it back to Starwest. The way we figured it out, somebody got into my locker while I was upstairs. Maybe she had bolt-cutters of her own or maybe she was trained as a safecracker and just opened the lock. My God, a little pipsqueak combination lock wouldn't even slow down a professional."

She raised one hand and looked at her wristwatch. It looked like a good one. Lindsey didn't doubt that.

"She must have timed it exquisitely," Whelan went on. "Either that, or just took one hell of a chance and got lucky. She took my lock off, took my emerald card out of my locker and substituted the phony. I don't know how she got my signature, unless she's some kind of instant copyist, or maybe had a miniature scanner and electronic pantograph."

"How would that work?"

"I don't even know if such a gadget exists. But if it does, she could scan my signature off my emerald card and lay it back onto the phony card. Then she put it back in the locker and relocked the locker with an extra lock she brought with her. That would have bought her an extra hour by the time I got things sorted out with Starwest."

"Why do you keep saying 'she?' How do you know it was a woman?"

"It was the women's locker room. Starwest is a coed gym but the locker rooms aren't coed. Even San Francisco isn't that liberated."

Lindsey pondered. "But why was the extra hour important? You didn't discover the theft until Saturday night."

"The crook couldn't know that. For all she knew, the fake card scam—I think that was brilliant, by the way, I really admire it—might fail. And I'd cancel the card and send out an alert within minutes once I discovered what happened. Even as it is, I know that the money was spent within three hours. If the theft took place at six o'clock Thursday, those big-ticket purchases were made by nine o'clock that night. She must have had her program worked out to the minute. Not only did she get expensive goods, they're all fencible. I'll bet those cars are in Mexico already. Or in the hold of a ship headed for Japan. Or Kuwait."

Lindsey frowned, concentrating. "One other question."

"Yes?" Whelan waited for him.

"The emerald card—your emerald card—has a no-question-no-limit feature. Did I understand you correctly about that?"

"Yes, you did."

"Then why didn't the thief just grab a fortune in cash? She could use the card for cash advances, couldn't she? Why bother with these complicated transactions, buying cars and HDTV's and computers and fencing them for cash? Why not just take the money to start with?"

"I thought of that myself, Lindsey. And here's the answer. While the emerald card has no limit, the AFR card cash fund itself has a limit. Even American Financial Resources doesn't have an inexhaustible cornucopia of plenty. So AFR Central monitors the cash account balance in real time, through our computer network. If she'd tried to get too much cash, she would have alerted the system that something abnormal was going on, and somebody would have been called in to look into it. Maybe even me!" That brought a smirk to her lips.

"So whoever did this knows the inner workings of the AFR system," Lindsey suggested.

"That's right. It might be an inside job. But whether it is or not—this is a smart broad we're dealing with." She ground out the words like small, sharp rocks. "But I'm a smarter broad. And I'm gonna burn her ass!"

Ω

MARVIA PLUM

Marvia Plum left Jeff Felton in charge of the crime scene and had Anise MacDougald take her to the Autumn House infirmary. MacDougald introduced her to the nurse, Amy Brown. The nurse had dark mocha skin and was overweight and friendly and was sitting beside Jack Collins, holding both his hands.

Marvia introduced herself, staring all the while at Collins. For an instant she thought she knew him, then realized that he seemed familiar because he looked so much like the dead Henry Smithton. Both men were short, probably shorter than they had been in earlier decades. Both had pale, almost transparent skin. Collins' hair was pure white while Smithton's had shown the remnants of once being blonde.

Even their eyes were a similar color, but Collins' eyes shone with life while Smithton's had held the glaze of death.

Collins was staring straight ahead, moving his lips silently and nodding from time to time. Marvia had no idea what he was saying. She stood in front of him and took his hands from Amy Brown. She introduced herself and asked Collins if he would speak with her.

He raised his eyes to hers, paused, then nodded.

"Mr. Collins, do you want to tell me what happened?"

"The Nazi is dead," he whispered.

"The Nazi?"

"The Nazi is dead."

"Mr. Collins, your roommate is dead. Henry Smithton is dead. It looks as if somebody hit him in the head with a heavy glass ashtray."

Nurse Brown interrupted. "We don't allow smoking here at Autumn House. Health and safety code, Miz, uh, Officer."

"Did somebody do it to Mr. Smithton, Mr. Collins? Did someone hit him? Do you know who hit him? Or could it have been an accident?"

Among younger men, it would surely not have been an accident. But among these frail, aged people, a loose shoelace, a ripple in the carpet, a momentary loss of balance, and you could have injury or death.

"I should have done it years ago," Collins said. "Years ago. The Nazi. But I was never certain. He could lie and lie." He nodded in agreement with himself. Then he added, "So could I." He smiled a secretive, inward-turning smile.

Should she mirandize him? Should she take him into custody? *Could* she take him into custody? It certainly looked as if he had wielded the heavy glass weapon, but there was no way she could book him into City Jail. She'd have to take him to the county hospital and have him admitted to a locked facility—if she decided to take him into custody at all.

"Mr. Collins, can you tell me what happened today? What happened to Mr. Smithton?"

"He had a visitor. His daughter came to see him. She brought it."

Marvia turned to Amy Brown, then to Anise MacDougald. She tensed, sending her question telepathically first to the nurse then to the facility manager.

MacDougald answered. "I'll get the log." She disappeared from the infirmary, returned almost at once with a notebook. She laid it in front of Marvia, then ran her finger down the page. "Here it is. Marjorie Dowling. Mr. Smithton's daughter. She brought him here, she visits regularly."

Marvia blinked. "Don't you control access to this building? All these old people must be—vulnerable."

"We do our best. We ask everyone to sign in and out. We keep a file of authorized visitors with each guest's records, and their photos. But this isn't a prison, you know, Sergeant. We operate more or less on the honor system. But you see—*Marjorie Dowling—in—out.* She was only upstairs for fifteen minutes."

"What about the ashtray?"

Mr. Collins was tugging at Marvia's hands. "The ashtray, the ashtray," he whispered. "It was the monsters. Both of the monsters. Both of them!"

"I don't understand, Mr. Collins. What monsters are those?" If the old man was delusional, seeing monsters in ashtrays, he might have thought that Smithton was one of them. He would have picked up the ashtray . . . .

Could Collins have picked up the ashtray at all? Marvia wondered. The aged man with his pipestem arms, his thin, fragile bones and withered muscles? It was heavy glass, it must have weighed the better part of ten pounds.

But if he was panicked by his imagined monsters, he might have found the strength to lift the heavy glass implement and bring it down just once, its sharp corner colliding with Smithton's thin temple. Once would have been enough.

"Did you do it, Mr. Collins?"

She was getting close to Miranda territory, she knew that. But if Collins was willing to speak freely, to offer a spontaneous statement, she should be able to use it. But that would mean she was putting together a homicide case, which would mean that he couldn't have been delusional.

"I should have done it a long time ago." He smiled up at her.

"Why is that, Mr. Collins?"

"You weren't there. You didn't see. He looked at the monsters and he—" He stopped speaking and a series of expressions raced across his features, anger, terror, grief.

Through all their conversation, Marvia had been standing in front of Collins, holding his hands in her own. Now he lowered his face and wept, his tears falling on the backs of Marvia's hands.

He pulled himself erect and dropped her hands. Nurse Amy Brown handed him a wad of tissue paper and he blotted his eyes. He reached for Marvia's hands and blotted them as well. "My apologies." A gentleman.

"Mr. Collins." She decided to try once again. "Who were these monsters you saw? Where were they?"

"In the ashtray."

"You mean—like in the ashes? Like seeing the devil in a flame?"

"No, no," he shook his head. "The devil, I'd take my dinner with the devil, I'd drink wine with the devil before these two. With the devil I'd play pinochle before these two."

"Then I don't understand."

"I won't even say their names. My mouth I won't soil by speaking those syllables. I could never spit enough to make my mouth clean if I said those names. At my age I don't have enough saliva."

Marvia turned. "Ms. MacDougald, can you call upstairs to Mr. Collins' room and get Officer Felton on the line for me? Thank you."

A moment later MacDougald handed her the phone. She asked Felton to sign for the ashtray and bring it down to the infirmary in an evidence bag. The techs could safeguard the crime scene until the coroner's squad arrived to remove the body.

To Collins she said, "Sir, I have to ask you, Do you understand what happened upstairs? Do you understand what's going on now, who I am?"

The old man smiled wistfully. "You know the best thing about Alzheimer's, Miss Police Sergeant? Those are sergeant's stripes, yes? At my age, your eyes aren't always so reliable. You know the best thing about Alzheimer's? You meet interesting new people every day."

Marvia said nothing.

Collins said, "Ah, I'm so old I can't even get a laugh no more. Well, a Henny Youngman I never was anyhow. So, Miss Police Sergeant, ask me again the question."

"Do you understand what happened, sir? Do you understand where you are and who I am?"

"Oh, yes." He nodded. "Oh, yes, believe me I understand."

"It looks as if Mr. Smithton was the victim of a homicide. If you're willing to chat with me about it, informally, we can chat. But if you want your Miranda rights, I'll read them to you and—"

The old man laughed. "I know my rights. I watch TV. What else do I have to pass the time? I see cop shows galore, Miss Sergeant. I know the niceties from NY to LA and back. Don't worry your head about my rights."

The door swung back and Jeff Felton entered. At Marvia's direction he carefully placed the ashtray, still in its bag, on a counter.

Marvia said, "Mr. Collins, would you pick that up for me?"

Collins swung around and peered at the ashtray.

"You want me to pick that up?"

"Please."

The old man rose unsteadily to his feet. Moving slowly, he crossed the short distance to the counter. He slid one hand under either end of the heavy ashtray. His powdery white face reddened with effort. The ashtray did not budge.

Ω

HOBART LINDSEY

International Surety had opened a prestigious regional headquarters in the upper reaches of the Transamerica Pyramid. Lindsey walked there easily from 101 California, rose skyward in an express elevator and used his Special Projects Unit ID to borrow a private office.

He was concerned over the timeline in Jeannette Whelan's story. If, as she claimed, she had reached the Starwest gym at six o'clock on Thursday night, and if the thief had completed her illicit purchases by nine o'clock, that meant that she had bought three automobiles, something close to a truckload of computers and other office equipment, an expensive sculpture and two of the most advanced television sets in existence in less than three hours.

Didn't the stores ever close around this town?

A few telephone calls settled that problem. The purchases had been arranged in advance. The customer had arranged to come back, pay for everything, and take delivery between six and nine o'clock Thursday night.

"Well, actually," a nervous Mercedes salesman told Lindsey, "she was going to come in Tuesday night. She never showed up, but she postponed to Wednesday. She's a V-VIP, you know, and we try to accommodate. She's a vice president up at AFR and she got stuck in a meeting and she actually had her executive assistant call us. A very impressive person, very authoritative. What was his name, now? Garrison, yes. Bernard, no, Barnard Garrison. He was all apologies but I could tell that he didn't like apologizing. Still, he explained Ms. Whelan's situation and of course we said, well, certainly. I mean, when someone has committed to a purchase of this magnitude, one does everything to accommodate. But everything."

Lindsey said, "Wednesday."

"That's right."

"She bought the car Wednesday?"

"No, Ms. Whelan's assistant called again Wednesday night and apologized again in behalf of Ms. Whelan. He said she was positively humiliated, she'd like to buy our whole staff dinner at the Carnelian Room to make up for the inconvenience, and could she pick up the car on Thursday. And we acceded, of course. My manager was hovering like a vulture and of course we agreed to do what the customer requested, and Thursday night Ms. Whelan did arrive with her assistant. A very charming, delightful person, I might add. She paid on the spot and they took delivery and drove off."

"Paid how?"

"AFR emerald card."

"You didn't check to see if the card was legitimate?"

"But I did. I punched it into the system and it came up clean but just to be certain I called the AFR 800 number and spoke with a human being who told me this was one of their NLNQ's. I asked what that was and she said, and I quote on this, Mr. Lindsey, 'no limit, no questions.'"

Lindsey thanked the salesman.

The salesman said, "Were we scammed, sir?"

Lindsey thought for a while before he answered. Finally the salesman said, "Sir? Are you there, sir?" And Lindsey said, "No, you weren't scammed. You sold the car. Congratulations. But I don't think you'd better count on that dinner at the Carnelian Room."

The story was the same with the second Mercedes dealer, with the Acura dealer, with a very-very upper-upper Post Street art gallery, three computer stores, two home-electronics stores, and the city's top-rated, cutting-edge, we-always-have-everything-first-and-you'll-pay-through-the-nose-if-you-want-it, television dealer.

There was no telephone listing for Patriot War Goods and Weapons, Incorporated, but there was an address in the blazing red case folder so Lindsey decided to visit the establishment in person. He picked up a cab in front of the Pyramid and gave the cabbie the address.

The cabbie was a grizzled veteran. His African features were covered with a week's worth of white bristles and a snowy fringe peeked out from beneath his old-fashioned cab driver's military-style cap. He craned his neck to get a good look at Lindsey. "You sure of this, mister?"

Lindsey said he was sure.

"Sir, I gotta take you anywheres you want, just so as it's in the city limits. But I really don't think you wanna go to this address."

Lindsey looked at his watch. It had been a long day and it looked as if it was nowhere near being over. "Why don't I want to go there?"

"You're not from the city, are you?"

"Walnut Creek."

"You do better in Hunter's Point, you look like me. You know what I mean?"

"Could I hire you to stand by, then, while I make this call? I wouldn't ask you to do anything improper. Just provide a little—"

"Local color?" The driver chuckled.

They cut their deal and the driver pointed his cab toward the Embarcadero. He accelerated up a freeway on-ramp and headed for his destination.

Shortly, the cab pulled to the curb in front of a ramshackle frame house.

A couple of ragged kids offered to watch the cab for a small fee and Lindsey nodded to the driver.

They had to pass a metal detector to get through the front door. Lindsey had to hand his electronic pocket organizer around the sensor. There was no sign on the building, nothing to identify it as Patriot War Goods and Weapons. He wondered if this was a crack house, but inside he found himself surrounded by an astonishing array of military collectibles as well as modern weaponry. The proprietor was an African American in a blue pinstriped suit, spotless white button-down shirt and maroon silk tie. He was standing behind a display case filled with glistening Samurai swords and World War II Japanese helmets. He set aside the slick journal he'd been studying and gave Lindsey a curious look.

"How did you get this address?"

Lindsey showed his International Surety credentials. "I'm following up a case of credit card fraud."

The black man shook his head. "I run a straight business here. I don't even like to take credit cards. I tell 'em to take a cash advance and pay me in greenbacks. But once in a while I'll make an exception."

"You made a large sale last Thursday evening, to a customer who paid with an American Financial Resources emerald card."

The other shook his head. "No."

"Sir, we have records of the transaction. There's no point in denying it."

"No point in buck you, fuster. Get out of my store, and take your slave there with you." He started to come around the display case.

Lindsey held up his hands placatingly. "You needn't get rough with me. You order me out of here, I'll go. But the police will be in here before you can blink your eyes, and you can expect a visit from the ATF and very likely the IRS. Or you can choose to talk to me. That's all I'm asking you to do, just talk to me."

Blue Suit backed a step and reached toward the display case, his fingers inches from the ornate handle of a Samurai sword.

"No need, brother. You want us out, we gone." It was Lindsey's cab driver. Suddenly he was standing between Lindsey and Blue Suit, and suddenly he was half a foot taller and thirty years younger than he'd been when they arrived.

Blue Suit dropped his hand and leaned on the counter.

The cabbie was a small old man again.

Blue Suit said, "What do you want?"

"Someone came in here last Thursday night and made a large purchase, and paid for it with an AFR emerald card. I've seen the charge slip. The card was stolen."

"I checked with the company. The card was okay. They said it was a no-limit-no-question card. I never heard of such a thing before. If they try and stick me for it—"

"You won't be stuck," Lindsey reassured Blue Suit. "But I need you to describe the customer. And I need an itemized list of what the customer bought."

"It was some white woman. Never saw her before."

"Describe her."

Blue Suit pondered. Then he said, "The Whelan chick, sure. Light brown hair, real light, with streaks. She colors it, definitely. About fifty. Slim, maybe five-three, five-four. Wearing sweats and running shoes, but no gym hanger-on, if you know what I mean. She didn't look real happy, but she slapped down that card and signed the slip, that's all I wanted from her."

The description didn't ring any bells with Lindsey. Blue Suit called the woman the Whelan chick but she did not sound at all like Jeannette Whelan.

"Was she alone?"

"Oh, no." Blue Suit shook his head. "She had her man with her."

Something gave Lindsey a hunch. "You didn't know her. Did you happen to recognize him?"

Blue Suit broke into a big grin. "Recognize him? Listen, I know him. His name's Billy Tarplin. My customers' names are sacred secrets to me, but not Billy Tarplin. That chump is too weird. Dresses like a fashion plate. Puts me in the shade, and I try to look good at all times, it's part of the image, you understand? But Billy is just too far off the beaten track for my taste. He loves that Nazi stuff. Plenty of customers for that, but Tarplin pays top dollar for first shot at new lots."

"Do you have his address?"

"This is strictly a cash and carry business, but Billy's such a good customer, I have to send his orders out by truck. Late at night, too—you wouldn't believe the things he buys. He must be planning a revolution with some of his weapons. Heavy machine guns, bazookas, BAR's. That chump even bought a .57 millimeter reckless rifle. But, hey, he didn't get anything illegal from me, you understand what I'm saying?"

Lindsey agreed that he understood what Blue Suit was saying. "I just need to track down this one purchase, the purchase made on the Whelan AFR emerald card."

"Here, here's what they bought," Blue Suit told Lindsey. He showed Lindsey a customer order sheet. A ceremonial SS dagger, uniform cap with death's-head insignia, an array of World War II era German medals.

"I don't like Nazis," Blue Suit said. "I don't like Nazi paraphernalia. Brings out some nasty types. But it comes in from time to time and there's always a market for it. If I lose Billy Tarplin I'll never miss him. These Nazi nuts get off on that sick stuff, and Billy's the sickest of the bunch."

Lindsey was busy jotting information into his organizer. When he finished he handed the order sheet back to Blue Suit. "You won't encounter any trouble from AFR," he assured him. "I just need the address where you ship Tarplin's orders."

"You didn't get it from me," Blue Suit said. He pulled open a file drawer, riffled through folders and pulled out a sheet of paper. Lindsey reached for it but Blue Suit pulled it back. "No way!"

But he held it while Lindsey tapped the address into his organizer. It was in San Anselmo in Marin County. This case was neatly triangulating the bay. "If you hear anything from Tarplin or, uh, Whelan, give me a call at once, please." Lindsey laid an International Surety card on the counter. "Or you could contact the police," he added.

"Yeah, sure." Blue Suit looked at the card without touching it.

"There will be a very large reward," Lindsey added.

Blue Suit picked up the card and slipped it into his pocket.

Lindsey started for the door.

"Hey, hold it there." Blue Suit brushed past him. "I have to let you out."

The cabbie stepped through the doorway ahead of Lindsey. As Lindsey moved forward, Blue Suit said, "Oh, yeah, there was one more thing those two got. The man was mainly interested in the hard-core military goods but the woman asked me about this one other thing that came in with a batch of Nazi merchandise. I had it in the case and she was interested so I said she could take it. I don't know what the hell it was doing with those other things anyhow. I threw it in gratis, and that's really something, for me."

Lindsey said, "What was that?"

Blue Suit said, "Some ugly old ashtray."

Ω

101

"What do you think, Jeff?"

"I really don't think he could have done it. He didn't have the strength."

"Even in a special moment? You know, the father who lifts a car off a child, that kind of thing?"

Felton shrugged. "Anything is possible, Sarge. But I don't think so. No."

Marvia studied Jack Collins. He was sitting quietly now, clutching one of Amy Brown's big competent hands with both of his small, fragile ones. "I don't think so either," Marvia said. "But I think I'm going to request a hospital evaluation. What's your opinion, Ms. MacDougald?"

"Actually, I think it would be a good idea."

"Does Mr. Collins have any family we can consult?"

The old man reddened and rose halfway from his seat, then sank down again. "Stop talking about me as if I wasn't here! You got a question, ask me, Policer."

Marvia leaned back. "I'm sorry. You're right, sir. Would you agree to a hospital evaluation? Voluntarily, that is."

Collins tilted his head thoughtfully. "In America, I guess a hospital is a hospital, eh? Not a murder house. No, I don't mind. I got nothing to hide."

"And do you have any family, sir?"

"Not in this world. In the world to come, they're all waiting for me. We got caught in the middle. In Poland. The ones Hitler didn't kill, Stalin killed. Our great friend and protector, Comrade Stalin."

Now Marvia was confused. "I'm sorry. Jack Collins? Is that a Polish name?"

"Jack Collins. So." He shrugged. "In Poland, Jacob Chmelkovitz, in America, Jack Collins."

"No children, grandchildren, no wife?"

"The monsters got them all. Why didn't they get me? I don't know, Policer, I don't know, I wish they had."

Marvia said, "Jeff, call this in, will you? Let's make sure Mr. Collins gets good treatment." She turned back to Collins. "They'll have an ambulance out here for you in a little while."

Collins shrugged again, turning his hands palm up as if to show that they were empty. "I could ride in your car, too, but I don't mind the ambulance neither."

Once Jack Collins was taken care of, Marvia went to the Autumn House office with Anise MacDougald. She asked to see their records on both Collins and the victim, Henry Smithton.

MacDougald hesitated briefly, muttering something about confidentiality, but finally she acceded.

Collins' record was as he'd indicated. Born in Lodz, Poland, in 1914 as Jacob Chmelkovitz. One brother, three sisters. Married in 1932. Twin girls born 1935, no other children. Twins taken by Nazis for genetic experimentation in 1942, never heard of again. Parents died of starvation. Brother and sisters all killed in Warsaw ghetto uprising. Chmelkovitz imprisoned at Bergen-Belsen, liberated 1945. Classified as displaced person, admitted to US on humanitarian grounds in 1947. Changed name to Collins, worked for Post Office Department, 1948 to 1979. Retired.

There were no photos of authorized visitors in the file.

Smithton's was far less dramatic. Born Bayonne, New Jersey, 1916. Worked in war plant assembling trucks during World War II. Married, 1948; daughter Marjorie born same year. Wife deceased. Daughter married and widowed, name Marjorie Dowling. There was a photo of Marjorie in the file, and one of another authorized visitor, a man named Barnard Garrison. Marvia asked MacDougald for copies of the photos; MacDougald ran them through a copier and gave her one of each. Since Dowling was Smithton's next of kin and his designated emergency contact, her telephone number and address were included. She lived in San Anselmo, up in Marin County.

Apparently Marjorie Dowling cared for her father, at least enough to visit him at Autumn House. Marvia would contact her with the sad news. She would also have some very serious questions for Ms. Dowling about the heavy ashtray that had crushed Henry Smithton's skull.

Ω

HOBART LINDSEY

"You a pretty standup guy for a overweight, middle-aged white man."

Lindsey decided to take that as a compliment and thanked the cabbie for backing him up in his confrontation with Blue Suit.

"Thanks are nice, they don't buy no groceries."

"You'll get a good piece of change for this day's work," Lindsey told him. It was I.S. money, not his own. He could afford to be generous. And the cabbie had certainly earned it. The cab was untouched when they reached it outside Patriot War Goods and Weapons, and the cabbie rather than Lindsey had paid off the kids who had guarded it so well.

The cabbie dropped Lindsey at the Civic Center station of the commuter rail line. Lindsey paid him off, reimbursed him for his time and the out-of-pocket expense that had gone to the kids, and added a very generous tip.

"Any time you need my help, cap," the cabbie offered. He pulled a stub of a pencil out of his pocket, found a soiled envelope and wrote his name and telephone number. He handed them over. Lindsey thanked him and climbed from the cab.

The train would carry him to Walnut Creek along with hundreds of other commuters, shoppers, and students returning from a long day at San Francisco State or USF.

The train barreled through the tube beneath San Francisco Bay, roared above ground in West Oakland, ducked into another dark tunnel downtown, then emerged for its run to the East Bay suburbs. Lindsey sat with his pocket organizer in his hands, reviewing the case.

Somebody inside AFR understood the card system well enough to know that no-limit-no-questions wasn't as simple as it sounded. A scam artist with a stolen no-no emerald card looking for the main chance would have to buy and fence big-ticket merchandise rather than go for a killing in cash. How many people in AFR were thoroughly familiar the system? There must be dozens, maybe hundreds, starting with Jeannette Whelan herself.

And somebody at Starwest, a woman, had to know Whelan's routine and be able to get in and out of the locker room fast, without being detected. Whoever was doing this had set up her caper for Tuesday, then had to postpone it to Wednesday and finally to Thursday before it worked. She was smart, quick, and self-controlled enough to put off her action twice, waiting for the right moment.

He didn't know who the woman, the false Jeannette Whelan, was, or where she was. But he had an address for Billy Tarplin.

He climbed into his car and started for San Anselmo.

It was a long drive from Lindsey's home to the Richmond Bridge, through downtown San Rafael and past one Marin County bedroom community after another before reaching San Anselmo.

Billy Tarplin lived in a modest single-story home on a curving road. The neighborhood had the look and feel of a 1950s development. The original homeowners would all have sold their houses and moved away by now, or died off and left them to their adult children.

Ten-year-old cars lined the street. There was a tangible feeling of seediness and slow deterioration in the air. Most of the houses had small swimming pools. Children shrieked under the watchful eyes of overweight mothers smoking cigarettes.

Lindsey double-checked the house number, then rang the doorbell. He heard muffled sounds, as if someone was stumbling around inside the house, sobs and fragments of speech.

He tried the door and it swung open.

A woman handed him something and he took it instinctively. It was sticky. It was covered with blood. It was a ceremonial dagger decorated with a swastika and Nazi eagle.

The woman was sobbing and babbling. She was spattered with blood, blood in her blonde-streaked light brown hair, blood on her white tee shirt and khaki shorts, blood on her face, her bare arms and legs and running shoes.

Lindsey heard a car screech to a stop and a voice behind him call out, "Freeze!"

He turned toward the voice. The blood-covered woman was behind him now. He was holding the bloody dagger. A black and white police cruiser stood in the driveway and a uniformed police officer was pointing her service automatic at him.

"Bart?" There was shock in her voice.

"Marvia."

"Put the weapon on the ground."

He obeyed.

"What's going on here?"

"I don't know. I just got here. I opened the door and she handed me the knife."

Marvia Plum moved past Lindsey. She addressed the blood-soaked woman. "Are you all right? What happened?"

"It's all over now," the woman said. "All over. The Nazis are dead. Both dead."

Marvia asked, "Are you wounded?"

"No." The woman shook her head. She seemed calm now, and fairly coherent although dazed. "I—he's in the pool. Come on, I'll show you."

Marvia said, "Come along, Lindsey. Stay where I can see you."

The three of them walked through the house, out the back door into a modest, fenced yard. The pool was filled and the water was stained with a pink cloud. A fully clothed man was floating face down in the pool.

Marvia holstered her weapon and picked up a long-handled leaf net. She used it to draw the man to the edge of the pool. "Come on, help me."

With Lindsey's assistance she dragged the man from the water and turned him onto his back on the concrete apron. She felt for a pulse but there was never any chance that she would find one. There were major wounds in the chest and abdomen, and one in the throat that would have been fatal even if the others had not been.

"He was right," the blood-covered woman said. "I wouldn't believe him but he was right. So now . . . so now . . . so now it's all over, it's all right, it's all over."

Marvia led the woman to a chair. She directed Lindsey to another. Lindsey watched, half in a state of shock, and listened as she asked the woman her name.

"Mrs. Dowling. Marjorie Dowling. Marjorie Smithton Dowling. Marjorie von Schmitt."

Marvia shook her head. "What's that? I don't understand."

"I killed Billy," the blood-stained woman said. "I killed my daddy and I killed my boyfriend. Bill Tarplin is dead dead dead." She grinned crazily.

"That's Bill Tarplin?" Marvia asked.

"Yes."

Lindsey shook his head. "That's Garrison. That has to be Barnard Garrison." Marvia Plum shot him a sharply questioning glance. "I met him at Jeannette Whelan's office. He was her executive assistant."

"Who the hell is Jeannette Whelan?" Marvia asked.

"She's a VP at American Financial Resources. She was the victim of a credit card scam. If that's Billy, what's his name, Tarplin, he worked for AFR under the name of Barnard Garrison. He was the inside man on the scam. Mrs. Dowling here, I take it, was the outsider. Garrison got the information inside AFR. Mrs. Dowling stole a no-limit emerald credit card from Ms. Whelan's locker at the Starwest Spa in San Francisco. They cleaned up on it. Cars, HDTV's—and Nazi paraphernalia."

For the first time he looked around the house, as much of it as he could see through the back door. The living room was straight out of an Eisenhower era *Saturday Evening Post*, only the colors were faded and worn by decades of sunlight and use.

"Would you like to see my lovely home?" Marjorie Dowling asked.

Lindsey shot an inquiring look at Marvia Plum. She nodded almost imperceptibly and he said, "Oh, I'd love it."

Marjorie Dowling rose and led Lindsey on a tour of the house. He could sense Marvia Plum following them, observing them, mostly observing Marjorie Dowling. The construction and furnishings were conventional, almost banal, until they came to one ordinary door with an unusually heavy lock on it. Unusual for a door inside a private home.

A sly smile on her blood-spattered face, Marjorie Dowling said, "This was Billy's special room. He put in the lock himself. I wasn't allowed in here, even though this is my house. My own house. I used to call it Bluebeard's secret room. Billy got mad at me when I called it that."

She extracted a key from her pocket. "He didn't know I knew where he kept the key. I took it and I had a copy made and then I put Billy's key back. He never knew."

She slipped the key into the heavy lock and turned it. She swung the door open and reached for a light-switch.

It was like museum lighting, and the room—larger than Lindsey had expected—looked like a room in a Nazi war museum. Flags, posters, military regalia. A fully articulated lifesize dummy in Wermacht winter uniform crouched behind a machine gun. A portrait of the Fuhrer hung in a place of honor.

Behind him, Lindsey heard Marvia Plum gasp. He felt light-headed.

"Billy was such a good customer at Patriotic. He always used to pay with his own money, he never let me go there with him until this time. You know what else he did with his money?"

She led them out of the display room, back to a modest bedroom. Through the bedroom was a private bath. A jar the size of an ordinary spaghetti sauce jar stood on the counter, a thin residue of white powder caked in the bottom.

"Up the nose," Marjorie Dowling said. "I tried to make him stop and you know what he said? 'Herman did it, even Adolf did it. I'll do it, too.' That's what he said. He made a good salary but it all went up his nose. Up his nose and to Patriotic for his, his *hobby* he called it. Just a little hobby. Just history. Didn't mean anything. He wasn't one but he was one, I knew. And he said my daddy was one and I said he wasn't, and Daddy always said he wasn't, but Billy said he'd studied, he knew, he knew Daddy was one and one day I'd know it too."

They had drifted back to the living room, like an ordinary suburban homemaker entertaining two guests, but Lindsey could see that Marvia's eyes were fixed on Marjorie Dowling while her hand hovered near her weapon. At least she'd holstered the automatic, but she could draw it again at any moment. He was surprised that she hadn't taken over the interrogation, but she seemed content to permit him to ask the questions and Marjorie Dowling to answer them.

"Your father," Lindsey prompted.

". . . and the ashtray," Mrs. Dowling volunteered.

Lindsey was aware that Marvia became suddenly attentive.

"He saw the ashtray. Billy was the only one who knew what it was. He said all along that he recognized my daddy from old photos, that he wasn't really from New Jersey, that he wasn't really Henry Smithton, he was really Heinrich von Schmitt. I always hated the Nazis, I knew what they did, and he said my daddy was a Nazi who came to America and hid out all these years under a false name. He was able to get a complete set of false records made. Somebody helped him, I don't know who. But I know that my name is false too."

"But you stayed with him," Lindsey said.

Marjorie Dowling shrugged. "I didn't know." She closed her eyes, then opened them again. "I did know. I didn't know. I did know." She grimaced. She looked like Joanne Woodward suffering in *Three Faces of Eve.* "I never knew and I always knew." She began to cry.

"Did Mr. Tarplin kill your father?" Lindsey asked

"No. Billy didn't kill Daddy. I killed Daddy. Billy said, 'We're going to buy this ashtray. Nobody knows what it is but I know what it is.' Billy studied his history, he studied all the time. He had a degree in history, you know. From the University of California. He could have been a professor but he made more money at AFR."

"You killed your father?" Lindsey asked. He was trying to read Marvia Plum's mind, trying to get Marjorie Dowling back on track.

"Billy said Stalin sent that ashtray to Hitler when they signed their treaty. Their pictures are etched in the glass, with the pledge of eternal friendship in German and Cyrillic. And Hitler didn't even smoke, wasn't that funny? When Daddy saw the ashtray he knew what it was. He was so shocked when I gave it to him. Then he said who he was. He didn't deny it any more."

She looked at Lindsey, then at Marvia Plum, then at Lindsey again.

"I couldn't stand it," she resumed. "I couldn't live with that. I knew what the Nazis were, I knew what Billy was. I knew who Daddy's roommate was, too. I knew what they did to him. He couldn't fool me. None of them could fool me. I killed my father and I came home and Billy asked me what was the matter and I picked up his favorite dagger and I pricked him. And he bled. I pricked him and he bled. Daddy's roommate saw the whole thing at Autumn House, he stood there watching and then I walked out and came home and Billy was here in his special room, in Bluebeard's special room, and I picked up his new toy, his new dagger from Patriotic War Goods and I killed him. He was so surprised, it was really funny."

As Lindsey watched, Marvia Plum stood up and took the few strides to Marjorie Dowling's side. She held up a pair of handcuffs and Marjorie Dowling held up her hands, unresisting and cooperative. Marvia muttered a few words of magical incantation to Marjorie Dowling, then she picked up the telephone and dialed. Without being told, Lindsey knew she was calling the San Anselmo PD.

Ω

Farmer snapped his fingers and gestured and Bink, the big Rottie bitch, hopped out of the Olds Ciera and stood waiting for his next command. He snapped the chain-link leash onto her collar, patted her on the head and started into the park. She ambled along at his side, pausing here and there to sniff a tree-trunk, a clump of ivy or a fallen limb. She looked at Farmer as if she could talk him into throwing a stick for her, but he gave a tug at the leash and she assented, trotting now alongside his US Keds.

The park was narrow and winding, the equivalent of two or three city blocks in length, and blue maple and California scrub-oak limbs met overhead, making a shadowy tunnel that ran the length of the park, only a dappling of sunlight breaking through every few score yards,

He saw the old man with the basset heading toward him, the old man placing his feet gingerly, one ahead of the other, careful to avoid roots and rocks that might cause him to twist an ankle and tumble to the earth, bruising his aged flesh or, worse yet, fracturing a dry, aged leg or hipbone. The basset, overweight and clearly short on exercise, waddled and panted beside his master.

Farmer smiled and waved. "Isn't it a glorious morning?"

The old man smiled back and mumbled something that Farmer couldn't make out, but it seemed vaguely agreeable. Farmer had seen the old man a few times before, in the park. Maybe it was the gray in Farmer's medium-length hair and in his mildly unkempt mustache that helped the old man feel comfortable with him.

Bink bent over the basset and snuffled.

The basset made a soft sound and wagged its long tail.

Bink wiggled her own tiny, cropped tail and looked up at Farmer. He said, "Come on, girl," and to the old man, "have a great one," and maneuvered the big Rottie around the old man and the fat basset and continued up the trail. He whistled a catchy tune he'd heard in an Alice Faye musical on AMC the night before. *You're a Sweetheart.* It stuck in his mind. *If there ever was one.* There was a kind of song, Farmer had never figured it out exactly, but they just did that to him. Just stuck in his mind. *If there ever was one, it's you.* Sometimes he thought he was in love with Alice Faye, even though she was born in 1915, the daughter of a cop, no less.

Traffic rolled past the park on either side, new Hondas and Acuras and Nissans, a Suzuki Samurai and a Mercedes, a family in a big Volvo wagon packed to the roof with camping and fishing gear, heading out on wholesome family vacation.

Farmer heard voices approaching from behind him, and the crunching and rustling sounds of wheels rolling over dry twigs and brown leaves. He turned and saw a procession of boys and girls on bikes pedaling along the path. From the looks of them they averaged twelve years old. They were jabbering and screaming about their summer plans. Farmer stepped off the path, into a patch of lush green ivy. He pulled Bink with him and waved at the first of the bicyclists, a pretty girl with blonde hair streaming out from under her helmet.

The pretty girl waved back at Farmer as she wheeled past. She yelled, "Thanks, Mister." Farmer stood with his hand upraised, waving at the kids as they rolled along the path. Nice kids. Polite to an older man, as Farmer himself had been to the senior citizen walking his basset. Civil, their conduct was civil, as it ought to be.

Once the kids were past, Bink pulled him along the path impatiently. She leaped into the ivy, almost jerking Farmer off his feet. He yelled and caught his balance. "Silly girl, you know you can't climb a tree. Leave the squirrels alone." It had been a good winter, adequate rainfall for a change, not too cold, The spring vegetation had been lush and by summer the population of squirrels and birds in the parks had reached levels Farmer hadn't seen in years.

Halfway through the park a flight of cement steps led to the parallel street and the narrow sidewalk that marked the edge of the park. The houses that flanked the park varied in size and architecture. Those on the uphill side of the park were larger than those on the downhill side. There were Tudors and California Mission style homes and a few redwood or brown shingle traditionals. No Victorians in this part of town; that style seemed not to fit in with the genteel suburban feel that the neighborhood managed to achieve despite its proximity to the university and the commercial areas that nourished the city's economy.

A classic little old lady was standing at the top of the cement steps. She clutched a leash, at the end of it a white toy poodle that squealed and tugged. The LOL grasped the metal handrail that slanted beside the steps. A look of panic swept across her papery features like the shadow of a fast-moving cloud sweeping across a leached-out, lifeless field.

Farmer found the encounter intriguing. He knew the poodle, even knew its name. He'd seen it walking sedately with a plainly dressed black woman on a number of occasions. But today, the person on the other end of the leash was this elderly female who gave off a distinct emanation of wealth.

Farmer laughed. "There's nothing to be worried about."

The LOL seemed to relax a little, but she still clung to the handrail and the poodle continued to pull. Farmer said, "That's Dulcie, isn't it?"

The LOL nodded, seeming to relax a little more.

"This is Bink," Farmer said. "Bink and Dulcie are friends, see?" He let the Rottweiler approach the poodle. Dulcie squealed and rolled over. Bink nuzzled the poodle. The Rottie's squarish black-and-gold head was as big as the entire poodle.

The LOL relaxed some more. She reached a hand, tentatively, toward Bink, looking questioningly at Farmer. He said, "It's okay, Bink loves people, don't you Binky girl?"

The Rottie wagged her stubby tail and massive hindquarters.

"We meet Dulcie almost every day," Farmer said. "But usually the other lady always walks her. I hope . . ." He let the sentence trail away. The LOL would probably finish it for him. He was counting on that. He could see the hand on the iron rail, not the one holding the leash, was decorated with an expensive wedding ring and a matching engagement ring with a rock on it that set his mind to dancing.

"Oh, Claudie is my maid."

"I'd never have known."

"She's my friend, too."

I'll just bet she is, Farmer thought.

"She's been with me ever so long. Years and years."

Yes, but? There has to be a yes but, Farmer thought. Yes, but what?

"I couldn't get along without her. Especially since my husband..."

This time it was the LOL who let the sentence drift into silence. In that silence a motorcycle roared past, the driver gunning the engine as he climbed the hill.

"I understand," Farmer said, even though he didn't. He had an idea, he had an inkling, and a gentle breeze stirred the scrub-oak leaves over the stairs letting a shaft of bright sunlight through to dance off the LOL's diamond ring. Yes, Farmer definitely had an idea. "And Claudette . . ."

"No, just Claudie. You know, they have these funny names sometimes."

"But she's still your friend."

"Of course."

"Claudie."

"Oh, her grandmother, she told me, you know they live so long sometimes, but her grandmother, and of course I couldn't insist that she stay. She offered to get me someone while she's gone. Especially since my husband . . ."

"Of course, your husband."

"But I told her, No, you go ahead, your family has to come first. I can manage. You come back as soon as you can. I'll take care of everything while you're away."

The poodle sniffed at a pile of leaves, turned in a circle, and squatted. The LOL looked at Farmer.

"Well, I think Binky wants to get home for her breakfast." Farmer extended his hand to the LOL. She looked confused for a moment, then transferred Dulcie's leash to the hand holding the railing and shook Farmer's hand with the other.

"A pleasure," Farmer said. "I hope Claudia's grandmother gets better soon, and I'll see you and Dulcie here, Mrs . . ."

The LOL's hand was like a dry, empty husk in Farmer's. He had to be careful not to crush it. Not to crush it. "Mrs . . ." he said again.

"Clyde," she furnished, even though he'd had to clue her twice to get the answer. "And Claudie, not Claudia."

Farmer shook his head self-deprecatingly. "I'm terrible about names. Terrible. Mine is Farmer. You know, sometimes I think I'm going to forget my own name. But I always remember pets. I'd never forget Bink. Or Dulcie. Well, then . . ."

He let Bink lead him up the path, turned back for an instant and saw Mrs. Clyde and Dulcie heading in the opposite direction, the LOL walking steadily in sensible shoes and a dress. You never saw women in dresses in the park, but Mrs. Clyde was an exception.

Bink and Farmer reached the top of the park, headed out and across the street, then walked back to where he'd left the Olds Ciera. He unlocked the passenger-side door and said, "Okay, Bink old girl, let's go home." The Rottie jumped in the car and settled down on the faded upholstery. Farmer thought, I ought to get her a mat or something before she wears right through that seat. He walked around the car and opened the driver's -side door and climbed in. On the way home he listened to an oldies station. After a commercial the disk jockey put on a cover version of *You Turned the Tables on Me*, another Alice Faye standard, by some present day vocalist. She was plenty good, but she was no Alice Faye.

At home he put out Bink's breakfast and set to work with a telephone book and a city map. There were a dozen Clydes listed. Farmer searched for their addresses on the city map. He managed to eliminate eight that way. They just didn't live anywhere near the park, and he knew that Mrs. Clyde—*his* Mrs. Clyde—wouldn't have come from another neighborhood just to walk Dulcie in the park.

Of the four remaining Clydes, two were listed as *Mr. and Mrs.* Farmer eliminated them. The elimination tourney was down to the finals. One of the two remaining Clydes was listed as *P. Clyde, DDS.* The other was simply, *R. Clyde,* and an address that Farmer knew was just a stone's throw from the park even without checking the map. Many women listed their telephone numbers with only first initials. Nice, androgynous initials. They discouraged obscene phone calls, or they had, maybe, until the obscene phone callers had caught on to the trick.

Farmer knew that *R. Clyde, 55 Ferndale,* was his Mrs. Clyde. R. Was she Roberta? Rachel? Rona, Rhonda, Rolanda?

Close attention to detail, that was the key to success in any business, including Farmer's. He chose his targets with care, did not strike too often, did not return to a neighborhood where he had previously worked. He had never been arrested, never been in serious trouble, earned a good living for himself, had money in the bank and conservative investments in his portfolio and lived a quiet, respectable life in his comfortable home with his faithful four-legged companion.

Farmer went into the bathroom and scrubbed the gray out of his hair and mustache, and combed his hair carefully and brushed his mustache into neat order. He smiled ruefully at his reflection. Mother Nature was doing her work. It wouldn't be long, at this rate, before he had to *cover* the gray instead of adding it, to change his appearance.

He let Bink out in the back yard to do her stuff, then they spent half an hour on their drills. Bink was good at the drills, she was one smart bitch, and Farmer ought to know. He loved Bink. Love, that was part of the secret of his success.

Actually she was Bink III. He'd raised the first Bink from a puppy, had built his career with her help, and had cried hot, salty tears when he'd had her put down. She was getting old and her hips were starting to go. These big, heavy dogs just didn't have the longevity of smaller, lighter breeds.

And then there had been Bink II. Rottweiler pups were expensive, but Farmer wouldn't settle for less than the best. And in due course Bink II had gone the way of Bink I, and Farmer had cried again, and taken some time off, and then bought Bink III and started training her. She was a great bitch, maybe the best of the three. By the time she was ready to retire, if things went well, he might be ready to do the same.

It was quite a thought.

He had a class at the community college that night, and he took Bink with him and made her stay in the Ciera while he sat through the lecture. He never used his real name when he enrolled in courses, and between such simple precautions, and moving on every so often, he figured he'd never get his degree. But what the heck, the classes were interesting and they filled the empty evenings. And once in a while he met some lonely divorcee or plain-featured middle-aged woman, and had a fling. Nobody ever got hurt, more empty evenings got filled, and when he moved on he left pleasant memories behind to warm those lonely hearts on cold, lonely evenings.

The next day, after he'd added the gray to his hair and mustache, he let Bink out as usual. They ran through a training session, then he brought her back through the house and out the front door. They jumped into the Ciera and drove back to the park. Farmer parked the Ciera on Wilton, just off Ferndale a couple of blocks from number 55.

He walked Bink along Wilton, then turned onto Ferndale, casing the houses. He kept an eye out for pedestrians or nosy neighbors. Ferndale was a quiet street. There was nothing pretentious about it. This wasn't a section for the super-wealthy. There were few if any of them in this town. But the people who lived on Ferndale were upper middle class. Very upper. They tended to have good jewelry and often serious cash in their houses. Certainly Mrs. R. Clyde had jewelry. Nice and compact and portable and convertible jewelry. And Claudie was out of town because of her grandmother. And since Mrs. Clyde's husband . . .

Farmer smiled to himself.

Number 55 Ferndale was a Tudor, down to the white stucco and half-timbers and the kitschy diamond-pane windows. A winding driveway led to an attached double garage. A row of firs lined the driveway, blocking part of the house's well-tended lawn from the street.

Perfect.

Perfect.

Fucking perfect.

He strolled around the neighborhood waiting for Mrs. Clyde to emerge from her house with Dulcie. Or—huh, maybe he'd blown the timing and the LOL was already out walking her poodle. Well, that was okay too. He just wanted to meet them again, wanted Mrs. Clyde to see him and Bink once more, preferably nearer her house than the park. Just to get her accustomed to the idea.

Just as he was thinking of giving up, of putting the whole project off 'til tomorrow, he heard a soft voice. "Mister—was it Mister—"

He turned around, smiling. "Farmer," he said. "And you're Missus, uh . . . I'm so bad with names."

She smiled back at him. "Mrs. Clyde." Dulcie yapped.

"Maybe I'm just getting old," he said.

She shook her head. "Oh, no. You're a young man, Mr. Farmer."

He gave her his grateful look. "At least I remember Dulcie's name. I never forget pets."

Mrs. Clyde said, "Do you live near here, Mr. Farmer?"

"Fairly. It's just that Bink loves the little park so, and I enjoy looking at the lovely houses. Is one of them yours?" As if he didn't know damned well which was hers.

"Oh, the Tudor, you see." She gestured. "My husband and I built that house. Forty-three years ago. Forty-three years." She took a breath. "But since he—I just don't know if I—"

Farmer assumed his sympathetic expression and nodded and mumbled.

Dulcie and Bink were sniffing each other. Mrs. Clyde said, "You know, they say that certain breeds of dogs are so fierce. Dobermans and pit bulls and Rottweilers."

Farmer shook his head. "Not if you love them. Not if you raise them to be gentle and to know love and not violence. Just look at those two." He laughed.

Mrs. Clyde pulled back a sleeve of her expensive dress. The sky was clear again today, and the sun glinted on a diamond-studded wristwatch. Farmer admired it silently. Mrs. Clyde looked a little concerned.

Farmer said, "Well, we shouldn't really keep you and Dulcie any longer. It's just such a pleasure—" He reached down and scratched the poodle behind its ears. Its coat was as curly as a lamb's.

Mrs. Clyde said, "It was so nice," and tugged at Dulcie's leash, and headed back to number 55.

That night he got ready to move. He packed his few belongings: half a dozen favorite books, a few CD's (a couple of Sinatra compilations, Mary Martin's *Songs from Rodgers and Hammerstein's The Sound of Music*, and of course *Alice Faye's Greatest Hits*), and his little cable-ready TV. And of course Bink's spare water dish, dinner dish, her favorite toys, and her spare leash and collar.

It might be nice, someday, to own a house instead of always having to rent. But when your business kept you moving around the country, that just wasn't practical. He only had to hit once every few years, once every time he moved. He'd lived in Vermont, in Oklahoma, in New Jersey, in Florida, and now in northern California.

And of course he knew where he was headed next. He believed in careful planning. He was headed up north again, but not to Oregon. He had his eye on Idaho. Boise, Idaho.

He always hit the same way when he hit, when he and Bink hit. But each time out brought enough to last for years, and who was going to remember a hit five years ago and two or three thousand miles away? Farmer remembered. He remembered the little Sheltie in Montpelier and the miniature schnauzer in Enid and the unusual, wirehaired dachshund in that little town near Trenton. They bothered him, they really did, every one of them. But business was business. It was a safe way to work, and Farmer liked to be safe.

He got a good night's sleep. Bink always seemed to sense a big day coming up, and she climbed onto Farmer's bed when she thought he was asleep and snuggled against his legs and went to sleep, too. Farmer had a funny dream that night. He was in an old movie, wearing a scratchy woolen suit and a stiff-collared shirt, and Alice Faye was there in a low-cut Naughty Nineties gown and with an ostrich feather in her hair, and they were doing a song-and-dance act to the tune of *You Say the Sweetest Things Baby*. He woke up and the woolen blanket was itching under his chin. He rubbed his eyes, reached down and rubbed Bink's muscular flank and climbed out of bed.

An hour later he parked the Ciera a couple of blocks from Mrs. Clyde's house and got out of the car. He was in his gray-hair-and-mustache persona. He snapped the leash on Bink's collar, took a small plastic bottle out of the Ciera's trunk, and walked the Rottie toward Mrs. Clyde's house. Farmer looked around cautiously, led Bink into the cover of the firs and knelt beside her. He pulled a large, heavy-gauge rubber band from his pocket and worked it up over Bink's right front leg, all the way to the shoulder. He opened the plastic bottle and poured its contents over Bink's right front shoulder. He tossed the empty bottle into the fir trees. He straightened up, grasped Bink's leash in his hand and started running toward the front door of Number 55.

He wasn't in great shape, actually, and he managed to look disheveled by the time they reached the front door. He was panting a little, maybe a little more than he needed to. Bink had tried to run with him, but the heavy rubber band around her shoulder was uncomfortable and she wound up with a limping, rolling gate.

Farmer pounded on the door, gasping and calling softly, as if he didn't have the breath to raise his voice, to be let in. Bink raised her dripping and rubber-banded leg and scratched at the door.

After a few seconds that seemed like a year, the door swung back a couple of inches. Mrs. Clyde looked out, her pale blue eyes wide and her china-white skin looking more delicate than ever. Somewhere out of sight, the toy poodle Dulcie was yapping.

Farmer gasped, "That hoodlum! He hit poor Binky and he never even stopped. He could have stopped. He could have taken us to the vet's."

The rubber band must have made Bink's shoulder sore because she whined and bit at it. Perfect. Per-fucking-fect.

"Can you—she's bleeding." Some of the phony blood from the plastic bottle must have splashed on Farmer's face. He hadn't even thought of that, but it was even better that way.

Mrs. Clyde said, "Mr. Farmer . . ."

"Please—Binky."

"Of course. Come—" She stepped away from the door. Farmer pushed it wide open. He took a couple of wobbly steps inside, Bink leaning against his thigh. Mrs. Clyde said, "I'll telephone. They'll send somebody."

Farmer sank to his knees. He put his arms around Bink and worked the heavy rubber band loose. More of the phony blood got on his face and hands. Mrs. Clyde had picked up the telephone. Little Dulcie had run into the room and was staring at Bink.

The room had a high, cathedral ceiling with dark wooden beams. The walls carried out the kitschy Tudor theme. The floor was of huge flagstones with expensive-looking area rugs and an antique-looking refectory table.

Dulcie had run up to Bink. The big Rottie leaned over the poodle, baring her teeth. The poodle rolled on her back, squealing.

Farmer surveyed the room one last time, to make sure that everything was right. It was. "Now, Binky, get 'er!"

Mrs. Clyde and Dulcie screamed simultaneously as Bink sank her teeth into the poodle's guts. She picked up the poodle, gave it one furious shake and flung it across the room. The poodle's screaming stopped as it smacked against the refectory table and tumbled onto a rug. Mrs. Clyde's screaming got louder.

Farmer pointed at the LOL and grunted, "Now, Binky, get 'er!"

The Rottweiler sprang at the old woman.

Farmer heard a whining sound and looked around. From a back hallway, an electric wheelchair rolled steadily into the room. The man in it was ancient, wizened. A lap-robe covered him from the waist down. Farmer hadn't seen anything like that since some Raymond Chandler flick on TV.

The old man.

Mrs. Clyde had said, "Since my husband . . ." And again, "Since my husband . . ." Farmer had thought she meant, since her husband had died, and was too bereft to speak the words. But she must have meant, since her husband became crippled.

But only from the waist down.

From the waist up he looked okay. Old and weak, but okay. And too far away from Farmer or from Bink for either of them to keep him from firing the double-barreled shotgun that he was pointing in front of him.

Still, Farmer pointed at the old man and ordered, "Now, Binky, get 'im!"

The Rottweiler abandoned what was left of Mrs. Clyde and charged across the room. Farmer saw the flash of the shotgun, then heard its explosion, then felt the impact as a full load of pellets smashed into his chest and hurl him back through the still-open front door. He looked straight up at the brilliant afternoon sky. He heard the shotgun roar a second time but he didn't know whether Mr. Clyde had hit Binky or missed her.

Ω

A single loud report. Shards falling, colliding, tumbling, red, green, purple, yellow, glittering, reflecting flickering gaslight, crashing to the parquet, all against the sounds of the orchestra playing, four hundred voices in anthem raised . . .

Ω

I was "womanning" the counter, waiting upon customers, accepting payments and wrapping baked goods, when the postman's bell was heard in the courtyard. I refuse to refer to myself as "manning" anything. Such usage demeans the female gender and implies that I am in some manner inferior to and subservient to the male.

Mr. Tolliver leaned his bicycle against the postern and, after taking a moment to sort through his sack of mail, came forward and handed me a small bundle of missives. He smiled through his gray moustache. "Mum all right, Miss Holmes?"

"She would rather work," I replied, "but the doctor insists that she rest during these final weeks. Once the new arrival is here, he says, she will have work enough to do."

"Aye. And Dad, what has he to say?"

"He is in league with Doctor Millward. As am I. Mother insists on cooking for us all, but at least she has consented to yield her duties in the shop."

"You take care of your mother, Miss Elisabeth. She is a dear lady."

I handed Mr. Tolliver a complimentary crumpet and he retrieved his bicycle and pedaled away.

The shop was busy this day. It was all that young Sherlock could do with mixing batters, keeping the ovens in order, and placing fresh goods on display. Dad alternated caring for Mum and napping so he would have his strength to tend to the heavy baking duties overnight. And of course Mycroft sat in the nook that passed for an office, working as he ever did over the bakery's books and studying formulas for new products.

Mycroft also handled our correspondence, such as it was, ordering supplies and paying bills. Ours was a reasonably successful family business, but a most demanding one in this busy section of London. Competition was keen, as well.

By the time the shop was closed for the day darkness had fallen over London and gas lamps were casting soft shadows outside our dwelling.

Gas had also been installed indoors despite the grumbles of older residents who insisted that the new lighting was unnatural and unpleasant compared to traditional oil lamps.

Father had risen from a nap. Mum had made a rich soup of orange pumpkin and had roasted us a piece of beef with potatoes and greens. There were, of course, baked goods from our own shop. Mycroft was as usual prompt to reach his place at the family table. It seems that Mycroft spends his entire life in a stationary posture, save for his rare and unexplained "expeditions." At irregular intervals he will rise ponderously, don headpiece, take walking stick in hand, and disappear for an hour or a day.

On one occasion that I recall he was gone for an entire year. My parents had given him up for lost when he strode into the shop, greeted a number of our regular customers familiarly, and returned to his accustomed place without a word of explanation. My elder brother is as portly as my younger is scrawny; could they but exchange a few stone of avoirdupois I believe they would both be the better off.

But this night it fell to me to summon Sherlock who had retreated to his room to practice his fiddle-playing.

I do not know which is more distressing, the sounds of scraping and screeching that he calls music or the unpleasant odors of the experiments which he conducts from time to time. Why my parents had gifted me with this bothersome string bean of a younger brother is beyond human comprehension. I hoped only that the next addition to the Holmes household would be a pleasanter companion. The Fates willing, a girl!

Of course, this pregnancy is a late and unanticipated one. Still, Mother gives every evidence of pleasure at the prospect of having another Holmes about the house. Father worries about expenses. Mycroft appears oblivious.

As for the execrable Sherlock, I suppose that he is accustomed to the privileges associated with being the youngest member of the family. When mention is made of the fact that he will lose this distinction his expression resembles that of a person who has bitten into a fruit, thinking it an orange, only to discover that it is a lemon.

To be honest I will confess that my little brother is not entirely brainless. On one occasion which I recall he asked me to assist him in his so-called laboratory. He explained that he was developing a technique to transmit energy by means of sound waves. He had arranged an experiment in which he mounted a metallic object in a brace, surrounded by sound-absorbing batting. He stood nearby, scraping hideous sounds from his fiddle. He played notes higher and higher in pitch until, to my astonishment, the metal object began to vibrate violently.

"Now, sister, I want you to stand on the other side of the apparatus and match that note on your flute."

I complied, with similar results.

"And now," Sherlock proclaimed, "for the peas of resistance. We shall stand on either side of the apparatus, and upon my signal, both sound the keynote."

I did not correct his solecism but merely shook my head in exasperated compliance.

Sherlock placed his fiddle beneath his chin, laid bow across strings, and favored me with a nod and a wink. The grotesquery of his bony visage thus distorted far exceeds my mean verbal powers. Indeed, the awfulness of it must be imagined rather than described.

We both sounded the crucial note, he upon his fiddle and I upon my flute. Within seconds the metal object began to vibrate violently, then to glow with red heat, and finally to liquefy and fall in a silvery rain upon the floor.

At this moment, Mother entered the room. "Elisabeth, Sherlock, dears, has either of you seen my precious silver spoon from Her Majesty's Silver Jubilee?"

Alas, there it lay, a formless puddle of molten metal upon the floor of Sherlock's laboratory.

Ω

The meal proceeded pleasantly enough, each family member in turn describing his or her day as is our longstanding custom. Talk had turned to affairs of the world as they filtered into our household through the conversation of our customers when Mycroft announced that he had found a missive addressed to our parents in the day's arrivals.

Mycroft is by far the most brilliant man I have ever encountered. I cannot imagine him spending his life in our family bakery, but for the time being he performs invaluable service. He can also be the most exasperating of men, surpassing even the annoying Sherlock. Wiping his chin free of a drop of grease he muttered and patted himself here and there, searching for whatever it was that he meant to share with us.

At last he found it. He drew it from an inner pocket and handed it to Father.

It was an envelope carefully addressed to *Mr. and Mrs. Reginald Beasley Holmes, in care of Holmes Family Bakery, Old Romilly Street, London,*

England. The stamps were of an unfamiliar hue and design, denominated in something called "cents." A return address in the City of New York in the United States of America provided the solution to the mystery of the odd stamps.

There followed an act that could have been performed as a comic turn at a Cheapside music hall. Father patted himself upon the chest, blinking all the time. "I cannot find my spectacles," he announced at last, handing the envelope to Mother.

Mother shook her head. "I must tend to my kitchen duties. Perhaps one of the children will read this letter to us all."

Somehow the duty fell to my lot. Somehow, it seems, in this household it always does.

I opened the envelope. It was unusually stiff and of a finer grade of paper than most ordinary correspondence. From the envelope I extracted a card. In embossed lettering it read as follows:

Mr. and Mrs. Jorgen Sigerson
Request the pleasure of your company
At the wedding of their daughter,
Miss Inga Elisabeth Sigerson
To Mr. Jonathan Van Hopkins
In the City of New York
On the Sunday, the twentieth of June, 1875

I had read the card aloud. Upon hearing it Mother clapped her hands. "My dear brother's child is to be married! It seems but yesterday that she was an infant."

"I knew it," I exclaimed. "I knew that a wonderful event was about to befall my Cousin Inga."

"A joyous occasion indeed, but of course we shall send our regrets," Father stated. "The twentieth of June is mere weeks ahead. There is no way that Mum could possibly undertake an ocean voyage, nor would I under the circumstances even consider traveling to America while she remained at home."

Mother reached for the envelope and I extended it toward her. As I did so a slip of paper fell from it, barely missing the vegetable bowl and landing in front of the bony Sherlock. He snatched it up and refused to surrender it until Father commanded him to do so. Even so, I had to tug at the slip before he would release it.

The note was written in the familiar hand of my cousin. *Dearest*

Elisabeth, I read silently, *My Jonathan is the most wonderful man. He is a skilled printer and editor and we plan to move to the West once married. Please, please, Cousin dearest, do find a way to come to my wedding. I shall be heartbroken if you do not. I want you there as my Maiden of Honor.* The note was signed, in my cousin's customary manner, with a cartoon drawing of the two of us, our arms linked familiarly.

Although we have never met, I believe that we have had a psychic link throughout our lives. My mother and Inga's father were twins. Mother remained here in England while her brother emigrated to the United States, where he married an American woman, Miss Tanner. We two cousins were born on the same day, and as far we have been able to determine, at the same moment. My cousin was named Inga Elisabeth and I was named Elisabeth Inga.

The invitation to my dear cousin's nuptials was confirmation of a knowledge that I had carried for weeks.

Gathering my courage I announced that, in view of my parents' inability to do so, I would represent the English branch of the family at Inga's wedding.

Father shook his head. "Out of the question, Elisabeth. We shall obtain a suitable gift for your cousin and dispatch it by transatlantic transport. You will not travel to America, certainly not alone."

Mother fingered the strings that held her apron in place, tying and untying them in distress. "Inga is my brother's only child, Reginald. She is Elisabeth's only cousin. It would be sad if she could not be present on this occasion."

"No," Father insisted, "a young woman traveling alone under these conditions would be most improper."

"Perhaps her brother could go with her, then. Mycroft is a responsible young man. Surely he would be a suitable chaperone for Elisabeth, and I have no doubt that my brother and sister-in-law would welcome him into their home."

I will confess that even in this moment I found it amusing to think of Mycroft boarding a ship and traveling to America. Mycroft, whose daily movements seldom vary in route from bedroom to office, from office to dinner table, from dinner table to parlor, and from parlor to bedroom.

With a single word Mycroft negatived our Mum's suggestion, nor was any further discussion useful.

Following dinner and coffee we retired to the parlor for our customary Family Hour. Some evenings Mother will read aloud from a popular work of fiction. Others, I play familiar airs on my flute, on occasion accompanied by Sherlock's execrable fiddle-scratching. Rarely, Mycroft deigns to entertain us with a recitation. He has committed to memory the complete *Dialogues* of Plato, Plutarch's *Lives of Famous Men*, the scientific works of the great Mr. Charles Darwin, and the Reverend Dodgson's *Adventures of Alice in Wonderland*, a favorite of my own from earliest childhood.

But this evening there was but a single topic of conversation. It was the wedding of my cousin.

Mother and Father having ruled out their own presence at the nuptials, Father having forbad me to travel alone, and Mycroft having refused to contemplate the journey, there remained but one possible solution to the puzzle. I swallowed my pride and proposed that Sherlock accompany me.

I half hoped that he would reject the idea. To be honest, I more than half hoped as much. But my dear younger sibling took this occasion to torment me by giving his assent. Of course he did so with a demonstration of reluctance bordering upon martyrdom.

Mother seemed ready to give her blessing to this plan when Father raised the question of money. Fare for two persons traveling from England to America and back would come to a substantial amount. It might be possible to run the bake shop without Sherlock and myself for a time. But there was simply not sufficient funds in the till to provide passage for Sherlock and myself.

Father rose from his chair and stated, "We will send a suitable gift, perhaps a gravy boat or salver, to the happy couple."

"Not yet." Mycroft's words, spoken in the same rich voice which he used for his learned recitations, brought Father to a halt.

"Not yet?" Father echoed.

"Sir," Mycroft replied, "do not be so quick to give up on our family's being represented at the wedding. Remember that Inga is my cousin as well, and I would wish to see my sister and her cousin together on the happy day."

Father reached for his spectacles, unfolded their arms and placed them on his face to get a better look at his elder son. "I trust you do not plan to rob a bank, Mycroft, on behalf of Elisabeth and Sherlock." Father seldom makes jokes but I believe he thought he had just done so.

"Never mind what I plan, Father. Please trust me. I make no promise, but I venture that Elisabeth and Sherlock will be at Inga's wedding." He reached into his vest pocket and extracted a turnip. After consulting it he shook his head. "Too late this evening," he said. "Give me twenty-four hours, Father. I ask no more."

The next morning found our bake shop fully stocked as usual, the product of Father's industry. I took my place at the counter; Sherlock, his in the area reserved for handling goods; and Mycroft, at his desk, tending to his administrative duties. Nothing further was spoken of last night's family conference.

At noontime Mycroft rose, took hat and walking stick, and strode from the shop. He disappeared into the pedestrian traffic on Old Romilly Street. He did not appear again until the family had gathered at the dinner table.

Mother had roasted a chicken and small potatoes, hot and cold greens, and of course dinner rolls and butter. She assumed her place at the head of the table; Father, at the foot; Sherlock and I, facing each other across the cloth and dishes. Father had just taken carving implements in hand and reached for the brown-crusted bird when Mycroft entered the room. He rubbed his hands together, smiled at each family member in turn, and took his place.

He spoke at length during the meal, but his sole topic was the excellence of Mother's cooking and Father's baking. "We are not the possessors of financial wealth," he stated, "but we are a fortunate family to have a comfortable home, a successful business, one another's company, and the finest cuisine, in my humble judgment, in all the realm."

He may have exaggerated but none at the table chose to dispute him. Not even Sherlock.

Following our meal the family assembled in the parlor, at which time Mycroft actually stood rather than sitting, and made his announcement.

"All is arranged," he said. "I met this afternoon with certain persons, and it is done."

"You have tickets for us?" Sherlock asked. His voice is less discordant and irritating than his playing upon the fiddle, but not much so.

"Tickets? No, Sherlock. You will not need tickets."

"Oh, a riddle, is it, Mycroft?" Sherlock ground his teeth audibly.

"If you wish, stripling. Or if you would rather, I will simply explain matters in words comprehensible even to so mean an intellect as yours."

"Please," I put in. "Mycroft, do not lower yourself to the child's level." Even though, I thought, the scrawny beanpole is already the tallest member of our household. "Just tell us what you have done."

"Very well." Mycroft did lower himself now into his chair. Mother had served coffee and sweet pastries from the shop and Mycroft placed an apricot confection upon his tongue. He chewed and swallowed with evident pleasure. "As you may know," he said, "the *Great Eastern* departs

126

from London on the twenty-fourth of May. She crosses the Atlantic in eleven days, arriving in New York on the fourth of June. I believe that will provide ample time for you and Cousin Inga to work with Aunt Tanner upon the trousseau."

"Yes, yes, Mycroft. But how can Sherlock," I shuddered at the thought, "and I travel on the *Great Eastern* when we have no tickets and no money with which to buy them?"

"Dinner music and entertainment is provided aboard the *Great Eastern* by the orchestra of Mr. Clement Ziegfried. You are an accomplished flautist, dear sister, while young Sherlock," and Mycroft shuddered visibly, "does on occasion manage to scrape a recognizable melody from his instrument. I have arranged for you both to become members of Mr. Ziegfried's orchestra. Passage and meals will be provided, and a modest stipend will be paid."

There was a silence in the room, broken at last by Mycroft himself, "There is one minor consideration, however."

Sherlock grinned.

I waited.

"A small cabin will be made available for your use, but you will have to share it. In the interest of propriety you will be expected to travel as brothers."

I moaned.

Sherlock laughed.

"Why not as sisters, then?" I asked.

Mycroft grinned. He has a most adorable, winning grin, has my elder brother. "A splendid thought, Elisabeth. Most amusing." He paused to sip at his coffee. "Alas, it is already arranged that the Holmes Brothers, Sherlock and Ellery, will perform with the Ziegfried orchestra."

Eleven days, I thought. The voyage would take eleven days. That would mean eleven days of passing for a male and eleven nights of sharing a stuffy ship's cabin with the noisome Sherlock. I shuddered.

And so it was settled. I persuaded my good friend Clarissa Macdougald who lives two houses from us and with whom I attended school for many years, to take my place in the shop. Her brother would substitute for Sherlock. Father approved the arrangement. I take pride in my skill with needle and scissors, learned from Mother. The two of us altered male clothing to fit my needs and to conceal my gender.

Sherlock and I arose long before dawn on the twenty-fourth of May and made our way by rail from London to Southampton. Once in that southerly city it would have been impossible not to find our destination.

To me the *Great Eastern* was a great and famous ship, but to Sherlock, of course, it was an occasion to deliver a learned lecture.

"The *Great Eastern* is undoubtedly the greatest nautical achievement since Noah's Ark." Oh, that nasal voice! "Her designer, the genius Isambard Kingdom Brunel, perished at an early age, doubtless due at least in part to the stress of his enterprise. The ship's bottom was ripped by a hitherto unknown underwater mountain on one of her early voyages, and only Mr. Brunel's brilliant design of a double hull saved her from sinking. She was designed to carry as many as 4,000 passengers but, alas, has never been a commercial success."

Thank you, dear brother. I restrained myself from throttling the weedish know-it-all.

Even so, and despite my having seen many images of the nautical behemoth, my first sight of her took my breath.

Sherlock and I were clothed in similar garments. We wore tweed suiting, elasticized knee breeches and long stockings, plain cravats, caps upon our heads and brogans upon our feet. I found the male garb uncomfortable and impractical. I yearned for a proper frock and flowered spring hat, even an outfit of blouse and jumper. But if this unpleasant costume was the price of my being accepted as Ellery rather than Elisabeth, it was a price I was willing to pay.

While Sherlock was in fact my junior by some five years, whiskers were already beginning to make themselves visible upon his upper lip, while my own countenance, of course, was unblemished by such excrescences. Thus, it had been decided that Sherlock Holmes would pass as the older of the musical siblings while Ellery Holmes would be the younger. A further insult to me, I felt.

Sherlock and I each carried a gripsack containing toiletries and changes of costume, and a separate case containing our respective musical instruments. We had been warned that the ship's orchestra were expected to appear in proper dinner costumes, and with Mother's deft management and my own long hours of sewing, Sherlock and I had so furnished ourselves. We made, I am sure, a picturesque pair.

We were met at the head of the *Great Eastern's* gangplank by a ship's officer, who directed us to our quarters. There we met Mr. Clement Ziegfried, our maestro. He was a harried-looking person. He wore his dark hair quite long, as was, I believe, not uncommon among members of the musical fraternity, and a luxuriously drooping moustache that seemed too heavy for his small face and thin neck.

He smiled and shook Sherlock's hand and my own. He said, "Holmes

Major and Minor, yes, welcome. I see you have brought your instruments with you. Good! You are of course unfamiliar with my orchestra's repertoire." He paused and consulted a turnip that he pulled from a brocade weskit. "We have rehearsal in twenty-two and one-third minutes in the grand salon. Place your belongings in your cabin and present yourselves promptly, if you please!" He spoke with a peculiar accent, obviously Continental.

He turned on his heel and strode away.

He was a very strange little man.

Because the *Great Eastern* was so huge – longer than two football pitches laid end to end – and had space for so many passengers, room was not at a premium. I had expected to have to live in cramped quarters with dozens of smelly males. Instead, Sherlock and I were housed in a comfortable cabin of our own. Each of us would of course have a bunk of her or his own. And having lived for twenty-two years as Mycroft's younger sister and for seventeen as Sherlock's older, I was not shy about enduring the mundane presence of a male.

We deposited our gripsacks in our cabin, found a crewman on deck and were directed to the grand salon. This was a spacious chamber, clearly a living souvenir of the *Great Eastern's* glory days. The walls were decorated with friezes of classical scenes. Satyrs and caryatids stood in classical poses, supporting the high, domed ceiling of the salon. That ceiling was of stained glass, a magnificent design that would have done proud any architectural showplace in the land.

The musicians assembled upon a small dais. Sherlock and I were apparently the last to arrive. Maestro Ziegfried stood before us, half hidden by a black music stand, turnip in hand. The watch buzzed audibly. Maestro silenced it by pressing a lever and returned it to his pocket. He surveyed the assembled musicians and nodded his satisfaction.

"Gentlemans," he announced, "we have three new musicians with us for this journey. I will introduce them to you." He lifted a baton and tapped it on his music stand.

"Mr. Holmes Major."

Sherlock bowed slightly, holding his fiddle at the height of his shoulder.

"Mr. Holmes Minor."

I emulated my brother, showing my flute to my fellow musicians.

"Mr. Albert Saxe."

A portly musician standing in the second row bowed slightly, holding a glittering cornet in the air. He wore a moustache and beard. How he could maneuver his cornet through that hirsute decoration was a puzzle to me.

Speaking in his oddly accented manner Maestro Ziegfried announced that each of us would find sheet music before us. "You will take six minutes and twenty-three seconds to acquaint yourselves with the notes. Then we rehearse."

What an odd man he was! Still, one followed his directions. My parents had replied telegraphically to my Cousin Inga's wedding invitation, expressing their regrets and indicating that a gift would follow in due course. I had dispatched a personal message as well, telling Inga that Sherlock and I would arrive on the *Great Eastern* and anticipated the occasion of her nuptials with the greatest joy.

And of course, I would be happy, thrilled, honored, and delighted to participate as Maiden of Honor. I was certain, also, that her fiancé, Mr. Van Hopkins, would prove a splendid individual whom I would be pleased to accept as a cousin-in-law, were there such a position in the rules of family relationships.

With a blast of her whistle the *Great Eastern* pulled away from her dock and moved into the channel toward Portsmouth, rounded land and headed in a westerly direction. By the time we passed Penzance the orchestra was warmed up. Maestro Ziegfried was a stern leader. There was no concertmaster; he coached and prodded the musicians himself, shaking his head with joy or anger or passion at each passage until his long hair flew around his head like the wings of an angry black bird.

When rehearsal ended, Maestro laid his baton upon his music stand and pulled his turnip from his pocket. He pressed a lever and the watch's engraved metal cover sprang open. He studied the watch's face, then nodded and announced, "Gentlemans, you will assemble here ready to perform in one hour, fifty-six minutes and eleven seconds."

He jammed his watch in his pocket, turned on his heel, and took his departure.

Although I had stood for Mother to prepare my suit of dinner clothes I had never worn this strange black-and-white costume for any extended period of time, nor attempted to perform even the meanest of tasks in it. How strange and uncomfortable it was, with its stiff wing collar, miniature black cravat, satin lapels and itchy woolen trousers. What in the world is the matter with the male gender that they choose to get themselves up in such impractical outfits!

The *Great Eastern's* passengers had already begun filtering into the grand salon when the orchestra assembled, strictly on time per our Maestro's eccentric directions. I found myself seated beside another flautist, a gentleman with round, rose-colored cheeks. I could not tell whether he was prematurely white-haired, amazingly well-preserved, or perhaps was simply the possessor of Scandinavian blood and blond hair so pale as to resemble snow.

My Brother Sherlock, I saw, was immersed in a section of violins, violas, and violoncellos. *Good,* I thought, *there are enough of them to drown him out. Or may he have the sense to hold his bow a fraction off the strings and avoid making any noise at all!*

Waiters were serving beverages and food to the passengers. The *Great Eastern* is so huge that a virtual barnyard of cattle and poultry is kept on her deck, providing fresh provisions during her voyages.

Maestro had planned a program that mixed recent works by the great composers of Europe with popular tunes suitable for performance in the music halls of England and America. For some selections only parts of the orchestra were required to perform. Maestro called upon the string section for a new quartet by the young Bohemian musical folklorist Dvorak. This was followed by a full orchestral rendering of an American tune by Luke Schoolcraft. Clearly influenced by what I believe is called "darkie music," this jolly piece, titled *Oh! Dat Watermelon!* was indeed a rouser.

Between numbers when I was not busy shuffling the sheets upon my music stand, I scanned the tables of well-dressed diners. For all that the *Great Eastern* had proved a commercial failure as a passenger liner, she had been turned to a number of other uses with far greater success. That she had been refitted for her original purpose was a melancholy matter. Word was that she was to be sold and turned into some sort of commercial showboat, a floating advertisement hoarding, and moored in a resort town, perhaps Brighton or Torquay. This, the greatest ship in the world, which had been visited by Her Majesty herself, and by His Highness the Prince of Wales, on several occasions!

Still Captain Halpin and his officers maintained the appearance of grand sea sailors. Their uniforms were elaborate, as neatly tailored and sharply pressed as those of any naval officer, their buttons sparkling, their decorations looking like the awards granted to the victors of great marine engagements. The captain himself was a portly man, bearded and mustachioed in the manner made popular by the Prince of Wales. He was seen from time to time striding the *Great Eastern's* deck in company of his wife and three lovely daughters and their great dog Harold. How I envied those three girls their freedom to be themselves and not play-act at being boys!

The other diners in the salon were an assortment of well-dressed and groomed ladies and gentlemen. A few of them, I surmised, might be emigrants intending to make new lives for themselves in the Western Hemisphere. Canada and Newfoundland sounded attractive to me, especially the former. The United States with its red Indians, its many thousands of black former slaves, and its Irish gangs must be a dangerous and exciting nation. Soon enough I should find out for myself!

One man I noticed carrying on a particularly animated conversation. He chopped the air with hands in time to the music and jerked his head up and down in agreement with himself at every moment. He was apparently without companion, but was seated at a table with several couples who gave every appearance of discomfort with his expostulations. When he paused for breath he drew back his lips to reveal teeth that reflected the salon's gaslights, causing me to wonder if he had not had them drilled by the new electrical apparatus of Mr. George Green, and filled with a metal amalgam.

My attention was drawn back by the tapping of Maestro's baton upon his music stand. We were to perform a suite of flute duets by Wolfgang Mozart. The rosy-cheeked flautist at my side smiled encouragingly and we set out upon a sea of the loveliest melodies ever composed.

It pleases me to state that we started and ended together, the performance was not a disaster, and most of our auditors actually lowered their implements and hushed their conversations while we played. Maestro Ziegfried smiled and gestured to us to rise and take a bow at the conclusion of the suite, and the room applauded most generously. My fellow flautist shook my hand and gave me his name, Jenkins. He had, of course, already learned mine.

That night I sat up in my bunk composing a letter to Mother and Father. I would post it when the *Great Eastern* reached New York. I was bursting with happiness. I was in the world at large. I had performed musically to acclaim. Even the presence in the other bunk of the annoying Sherlock could not dampen my cheery spirits.

As the voyage proceeded our days on shipboard were not unpleasant. Our meals were excellent in quality and generous in portion. When not rehearsing or performing, we musicians were free to roam the *Great Eastern*'s extensive decks, to borrow volumes from her library, even to explore her gigantic engine rooms. These were extensive. She carried volumes of coal with which to fire the huge boilers that powered her twin paddle wheels and her screw propeller. The ship even bore tall masts, but her sails were seldom unfurled.

From time to time I would encounter my friend Mr. Jenkins. We even shared a glass of wine on occasion, discussing the great ship, Maestro Ziegfried, and various members of the orchestra. Mr. Jenkins seemed to have tidbits of gossip, most of it not unpleasant, about each of our fellow musicians, with the exception of the cornetist, Mr. Saxe. When I asked if Mr. Jenkins knew anything of this gentleman he quickly changed the subject.

Our musical repertoire was varied, with each evening's performance including both orchestral and solo performances. Maestro Ziegfried proved an expert pianist, interpreting compositions by Joseph Haydn, Frederic Chopin, and several of the Bachs, most notably my favorite, the underrated Carl Philipp Emanuel.

During Maestro's solo performances I was able to observe the audience. Time and again my attention was drawn to the man with the metallic teeth.

His behavior changed but little each evening. He would arrive at the appointed hour and take his place, the sole unaccompanied male sharing a table with three couples. At the beginning of the meal his mien was respectable, but he inevitably consumed copious alcoholic beverages. As he did so he became increasingly animated and, apparently, belligerent. On an evening near the end of our voyage, two days before we were due to make landfall at New York, his six companions rose in a body and departed from the table, leaving him to fume amidst empty bottles and soiled napkins.

Early the next afternoon Sherlock and I strolled upon the *Great Eastern's* deck. The starboard side was reserved for the ship's sea-going cattle ranch, as I had come to think of it. The port side was the promenade deck, so lengthy and broad that it had come to be known as Oxford Street.

Sherlock was speculating upon the availability of scientific instruments in the savage streets of New York. I listened patiently, or half-listened, pretending a greater interest in his monologue that in truth I felt. The *Great Eastern* must have been breasting a warm Atlantic current, perhaps the fabled Gulf Stream, for the air was warm and so moist that it seemed almost to hold a heavy mist. Figures appeared and disappeared as they approached or distanced themselves in what I finally came to think of as a displaced London fog.

A well-dressed couple approached us. The gentleman bowed politely. "Mr. Holmes and Mr. Holmes, is it not?"

My brother and I conceded that we were indeed the Holmses.

"You are not really named Major and Minor, however?" Apparently these people were Americans, returning to their homeland. Had they been British they would have been familiar with the customary identification of elder and younger brothers.

"My name is Sherlock Holmes," my beanpolish sibling explained. "My little brother is Ellery."

"Boatwright. Bertram and Bonnie Boatwright, of Back Bay, Boston," the gentleman said.

There followed much tipping of hats and shaking of hands. I had to remind myself that I was one of three males in the presence of but one female. I would have liked to identify myself by my gender; I could imagine how Bonnie Boatwright must yearn for the companionship of a fellow woman, but I determined to maintain my disguise.

The Boatwrights invited Sherlock and myself to join them in their stroll along "Oxford Street." Both of these Bostonians were kind enough to compliment me at length upon my rendering of the Mozart flute duets with Mr. Jenkins. No mention was made of Sherlock's violin performances. It was well, I thought, that Maestro had not singled my brother out for any solo.

The prow of our great ship split the waters gracefully. A thin spray on occasion rose above the ship's railing, reminding one and all that we were not in truth at home, but many hundreds of miles from the nearest land.

At length our conversation, which had consisted for the most part of what is sometimes known as "small talk," turned to the Boatwrights' dinner companion.

"It is a good thing that we are Americans," Mr. Boatwright announced. "That fellow – what is his name, darling?"

"Beaufort. John Gaunt Beaufort, or so he fancies himself."

"Thank you, my dear. Beaufort. Yes. As I was saying, it is a good thing that we are Americans, and your English politics with your dukes and princes and suchlike don't mean much to us."

"And why is that?" piped Sherlock in his irritating voice.

"Why, young fellow, this Beaufort pipsqueak seems to think he's the King of England."

There was a shocked silence.

Then Sherlock and I exclaimed simultaneously, "What?"

"Yes, that's what he says."

Mrs. Boatwright nodded agreement with her husband. "Yes, he claims to be the rightful King of England."

"Surely he means that as a jest," I put in.

"I think not. Have you seen his conduct? He became so agitated that he knocked over a bottle of wine and ruined my poor darling's frock."

"He is serious, then?"

"Very."

"Upon what does he base his claim?"

"He says that he is the legitimate heir of the Plantagenets. That each monarch since Henry the Seventh has been an usurper and a fraud. That upon the death of Richard the Third the crown should rightfully have passed to Margaret Pole, eighth Countess of Salisbury. That her beheading in 1541 was an unforgivable crime and that only the recognition of this fellow, this—what was his name again, darling?"

"John Gaunt Beaufort," Bonnie Boatwright dutifully supplied.

"Yes, this Beaufort fellow claims that the crown is rightfully his and that once he is recognized as rightful monarch of Great Britain and her Empire, he will take the name Richard the Fourth." He shook his head in disbelief. "Kept muttering about houses. Do you think he's a real estate developer?"

Bonnie Boatwright said, "No, dear."

Bertram Boatwright ignore her. "Don't know why a real estate developer would complain about kings, eh, Holmeses?"

I felt compelled at this point to give the poor overlooked Mrs. Boatwright her due respect. Calling upon the authority of my *faux* manhood I interrupted. "Mrs. Boatwright, what was your point regarding real estate?"

Her gratitude at even this small recognition of her worth was manifest. She said, "Beaufort's reference to houses was directed at the dynasties of the British monarchy. At least, such was my education, even in Boston. He mutters about the Angevins, the Lancasters, and the Yorks. He is quite opposed to those who came later. To the Tudors, the Stuarts, and the Hannovers."

Bertram Boatwright said, "Quite right, my dear, quite right." Then he shook his head. "My manners, my manners," he exclaimed, patting himself on the chest. From an inner pocket he drew an elaborate cigar case of yellow metal and green stone—I guessed, gold and jade—and opened it. "Will you have a smoke, Mr. Holmes? I prefer the torpedo myself, but you may prefer a smaller and milder product. Perhaps this panatela."

He extended the cigar case to Sherlock and to me. It contained a variety of smokes. We each extracted a cigar from it.

"The finest Havana," Bertram Boatwright announced. He drew a packet of Lucifers from another pocket and struck one to light.

Sherlock bit the tip from his panatela, bent toward the flaring Lucifer that Mr. Boatwright held for him, and drew a flame into the cigar.

This, I thought, will be the supreme test of my masquerade. I imitated my brother and managed to get the cigar going. I had expected to collapse upon the deck in a coughing fit, but instead I found the flavor of the smoke not unpleasant.

We soon parted from the Boatwrights and returned to our cabin. Sherlock sat upon his bunk, making arcane computations in a note book while I penned another missive to our parents in London.

I made it my business to arrive early that evening at the grand salon. Our voyage was drawing to a close. We expected to make land on the second day following, and a peculiar air had descended upon the ship. It was an amalgam of melancholy and excitement; the former, I suppose, deriving from the imminent dissolution of the little aquatic community that had formed on our ship; the latter, as women and men thought of the homes that awaited them or of the adventures they might experience in an exotic and undeveloped nation.

Mr. Beaufort made his entrance as usual. I thought that the night before he had drunk almost to the point of unconsciousness, and I rather expected him either to miss tonight's meal altogether, or to arrive shaken and contrite. No such symptoms, however, were visible.

The Boatwrights of Boston and the other couples who shared their table arrived in turn. They exchanged greetings with one another and even ventured a polite nod to the self-styled monarch who favored them with his company.

Maestro's selections of music for the evening were subdued for the most part, although the performance climaxed with a chamber arrangement of Peter Illich Tchaikovsky's *Pathetique* symphony—not the lugubrious piece that its title implied, but in fact a rousing composition.

Mr. Beaufort—I still thought of him as "the man with the metal teeth" —managed to avoid any outbursts, and retired even before coffee and brandy had been served.

The next day was to be our last full day at sea. The *Great Eastern* had performed admirably and I was saddened to think that this would, in all likelihood, be her last oceanic crossing save one. That, of course, would be her return journey to England. I stayed up late composing another missive to my parents, then lay in my bunk, imagining the wedding to which I was journeying.

If I was in truth to serve as my cousin's Maiden of Honor I would of course need a suitable costume. Knowing my Cousin Inga from a lifetime of correspondence, I was aware that she and I are of similar proportions. Inga would have served as a draper's model in my stead, and a lovely gown would await me. Of this I was certain.

I passed from wakefulness into the land of sleep without being aware of the transition, and dreamed pleasantly of the experiences that lay ahead of me in the company of the wonderful cousin whom I had known all my life through the medium of correspondence but whom I had yet to meet *in propria persona*.

The morning before our planned arrival in New York dawned hot, with a brilliant sun, a lovely blue sky, and the even a great white albatross circling above our ship, the traditional symbol of good luck to all nautical enterprises. I breakfasted in company of my brother and several other members of Maestro Ziegfried's ensemble.

It was, perhaps, indication of nervousness upon my part that I was able to take only a cup of fragrant Indian tea and a half-slice of toast lightly coated with orange marmalade for my meal. Need I describe the quantity of scrambled eggs, the slab of broiled ham, the potatoes and biscuits with warm honey which Sherlock consumed, accompanied by a series of cups of rich, steaming hot chocolate *mit schlagsahne*.

My traveling gear was small and so I was able to pack everything into my gripsack quickly enough. I spent the next hour strolling on Oxford Street. At one point I had the misfortune to cross paths with the terrible Mr. Beaufort. Clearly, he recognized me, certainly because of my appearance each night with the *Great Eastern's* orchestra.

He tipped his hat and offered me one of his metallic smiles. In that moment I felt a chill as I feared that he had penetrated my disguise and recognized me as a member of the female sex. Should this be the case a most unpleasant conversation might all too easily ensue.

But he merely bowed slightly as we passed, walking in opposite directions. "Mr. Holmes," he hissed.

"Mr. Beaufort," I returned.

I walked on as rapidly as I could, hoping that he would not turn and follow me. Fortunately, he did not.

The hours seemed to drag that day, and yet I was taken by surprise when I realized that night had fallen and it was time for me to repair to my cabin and don my evening outfit.

As is traditional, the last evening of the voyage was observed with a gala dinner. Captain Halpin and his officers were present, each of them wearing his most splendid uniform. The captain's lady and their three daughters were gowned in the most charming fashion. The passengers who filled the salon were similarly garbed in their finest.

The meal featured cold lobster, roasted squab, lamb chops with fresh mint sauce, baby peas and carven potatoes. Champagne flowed freely. The repast ended with coffee and brandy and portions of trifle.

Toasts were offered to Her Majesty, to Mr. Disraeli, to the American President, Mr. Grant, and to Vice President Wilson. A special toast was offered, to the memory of the great Isambard Kingdom Brunel. A resolution of thanks to Captain Halpin and his officers and crew was proposed and adopted by acclamation by the passengers.

Maestro Ziegfried's orchestra performed a series of numbers alternately stirring and amusing. Our American passengers were clearly pleased to hear the jaunty *Carve Dat Possum*, by Messers. Lucas and Hershey. A great cheer greeted the *Water Music* of George Frideric Handel. The Maestro had chosen to end the program with a salute to the United States of America and to our own blessed isle. Alas, the Americans have no accepted national song. Many of them, I have been led to understand, enjoy singing a set of lyrics by the poet F. S. Key, set to the tune of the *Anacreontic Song*, but those very words are deemed to be anti-British. Instead, there was an instrumental rendering of their so-called *Battle Hymn of the Republic*, Mrs. Howe's reminder of their own Civil War.

At last came the great moment, the orchestral rendering of our own glorious anthem. For this occasion the Maestro elected to add his pianistic talents to those of the rest of the orchestra, whilst conducting, as the expression has it, "from the keyboard." All present, further, were invited to give voice to the patriotic words.

Throughout the evening I had cast an occasional glance at Mr. John Gaunt Beaufort, the man of the gleaming teeth. He had drunk a great deal, this much was obvious, but to this moment had behaved himself in an acceptable manner.

All rose.

Maestro raised his hand in signal and the first notes rang out stirringly.

I could see Mr. Beaufort leave his party and stumble drunkenly toward the front of the grand salon. He climbed clumsily onto the vacant conductor's podium and began to wave his arms as if conducting the orchestra.

Four hundred voices rang out:
God save our gracious Queen,
Long live our noble Queen,
God save the Queen.

Mr. Beaufort reached inside his evening jacket and drew an old-style, two-barreled pistol. He pointed it upward and fired. *There was a single loud report. Shards falling, colliding, tumbling, red, green, purple, yellow, glittering, reflecting flickering gaslight, crashing to the parquet, all against the sounds of the orchestra playing, four hundred voices in anthem raised . . .*

Half the orchestra ceased playing. Half the room ceased to sing. The other half, perhaps unaware of what had transpired, perhaps too stunned by the suddenness of Beaufort's act, played or sang on:

Send her victorious,

Happy and glorious,

Long to reign over us.

Beaufort lowered his pistol, pointed it before him. He shouted, "*Deo, regi, patria!* Bow before your rightful monarch, Richard the Fourth, *Rex Anglorum!*"

Mr. Albert Saxe, our cornetist, stood forward, his massive chest expanded like the breast of a pouter pigeon. He spread his arms, the salon's lights glinting from his silver cornet. "Shoot," he commanded, "if you must. I am your target. Aim well!"

But the delay had given Sherlock time to raise his fiddle and bow, and I, my flute. At his grotesque signal I breathed into the air-hole of my instrument, and he drew his bow across the strings of his. The two sounds converged upon Mr. John Gaunt Beaufort. He screamed in pain and tossed his pistol into the air. As it crashed to the parquet he tumbled from the conductor's dais and rolled on the floor, clutching his jaw in agony as smoke rose from his mouth.

In moments he had been seized by crewmen and hustled from the room to end the voyage in irons, as he well deserved.

An hour later I sat upon my bunk, trembling. I had decided to end my charade a day early and was garbed in comfortable female costume. Sherlock had doffed his performer's finery and donned his tweeds.

There was a knock upon the door. Sherlock rose and answered it. Standing in the doorway we beheld the rose-cheeked Mr. Jenkins, my fellow flautist. He nodded, smiling, and said, "Mr. Holmes, and"—he hesitated but for a moment—"may I presume, Miss Holmes. Would you be so kind as to accompany me."

Mr. Jenkins offered no explanation, but there was something in his manner that persuaded my brother and myself to comply.

Without further speech we accompanied Mr. Jenkins to a suite guarded by two armed ship's officers. At Mr. Jenkins' knock the door was opened and we were ushered into the presence of two bearded, portly gentlemen.

They were remarkably similar in appearance. One was Captain Robert Halpin, master of the *Great Eastern*. The other was Mr. Albert Saxe, the talented cornetist.

Mr. Jenkins addressed the latter personage. "Your Highness, may I present Mr. Sherlock Holmes and Miss Holmes."

"Elisabeth, please," I corrected.

Sherlock and I were in the presence of none other than the Prince of Wales, the Heir Apparent to Victoria's throne. Sharing the suite were Mrs. Halpin and the three Misses Halpin, and a woman whom I recognized as a leading beauty of the London stage.

The Prince shook Sherlock's hand heartily, then reached and embraced me in his great arms. I was bereft of words.

"How can I thank you both," His Highness said. "My equerry, whom you know as Mr. Jenkins, was kind enough to tell me who you both are. Your courage and resourcefulness are quite amazing."

Not one to hold his tongue at a moment like this, Sherlock asked, "Who was that drunken fool, Your Highness?"

The prince uttered half a laugh, then became more serious. "Apparently he is a Plantagenet pretender."

"A criminal!" Sherlock expostulated.

"Perhaps," said the Prince. "Or more likely a madman. It is not for me to say. Everything will be sorted out in due course, I am certain." He issued a sigh. "I wish I could reward you both suitably but at the moment I am traveling incognito and any ceremony would be unsuitable. But when we return to England, rest assured, you shall hear from me."

Sherlock scrabbled in his tweed jacket for pencil and paper. "Here, Your Highness, I'll give you the address."

The Prince waved his hand. "No need. No need, young man. I well know your older brother."

Ω

By morning he was at Moisant International Airport in New Orleans. The pilot announced that a cold front had beaten the jet down from the Chicago and New Orleans had experienced a freak snowfall during the night, and everybody should watch out for slippery surfaces.

He rode into town in a van full of tourists, climbed out in front of a hotel in the French Quarter and just wandered away while the rest of them dealt with their baggage.

He walked in a straight line until he came to a broad thoroughfare. The street sign said Canal Street. He found a fleabag movie theater and bought a ticket and a hot dog and slathered relish and sauerkraut on the dog and sat in the dark, stale-smelling, mostly empty auditorium. He was too warm in the jacket he'd worn on the airplane, so he laid it across his lap for safekeeping. He ignored the movie, eating his lunch and trying to get his act together.

He'd walked out of the joint expecting to be met by a team of Feds armed with a subpoena. It was going to be a matter of giving his testimony and then disappearing into the Witness Protection Program, and from everything he'd ever heard about the program he didn't want any part of it.

Instead he'd been met by a couple of guys in blue suits and black glasses and whisked to Chicago by limousine, no less. A fancy dinner with the old guy in the soft houndstooth jacket and then it was another limo ride, this time to O'Hare with a couple of hundred fish in his pocket and a ticket on the redeye headed south.

The old guy kept making small talk and calling him Charlie and he kept telling him that his name wasn't Charlie but the old guy didn't pay any attention. The old guy did look familiar, but when he asked who he was all he could get was, "You don't know me, Charlie." He only asked once, and when he saw the look in the old guy's eyes he wished he hadn't asked at all.

In late afternoon he wandered through the French Quarter again. He let a barker lure him into a bar. Once he got inside the bar he scoped around. The place was full of people in tee shirts and short pants. He asked the bartender what kind of beer they had and he said to try an Abita and he said okay, and it was actually pretty good.

On his way out of the bar he bent over and picked up a square plastic badge. It said,

YO, DUDE!
YOU CAN CALL ME JOHN

OR YOU CAN CALL ME JOHN
BUT DON'T CALL ME LATE FOR COCKTAILS
World Consortium of Q-Zix Processor Engineers
Novum Orleansis

It was a convention badge, and across the bottom where the date should have been was just a row of ones and zeroes.

He pinned the badge to his jacket pocket. It helped him blend in with the people wandering around getting drunk. He'd never heard of a place like this, but then when you've never been anywhere except Indiana, Ohio and Illinois in your life, and more than half of that in the joint, there must be a lot of strange places in the world.

He needed a place to stay and he needed a way to make some money. At first glance this town looked like dip heaven, all these overweight tourists wandering around, the men with their wallets in their back pockets and the broads with their purses on their arms. But he'd dipped a few times in his life and learned that it wasn't for him, he didn't have a light enough touch to be really good at it, and he didn't want to get picked up by the local minions of the law. Especially not on his first day in town.

Besides, there were too many blue uniforms in evidence, and too many units visible on the streets here. It made sense. In a tourist town, keep the tourist neighborhood under control. Let 'em spend their green, the more the merrier. And look the other way if the girls in the bars want to cut their own deals with the visiting firemen, even if the powdered sugar that gets sold is maybe not just sugar.

But try to keep the dips and the muggers under control.

Somewhere along the line he'd attended enough school to know that New Orleans was on the Mississippi River but he was astonished to find himself looking at it. The water was yellowish-brown. He turned away and wandered down the street into a neighborhood dotted with warehouses and marine supply outfits and job printers. He stood across the street from a row of saloons and restaurants, studying them, trying to choose the one that would be just right.

He'd never seen so many liquor dispensaries in one town in his life, and they were all busy. He picked one that looked like it served food and booze both. The only thing he'd eaten all day was the hot dog in the movie house and it was squirming around in his belly now as if it didn't like him any better than he liked it.

He picked a place that looked right and crossed the street and stood on the sidewalk in front of the establishment. The air was warm and moist. His clothes stuck to his skin.

The front window was a big rectangle of plate glass with a tank in it half filled with water with a quarter-grown alligator in it lying on a rock. A few fat goldfish swam lazily around the alligator. He wondered if they even knew the alligator was there, and if the alligator knew the goldfish were there. The alligator looked like it was asleep until you looked at it closer, then you saw that its eye was open a slit and it was watching you. It had an expression on its face that said, *Come ahead, buddy, you look like you'd make a lovely morsel.*

The sign in the window said:

KING ARTHUR'S ALLIGATOR ROUNDTABLE

The place was cool inside and it wasn't as crowded as the restaurants and saloons that pulled in tourists in the French Quarter were. There was a single big room in the place, with a little office to one side and a couple of doors that must lead to the kitchen at the back. If King Arthur had a roundtable, it might have been any one of twenty or thirty tables that filled the big room. There was a bar running along the wall opposite the office, in the back half of the place. The ceiling was high, covered with patterned metal squares. Big wooden fans turned slowly above the customers' heads.

He slid onto a barstool and surveyed the room more closely in the backbar mirror. He could see the office door in the mirror, and people eating an early dinner at four or five tables. It was too early for the real dinner crowd. These people must have a terrific appetite; maybe they were stoking up for a long night soaking up booze and jazz and the hot smell of strippers. They were eating some kind of stew, most of them, or some kind of mess of rice.

There were a few drinkers at the bar. A couple who looked like they were on their honeymoon, touching each other and drinking ridiculous drinks with pieces of fruit in them and whispering in each other's ears. A sad type who looked as if his wife had walked out on him leaving her mother in her place. He could have been the happy bridegroom, twenty or thirty years down the road, desperately trying to wash away a lifetime of mistakes with a glassful of bourbon.

There was a guy who looked a little smarter and a little tougher than the others. He had a double shot glass in front of him. It was mostly empty.

There was a woman at the end of the bar, with gray hair like steel wool and a blouse with some kind of collar that rolled away from her chest. She wore a bead necklace that disappeared into her cleavage. You couldn't help looking there. She must have been a looker twenty years ago. Now she looked like she was barely hanging on, one day at a time. Just like the AA people, only her one day at a time wasn't a day clean and sober, it was just a day.

She was drinking something that sent up steam. Maybe the air conditioning in the place was too much for her. Her drink looked like a hot rum toddy. It must be doing a swell job of keeping her warm because there was a sheen of moisture on her face.

He watched a drop of sweat roll down her neck and slide down her chest and disappear into her cleavage. It left a little trail behind it, a narrow stripe of skin washed clean of the day's accumulated grime.

She caught him watching her chest and gave him a peculiar look.

He said, "Excuse me."

She gave him some more of the look.

He said, "I'm sorry. I didn't mean to . . ."

She said, "Of all the gin joints in all the towns in all the world . . ."

The bartender looked at him. The bartender had a pale face, as if he never got out in the sun. It was almost a prison pallor. He had a fringe of black hair around his bald dome. His face was smooth. He was either old and well preserved or young and prematurely bald, it was really hard to tell. "Something for you, mack?"

He said, "Gimme an Abita." You had to like a town with its own beer, that was as good as this stuff.

The bartender put a bottle and a glass in front of him, took his money and slapped his change on the wood. He looked at it and thought about picking it up, then decided to leave it there.

In the mirror he watched a waiter come over and serve some food to a quartet of customers. They were all wearing little square plastic badges. They were all wearing *I Survived the Great New Orleans Blizzard* tee shirts. They were all overweight. The one who was most overweight was a woman. She caught his eye in the backbar mirror. She wasn't wearing any brassiere. The two men at the table were smoking cigars and gabbing a mile a minute. They looked as if they were working on a business deal. The other broad was busy looking the waiters up and down but the waiters didn't look the least bit interested.

The fat woman without the brassiere smiled at him in the backbar mirror. Christ, was she giving him the come on? Was she trying to get something on with him, right there while her husband yakked up a storm with the other broad's husband? That was all he needed. Christ.

The bartender said, "You want another one, John?"

He said, "Sure."

At the same time the guy with the double shot glass said, "Nope."

They looked at each other.

The bartender looked at the guy with the double shot glass and said, "Your name John, too?"

The guy with the double shot glass said, "Yeah."

The bartender said, "What a remarkable coincidence. I just read John's badge here." He took away the empty bottle, popped the cap off another Abita and clunked it onto the wood. He took the price of it out of the change that was left from the first Abita.

"Hey, John." The guy with the double shot glass looked at him. "What the fuck is a Q-Zix Processor? Sounds like some kind of ice box."

He poured a little Abita into his tall glass, watched it foam into a thin white head, said, "What ice box?"

The other guy laughed, if you could call one short, sharp bark a laugh. "And what the fuck is that one-zero-one-one shit?" He pointed to the badge.

Damn! Try and blend into the population and some wiseacre asks questions that you can't answer.

The woman with the steel wool hair saved him. She said, "Didn't you read about those Q-Zix people? Some kind of computer wizards. Hey, Johnny, you're the first one I've seen without a plastic pocket full of pencils."

He tried to keep quiet and ride this one out.

The woman with the steel wool hair said, "I thought you superbrains were all gone a couple of days ago. Doesn't that one-and-zero stuff mean the dates you were going to be here?"

He stole a glance at the badge himself, then tilted it up so he could read it upside down.

The bartender chimed in, "That's binary code. Lemme see." He scrounged around under the bar, came up with a plastic pen with a tiny woman trapped inside the plastic. When he held it one way she was wearing a green brassiere and panties. When he held it the other way the brassiere and panties slid down and you could see her tiny red nipples and dark triangle.

The bartender scribbled on a cocktail napkin. Then he said, "Yeah. Your convention ended last week."

Everybody seemed to be waiting for an answer.

The honeymooning bridegroom slipped his hand inside his wife's New Orleans Blizzard tee shirt and she squirmed and giggled. The older guy whose wife had left him gazed deeper into his shot glass.

"Yeah. The convention ended but I had a few extra days to kill. I'm taking a little rest. I been working too hard."

The giggling bride pulled her husband's hand out of her shirt and he dropped it into her lap. She squeezed her legs tight around his hand. She said, "We use computers all the time in my office. The boss says we're going to get a Q-Zix processor next year."

"I never talk about that when I'm on vacation." He fumbled with the plastic badge, undid the shiny metal pin that held it to his jacket and slipped it inside his pocket. He was still wearing his Chicago clothes. The jacket was too hot for this place and he pulled it off and laid it across his lap like he'd done in the movie theater.

The tough looking guy said, "So you're John and I'm John. What a coincidence. But they call me Jack. And you're Johnny. That's good. That'll keep us separated okay."

He said, "Yeah. That's good. Jack and Johnny."

Jack said, "Pleased to make your acquaintance." He held his hand out.

Johnny hesitated a tick, then shook Jack's hand. Jack gave him a look. Johnny didn't like the look much. It was a funny look. It wasn't quite a faggot look. It was more a sizing-up look like new fish got when they hit the yard. There was nothing like the first day in a new joint. You look around for a familiar face and you sense the sizing-up that you're getting, from the jockers, from the killers, from the professional bullies, from the gang recruiters.

He didn't like the look.

Jack said, "You staying in the Quarter?"

Johnny said, "Maybe."

Jack held his head sideways. Johnny didn't like that look, either. Jack said, "You need a place to stay?"

Johnny said, "I'm set."

Jack lowered his voice. He said, "Just finish your beer and head up the street to the corner. There's a boarded up gas station there. Take your time, Johnny." To the bartender he said, "I've had enough." To everyone at the bar he said, "Don't eat no yellow snow." Then he left the bar.

Johnny did a little mental math and ordered a bowl of the brownish stew. The bartender said it was gumbo. He ate it and drank another Abita.

A couple of times single guys dropped in to the bar, slid onto the stool next to the woman with the steel wool hair, and tried to pick her up. She brushed them off. She drank her hot drinks. Every time a drop of sweat rolled between her tits Johnny followed it with his eyes. The woman caught him looking every time.

He looked at a clock above the backbar, slid off his barstool, pulled his jacket back on, found his way to the toilet and took a piss, then headed for the door. He stopped to look at the quarter-grown alligator. He counted the goldfish. A couple of them had disappeared but the others swam around looking as happy as ever. The alligator had switched ends of its tank. It gave him the same look it had given him before. Like it would still be glad to take off his hand for dinner. No couple of goldfish could satisfy this gator's appetite.

Outside in the street, Johnny stopped and looked at the sky. The sun was gone and a combination of low clouds and mist covered the stars. The moon made a pale, soft-edged blob over the Mississippi. His jacket felt like it weighed a ton but he had his hands free if he wore it and didn't carry it.

Jack was smoking a cigarette in the boarded up gas station. He was wearing a blue Hawaiian shirt with hula girls on it. He was standing on a concrete island where gas pumps had been removed, leaving a couple of iron pipes sticking out of the island. He said, "Where you from, Johnny?"

Johnny said, "Chicago."

"What joint?"

"Fuck you."

Jack grabbed him by the front of his jacket. "Don't tell me fuck you, Johnny. I said, *What joint?*"

Johnny tried to get free but Jack wouldn't let go. Johnny said, "What makes you think I been in the joint?"

Jack shoved him away and Johnny stumbled over the concrete island. He caught himself without going down but now he was shaking a little. Jack said, "Don't shit me, it's all over you. I can see it. I can smell it. You got con stink on you, Johnny. What's this computer shit?"

Johnny said, "I found the badge."

Jack said, "You got a place to stay? You just got into town. You're dressed too warm. If you had a place you'd leave the coat in your room."

Johnny said, "I guess not. I'll find a place. You're not a cop."

Jack barked like he did back in the bar. "You'll stay with me. I got room. You can sleep on my couch."

Johnny looked around. He could see lights a couple of blocks away, back where the tourist crowds were dense. They were definitely out of the Quarter but it wasn't far away. It was darker here and there were no crowds. He could see the front door of King Arthur's Alligator Roundtable. The honeymoon couple were coming out. They headed the other way, toward the bright lights and the crowds. The guy had his hand on the broad's ass and he was squeezing as they walked.

Jack said, "Come on." He grabbed Johnny's arm. His fingers were strong. Even through the too-heavy jacket the fingers dug into Johnny's arm and hurt. Jack had a beat-up Plymouth Sapporo parked around the corner in front of a factory building. He unlocked it. Johnny stood next to the car. Jack said, "Fuck you, get in the damned car."

They drove under a couple of interstates and wound up on a street with old houses on both sides, scraggly lawns, a wide island in the middle of the street. Jack pulled the Plymouth into a driveway and led the way into the house. It was divided into apartments. Jack had a couple of rooms. The furniture was old and the place smelled of mildew and sweat. There was a kitchen sink and a counter with a hot plate and a small, battered looking refrigerator in the room. There was a scratched up TV in one corner with a coat hanger for an antenna and a short metal shaft sticking out where the tuner knob should be.

Johnny took off his coat. He sat down hard on an overstuffed chair. There were stains on the upholstery and whatever color it might once have been had turned to a kind of neutral nothing. It was hot in the room and the chair felt damp and it smelled musty. He laid his coat over the arm of the chair. He said, "What do you want?"

Jack stood in the middle of the room. He looked at Johnny. He didn't say anything.

Johnny said, "You're not a fag. You're not a roll artist. You gotta be after something. You sure as hell didn't just take a liking to me."

Finally Jack said, "You got any money?"

Johnny said, "Maybe you are a roll artist. Why the fuck did you bring me here?"

Jack said, "I'm not a roll artist. You have some money or you wouldn't have spent like you did in Arthur's."

Johnny relaxed a little. "I got a few bucks."

"But not many or you wouldn't have been so eager for a free flop."

"Ain't you smart."

"Look, Bo, you're a con and you got a few bucks and you're new in town and you got no prospects. You want to make some green?"

Things were rolling his way, now. Jack wanted something. Johnny played it cagey. "What's your proposition?"

Jack said, "I need a helper."

"Sure you do. A helper with what?"

"Real easy job. A nice heist, real easy."

Johnny said, "Tell me."

Jack walked over and stood in front of Johnny's chair. He said, "Sure I'll tell you." He reached down and grabbed Johnny and pulled him out of the chair and spun him around and threw him against the wall. Johnny hit the wall face first with a crash. Jack said, "Position, fucker! You're too curious. You're wired."

Johnny put his hands on the wall and crossed one ankle over the other. Jack patted him down. He grabbed him by the back of the neck and threw him back into his chair. Johnny said, "No wire, okay?"

Jack said, "Okay. And no heat. Not even a shank. What the fuck— ?"

"I'm clean. I just hit town. Whadda you expect?"

Jack lit a cigarette. Johnny held his hand out. Jack gave him one, threw a book of matches at him. "Christ, what happened to you? You get born this morning?"

"You're so fucking smart, I'm just out of the joint and I'm new in town. Okay, I need a score."

"You're no junky. I coulda spotted that."

"I need to score some bread. I got a little roll but it won't go far and there's no more coming."

Jack nodded. "Okay. What brought you into Arthur's?"

Johnny said, "Nothing."

Jack gave him a look.

"I wanted a drink and a meal."

"Arthur's is a little off the beaten track, Bo."

"That's why."

Jack looked at him. "Maybe you ain't so dumb." He drew on his cigarette, walked over to the sink and turned on the tap. He held the cigarette under it and when the water hit the burning tobacco the cigarette went out with a hiss. Jack threw it in a garbage pail under the sink.

Johnny crossed his legs and rubbed out his cigarette on the bottom of his shoe.

Jack said, "I been stopping in Arthur's pretty regular."

Johnny said, "So what?"

"How much money you think goes through that place every day?"

"I don't know."

"Want to guess?"

"I have no idea."

Jack said, "Call yourself a computer whiz."

Johnny said, "I told you, I found that badge. I don't know squat about computers."

Jack said, "Right." He said, "Stay put." He started looking for something, shoving piles of old *Times-Picayunes* around on top of a table and tugging drawers open and slamming them shut again. He grunted and came back to where Johnny was sitting. He sat on a chair like Johnny's. He had a yellow pad and a wooden pencil and a little calculator in his hand. He balanced them on the arm of his chair. He said, "Look at this."

Johnny grunted.

Jack said, "King Arthur's opens at ten o'clock every morning. They serve breakfast, lunch, dinner. They serve dinners 'til ten thirty at night. The bar opens when the restaurant opens and it stays open 'til eleven thirty at night."

Johnny said, "I'd think they'd stay open later."

"If they was on Bourbon Street they would. Or Decatur Street. Anyplace in the Quarter. Maybe in the Garden District. But not in the Warehouse District. There's no foot traffic there late at night. Wouldn't pay 'em to stay open."

Johnny said, "Christ it's hot. Gimme a glass of water."

Jack said, "Take it." He gestured toward the sink.

Johnny opened a cupboard, found a jelly glass, filled it with tepid water and came back to his chair. He took a sip of water. "Wonderful," he said. "You planning to go in the restaurant business and you want me to manage the place for you."

Jack said, "Don't be so fucking smart. I asked you if you had any idea how much money goes through Arthur's every day."

"And I told you I have no idea what so fucking ever."

Jack was writing numbers on the yellow pad. He said, "Look, fuck-ass, here's how many customers Arthur's seats at the tables. Here's how many times they turn over those seats for breakfast on an average day. I been watching them, see? And I worked in a couple of saloons in my time, and a couple of dinner houses."

This time Johnny laughed. "I was right. You want to go in the restaurant business."

Jack hit him in the face with back of his hand, pretty hard. Not hard enough to knock him out of his chair, but hard enough to let him know he meant it. He said, "Pay attention."

Johnny rubbed his face. "Shit," he whispered. "Shit, shit, shit."

Jack said, "Here's how many lunches they sell. Same principle, you take the number of seats times how full they get times how many times they turn over."

Johnny said, "You really did work in one of those places."

"A lot of 'em. Shut up and pay attention. Don't interrupt me unless you don't understand something. Look, dinner's the big meal. They got a real long dinner hour in this town, the place gets the fullest then, and the meals cost the most. And the customers drink the most. You got to calculate bar business in there too. Sometimes that'll carry a dinner house all itself."

"Yeah. Yeah."

"Bar drinkers plus table service, figure they sell—hey, pay attention, shit head—you got straight drinks, you got mixed drinks, you got wine and beer. You—fuck, just sit still." He scribbled numbers, poked the calculator *On* button and punched the keys, scribbled some more numbers, wrote the final total big at the bottom of the page.

There was a rattling sound.

Johnny jumped.

Jack said, "It's raining, that's all."

Johnny said, "I thought it snowed here."

Jack said, "That was a freak. It's raining."

"Okay." Still, a window was open and a cool, moist wind swept through it. The temperature dropped and Johnny was almost cold. It was still as moist as ever, close and sticky, but no longer hot.

Jack shoved the pad under Johnny's nose. "Look at the numbers, fuck-o. Look at the bottom number."

Johnny did. He nodded his head.

Jack said, "All right. I'm gonna watch TV. We'll talk some more tomorrow." He turned on the TV, jiggled the coat hanger. The news came on. There was a story from Illinois about how the Feds were pissed at the local cops because they'd gone to pick up a con and the local guys had turned him loose an hour early and they couldn't find him.

Jack gave Johnny a sour look. He stood up and found a pair of pliers to turn the dial on the TV. "Nothing any good on. Fuck. If you ain't here in the morning I'll find your ass and I'll kill you, Bo." He snapped off the TV and disappeared into the other room.

Ω

The sun came through the window and hit him in the face and he sat up, startled. He blinked and Jack was standing there watching him, wearing a pair of stained khaki pants and an old-fashioned undershirt, smoking a cigarette.

Jack said, "All right. Here's how it works. All you need is a cosh, fuck-o."

"A cosh?"

"Christ! A sap. A blackjack. You're going to hit a guy on the back of the head. That's all you have to do and you get a quarter of that money we were talking about last night."

"A quarter?"

"Do you know how much that comes to? Are you smart enough to figure that out?"

Actually, Johnny hadn't figured it out. He looked around the room. Jack's yellow pad was still there. He looked at the bottom number, cut it in half in his head, cut it in half again. "If I'm your partner I get half."

"You're not my partner. You're my helper."

"Hey, if we take a fall I do the same time you do."

Jack hit him again, harder this time, right in the same place he'd hit him last night. "Shit head, I spotted this thing, I worked it all out, I made the plan and I'm running the job. All you got to do is do what I tell you. All you got to do is slug a guy. You got to do about ten minutes work. This'll be the best night's work you ever did."

Johnny said, "Who do I have to slug?"

Jack said, "You'll find that out later. You had breakfast yet?"

"How'm I gonna have breakfast?"

Jack sucked on his cigarette, took it out of his mouth and looked at the coal as if he expected to find a message there. He hung the cigarette from the corner of his mouth and squinted at Johnny through the thin column of smoke that twisted past his eye. He didn't say anything.

Johnny said, "You got any grub? And you got an extra set of threads I could borrow? I'm starting to feel a little ripe. I need some other stuff, too." He scratched the stubble on his face with the tips of his fingers. His face was sore where he'd taken those shots from Jack. He didn't say anything about that but he stored it away. He always stored things like that away.

Jack said, "I'll do better for you than that. You're gonna help me make a nice score, I'll front you the bread for a couple meals and a set of threads. Come on."

Johnny was sitting on the couch in his underwear. He pulled on his heavy pants and his shirt, his sweaty socks and shoes. While he rubbed toothpaste on his teeth with his finger, Jack boiled water on the hotplate. They drank some instant coffee. Johnny asked why it tasted funny and Jack said that was the chicory in it, you better get used to it.

They took Jack's struggling Plymouth down to Canal Street and Jack parked it and they went into a huge old department store that looked like they hadn't changed the stock in thirty years or the equipment in forty. Johnny still had most of his bankroll from Chicago but if Jack was willing to front him the cash for a couple of pairs of khakis and some Hawaiian shirts, that was fine with him. He picked up a toothbrush and a razor at Woolworth's.

Jack drove him back to his apartment and waited while Johnny shaved and washed the sweat off his body and put on new clothes. He felt a thousand times better.

They drove back downtown and ate lunch at Kolb's on St. Charles Avenue. Jack ordered red beans and rice. Johnny had a fried oyster po' boy. He drank a few beers with his meal and a cup of coffee after. They talked about great joints of America.

Johnny tried to be careful but Jack knew people he knew and the beers seemed to have more effect than they should. Maybe it was the hot, muggy weather. It was almost winter in Chicago and it should be getting colder in New Orleans, too, he thought, but you could take a bath in the steamy air.

Jack said, "I gotta piss." His chair scraped on the old tile floor and he strode away.

Johnny thought about just getting up and leaving. New Orleans was a big city. Jack wouldn't find him, probably wouldn't even try, and if he did, so what? But a score sounded good. His roll wouldn't last long, and Jack was the only person he knew in town. He signaled the waiter for another beer.

A couple of suits at the next table were looking at a copy of the Chicago *Tribune*. Wouldn't you know it. One of them was pointing to a story, saying, "You can bet he's dead. They'll fish him out of the Lake or maybe he's in New Jersey with Jimmy Hoffa. They'll never let that guy talk."

The other suit grunted. Then he said, "I don't know. More likely New Jersey. Yeah. They wouldn't want him anywhere close to home, not even dead. Draw too much heat."

"Yeah," the first suit said. "I'll tell you what I bet, they'll send him away someplace and set him up and just when he figures he's safe they'll take care of him. Serve the fucker right, anyhow." He laughed like he thought that was real funny.

The second suit said, "I guess you're right. Fuckin' criminals, deserve what they get."

Johnny felt like somebody had dropped an ice cube down his back. He looked away from the suits. There was no sign of Jack coming back from the pisser.

The first suit said, "Listen, we got one more appointment this afternoon and then we don't have to fly back 'til tomorrow. How do you feel about tying one on tonight? We can get a couple of bimbo's up in the room, a couple of bottles, maybe a little powder. Just keep the expense account clean . . ."

Jack pulled out his chair and slid into it. "God, nothing like a good piss to make you know you're alive. You had enough? I haven't." He signaled the waiter and ordered a slice of cheesecake. He stuffed his mouth full of cheesecake and said, "How'd you work that thing in Illinois?"

Johnny shot a look at the suits. They were halfway to the front door, headed out of Kolb's. He said, "Work what thing?"

Jack put his fork down on his plate, loud. "Don't bullshit me. You saw the story on TV."

Johnny said, "I didn't work nothing. I served my time and I got my release. That's all."

Jack said, "Yeah." He chopped off another bite of cheesecake and shoved it in his mouth. He said, "Look, you can take the afternoon off. Do whatever you want. Go to the zoo, listen to some jazz, find a whorehouse. You want me to take you to one? Christ, I feel like your father." Some cheesecake crumbs fell on his shirt as he talked.

Johnny looked into his coffee cup. How long had it been? But he said, "Not yet. I want to keep my edge. Let's make this score, then I'll want a broad. I always like to get laid after a score."

Jack shoved the last of the cheesecake into his mouth. "Yeah. Don't I know it." He looked around for the waiter and signaled for their bill. He told Johnny he was lucky he'd cleaned up and put on his new clothes before they got there. He'd never have got into a place like this, looking like he did before.

Johnny said, "We need a schedule."

Jack nodded. He paused while a couple of working girls in tight skirts swirled past. "Look, you take the afternoon off. We're going back to King Arthur's tonight. Not for dinner. Ten o'clock. Make it ten thirty. I wanna show you something. You know your way by now? I don't wanna get there together, that same name business last night was creepy. Sit at the bar and have a drink. You really like that Abita stuff, don"t you? I wanna show you something."

He spent the afternoon in the movies again. He watched a pretty good flick about a corpse loose in a girls' school, lots of shots in the dorm and in the showers before the corpse killed his quota of teenagers and some faggoty-looking jock blew up the corpse.

After the movie Johnny worked his way down Bourbon Street. He picked up a street map. It was easy to get around in New Orleans, especially in the Quarter. He watched a few strippers, drank a couple of beers. Christ, but this would be heaven if he was still dipping for a living, but he kept his fingers to himself.

He cut over to Jackson Square on Saint Something street. He bought a hot dog from a vendor and sat on a bench watching a kid tap dance to a boom box until it was dark and the air was starting to cool off a little. He walked up Decatur, back to Canal Street, then crossed Canal to Magazine Street.

He stood opposite King Arthur's Alligator Roundtable and watched people go in and come out. Most of them looked like tourists, a few looked like locals. He tried to count the customers. Jack knew so fucking much about the restaurant business, why didn't he open a restaurant? In Chicago, he knew if the man in the soft houndstooth jacket wanted a restaurant, he'd send a couple of guys in blue suits and black glasses around and they'd arrange it.

He looked at his watch. It was a quarter after ten.

Jack's Plymouth wobbled past King Arthur's and disappeared around the corner onto Natchez. Ten minutes later Jack reappeared on foot smoking a cigarette. He crossed Magazine Street. Johnny ducked back into an alley. Jack walked past him, close enough for Johnny to reach out and touch him if he wanted to.

Jack reached the corner of Gravier, crossed Magazine again, and went into Arthur's.

Johnny gave him five minutes to get settled, then crossed Magazine in the middle of the block and looked through the window of Arthur's. The alligator was still in its tank. There was one goldfish left. The alligator gave Johnny the *you-look-good-enough-to-eat* look. Johnny said, "Fuck you, alligator." The alligator didn't say anything back.

Inside the place, Johnny could see Jack silhouetted against the far wall. He was sitting on a bar stool with a double shot glass in front of him. At the near end of the bar the woman with the steel wool hair was on the same stool she'd been on last night. Johnny could see she was wearing a rusty-orange colored shirt and a pair of dark jeans. He couldn't see her drink but he thought he saw a little wisp of steam rising from it.

He pushed open the door and stepped inside. A party of two plain-looking women and a muscular guy with a dark mustache went by him, leaving the restaurant. A waiter spotted him and started to say something about the kitchen being closed but laid off when Johnny shoved past him and headed for the bar.

There were a couple of strangers soaking up booze but Johnny slipped into a seat next to Jack. He didn't look at Jack. He looked around, surveyed the other drinkers, zeroed in on the woman with steel wool hair. Tonight's shirt buttoned up the front and the top few buttons were open and she wasn't wearing a brassiere. Christ, she must have been something before she got so old.

She looked at him and made a little motion with her head.

Maybe she wasn't so old after all. What was the saying about how all cats were gray in the dark? All pussies. He smiled back at her. He felt a sharp pain in his side. He made eye contact with Jack in the backbar mirror.

Out loud Jack said, "Hey, if it ain't Mr. Skeezix!" Under his breath he hissed, "Watch this, you fuck." He picked up his double size shot glass, laying one finger alongside it, pointing to the mirror.

Johnny watched.

The owner was coming from the far end of the dining room. One look, you knew this guy was the owner. King Arthur him fucking self. He gave the bartender the high sign and the bartender pulled his cash drawer out of the register and followed the owner into the little office. One of the waiters came over and took over the stick. None of the customers complained. Everybody drank his drink.

Johnny looked at his watch. It was eleven o'clock.

The office door opened and the bartender stepped out, carrying a cloth satchel. The owner came out behind him and stopped long enough to lock the door. Then he took the satchel from the bartender and headed for the door. The bartender followed him out onto the sidewalk.

Through the front window of Arthur's, beyond the alligator and its goldfish pal, Johnny saw the owner head up Magazine Street. The bartender waited a few beats, then followed him.

To Jack, Johnny said softly, "Is that all?"

Jack said, "Shut up."

Jack drank his Abita and admired the tits on the broad with the steel wool hair. Christ, she was looking younger by the minute and better by the beer.

At twenty after eleven the owner and the bartender came back in, together. The owner disappeared into the office with the cloth satchel. The bartender took back the stick and the relief bartender disappeared into the kitchen.

Ω

They drove back to Jack's in silence, smoking cigarettes and listening to the radio. The disk jockey played nothing but punk rock. There was a news and weather break. The news was mainly about a political scandal in Baton Rouge, followed by a couple of sports headlines. The weather forecast was hot and muggy with a good chance of thunder showers blowing in from Lake Ponchartrain. Not a word about the missing witness in Illinois.

In the apartment Jack brought out a bottle of scotch and two jelly glasses and poured them drinks. They lit cigarettes. Jack said, "Did you get it?"

Johnny shook his head.

Jack picked up his hand like he was going to backhand Johnny again but he stopped. "Maybe I made a mistake. You're so fucking dumb."

Johnny put his glass down. He wasn't going to take a beating from this creep. "Can the tough talk and say it."

Jack looked at him with a little respect for once. "Didn't you understand what you saw tonight? Look, Arthur has a safe there in his office. Every couple of hours they transfer all the cash from the dining room register into the safe. Same for the bar register."

He dragged on his butt, swallowed a slug of scotch. "At eleven o'clock Arthur carries the last restaurant cash into the office, the bartender brings his cash drawer in. They total up the day's cash and put it in that satchel. Then they carry it to the night deposit at the bank."

Johnny nodded.

Jack said, "You're starting to follow, hey?"

Johnny said, "Yeah. Go on."

"Arthur carries the satchel. The bartender follows a little ways back. They don't look like they're together. If anybody tries to put the arm on Arthur, there's Arthur's little helper to the rescue. Any money comes in at the place, meanwhile, they put in the safe overnight. But that's peanuts."

Johnny rubbed his face. He'd shaved off the stubble and he was only a little bruised and swollen from Jack's backhand shots. You didn't know to look, you'd just think that he was kind of fleshy around the jawbone, a little fleshy and a little blotchy.

He said, "You want to put the snatch on the receipts."

"You figured it out."

"Half."

"A quarter. All you got to do is slug the bartender. That comes first. Then I hit Arthur. Nice and quiet over there, not too light, nobody walking around. We come back here and split the green. Then, who knows, maybe we'll stay partners."

"Half."

"A third." They bargained a little more. It would be a good score. Maybe he could partner with Jack. This was a nice town, looked like there was plenty of loose cash around, he sure as hell didn't want to head back to Chicago. He didn't want to see the old guy in the houndstooth jacket again, or the guys in the blue suits and black glasses. So—why the hell not?

"Fuck you. A third."

Ω

They had a day to kill so they left the Plymouth in the alley by Jack's house and took the St. Charles streetcar out to Audubon Park and walked around the zoo with the tourists and the school kids. They looked at tigers and bears and some alligators that could have swallowed the one in the window at King Arthur's in one bite.

They rode the streetcar back and sat in Jack's place and drank scotch and smoked cigarettes until it was time to go. Then Jack drove the Plymouth down to Magazine Street and parked around the corner from King Arthur's.

Jack provided the saps.

They sat at a table like a couple of guys in town for a convention or like two faggots celebrating the first week anniversary of their beautiful romance. Jack ordered a plate full of crawfish and Johnny ordered a blackened steak. Jack was still picking up the tabs, but he was keeping careful track of everything Johnny spent. Once they'd scored, he'd take it all back.

Somehow that made Johnny more confident. If Jack had been planning anything funny, he wouldn't be fronting cash. Would he?

Jack had his back to the street door so he could see the kitchen doors, the little office and the bar. Johnny could see the alligator tank behind Jack. He had a better angle at the bar. Steel wool hair was there as usual. She didn't seem to have noticed Johnny. She was wearing an off-white tee shirt with a picture of a spotted cat on the front. She must have picked it a couple of sizes too small. Her little tits were pointed and they looked really nice to Johnny. Maybe once he and Jack had made their score, there might be something there after all. The old ones were so damned grateful.

The waiter brought coffee with chicory and bread pudding. Jack looked at his watch. Johnny looked at the clock over the bar. They were running ahead of schedule. Shit, they didn't want to be conspicuous.

Jack signaled the waiter and said, "How about a liqueur?"

A liqueur, for Christ's sake!

The waiter brought over a bottle of Drambouie and a couple of tiny little glasses and poured them both drinks right there at the table and took the bottle away again. They nursed the Drambouie and that made the timing right. Jack paid their check and left a tip on the table and they walked outside, ignoring the bartender and the woman with the steel wool hair, past the sleepy looking alligator. There were no goldfish in the tank tonight.

Jack and Johnny walked up Magazine toward Gravier. Jack pulled Johnny into a narrow alley between two building. There was a flash of lightning and Johnny got a look up the alley before the thunder rolled in. The alley was filthy but otherwise it was empty. What a joke it would have been if they'd interrupted some conventioneer getting a blow-job from a whore when they were just there to knock off a restaurant's receipts!

The wind blew along Magazine Street, carrying some newspapers and fast food wrappers with it. It whipped around the corner, wrapping a piece of paper around Johnny's ankle. He bent over and pulled it off and threw it away.

Jack's sharp fingers dug into Johnny's arm. Johnny reached into his pocket and felt the sap there. He wrapped his fingers around it. He heard footsteps and in a couple of seconds King Arthur walked past the alley. There was another flash of lightning and Johnny could see the cloth satchel in Arthur's hand.

Arthur disappeared.

Jack shoved past Johnny and followed Arthur. If there was a flaw in Jack's plan, this was the moment it would appear. If the bartender saw Jack pop out of the alley and head after Arthur he might yell a warning or even pull a heater on Jack. As far as Johnny knew, Jack wasn't heeled except for a sap, just the same as he was.

If that happened, Johnny might still be able to sap the bartender, but it would be a messy thing, a risky thing. If that happened, he decided, he would just pop out of the alley and scamper off the other way. Forget it. Let Jack take the fall. Johnny still had most of his Chicago bankroll. He'd start over, maybe in New Orleans, maybe in some other town.

But Jack was gone and now the bartender moved past the alley. A gust of wind came up and brought the first rush of hot, fat raindrops spattering down as Johnny stepped out of the alley a few paces behind the bartender. He could see Jack farther ahead, and Arthur beyond him. Everything was working perfectly.

He raised the sap and brought it down very hard. The lead-weighted, spring-loaded, leather-covered sap smacked against the bartender's hairless skull. The guy didn't go straight down. It was funny. First he jumped like he'd been goosed instead of sapped. Then he seemed to go limp in mid-air. He crumpled to the sidewalk and he didn't make a sound and he didn't move.

Behind Johnny a woman's voice yelled and he turned around and saw a woolly-looking head silhouetted against a distant streetlight. The woman with the steel wool hair was running toward him. She had a rod in her hand. She was pointing it at Johnny.

She yelled again and he put his hands up and dropped the sap. He thought, fuck, fuck, fuck.

The woman was coming up fast and something spat past him and then he heard the shot and the woman hit the sidewalk with a dive and pointed her gun again. He couldn't figure out what was happening. Did somebody plug her? He started to turn around, to see where the shot had come from.

He saw Jack facing toward him, a heater in his hand. The guy was heeled after all. He saw twin flashes, one from behind Jack and one from Jack's gun. He saw Jack jump toward him as if somebody had punched him hard between the shoulder blades. He heard another crash, this one from behind him. He felt a whack as a round hit him. He'd already been turning and he didn't know whether Jack had shot him or the woman with the steel wool hair. He tumbled and rolled and felt a little shock as he fell off the edge of the sidewalk into the gutter. He lay on his back looking at the sky.

He lay in the street in the trash, waiting for the wail of sirens, feeling the hot, heavy raindrops on his face. He didn't think he was dying. He blinked and the woman with the steel wool hair was standing over him, the gun still in her hand. He wondered if she had shot him, or if Jack had. He wanted to ask her but he couldn't talk. He could hear footsteps pounding, and he knew they belonged to Arthur, not to Jack.

The rain was really coming down and the woman with steel wool hair's tee shirt was soaked and plastered tight against her skin and he could see that she still wasn't wearing a brassiere. He could feel himself bleeding and everything was starting to look a little fuzzy and now he wasn't so sure after all that he wasn't dying.

The woman bent over to look at him and there was a flash of lightning and he thought, *Christ, does she ever have beautiful nipples.*

Keweenaw Bay Gazette
Keweenaw Bay, Michigan
July 5, 1940
Mr. Zachary Grand
Editor-in-Chief
Grand Publications
143 West 43rd Street
New York, 16, New York

Dear Zach,

Well, you'll never guess who turned up here in Keweenaw Bay a couple of days ago. Tony LoPresto! What the heck was Tony doing in this little town? Bet you've never heard of it. But there he was.

I was on my lunch break, stopped into Helen's Café for a chicken salad sandwich and an iced coffee, and there he was sitting at the counter. You could have knocked me over with a feather.

Tony LoPresto! Carried me right back to the days of the Three Cheshire Cats. Remember the Three Cheshire Cats? Of course you do! Tony was as surprised to see me as I was to see him, but as soon as we both got over the shock we started exchanging biographies. It's been what, six, seven years, right, seven years since we said good-bye to North Cheshire Central College. Funny how three fellows who were roommates for four years, formed the best little swing trio that northwestern Massachusetts has seen, chased co-eds, shared homework, got into and out of trouble with the local law, and somehow managed to escape with bachelor's degrees, can disappear out of each other's lives as if they'd never known each other.

But I guess that's life.

Would you believe that Tony is police chief of Napoleonville, the flower city of Bayou Richelieu, Louisiana? He still loves bird-watching and he was up here on vacation, field glasses in one hand and notebook in the other, studying the local feathered wildlife. Stopped into Helen's for his ham and eggs and ran into me.

Two of the Three Cheshire Cats back together! Naturally we reminisced about good old North Cheshire Central College, good old President Lucas Smith, poor old Professor Percival Dunning, and all the great times we had together. And of course, the Three Cheshire Cats. I still play a little piano, although just for fun. Tony says he hasn't touched his trumpet in years. Do you still keep your old bull fiddle around, Izzy—or should I say Zach?

When your name came up, Tony told me that you went back to your old hometown and got a job in the publishing world. How things change, don't they? Good old Isaac Goldberg, editor of the *North Cheshire Literary Quarterly*, is now Zachary Grand, editor of *Grand Adventures*, *Grand Western*, *Grand Mystery*, and *Grand Ghost Stories*.

Did I leave anything out?

Those pulp magazines are a far cry from the *Literary Quarterly*, I guess, but everybody has to earn a living. Who would have thought I'd become production manager of the Keweenaw Bay *Gazette*?

Tony says you're always looking for new talent, which is how he discovered you're "Zachary Grand." I'd like to try my own hand at something like that. Being over on the production side of the *Gazette* is okay, but I sometimes get an itch to try writing the stuff instead of printing it. Thought maybe the sad end of poor old Dunning might furnish the ingredients for a story. Might even find a place in your *Grand Mystery* pulp. Just let me know, old roomy.

It's been fun reminiscing about the old days anyway, please write back when you get a chance.

Meow, Cats, Meow!

Robert "Bobcat" O'Brien

Ω

Keweenaw Bay Gazette
Keweenaw Bay, Michigan
July 15, 1940
Mr. Zachary Grand
Editor-in-Chief
Grand Publications
143 West 43rd Street
New York, 16, New York

Dear Zach,

It was great to hear from you after all these years. I know you must be dreadfully busy there at Grand Publications, running all those magazines, and I'm actually flattered that you remembered me as you did. I'm also flattered that you asked about my job here at the Keweenaw Bay *Gazette*. A small-town weekly is a far cry from your line of big magazines.

Actually, what I do here at the *Gazette* is not so different from the work I did on the *North Cheshire Literary Quarterly* when you were the editor-in-chief. My title here is "production manager" but in fact I'm pretty nearly the whole production department. The owner is a fellow named Jack Miller. Editor-in-Chief is Tim Holcomb, although in fact he's also our chief reporter, feature writer, and advertising salesman. I'll send along a half dozen recent issues so you can see what we're all about.

What passes for hard news in Keweenaw Bay is the opening of hunting season in the fall and fishing season in the summer, weddings, funerals, and births, and graduation at the local high school. Come out here for a visit and you'll think you're in an Andy Hardy movie.

My job—well, I set type, pull and read proofs, lay out pages, and even run the press. We set type on a second-hand Mergenthaler Linotype that we got at a bankruptcy sale at the Kearsarge *Recorder* when they went belly-up. Of course at the *Quarterly* we hand-set type and ran vellum on a letter press. Out here we run newsprint on a small rotary, a Goss Sextuple that's older than Methuselah but still runs okay. Not nearly as pretty as the *Quarterly*, but a whole lot cheaper.

You know, I've been thinking about the old gang at North Cheshire since Tony LoPresto was here. You and Tony and I were quite the trio, weren't we, and I mean that in more ways than one. I've been thinking about some of the young ladies we chased, too. Remember Carolyn Deering, Annie Mayfield, Jennie Lipton? I'll admit, I used to dream about Annie. What a girl! What a figure! I wonder what ever became of Annie and the others.

And the professors, oh, weren't there some characters in the faculty? Shakey Simmons, Henry von Eisen, Percival Dunning. Poor guy. Remember how he used to whisper his lectures? Well, not exactly whisper, but you remember that soft, breathy voice he always used. Remember how he got it?

Oh, you wouldn't, of course. He didn't like to talk about it, never mentioned it in class, I only remember him talking about it one time. It was at one of his Friday night soirees. He used to invite a few students in to his apartment there in Wellington Hall on Friday nights. He'd lay out sandwiches and serve brandy and put on music, and we'd talk about everything from the benzene ring to Schopenhauer to the history of the Hittites. Of course there was a certain amount of pairing off, too. Normally coeds wouldn't have been in a men's dorm but Dunning used to invite them to his parties and nobody complained.

I'm sure he would have invited you, Izzy. He always spoke highly of you.

But you were over in Great Cheshire at the synagogue on Friday nights. I had a lot of respect for you, Izzy. I think you were the only Jew at Central Cheshire, and you didn't bother to deny it, you took whatever you had to and you stood up for who you were.

That rat von Eisen, Henry von Eisen, I remember he used to rag you every chance he got. I don't know why he hated Jews but he certainly did, and he never missed an opportunity to slam you, pal. Percival Dunning would never have done that, it just happened that he held his gab-fests on Friday nights and you couldn't attend.

Anyway, one Friday Percival must have had a little too much brandy. I remember he had his radio on. He used to play records most of the time, he was a big fan of Ralph Vaughan Williams and Frederick Delius and Gustav Holst, but once in a while he'd turn on the radio instead. The news came on and there was something about the election in Germany, this thug who was running against old President von Hindenberg. Dunning got pretty upset about it.

When the news went off somebody asked him why he was so agitated. Dunning said that the Great War was starting up again, this bum Hitler was worse than the Kaiser and the slaughter was going to happen all over again.

Everybody else said, Look, Hitler lost the election, there's nothing to worry about, but Dunning just sat there looking unhappy and drinking brandy. Finally a coed, I think it was actually Carolyn Deering, put her hand on Dunning's hand and asked him why he cared so much about Europe, it was three thousand miles away anyhow.

Dunning was English. Of course you knew that, Izzie, you could tell from the way he talked, right? Everybody knew he was English.

What he told us was that he'd been a Tommy in the Royal Fusiliers in the Great War. He'd been in the Battle of the Marne. There were Spads and Fokkers flying over and cannons going off and both sides were using poison gas. I thought they had gas masks but I guess they didn't work very well, and poor Dunning wound up gassed.

He said he was nearly dead. His comrades to the left and the right in the trench were dead. He was lying in the bottom of the trench, water and mud nearly a foot deep. He had no food. He was so weak he couldn't move, just lay there with his rifle at his side pointing up in the air, the bayonet fixed.

The Germans tried a charge, and a German soldier must have lost his footing. He fell into the British trench, landed on Percival's bayonet. It went right through his gut. The German landed on Percival and Percival was too weak even to crawl out from under him. The German was as good as dead, he would have been better off dead but he was alive. He was screaming in pain. Then he just moaned and cried.

Percival said it took the German a day and a night to die. Finally a German graves registration unit came through and pulled the corpse off Dunning and took it away, and one of the Germans noticed that Dunning was alive. They pulled him out of there and sent him to a field hospital and he spent the rest of the war in a prison camp.

That was why he always whispered, Izzie. It was his lungs. They were ruined by that poison gas. It was a miracle that he didn't die. Didn't die then, I mean.

Say, I'm sorry to ramble on like this, Izz. I know you're a busy man and you have plenty of work to do. And I have to get back to setting type myself. You didn't say anything about my writing for your magazines in your last letter. What do you think? Do write when you get a chance, Izz. We old Cheshire Cats have to stick together!

Meow, Cats, Meow!

Robert "Bobcat" O'Brien

Ω

Keweenaw Bay Gazette
Keweenaw Bay, Michigan
July 20, 1940
Mr. Zachary Grand
Editor-in-Chief
Grand Publications
143 West 43rd Street
New York, 16, New York

Dear Izzy,

I'm glad you got a kick out of those copies of the Keweenaw Bay *Gazette* I sent you. The owner, Jack Miller, wanted to know if we might get a subscription out of you. When I told him I doubted it he made me pay for the copies and postage. What a cheapskate! Well, I guess he's a businessman and he has to watch expenses.

I hope you didn't mind my mentioning your being a Jew and all, and your attending synagogue in Great Cheshire. I wonder what Percival Dunning would think of the war in Europe if he were alive. He predicted it back in '31, I think it was, when Hitler ran for President of Germany against old Paul von Hindenburg. Was it '31? No, '32, I think. Of course Hitler lost but that was only a temporary setback for him, wasn't it?

And I wonder what Henry von Eisen thinks. He used to talk about Hitler and his theories of Aryan purity. I wonder what he thinks nowadays. Remember how he used to hate That Man in the White House, said he was secretly Jewish, his real name wasn't Roosevelt at all, it was really Rosenfeld and he was part of the International Zionist Movement and that we needed a Hitler in America to stop Rosenfeld from selling out the country to the Jews? And where is that rat von Eisen now?

Hey, I don't need to tell you about this, do I? Sorry, Izz.

I had a nice letter from Tony LoPresto this week. He's back in Louisiana, of course. Who would have thought our fellow Cheshire Cat would turn out to be the Sherlock Holmes of the Bayou Country? Back in our undergrad days it seemed as if Tony's only interests were the time he spent on the bandstand and the football field.

Man, could he play that horn! He could have given lessons to Ziggy Elman or Harry James. And when he put down his trumpet and put on a North Cheshire uniform, those pads and that leather helmet, he was something else! You wouldn't think a barrel-shaped guy like Tony, North Cheshire's own Two-Ton Tony, could move the way he did. But...

Remember the big game in '32 against Willow Lakes Institute? The way Tony snagged that pass from the Willow Lakes quarterback in our own end zone, and dodged his way the length of the field to win the county championship for us? Beautiful! And then he turned around and batted .380 for our baseball team in the spring of '33.

But now he's running Bayou Richelieu like J. Edgar Hoover. Who would have guessed?

I've been thinking about your magazines, Izzy. Somebody like Tony LoPresto could make a great character, don't you think? I don't mean to make a pest of myself and I always enjoy hearing from the old gang, but you haven't responded to my questions about writing for your pulps. I hope I'll hear from you soon.

Meow, Cats, Meow!

Robert "Bobcat" O'Brien

Ω

Keweenaw Bay Gazette
Keweenaw Bay, Michigan
August 2, 1940

Mr. Zachary Grand
Editor-in-Chief
Grand Publications
143 West 43rd Street
New York, 16, New York

Dear Izz,

You are a prince of a fellow, Izzy! Not a word from you in a week and a half, and suddenly there's a package on my desk at the *Gazette*, all the way from New York City. Once Tim Holcomb, the editor-in-chief, saw the return address he couldn't wait for me to open it, and when he saw what was inside he didn't know what to make of it. I think he suspects you're trying to lure me away from the bright lights and fast action of Keweenaw Bay and get me to come to the big town to work for Grand Publications.

And I just might do it, too, if I got the right offer. (That isn't a hint, old roomy, I'm just pulling your leg.)

Still, copies of *Grand Adventures, Grand Western, Grand Mystery,* and *Grand Ghost Stories* all in one heavy bundle made quite a stir around the *Gazette* office.

I took *Grand Adventures* over to Helen's Café and spent my lunch hour poring over it. It's quite a magazine. I know you've got your competition, but they'll have to go a long ways to top *Grand Adventures*. That was some picture on the cover. That guy Saunders can sure paint up a storm! That native gal was really something. I hope you don't get into trouble with the censors over it.

And the story was every bit as good as the picture. Splash Shanahan is some hero! I thought the nasty Sea Lynx was going to put a knife between his ribs at any time. Good writing, good story-telling. I'll bet you never dreamed you'd be publishing yarns like this one when we were working together on the *North Cheshire Literary Quarterly*.

Some of the other stories were just as good, and of course there are all the other magazines you sent me. *Grand Ghost Stories* is next up on my nightstand. I don't mind a good scare every now and then. You are one heck of a pal, Izzy!

You know, thinking about the old days, recalling the times we all had together puts me in a funny mood. Remember the night you rolled that old Cole roadster on your way back to North Cheshire from Great Cheshire? You showed up at our digs in Warren Hall with your clothes ripped up and blood all over, but you were mainly worried about your car.

What a night that was! I didn't think you ought to make your weekly pilgrimage to your synagogue, but I'm not a very religious person and I can only stand back and respect people who are, like yourself. Still, pitch black out, temperature down around zero, sleet in the air, ice on the roads, and what had to be an out of season nor'easter blowing. You were lucky to get home alive, Izzy.

Tony and I got a few of the gang to hike out to the Cheshire Pike in the middle of the night. At least the storm clouds had blown over and the moon was as big as a wagon wheel. Still, there were ice crystals in the air and the roadway as slick as a mirror. Took every muscle in the gang to set that old Cole back on its wheels, but once we did the flivver started up and ran. And you were lucky at that not to crash into the landfill out there, roomie. If you had you'd never have made it back to campus and nobody would ever have found you, most likely. But after all of that, your Cole got you back to the dorm. What a car! They don't make 'em like they used to, I'll tell you that, Izzy.

That was the same night that poor old Percival Dunning disappeared, and Henry von Eisen had apparently had all he could take of small town, small college, campus life and lit out for parts unknown, deserting his classes in mid-semester. What a guy! If I hadn't disliked him before that, I surely would have then.

Meow, Cats, Meow!

Robert "Bobcat" O'Brien

Ω

Keweenaw Bay Gazette
Keweenaw Bay, Michigan
August 12, 1940
Mr. Zachary Grand
Editor-in-Chief
Grand Publications
143 West 43rd Street
New York, 16, New York

Dear Izz,

Don't know if I ever mentioned Charlie Potts to you. Nice kid, finished high school last June, always wanted to be a big-time news hound. Used to cover Keweenaw Bay High news for the *Gazette*. Sports mainly, but class elections, dances, amateur plays, whatever would fill space around the ads. Anyway, Tim Holcomb, our editor-in-chief, took him on as an office boy and cub reporter and he's working out fine.

Brought a little radio to work and set it up on the desk we let him use, and he turned on a Detroit Tigers ball game. They were playing the Philadelphia Athletics. Made me think of our old pal Tony and the North Cheshire baseball team, and all the trouble there was over Coach von Eisen.

Young Potts is not just a baseball fan, he's a real scholar, studies up the old records, can give you every player's batting average since the game got started. The Tigers had a new pitcher this season, young right-hander named Dickie Conger, and Potts up and says the kid reminded him of Heinie von Eisen.

That made me perk up my ears. "Heinie Who?" I said.

"Von Eisen. Pennsylvania farm kid named Heinrich von Eisen. Lefty. He was supposed to have the wickedest curve anybody ever saw. Was a star in the bush leagues. Came up to the Tigers in twenty-six. No, twenty-five."

As if anybody in the *Gazette* office was going to catch him on that!

Well, Charlie Potts told the story to anybody who would listen, which meant Jack Miller, Tim Holcomb, and yours truly, Izzy. Seems like this von Eisen kid was a drinker and a brawler and something of a womanizer. Made it all the way up through the minors, got his first start with the Tigers and beat the St. Louis Browns one to nothing. Threw a three-hitter. Phenomenal.

Went out to a bar that night and a young lady he spotted there caught his eye and he tried to pick her up. Seems she already had an escort who took exception to Heinie's remarks. They got into a brawl and somebody pulled a knife. There are different versions of the story. One of 'em, Potts said, is that this all happened in darktown. Anyhow, the knife man swings, Eisen puts up his hand to defend himself and the knife slices right across the palm of his hand. He wound up in the hospital and got his hand stitched back together, but he could never throw that curve again. Never made it back into the lineup. Before long he was out of baseball and he completely disappeared.

Izzy, do you think Heinie von Eisen is our Henry von Eisen? You think he was baseball coach when you and Tony and I were at North Cheshire Central College? It makes sense, doesn't it? He seemed to know so much about baseball, at least Tony said, and yet all the players hated him because they felt as if he hated them.

What do you think, Izzy?

Say, I don't mean to bother you with this rambling. I'd better close this letter and get some shut-eye, tomorrow it's back to the old salt mine for yours truly.

Oh, before I close, I do want to thank you again for the magazines. I'm lying here on my bed, my feet propped up, watching the moths bang against the glass and wondering if it's every going to cool down again. I'll tell you something about this part of Michigan, it's so cold in winter you'd think those New England freezes we used to have were days on the beach in Havana. But then it gets so hot in July and August, you can't believe that you were ever cold. I swear, even the moths must be sweating on a night like this!

Going through the other magazines you sent, I find that a lot of stories seem to have continuing characters. I guess there's nothing new about that, Izzy, all the way back to the Three Musketeers and that Poe detective, what was his name, and then of course Sherlock Holmes. For that matter, didn't Mark Twain bring Tom Sawyer and Huck Finn back for a couple of encores?

You've got some good ones. I like that Crimson Wizard fellow that Arl Felton writes about, and the Golden Saint. And of course you've got those cowboys and detectives and that spook-busting crew in *Grand Ghost Stories*. Tell you what, I've scratched a few notes and if you don't mind I'll type 'em up on the old Blick Ninety down at the *Gazette* office and mail 'em off to you soon as I get a chance. I hope you'll find some ideas you like there. Let me know, hey, old roomie?

Meow, Cats, Meow!

Robert "Bobcat" O'Brien

Ω

Keweenaw Bay Gazette
Keweenaw Bay, Michigan
August 19, 1940
Mr. Zachary Grand
Editor-in-Chief
Grand Publications
143 West 43rd Street
New York, 16, New York

Dear Izzy,

That sure is exciting news, that you're starting up a comic book line there at Grand Publications. Of course I won't breathe a word about it, not that there's much of anybody to breathe it to here in Keweenaw Bay.

But sometimes we stop in at the Tip Top Tavern for a couple of wee ones after we close up shop for the day and people do talk. "We" being Jack and Tim and myself. Charlie Potts keeps trying to invite himself along but Marty O'Hara runs a tight ship down at the Tip Top and he says he can't have any minors in there or he'd risk losing his liquor license.

Funny, Percival Dunning didn't worry about people being over twenty-one to join his Friday night soirees and nobody ever said a word. But then I think the whole campus, from Prexy on down, felt sorry for old Percival and wouldn't say boo at anything he did, so long as he was quiet about it.

Everybody except Henry von Eisen, that is. I'm not just saying this because I know there was bad blood between von Eisen and you, Izzy. The man was a brass-plated son of a sea cook, if you know what I mean. I think Charlie Potts had the key to von Eisen. If he really was the same Heinie von Eisen who pitched that game against St. Louis and then got his hand sliced open and lost his curveball, that would explain a lot about him and why he was always so sour and so ready to jump down anybody's throat.

I think he especially hated Percival Dunning because Dunning was English and had been in the King's Fusiliers during the Great War. Von Eisen was a few years younger than Dunning and he couldn't have been in the war himself, and besides, we were on the same side as the English, weren't we? But von Eisen was Pennsylvania Dutch, not really Dutch, you know, *Deutsch*, German, and there was a lot of pro-Kaiser sentiment out there in western Pennsylvania during the war.

Oh, you know this as well as I do. We used to sit in the same row in Professor Trowbridge's modern history class, just Carolyn Deering between us to help us not concentrate on Professor Trowbridge's lectures. Wasn't that girl something, with those sweaters of hers and those plaid skirts she used to wear! You'd think she'd freeze herself half to death in those Cheshire County winters, but I don't think she ever did.

Anyway, I never heard von Eisen say a kind word about Percival Dunning. Used to mock the way he walked, hunched over as if his chest was killing him, and talked, in that soft, almost whisper of his. Well, his chest *was* killing him. He never got over that gas attack in France. And as for the whisper, I just don't think he had the breathe to do any more than that. But von Eisen loved to parade back and forth in his classroom, all hunched over like Dunning, and whispering so you couldn't make out what he was saying.

One sweet guy despite all his suffering, one brass-plated s.o.b. who brought his trouble on himself. I guess it takes all kinds.

Enough for now, Izzy. I hope you're well and happy. Take a look at those little ideas that I sent you last week and let me know if you think I could write for one of your magazines. It's getting a little bit dull here on the production side.

Meow, Cats, Meow!

Robert "Bobcat" O'Brien

Ω

Keweenaw Bay Gazette
Keweenaw Bay, Michigan
August 28, 1940
Mr. Zachary Grand
Editor-in-Chief
Grand Publications
143 West 43rd Street
New York, 16, New York

Dear Izzy,

Well of course I know about comic books. Jumping Jehosophat, old roomie, Keweenaw Bay isn't exactly New York or Boston but it's still on this planet. We even heard about that invasion from Mars a couple of years back, we have radios out here and running water and everything.

Hey, just pulling your leg, old friend. But you really don't need to explain comic books to me. The kids in this town are as addicted to the things as they are anywhere. The schoolteachers are outraged, the town librarian has banned 'em from her sacred precincts, but Bud Campbell, owner, manager, stock boy, cashier, and chief cook and bottle washer over at Pine Street News and Magazines, loves 'em. Says they've cut into his pulp magazine sales a little but more than made up for it by bringing every six-through-twelve-year-old in town through his door day after day. Once school starts again in a few weeks that may cut down a little, but right now Bud is as happy as a clam.

Favorite scene these days: Two kids standing outside Pine Street News and Magazines arguing to beat the band. Resolved: Superman could beat up Captain Marvel in a fair fight. Sometimes the kids get so carried away they decide to knuckle it out themselves. One of those muscle men wears red tights and the other one wears blue tights and I can never remember which is which, but I don't suppose it matters, I'm a few years too old to get involved. But I've even seen young Charlie Potts sneaking a read along with a sandwich when it's his lunch time down at the *Gazette*. Says his favorite is a fellow who can set fire to himself, fly around, throw fireballs at his enemies, and then come home without so much as a blister on his nose. Okay with me.

Seems to me, Izzy, these comic book heroes aren't anything different from the good old pulp heroes we used to read about back in Warren Hall when we didn't have our noses buried in chemistry or calculus texts or Shakespeare. The rough preliminary for *Captain Grand Comics* looks good, I didn't mean to take any shots at it.

Let's see if I have this one right.

Gary Grant is exploring in Antarctica when he discovers a lost race of wizards from Atlantis. They decide to initiate him into their sacred rites, which include walking through the hot lava of an active volcano right there at the South Pole. They've given him a magical cloak that will protect him as long as he exercises total will power and concentration; otherwise, he's a toasted marshmallow.

After a couple of years of study and discipline, the chief wizard decides that Gary's ready to give it a try. So off he goes, he passes the test, and he emerges as Captain Grand, Master of Mysticism.

Okay, pal. I guess the kids will go for it. Not so different from some of the pulp stories we used to read. Or the ones you publish, if you don't mind my saying so. Tell you what. I know you want to keep *Captain Grand Comics* under the rose for now, but when you're ready I'll bounce this thing off Charlie Potts or maybe some of the town kids if I can pry 'em away from Superman and Captain Marvel for a few minutes. I'll let you know what they have to say.

We could have used somebody like Captain Grand, Master of Mysticism, back at Central Cheshire, couldn't we? Somebody like Captain Grand could have saved poor old Percival Dunning's life. I'll never forget the way his disappearance hit the campus. Nobody knew where he'd gone or what had happened to him. Personally, I thought he'd gone back to England or at least up to Canada to try and enlist in the Army. Nobody on campus took this fellow Hitler seriously except for Dunning. You have to give him credit for that. Soon as Hitler announced he was going to run for President of Germany, Dunning predicted what was going to happen. And look at Europe now!

Then when his car turned up in Big Star Pond—Izzy, I still can't get over it. It must have been there since November of '32. Dunning must have driven that funny Pullman coupé of his onto the ice and it cracked under the car and the car sank with Dunning in it. Imagine being trapped in that little car, icy water coming in, and you can't get out.

And then we had our ice skating parties that winter, the annual Founder's Day Bonfire and all, and all that time poor old Percival Dunning's body lying there in his car on the bottom of the pond until the spring thaw. There were the Three Graces, Carolyn Deering, Annie Mayfield, and Jennie Lipton, out for a picnic by the pond and they spotted something in the water that scared the bejesus out of them.

Yep, it was poor old Dunning, still trapped in that little car of his.

Did I say that Dunning was the only one who knew what Hitler was up to in the old days? I shouldn't have left out Henry von Eisen. You'd think von Eisen had a direct line to Berlin, the way he spouted the Hitler line every chance he got. Heck, Izzy, it was really annoying. I know nobody stood up to von Eisen. That was cowardly of us, and I apologize.

Tony LoPresto and Jack Remington and Roland Stephenson and some of the gang used to sit around in one of the Double You Dorms—Warren or Winston or Watson or Wellington—and talk about it. We could all see what von Eisen was doing to you, Izz, but everybody was afraid of the son of a sea cook. We should have got together and made a petition to Prexy about it. We really should have.

But that's all past now. Percival Dunning is in his grave and Henry von Eisen is—wherever he is. You have to wonder, don't you, what ever became of von Eisen.

You know what I regret more than anything else that ever happened at Cheshire Central? It was dedicating our yearbook, the *Cheshire Cheese*, to von Eisen our senior year. How the heck did that ever happen, Izzy?

No, you don't have to tell me. That was just a rhetorical question. Von Eisen took over the job of faculty advisor for the yearbook when old what-was-his-name retired. Dr. Standish. That was the old gent's name, David Donald Standish, Ph.D. Must have been the head of the English Department from the day the college opened its doors. I've never seen anybody so old.

Dr. Standish must have been faculty advisor for the *Cheshire Cheese* as well as the *North Cheshire Literary Quarterly* since McKinley was shot. When he finally packed his bags and retired to sunny Florida, Hermione Zeller took on the job at the quarterly and von Eisen took it at the yearbook. Nobody was surprised that Miss Zeller got involved with the quarterly. She was already college librarian, she fit right in, and remember the fun we used to have with her? But nobody expected von Eisen to take on the yearbook.

Nobody except his personal toady, Gene Stullmeier.

I'm sorry, Izzy. I'm raking up too many old embers. And I'm going on too long anyway. You still haven't commented on the ideas I sent you. I could write those stories for *Grand Adventures* or some of the other pulps, or I suppose I could turn 'em into stories for some of your new comic books.

Let me know when it's okay to show the dummy *Captain Grand Comics* to Charlie Potts and the local urchin brigade and I'll send you back some comments. And let me know when you want me to start writing for you. I'm starting to get the itch.

Meow, Cats, Meow!

Robert "Bobcat" O'Brien

Ω

Keweenaw Bay Gazette
Keweenaw Bay, Michigan
August 31, 1940
Mr. Zachary Grand
Editor-in-Chief
Grand Publications
143 West 43rd Street
New York, 16, New York

Dear Izzy,

I couldn't believe my eyes when I got your wedding announcement. You and Carolyn Deering. I still don't believe it! Well, congratulations, roomie. Carolyn was one of the prettiest gals on campus, but of course you know that. And smart, and sweet. I envy you, Izzy. How the heck did you ever catch her? You must have been studying hypnosis.

Just kidding, Izz. Thinking about you and Carolyn makes me think about the six of us—you and Tony and me in the Three Cheshire Cats and Carolyn Deering and Annie Mayfield and Jennie Lipton, the Three Graces. Didn't we have great times together! And now Isaac Goldberg and Carolyn Deering are Mister and Missus Zachary Grand.

You know that Tony LoPresto and Jennie Lipton are married, don't you? Living there in Bayou Richelieu and raising a house full of bambinos, that's what Tony tells me. I never pictured Tony as a lawman or Jennie as a *mater familias* but that just goes to show you, doesn't it?

Where did Annie Mayfield go after graduation? Maybe I ought to look her up, see if the old spark is still smoldering. I'll tell you, Izz, there isn't much social life in a town like Keweenaw Bay. Not that I'm knocking this burg. I'm pretty comfortable here, I've got a decent job and I make a living. But I think I could use a dose of the bright lights every now and then.

Since you said it was all right to show the dummy *Captain Grand Comics* to Charlie Potts and some of the local kids, I've got some reactions to share with you. Everybody likes Captain Grand but they think he needs a good enemy. A guy who can do all the things Captain Grand can do is wasted on kidnappers and bank robbers. One of the local kids suggested a mad scientist for an enemy. Another kid says he'd like to see a beautiful, evil woman in the strip. Charlie Potts says he's starting to outgrow some of these wild stories. He's getting very literary, thinks you should read Steinbeck or Hemingway for inspiration.

Ho, ho, ho.

I was thinking of another character myself. So many of these heroes are musclemen, what about somebody who uses his brains to fight crime? I was thinking of a strip called "The Scholar." Something like Sherlock Holmes. He tackles crimes that the police can't solve because they're just not smart enough.

What would you think of that, Izzy? Do let me know.

I've got to turn in now, roomie. Tomorrow's a school day down at the *Gazette* and I can't stay up all night the way I used to back at North Cheshire Central, not if I'm going to be all full of pep and energy in the morning.

Oh, one more thing. Tony LoPresto says that he and Jennie are planning a trip back to Massachusetts for the big homecoming game next month. Going to bring all their youngsters with them, too. The old campus is in for a real treat! I wish I could make it but every time I look my budget in the eye and ask, How about it? the old budget looks right back at me and says, Not this year, old fellow!

So maybe next year, Izzy. I assume that you and Carolyn will attend, it can't be much of a trip from New York City. Say hello to Tony and Jennie for me, and congratulations again to yourself and Carolyn. You lucky dog—or should I say, Cheshire Cat!

Meow, Cats, Meow!

Robert "Bobcat" O'Brien

Ω

Keeweenaw Bay Gazette
Keweenaw Bay, Michigan
September 20, 1940
Mr. Zachary Grand

Editor-in-Chief
Grand Publications
143 West 43rd Street
New York, 16, New York

Dear Izzy,

This is a letter I never expected to write, old roomie. You know, Keweenaw Bay may be isolated and all, but we do have radios and we get out of town newspapers even if we have to wait a few days to see what's happening in the rest of the world. But Tony LoPresto telephoned and gave me the lowdown on what happened during homecoming weekend, and then there were reports in the Boston and New York dailies.

Now we know what happened to Henry von Eisen.

Who would ever have expected an Atlantic hurricane to make it all the way to Massachusetts, and then to sweep inland as far as Cheshire County, setting off that waterspout from Big Star Pond and then turning into a tornado and ripping up the old landfill near the old Cheshire Pike? Mainly, everybody was upset that the big homecoming parade was cancelled, the football game against Billerica Tech was called off, and the gymnasium was flooded so the homecoming dance never happened.

At least, that's what Tony LoPresto said when he phoned me. I don't know if he paid for the call himself or found some way to get the city fathers in Bayou Richelieu to foot the bill, but one way or another all that gab must have cost plenty.

The kids at North Cheshire were disappointed by the mess the storm made of homecoming weekend, but Tony was more interested in what the storm pulled out of the old landfill. Tony told me that the human remains that turned up were identified as belonging to some old tramp who'd fallen into the landfill years before and died there. The local authorities gave Tony the run of the place. Professional courtesy, they call it.

But Tony knew better. He didn't say so, but he knew better.

We both knew who that corpse was, or what was left of it after almost eight years lying there in the landfill. There are raccoons and lynxes and even a few wolves in those woods. There wasn't much left of that fellow. But Tony told me there was one odd thing about the body. You know how freakish Old Ma Nature can be, and somehow, for all the scavengers who'd worked over that body and then the effects of lying in the earth all these years, the flesh was almost perfectly preserved on the left hand.

Isn't that odd, Izzy?

Tony told me that the left hand of the body showed a big scar running straight across the palm. As if the owner of that hand had got into a fight and his opponent came at him with a really nasty knife, and that fellow put up his hand to try and stop the knife and wound up with a terrible gash running right across the palm of his hand.

Looked as if the cut had healed up all right, Tony said, but the scar was something to behold. And Tony figured that whoever owned that hand would never be able to do very much with it ever again, even after the wound had healed.

Oh, it was Henry von Eisen all right. Tony has some wild theory about von Eisen getting into a scrape with poor old Percival Dunning that icy night back in the winter of '32-'33, and maybe beating old Percival into a helpless state and then putting him in his old Pullman coupé and sending it out onto the ice of Big Star Pond.

And then, Tony figures, somebody else comes along, somebody von Eisen doesn't like to start with, and now this other person has seen von Eisen practically murder poor old Percival Dunning. So von Eisen goes after this other person, too. You'd think von Eisen would win a fight, but who knows, under those conditions, anything could happen. Anything. Right, Izz?

Even though I'm not a religious person, I know a few Bible stories. I know about David and Goliath. Do you think Henry von Eisen might have been a kind of Goliath? And who would be David?

Who, Izzy?

Well, I guess I missed all the excitement of homecoming weekend, the hurricane, the waterspout, the tornado, the body in the landfill. Things are quiet here in Keweenaw Bay. Must be more exciting back East where you are, Izzy.

Congratulations again on your marriage. Give Carolyn my best wishes. You are one lucky son of a gun!

Meow, Cats, Meow!

Robert "Bobcat" O'Brien

Ω

CINQUEFOIL

Regis Hardy

A MESSAGE TO THE READER

The world is in a sorry state. In Europe Herr Hitler and Comrade Stalin appear bent on outdoing each other in the pursuit of enormity. In my own homeland the vile Konrad Henlein will stop at nothing to establish his own brand of tyranny. Across the globe in Asia the militarists of the Mikado pile atrocity upon unspeakable atrocity in their terrible war against China. Here in the United States of America, That Man in the White House, after five years, appears unwilling or unable to offer relief to suffering humankind.

I have authorized my assistant, Mr. Winslow, to publish the following story in the hopes that his narration will provide readers with a few moments of relief from the stresses of the day. Mr. Winslow has drawn upon the files in my office, most notably the one labeled Hamlin, Andrietta, *and further marked* Case Closed—Account Paid in Full.

I do not, however, certify the accuracy of Mr. Winslow's account. He has been known to exaggerate.

CF
West Adams Place
New York

Ω

Whoever left the parcel on our doorstep might have rung the bell but obviously no one in the house had answered it. Foxx would of course not have stirred himself to do so even if he hadn't been busy in the greenhouse, and Reuter, Foxx's personal chef and general domestic factotum, was engaged in preparing a sauce *a la postole* for our lunch.

I drew my yellow Auburn roadster to the curb, figuring that I'd park it later on next to Foxx's twelve-cylinder Packard in the old carriage house. I left the radio turned up and permitted a syrupy voiced announcer to invite me to tune in to the next episode of *Dulcie Dixon at Deanville High*. The studio audience cheered. I switched off the engine and vaulted up the steps.

Then I studied the package lying on our stoop for a while before I touched it. My employer had made a number of dangerous enemies in his career, and I knew that some of them were not above leaving a deadly gift for him, but this one seemed innocuous enough. It was addressed to Caligula Foxx at his house on West Adams Place. It bore the return address of a messenger service in midtown, printed on a conspicuous sticker, but the name of the sender was also indicated and it was one that I recognized.

The package was pretty light, so I hefted it under one arm and brought it inside. I picked up the house phone and called Foxx in the greenhouse.

"What is it?" Foxx demanded in his usual growl.

"A package," I told him.

There was a brief, unpleasant pause, then he said, "Andy, an employee who values his position generally obeys standing instructions from his employer, does he not?"

I was way ahead of him. I said, "I know you don't like to be disturbed when you're playing with your roses, Mr. Foxx. But this is from Andrietta Hamlin, the motion picture star, and . . ."

"I know very well who Andrietta Hamlin is," Foxx interrupted, "and you know equally well that I am busy hybridizing and the package can assuredly wait until business hours resume this afternoon. But if your curiosity is overwhelming, Andy, you have my permission to take the item to the office and examine it there. Do be careful not to cause any disarray or Reuter will fret."

He placed the telephone handset back on its base with a click I could hear all the way downstairs. I carried the package into the office that Foxx and I share and placed it on his huge glass-covered desk. I used a pair of scissors to cut the string around it, peeled away the brown wrapping paper, and slit the sealing tape on the corrugated cardboard box.

It contained a selection of rose cuttings that I immediately realized would pique Foxx's interest. There was also a small, rectangular envelope that I opened. The card inside read, *Mr. Caligula Foxx, I am in terrible trouble. I must see you. Please contact me at once.* It was signed with a scrawl that I decoded as the signature of Andrietta Hamlin.

The most recent of her films was still fresh in my mind. It was a swashbuckler that I'd taken a young lady to see, and we had left the theater well before the feature ended. It wasn't Andrietta Hamlin's fault, either. She bore up mightily under the weight of a putrid script and a leading man who must have passed his prime during the Taft Administration.

Foxx likes me to show initiative, so I telephoned the number at the top of the stationery and spoke with a dame who identified herself as Miss Hamlin's confidential secretary. She spoke in a soft voice and a tone so dull and lifeless, she almost wasn't there.

Miss Hamlin was unavailable, the dispirited voice informed me. She was on the set of *Bachelor Girls on Broadway*, being filmed, conveniently, in the Superior Films studios in Astoria. But if I would care to discuss the matter with her, the secretary, she would do everything she could to accommodate me. Her name was Helene Jones.

I told her that I was Caligula Foxx's assistant, Andy Winslow, calling in behalf of Mr. Foxx, and if Andrietta Hamlin wanted to see Foxx I could give her an appointment. Helene Jones said that Miss Hamlin should be home from Astoria by eight and if Mr. Foxx would allow her a few minutes to freshen up he might join her at her apartment for a light supper while they discussed business.

That wouldn't work, for sure. Besides, what was this all about? I figured, if it was something worth Foxx's attention, he'd want as much info as I could give him. And if it wasn't worth his while, he'd want me to handle it and get rid of the pest. He wasn't in business for the fun of it and I knew that the alleged glamour of a movie actress would mean nothing to him. Foxx didn't go to the movies, and even though he'd said he knew who Andrietta Hamlin was, he wouldn't have cared.

Miss Jones was distressed when I told her that Foxx never discussed business over food, and that he almost never left his white frame house. She wanted to know the reason and I told her that was simply Mr. Foxx's policy, and if Andrietta Hamlin wanted to see Foxx, she'd have to come to West Adams Place. We were talking at cross purposes and Miss Jones was pretty upset by then but she said she'd take the matter up with Miss Hamlin and get back to me. I told her that would be utterly swell.

When Foxx came down for his noon repast he would hear nothing of the phone call or the contents of the package until Reuter had served the meal and Foxx and I had consumed our fill. For me, that meant a small salad, a medium-rare lamb chop with Reuter's brilliant sauce of apricot and half a dozen herbs, a roll and butter, and a cup of coffee. For Foxx, you can just multiply each item by a number anywhere from two to five, add a couple of chicken croquettes and several large ears of yellow corn, baked in the husk, liberally salted and dripping sweet butter, then top it off with three large slices of Reuter's freshly baked peach cobbler served hot and topped with raw vanilla ice cream.

Foxx wiped his lips carefully with a giant linen napkin and we repaired to the office. He'd complained that Reuter had diced the orange peels in the sauce when he should have grated them, but otherwise he'd found the meal satisfactory. He glanced at Andrietta Hamlin's opened parcel before settling into his giant leather chair. I caught a glimmer of interest when he gave those rose cuttings the once over, but as usual he said nothing until he was good and ready.

When he was, he said, "What do you make of these?" He'd picked up a pen out of the marble-based set on his desk, and used it as a pointer to indicate the cuttings.

"Looks like miniature eglantine. I think it might take in the soil upstairs."

"Very well." Foxx put the pen back in its holder. "I'll have Simon take a look at them this afternoon. You say these cuttings were sent by Andrietta Hamlin? Why do you suppose she would do that?"

"She wants to talk to you. I phoned her number and got a biddy named Jones." I told him about my conversation with the confidential secretary and he nodded a couple of times and made a barely perceptible movement. I knew what that movement meant. He had stepped on the button under his desk and given the signal that would bring Reuter into the office.

Sure enough, Reuter appeared promptly. He was carrying a silver tray with two bottles of Teplitz-Schönau ale along with a single chilled glass. Foxx had it imported especially for him from the town where he was born, in Bohemia. He maintained that no ale brewed west of the Erzegebirge Mountains was worth placing on his palate.

He opened the first bottle, poured himself a generous portion, and savored it for a moment. Then he put his glass back on the tray and turned toward me. "All right, Andy. I can see that you are barely able to contain yourself. What compelling news do you have for me?"

"I talked to the Hamlin broad's secretary, Helene Jones. Hamlin wants to pow-wow with you at her joint. I told her nix on that and she said she'd get back to me."

"She didn't indicate the nature of the problem?"

"Not a bit."

Foxx bent over some papers on his desk and I took that as a signal for me to make myself scarce, but before I could comply the phone rang. Foxx didn't budge. Either he was concentrating so hard on the papers in front of him that he was in a trance or he just didn't feel like dealing with it while I was around.

It was Jones calling me back. At least she got points for promptness. She had reached her boss on the set at Superior Films between takes. Hamlin was plenty steamed, she hated interruptions while she was busy playing movie star, but she said it was unavoidably imperative that she speak with Mr. Foxx, and if the mountain wouldn't come to Mohammed then Mohammed would have to come to the mountain. Considering Caligula Foxx's immense girth, I figured either she was a past mistress of the *mot juste* or she had scored a bull's eye by sheer chance.

Instead of heading straight home from the studio, Miss Hamlin would shower and change in Astoria, enjoy a light repast on the set, then have her limousine drop her at Foxx's house. Knowing Foxx and his habits, I told her to make one small change in that plan. Have Hamlin refresh herself and come to West Adams Place and take supper here as Foxx's guest. They could talk business afterwards.

Jones said she'd talk to Hamlin again and call me back if that was unsatisfactory with Her Highness. She didn't call, so it must not have been unsatisfactory.

Foxx worked alone until quitting time. I had my own fish to fry so I didn't bother him. At one point I stepped out to put the Auburn in the carriage house. It was a stifling August afternoon, but thundershowers were predicted and I didn't want to leave my little baby out in the rain. When I came back Foxx was sitting behind his desk, leaning back in his huge leather chair, his fingers laced over his belly. His eyes were shut but every now and then he would raise his right eyebrow, hold it that way for a few seconds, then drop it back. I knew that he was deep into his mind, working on a problem.

At quitting time he picked up the box of rose cuttings and ponderously ascended to the greenhouse. I knew he'd spend the next couple of hours conferring with Simon, clippers in hand and spray bottle at the ready, tending his roses. What Simon would have to say about Andrietta Hamlin's offering would bear heavily on the treatment she got from Foxx a little later.

Ω

When the doorbell rang at eight o'clock I was ready to answer it. I'd togged myself up in my latest Trippler suit, clean linen and regimental tie. I opened the front door and beheld the lovely Andrietta Hamlin. She must have stopped at her hunting lodge after leaving Astoria and shot something small and vicious, because she had its carcass draped around her shoulders. She wore a spiffy little thing on one side of her head with a tall feather sticking out of it, and a tailored suit that had to have come from Bendel's at least.

I introduced myself, she introduced herself, and we waltzed into the foyer. Her secretary, Helene Jones, followed. She was about the same size and shape as Hamlin, but that's where the resemblance ended. Hamlin had glossy black hair, Jones had mousy brown hair; Hamlin had flashing dark eyes, Jones had dull pale ones. Hamlin had a body that ran all the way from her shoulders to her hips, and a pair of legs that continued down from there, and down, and down, and down. What Jones had was hidden inside a baggy brown thing that S. Klein would have been ashamed to peddle.

Reuter showed up and took away Hamlin's dead animal and Jones's shapeless brown coat and I led the ladies into the front parlor. A couple of minutes later I heard the ponderous footsteps of my employer and Caligula Foxx made his majestic way into the room. I introduced him to our visitors and vice versa. He bowed over Hamlin's hand like a Continental boulevardier, nodded to Jones, and demanded to know why they hadn't been served aperitifs.

While Reuter remedied that situation Foxx settled into a great easy chair and turned on the charm. On the wall above Foxx's chair there was a portrait of Foxx's fellow detective, Abel Chase, painted by the great Jainschigg of Rhode Island. Chase was an eccentric character who practiced the snoop trade out on the West Coast. I never figured out whether Foxx kept his picture there because he admired Chase or as a reminder to himself that he'd better keep up his batting average and stay ahead of the competition.

He apologized to Miss Hamlin for not leaving the house and apologized again for never having seen one of her movies. He trusted that I'd treated the ladies with courtesy and inquired after their every comfort. He actually looked pretty good in his custom-made suit. I can't imagine anyone else bringing off that act with a shirt of glaring aquamarine silk, but Foxx managed to do it.

We were called for dinner promptly at the scheduled hour and placed ourselves around the mahogany table, Foxx at the head, myself at the foot, Hamlin at Foxx's right hand and Jones at his left. Reuter brought the courses, one after another, a simple meal of clam broth, mackerel poached in cream, calf's liver Venetian style served with scalloped cabbage and nut and potato croquettes, a spinach, mushroom and bacon salad with nut Pascagoula dressing, and espresso coffee with freshly steamed milk. Of course there were wines for our guests, but I stuck with my usual lemonade and Foxx with his bottles of Teplitz-Schönau ale.

It was easy to tell that Hamlin wanted to talk about her problem but Foxx told her in no uncertain terms that they would hold their business meeting in the office, after the meal was over. He kept switching the subject to Hamlin's career, and she didn't really mind too much, that was easy to see. She had one story after another about her adventures with this Barrymore and that Fairbanks, John Gilbert this and William Powell that. Somehow there didn't seem to be women in any of her stories, except herself of course.

Jones sat there quiet as a mouse. She was practically invisible. I enjoyed my meal and enjoyed gazing at Andrietta Hamlin. I wondered if she was married, and if so, how would her spouse feel about granting her one of those new marital vacations I've heard about. I'd like to share a vacation with Hamlin, that was for sure.

Finally the meal was over and we repaired to the office. Foxx made sure that Hamlin and Jones were settled in two leather chairs facing his desk before he placed himself behind it. I sat at my own desk but swung around facing the others, my notebook at the ready.

Foxx leaned back, laced his fingers over his belly, and said, "I am now ready, Miss Hamlin."

You could tell that Hamlin was getting fidgety by then, despite the meal she'd packed away. She said, "I'm being threatened."

Foxx raised an eyebrow at that, but since his eyes were open I knew he wasn't in his deep concentration state. He nodded encouragingly but he didn't say anything.

"Well?" Hamlin demanded.

"Well?" Foxx repeated. "I'm sorry. Did you ask me a question?"

"I said I'm being threatened. I want you to do something about it."

"Ah." Foxx nodded. He turned his head a little so he was looking at me. "Andy, make a note of this. Miss Hamlin is being threatened and wants me to do something about it. Perhaps she will elaborate as to the nature of the threats, and indicate just what it is that she wants me to do."

The Continental boulevardier had disappeared and Caligula Foxx was being his normal irritating self.

He turned back toward Hamlin. "If you please, madame, I can help you only if you furnish me with that which I need to do my work. And that is information. What is the nature of the threats? When were they delivered? Did you retain them? Do you know who is threatening you? Has this person made any demands?"

Hamlin looked at her secretary helplessly. For what seemed the first time in two hours, Helene Jones uttered human speech. "Miss Hamlin is exhausted, Mr. Foxx. She has worked a very long day. She has to be on the set by six every morning for makeup and costume, you know."

185

"No, I didn't know," Foxx responded. "I thought her life was one round of parties beside swimming pools, polo ponies and yacht journeys. That was the impression I received from Miss Hamlin's supper conversation."

"That's what the public think," Andrietta Hamlin put in. "The studios want them to think that. Actually it's just a job, and sometimes I wish I could trade places with a plain housewife or school teacher."

"Indeed, indeed," Foxx muttered. "One would never have imagined. But regarding these threats . . ."

"Yes. The first one came a week ago. Miss Jones would know. She took the call. I had the day off. They were shooting the other girls that day and I slept late and had a facial and a hair styling and lunch with Mr. Kilburn."

Again, Foxx's eyebrow rose. "I'm not familiar with the name," he admitted.

"Lance was a silent star. We had a fling a few years ago. He was one of the actors who didn't survive the transition to sound. He used to specialize in adventure films, he became quite an expert sailor, a fencer, a crack shot. He made a couple of unsuccessful talkies, then disappeared."

"While your career has prospered," Foxx added gallantly.

"I had a background on the stage. Those of us who had training could use our voices. Actors who never worked at anything but movies were badly at risk, Mr. Foxx. John Barrymore did just fine. Lance Kilburn—did not."

"I see." Foxx twirled one thumb around the other, a gesture that seemed to capture the attention of Hamlin and Jones. "But tell me, then, how Mr. Kilburn occupies himself these days. And how he earns his daily bread. Silent films have been dead for a decade or so, have they not? I ask out of ignorance, Miss Hamlin, not being an aficionado of the cinema myself." He didn't bother to add that, in addition to his agoraphobia, there was no way that Caligula Foxx could have fit into a theater seat.

Hamlin frowned. I hoped that the little line that appeared between her eyebrows wouldn't stay there, and as soon as she began talking it disappeared. I was relieved.

"Lance may not have much of a voice, but he still has his face. I'm sure you'd recognize him if you met him. He earns a very nice living modeling. Men's clothing, hair preparations, that kind of thing."

"Truly. One can make a living that way?"

"Oh, yes. Plus, he's taking voice lessons. He still hopes to make a comeback in movies or maybe on the radio. Radio actors are remarkably well paid, and they don't even have to learn their lines. A good radio actor can do any number of voices, even play several parts in one show. It's a great way to make a living."

Foxx absorbed that, then asked, "But what about these threats?"

Hamlin looked at Jones. "Helene received them. She can describe them better than I."

Jones seemed to be studying a spot on the floor between her drab, practical shoes. "There have been three," she said. "The first was from a man. I wrote down his exact words." She fumbled in a drab, shapeless purse until she found her own notebook, then read in her dull voice:

Andrietta Hamlin gitcher self outta town an' gitcher self back to Hollywood. You-all have been warned.

"When did the man call?" Foxx asked.

"Last Tuesday morning, while Miss Hamlin was at the beauty salon. That was just before her appointment with Mr. Kilburn."

"What did you do about the warning?"

"I told Miss Hamlin about it when she returned to the apartment, and she said we get crank calls all the time, ignore it, so I did."

"The caller did not identify himself? He left no clue as to his identity?"

She shook her head. I expected her to put on a pair of horn-rimmed glasses, but she stopped short of that. She said, "But he had a Southern drawl. He sounded like a poor, uneducated individual."

Foxx said, "Ah." He buzzed for ale and asked his guests if they would like an after dinner beverage but they declined. After Reuter had brought a tray with bottles and a glass Foxx poured himself a glass of Teplitz-Schönau ale, downed a long sip, and asked about the other warnings.

I watched Andrietta Hamlin tapping her lacquered fingernails impatiently on the arm of her chair. She crossed her legs and I watched that, too.

Helene Jones said, "The second warning came last Friday. I wrote it down, too. *You have failed to heed our warnings, Miss Hamlin. Leave New York and keep away from Dulcie Dixon or you'll be sorry indeed.*"

"The same man?" Foxx asked.

"No." Jones managed to shake her head, if you can call that twitch a shake. "It sounded like an Englishwoman."

"Really!" Foxx raised his eyebrow. "Fascinating. Do you think there is a gang involved? Never mind, you need not theorize, that's my job."

Jones looked relieved.

Hamlin said, "You don't seem to be doing anything, Mr. Foxx." She was getting agitated, I could tell.

Foxx unlaced his fingers and raised one hand placatingly. "All in good time. Let us hear Miss Jones' report of the third warning."

Jones looked as if she wanted to get out of her chair and run away. "That came early this morning, shortly after the limousine arrived to pick up Miss Hamlin. I called Miss Hamlin on the set and she said I should get Caligula Foxx."

Foxx nodded approvingly. "And whose idea were the rose cuttings?" he asked.

For the first time Jones showed some color other than dull brown, actually managing to blush. "That was my idea. You have a reputation, Mr. Foxx, of being hard to reach, and I knew you were a rose fancier, I read about your roses in the Sunday supplement, so I thought you'd . . ."

Her voice faded away as if she just didn't have the strength to continue, but Foxx urged her to, and she read the third warning message from her notebook:

"*You ain't Dulcie and you'll never be Dulcie. Try it and you won't be nobody at all.*"

"When I heard that I decided to get help," Andrietta Hamlin put in.

Foxx said, "One moment, please, Miss Hamlin. Miss Jones, was the third caller the same as either of the others?"

"No," Jones managed, "it was a man again, but a different man. He sounded like one of those Brooklyn toughs in the gangster movies."

Foxx thanked her. To Hamlin he said, "Do you know what these references to Dulcie mean?"

"The studio has obtained rights to the Dulcie Dixon character and is planning a series of films. They want me to star."

Sure, I thought. Andrietta Hamlin as a small town high school girl. Why not. And maybe I can play the Baby Jesus in next year's Christmas pageant.

"Would you be willing to give up the role?" Foxx asked. "If you were to make a public announcement to that effect, perhaps this gang would leave you alone."

"But they wouldn't be caught."

"Miss Hamlin." Foxx helped himself to another generous sip of Teplitz-Schönau ale. "Miss Hamlin," he repeated, "are you hiring me to catch the gangsters or to protect you from them? I thought it was the latter. If you take my advice and announce that you are giving up the role, they will almost certainly cease to annoy you, and you can pay me a modest fee for my evening's work and have done with it. Otherwise, I suggest that this is a matter for the police."

Hamlin stood up, her eyes flashing. I know that Foxx didn't like to talk to people who were standing while he was sitting, and it was a production for him to get out of his chair, but he leaned back and gazed up at her and let her rant.

"I have no intention of giving up the role of Dulcie Dixon. The Bachelor Girls series is totally played out, and I don't like being regarded as just one of the girls anyway. I am too great a star for that. I'm going to be Dulcie Dixon and that's that."

Foxx rose to his feet. I won't describe the operation, it was simultaneously magnificent and terrible to behold. He said, "Very well, then. I shall undertake to protect you from those who have threatened you. One more question, however."

The room was silent as Foxx stepped from behind his desk and crossed the carpet to the beautiful Colonial spinning wheel that adorns the room. "While I do not attend the cinema," he said, "I do on occasion listen to the radio, and I have heard the character of Dulcie Dixon portrayed there by another actress than yourself. Would she not be considered for the part in the motion picture as well?"

"You're speaking of Christina Gluck, Mr. Foxx, and you can be certain that she will never play Dulcie Dixon on the screen. Now, if you will be so kind as to have your Mr. Winslow summon my limousine, Miss Jones will attend to the business aspects of our relationship."

"If you feel that you are really in danger, Miss Hamlin, you ought not to return to your usual surroundings. There is room in this house, you and Miss Jones are welcome to stay the night. We will make other arrangements in the morning."

"No, no, I won't give in to thugs! Please send for my limousine, or let me use the telephone and I'll summon it myself."

"No need for that," Foxx told her. "We will bill you, fear not. And I am certain that Mr. Winslow will be happy to offer you and Miss Jones a ride to your home. Andy, I'm sure our guests will be more comfortable in the Packard than in that little yellow toy of yours."

Ω

When the phone rang I wasn't sure whether it was just getting dark out or just getting light, but I blinked a couple of times and gazed at my alarm clock and figured out that it had to be morning because I couldn't have slept all night and all of the next day.

The sun wasn't all the way up yet and already the air was hot. I peered out the window and the sidewalk looked wet. The thunderstorms must have come and gone without even waking me up, but they had done nothing to break the heat wave. Today was going to be a scorcher.

The phone was still ringing and I finally got awake enough to pick it up and mumble something about, "Caligula Foxx Investigations, Winslow speaking."

The voice on the other end was shrill and nearly incoherent. It took me a minute to realize that it was Her Highness the glamorous Andrietta Hamlin calling, and another minute to figure out what she was saying.

"She's dead! She's dead! She's been—I don't know—shot dead I think! Please get Mr. Foxx here at once!"

"Who's been shot dead?" I asked.

"Miss Jones. My secretary, Miss Jones. She's got a hole in her temple and she's lying on the floor in her own blood and she's dead."

I told her not to touch anything, stay where she was, and I'd be right there. I pulled on a lightweight outfit, raced to Foxx's bedroom and risked the wrath of the almighty by waking him up with the news.

"My fault," Foxx berated himself, "I should have insisted that they stay." He looked up at me. "Go up there at once, Andy. You'll know what to do. Report back to me as soon as you have anything."

I saluted and did a smart about face.

"And tell Reuter that I'll have my breakfast early today, Andy. I don't suppose there's any point in trying to go back to sleep now."

I slipped on a shoulder holster under my linen jacket and made sure my snub-nose .38 was fully charged before I tucked it under my arm. Then I got the Auburn out of the carriage house and headed uptown. It was a good thing I'd given Hamlin and Jones a ride home last night, I didn't have to ask Hamlin for her address this morning. She sounded so upset, she might have got it all wrong.

The morning rush was just getting under way, and I managed to make good time getting up to Hamlin's apartment in a big *belle époque* building on Park Avenue in the Sixties. She had a whole floor, divided into personal quarters and a little business office. There was even an extra bedroom where Jones put up, one of the perquisites of working for the rich and famous, I suppose.

The grand admiral under the marquee took my car keys and handed them to a commodore who hung around waiting for the chance to make himself useful, then a mere captain escorted me up in the elevator and dropped me at Miss Hamlin's private floor. I leaned on the doorbell until the door swung open. I didn't know whether to expect La Hamlin herself or a French maid in a short skirt and a funny cap, but it was neither.

It was some guy I'd seen a hundred times in the pages of glossy magazines hawking sports jackets, hand-painted neckties, brilliantine hair tonic or vacations in Bermuda. He said, "Are you Caligula Foxx?"

"No, but I work for him. Who are you?"

He didn't like being asked that, but said, "I am Lance Kilburn."

No wonder I recognized his phiz. He was the ex-silent star who turned his simoleons now by pretending that his latest employer's product was the absolute guarantee of a happy life.

I said, "I'm here to see Andrietta Hamlin. Step aside."

He looked unhappier than ever at that, but he stepped.

I'd only seen the ladies as far as their door last night. Now I saw that the apartment was furnished in the latest and the best that Wanamaker's could provide. I didn't wait for Kilburn to show me the way, I sounded off, "Miss Hamlin, Andy Winslow here, where are you?"

She didn't answer, maybe she was protecting her golden pipes for her next film role, but without delay I heard the pitter-patter of tiny feet and in two shakes of a lamb's tail she was in the foyer looking distraught. She was wearing silk pajamas of some golden color with a flimsy peignoir over them and high-heeled mules on her graceful tootsies.

"Oh, Mr. Winslow, it was terrible, it . . ."

I cut her off with a gesture. "Just show me," I told her.

She took my by the hand and led me, like a little girl leading her daddy to see his big birthday surprise. In a minute we were in a sunny combination kitchen and breakfast nook.

The windows were closed but the room wasn't yet as hot as I knew it would be on a day like this. There were light curtains over them but you could see clearly right through them. There was a tiny tear in one, just about at the height of a woman like Helene Jones or Andrietta Hamlin. Helene Jones was lying on the floor, a broken cup and saucer near her outstretched hand, coffee spattered where she'd dropped the cup.

She was lying on her right side. Her almost colorless eyes were open and staring. Blood had puddled under her head. I brushed her mousy-colored hair aside and found a hole about the size of a .38 round in her temple. If that was the entry wound there would be a similar hole in the other side of her head. The blood would flow out and pool up just as it had.

Lance Kilburn said, "Miss Hamlin called me as soon as it happened. I live right across Park, you see." He jerked a thumb at the window facing onto Park Avenue.

I didn't talk to him but I noticed that those voice lessons he was taking must be pretty good. At least, he sounded okay to me. I asked Hamlin, "Who else did you call?"

"Nobody. You told me not to touch anything and not to do anything and I did as you said."

"What about him?" I asked.

"I'd already phoned him. He was on his way here when I dialed Mr. Foxx."

"You didn't tell me Kilburn lived across the street from you."

"You didn't ask. He's an old and very dear friend, and when . . . when . . . it happened . . ."

"Okay," I told her, I didn't need to stand there and listen to her blubber. "You didn't call anyone else, right? The doctor? The police?"

"No." She shook her head. "You told me not to, so I didn't. Mr. Kilburn came right over and I—I told him about poor Helene. I couldn't go in there again, so Mr. Kilburn looked at her for me while I waited in the sitting room."

"All right. You can call the cops now. By the time they get here I will have seen what I need to see. And heard what I need to hear. Which is, how this happened."

I bent and took a closer gander at the dead Helene Jones. She was wearing pajamas and a robe but what they did for her wasn't anything like what the peejays and peignoir did for Hamlin. Of course, being dead wasn't any help either. Whoever had done the dirty deed had potted her at exactly the right spot, where the bone is both flat and pretty thin. There's always the freak case where a bullet creases somebody's scalp and leaves 'em with nothing worse than a prize headache but this one had hit smack on. The poor thing hadn't had a chance. The timid, pale woman who had so little going for her she was hardly there, now wasn't there at all.

It dawned on me that the killer might still be in the apartment so I pulled my snub-nose .38 out and held it at the ready while I did a quick inspection of the apartment. I was lucky at that. If the killer had hung around he could have got me before I had the brains to look for him, but as it turned out he'd skedaddled. I made a mental note to check with the Department of the Navy downstairs, but I had a feeling that the killer would have planned an exit through the basement and a back alley and was long gone by now.

There wasn't much else to see in the kitchen-breakfast nook. A new model refrigerator, a stove, a sink, a metal canister for kitchen scraps, and a half-size door halfway up one wall that had to open onto a dumb-waiter. I opened it and that's what it was, okay, with nothing to see in it but a couple of ropes for hauling the box up and down. I also got very smart and looked in the canister for a clue, but it was empty.

Somebody was giving the front door a knuckle tattoo and Kilburn was comforting Miss Hamlin, who had decided at last to open the dam and let the tears gush out, so I was elected to open the door.

There stood my favorite New York City flatfoot, Inspector Cromwell. There were a couple of plainclothes masterminds behind Cromwell, and a team of harness bulls bringing up the rear. Cromwell took one look at me and said, "What the hell are you doing here, Winslow?"

I said that Hamlin was a client of Foxx's and I was here to protect her from perils both known and unknown, and what could I do for him?

He said, "You can get the hell out of my way and mind your own business and show me to the stiff." I didn't bother to point out his inconsistency, but just stepped carefully past the weeping Miss Hamlin and the comforting Mr. Kilburn and led Cromwell to the breakfast nook.

Jones hadn't got up and left.

Cromwell knelt beside the body, checked for a pulse, shook his head, studied the neat hole in Jones's temple, and whistled between his teeth. He picked up her head—there was no rigor yet—and I could see the black hole where the bullet must have exited. That was just as I'd expected, but I had enough brains not to handle the *corpus delicti* and Cromwell's badge gave him the right to mess things up all he wanted.

He turned around and yelled at the harness bulls to seal off all means of entry and egress and secure the crime scene. It gave me a thrill to hear him spout that cop lingo.

"You know the victim, Winslow?" Cromwell stood up and gave me a look of displeasure.

"I know everybody, Inspector. This lady is Miss Helene Jones, deceased. The fountain of grief over there is Andrietta Hamlin, the famous movie star. And her tower of comfort and support is Mr. Lance Kilburn, late of the silent screen and currently of the product modeling trade."

Cromwell eyeballed the other two and nodded. At least he didn't fly into a tizzy when he learned who they were. He asked them each a few questions and got pretty much the same answers I'd been getting. I told him that I'd been at West Adams Place when I got the news. Kilburn said that he'd been sleeping in at his own digs. And Hamlin had been giving her glossy locks their wake-up strokes prior to reporting to the *Bachelor Girls on Broadway* set in Astoria. The studio sent a limousine for her every morning, and she wanted to be ready when it arrived.

Cromwell told her that she'd better cancel the limousine. Then he borrowed her phone and called for a meat wagon for Jones. Then he told Hamlin and Kilburn and me that we'd get a free ride downtown ourselves, and our statements would be taken at Homicide.

Hamlin thought about that for a minute, shot me a questioning glance, got a quick nod in return, and agreed. She repaired to her boudoir to exchange her peejays for something a little more suitable. Kilburn protested that he was a busy man and had an urgent business obligation to meet. Cromwell promised to get his statement and turn him loose lickety-split, and Kilburn quieted down.

I just sighed at Cromwell and he gave me his cat-in-a-fish-store grin. I also asked if I could use the phone after him so I could call in to Foxx. I figured my boss would be awake and functioning by now. Cromwell was slightly reluctant but I reminded him that I was entitled to a call and I'd save the city a nickel by making it from Hamlin's apartment instead of his office, so he relented.

Foxx was intrigued by the details I gave him, and I gave him everything I could in Winchell-paced prose. He said that I was to bring Hamlin back to West Adams Place with me as soon as Cromwell was finished with her. He was certain that Cromwell wouldn't try to hold her after she'd given her statement. The publicity would be too good for her and too bad for the city.

For once Cromwell was a man of his word. When we got our walking papers from the myrmidons of the municipality he even offered us a free ride to our next destinations. Kilburn declined and hopped into a convenient cab. Hamlin and I piled into the backseat of a green-and-white, a harness bull ferried us back to Park Avenue, and we transferred to my spiffy Auburn.

Back at West Adams Place we found Caligula Foxx settled into his favorite chair, hands laced over his belly, eyes closed, eyebrow elevated. When he came out of his trance he turned the charm back on to welcome Miss Hamlin, who responded in kind. I was mildly peeved at being ignored. Finally Foxx decided to notice me. He reached inside his jacket and pulled out a plain white envelope. "This came for you, Andy. I have no idea what it's about. You might wish to read it now."

I went and stood by the window and unfolded a sheet of simple white paper. I recognized the penmanship at once.

Go to the WRNY studios, Green Network Building, and see what you can learn about "Dulcie Dixon." Rendezvous with Solly outside Kilburn's building afterwards. Then return here.

There was no signature but that was okay, the handwriting was Foxx's. Solly was our best contract man. Foxx was putting some dollars into this case. I stuck the message in my own pocket and said, "It's an urgent personal matter, I have to go now." I bowed to Andrietta Hamlin, nodded to Foxx, and scrammed out of there.

When I got to the Green Network Building I checked my watch and reckoned that *Dulcie Dixon at Deanville High* should be going on the air in a little while. I found a receptionist sitting at a little desk in front of one of those "our founder" paintings. Their founder was some scrawny geek with a big nose and thinning hair.

I used the old Winslow charm on the receptionist and she was delighted to hand me a free ticket that would get me into the studio audience for *Dulcie Dixon*. She even told me how to find the right studio.

What a thrill.

There must have been a couple of hundred people in the audience. A cheery bozo was cracking wise up on the stage. I closed my eyes and listened closely. He was the syrupy voiced announcer I'd heard over the air.

When the magic moment arrived the big *On the Air* sign flashed on, the band started to play, a bunch of people appeared and planted themselves in front of microphones, and a new guy popped up waving a card that said, APPLAUSE.

It was quite a show. The guy kept holding up cards that said LAUGHTER, CHEERS, and APPLAUSE again. There were some ringers in the audience, I could tell that, who were always the first and the loudest with the noise.

The actors were pretty unimpressive looking but all I had to do was close my eyes for a beat and the characters came to life. Dulcie Dixon was a big surprise. She was supposed to be a svelte and bubbly sixteen-year-old, and when I listened to her she sounded exactly right. But when I looked at her she was clearly on the shady side of forty, with frowzy graying hair and a size sixteen figure or I missed my guess.

But her boyfriend, Rollo, was an even bigger surprise. He was squeaky voiced and had a high-pitched squeal when he got excited, which was always, and a way of stammering when he was trying to sound sophisticated, which was most of the time. The actor playing Rollo was no adolescent. He was my new-found buddy, Lance Kilburn. And if that wasn't enough of a stunner, Kilburn was also Principal Peter Palmer of Deanville High and Pastor Shepherd of the Deanville United Church.

Each of them had a different tone, a different rhythm to his speech, and a different way of pronouncing words. All I could think of was, whoever was giving Kilburn his voice lessons was doing one bang-up job.

Once the program signed off the announcer introduced the cast members and invited the audience to stick around and ask questions. The middle-aged frump who played Dulcie was one Christina Gluck. So that was the babe whose role La Hamlin wanted. I'd never heard of her before Hamlin mentioned her, but I'll say that she did a good job with her character. As for Rollo-Palmer-Shepherd, his name was Arthur Smith, not Lance Kilburn. At least that's the way he was introduced.

Right.

While the festivities were going on I beat it as inconspicuously as I could. I did not want Kilburn to know that I'd seen him. I followed Foxx's directive and drove uptown again, parking the Auburn around the corner from Kilburn's building.

I strolled around the corner in time to see a swarthy guy in a white workman's uniform, complete with visor cap, coming out of the service entrance. He had a metal toolbox in his paw. He looked surprised to see me but he managed to blurt out, "Mr. McGurk, was that work I did okay? You got any more problems?"

He fell in beside me and we climbed into the Auburn. On the way back to West Adams Place he told me what he'd been up to while I was laughing, cheering, and applauding on cue for Dulcie Dixon.

He'd gone into Kilburn's building to check out a gas leak, very dangerous, very urgent. The super had cooperated with him, even turning off the building's incinerator—Solly would notify him when it could be turned back on, probably after twenty-four hours or so. He'd done a quick read on the tenant directory in the lobby and noted Kilburn's apartment number, and wouldn't you know it, the gas leak was in that very apartment.

Once he was in there he did a quick but thorough check. There wasn't much of interest, in fact the only thing out of the ordinary was Kilburn's collection of memorabilia from his silent film career. I thought that the studios made the actors give back their costumes and props when a picture was finished, but I guess Kilburn had been a big enough star to get special treatment in that department.

In any case, Solly had found a terrific pirate suit complete with cutlass and flintlock pistol, a Revolutionary War uniform and accompanying rifle, a Roman centurion's outfit and sword, a set of forest green Robin Hood duds, and even a French cavalier's rig complete with epée or whatever the heck you call those long, thin pig stickers.

There were also a bunch of chummy photos of the cast of *Dulcie Dixon at Deanville High*, people partying and playing around, including a bunch of Kilburn smooching with Christina Gluck. There were even some damned steamy inscriptions on the backs of the snapshots, and Solly had slipped the most personal of them into his tool box. They were something to behold. I could see why Rollo was stuck on Dulcie, but what Kilburn saw in Gluck was a mystery to me. Still, there's no accounting for taste or we'd all be betting on the same horse, wouldn't we?

Nothing too exciting there, but still Solly hitched a ride with me back to Foxx's house. When we arrived Foxx was upstairs conferring with Simon again and playing with his roses. Andrietta Hamlin had retired to a guest room to meditate or do her nails or catch up on her beauty sleep or something. I wondered if production was stalled on *Bachelor Girls on Broadway*, but if Hamlin wasn't worried about it I wasn't either.

Half an hour later Foxx was back behind his desk. He picked up a gold-barreled fountain pen and used it to tap the rim of a little golden frame that stood on the desk. Even though the frame was turned toward Foxx I knew exactly what it contained; I'd seen it enough times. It was an autographed baseball card featuring the portrait of Jimmy Foxx, the recently-retired batting star of Connie Mack's Philadelphia nine. My employer always claimed that he and the ballplayer were twins, separated at birth, and that Brother James got a double share of physical prowess while Brother Caligula got a double dose of mental acuity. This was another thing that baffled me: Was Caligula Foxx serious about the relationship or was the whole story an elaborate leg-pull?

I was in my own chair, and Solly was settled in a client seat. While I gave my report Foxx sat with his hands folded and his eyes closed. When I finished he buzzed for Reuter. Foxx had his usual Teplitz-Schönau ale, Solly asked for a stiff scotch and got it, and I cooled off with an iced lemonade.

Foxx took a long draught of ale, sighed contentedly, wiped his mouth, leaned back in his chair, folded his hands on his belly, and nodded for Solly to begin. Foxx listened passively until Solly finished. Then Foxx nodded once and Solly picked up his metal toolbox and started to leave. Solly was a family man, and he insisted on taking dinner with his missus and their tykes, but Foxx asked him to come back afterwards and Solly agreed.

Foxx's eyes slid shut and his eyebrow rose and stayed raised.

When he finally lowered his eyebrow and opened his eyes there was a beatific expression on his face. He picked up the telephone and called Andrietta Hamlin's room on the inside line. I heard him ask her to come downstairs for dinner at the accustomed hour, and to invite Lance Kilburn to join us as well.

I couldn't hear her side of the conversation but Foxx's ended with, "Of course he'll come. You have immense powers of persuasion, Miss Hamlin, and he will respond to them. Besides, he knows of your influence in Hollywood and I'm sure he is still eager to resume his screen career. Posing for haberdashers' advertisements can hardly provide the satisfaction his ego demands. Yes, of course. Thank you."

To me, Foxx said, "Andy, call our friend Inspector Cromwell and ask him to join us after dinner for a little meeting. Have him bring a couple of uniformed officers, as well."

Ω

When cocktail hour arrived I'd showered and switched to a lightweight seersucker suit, pale blue shirt and, just for a change, a snappy patterned bow tie. Foxx of course was elegant as ever, despite his unique aquamarine silk shirt. As for Hamlin, I don't know how she managed to get her mitts on a change of outfit without ever leaving the house or even the guest room, but somehow she had.

She arrived decked out in an evening dress of white tulle, shorter than the fashion of the day but with legs like Hamlin's who could blame her? It looked like a Jacques Fath number, and she'd set it off with a glittering emerald choker and a simple platinum-mounted emerald ring. Even her high-heeled shoes were a perfect matching green, but then I shouldn't have been surprised. She was Andrietta Hamlin.

Kilburn showed up a few minutes late, which of course ruffled Caligula Foxx's feathers. Kilburn planted a chaste kiss on Hamlin's cheek. He shook Foxx's hand, eliciting an oversize pout in return. Me he gave a single, grumpy look. I wondered if he's spotted me in the studio audience at WRNY. I thought not, but I couldn't be sure.

Foxx insisted on cocktails and small talk before dinner.

Then Reuter summoned us to the dining room and we obeyed. The arrangement was the same as it had been the last time we'd assembled for a meal, except of course that Helene Jones was absent, her place at the table taken by Lance Kilburn.

The meal was one of Reuter's masterpieces, which is saying a lot in view of his customary level of accomplishment. He started us off with a cold salmon mousse, light on the cayenne pepper, heavy on the lemon as he tended to be. This was followed by chicken and oysters prepared in a chafing dish that he set in the middle of the table. Being Reuter he had declined to use sliced large oysters, but had somehow obtained Olympias, starting with fresh mushrooms sautéed in sweet butter, then adding the diced chicken, whole tiny oysters, cream, sherry, and salt.

The freshener was a simple dandelion salad with bacon, minced garlic, freshly ground black pepper, diced scallions and beef tomato wedges.

Desert was fine lemon pudding—Reuter's prejudice showing itself once more—accompanied by hot coffee and followed by assorted brandies.

During the meal Kilburn kept trying to pump Hamlin about her plans, especially whether she intended to grab the role of Dulcie Dixon in a forthcoming movie series. I personally thought that Hamlin was more than slightly long in the tooth herself to play a teen-ager, but she might be able to bring it off after all. Kilburn kept pushing to keep the radio cast intact when the show was transferred to the silver screen, and I thought that was hilarious. Him as Rollo? Christina Gluck as Dulcie? Come on, tell me another!

Foxx was more interested in talking about roses. He thanked Miss Hamlin again for the cuttings she'd sent. Simon was pleased with them, he told her, and was preparing to start them off in the greenhouse. Perhaps in the morning she would be sufficiently rested to visit the greenhouse and receive a personal tour of Foxx's fragrant darlings.

I don't know if Hamlin appreciated what that meant. Foxx was proud of his roses, always experimenting with new nutrients for them and trying various soils, levels of moisture, temperature settings and sunlight. He was both an artist and a scientist of the Family Rosaceae. He loved to exhibit his accomplishments at rose shows, entrusting them to Simon and anticipating Simon's reports like an expectant father waiting for news from the delivery room.

But he did not invite guests to visit his greenhouse. I couldn't remember his doing that before tonight. I wondered if he had actually succumbed to the charms of the glamorous Andrietta.

Ω

After dinner we assembled in the office. Foxx sat behind his desk, I sat at my own desk with my chair turned to face Foxx. Between us Foxx had seated our guests, Miss Hamlin and Mr. Kilburn. Inspector Cromwell was present, as was Solly Kanter, who had abandoned his white worker's outfit for a light jacket, pale shirt and a necktie hand-painted with a scene of some cowboys sitting around a campfire beneath a starry sky.

Foxx opened the proceedings.

"I trust we have all enjoyed a pleasant dinner. It is now time to turn to the business of the evening, which I fear will be of a less congenial nature."

He paused, gave the Colonial spinning wheel a silent twirl, then resumed.

"I was engaged to protect Miss Hamlin from the threats of a person or persons unknown, who had telephoned her private number repeatedly, delivering said threats to her confidential secretary, the lamented Miss Helene Jones."

"If you or anyone else can solve that murder," Andrietta Hamlin interrupted Foxx, "I will personally offer a reward of twenty-five thousand dollars."

"Very good," Foxx said. "It was my intention to waive my fee in this case, since I actually failed to protect you, Miss Hamlin. The fact that Miss Jones was the one to fall victim to a killer, rather than yourself, was the result of a twist of fate, and not of my own doing. However, since I have deduced the identity of the killer, I will be pleased to accept your check as a reward for the latter service. And once again, I shall be in your debt."

He made a small gesture with his massive head, as close to a bow as he could contrive without standing up.

"You know who killed Jones?" Cromwell exclaimed. "I doubt that, Foxx. You haven't left your house."

"Nor did I need to, thanks to the excellent work of Mr. Winslow and Mr. Kanter. They will tell you what they learned and if you cannot deduce the identity of the culprit from that information, I will be happy to do so for you, Inspector."

Cromwell was fuming. "Go ahead, Foxx. This better be good."

Foxx nodded toward me. "Andy."

I took my cue. I reviewed the death scene and I told them about attending Kilburn's performance at the WRNY studio.

"Thank you, Andy." Foxx glared at Lance Kilburn, then fixed Inspector Cromwell with a demanding stare. "Do you see, Inspector?"

"No, I don't. Are you saying that Kilburn is the killer? Why would he murder Miss Jones? And how?" He paused to catch his breath, then added, "Besides, Kilburn arrived at the Hamlin apartment *after* Jones was murdered, not before."

"Very well," said Foxx. "Perhaps Mr. Kilburn would care to explain how he committed the crime, and the terrible mistake that he made which cost Miss Jones her life."

"I don't care to explain anything," Kilburn snarled. "You're nuts, Mister, if you think you can pin this on me."

Cromwell gave him a look that showed no great affection. "But," he said, "I don't see it either, Foxx. What are you driving at?"

"Ah, well, we must continue. I'd hoped for a quick end to these proceedings, but such is not to be. Solly, would you be so kind?"

Solly Kanter explained his gas man stunt and described what he'd found in Kilburn's apartment. At the end of his little speech he held up the photos for everyone to see. Hamlin was the most interested in the shots of Kilburn smooching with Christina Gluck and in the inscriptions on their backs.

"It would appear," Foxx said, "that after his fling with you in Hollywood, Miss Hamlin, Mr. Kilburn found a new object for his affection."

He inhaled, then said, "Mr. Kilburn, I congratulate you on finding your voice at last. Or, should I say, your many voices. Was Miss Gluck your coach? I see by your expression that she was, and a most commendable job she did, too. You didn't want to see *Dulcie Dixon at Deanville High* filmed with an all-new cast, did you? And yet that was the producer's intention, I would warrant."

Kilburn didn't speak.

"Hell hath no fury like a lover spurned," Foxx resumed, "be he man or woman, eh? What rage would have filled your heart, had Andrietta Hamlin replaced your new paramour, Christina Gluck, in the role of Dulcie. And who would have been the new Rollo? For surely you could not have qualified for the role. Now that you can sound the part at last, you are too old to look it. A bitter irony, alas."

Foxx shook his head.

"I'm still lost," Cromwell muttered. "If Kilburn arrived after Jones was dead, how can you say he shot her? Besides, we never found the bullet. There was an entry wound and an exit wound, there should have been some lead in that kitchen, and there wasn't."

Foxx raised an eyebrow briefly, then lowered it again. "You found no bullet because there was no bullet to find. In addition, I might mention that there was also no gun, obviously."

Cromwell was getting red in the face, something that I've seen him do too often to find it amusing any more. He took a deep breath, let it out, took another and finally managed to speak. "Okay, Foxx, if there was no bullet and no gun, how did those holes get poked into Jones's skull—by magic?"

"Miss Jones was shot, Inspector." Foxx allowed himself to smile his tiny smile. "She was shot with an arrow propelled from a powerful bow." He turned ever so slightly. "Isn't that so, Mr. Kilburn? You're a very fine bowman, scoring a bull's eye on your first attempt from the other side of Park Avenue."

"You *are* out of your mind," Kilburn screamed. "I didn't do it and you can't prove I did. I don't even own a bow."

"Perhaps not any more, but you did as of this morning. Ask Mr. Kanter, Inspector Cromwell, if you doubt my word."

Cromwell peered at Foxx, then at Kilburn, and finally at Solly Kanter.

"I'm sorry, Mr. Foxx, I don't mean to let you down but I didn't find any bow in the Kilburn apartment."

"Of course not," Foxx replied. "You found the photos, for which I commend you, and you found Mr. Kilburn's Hollywood memorabilia, did you not?"

Kilburn was starting to squeak in his Rollo voice. "You had no right going into my apartment! You had no search warrant! I'll have the evidence quashed!"

"Mr. Kanter isn't a police officer," Foxx murmured, "so he didn't need a warrant. You might charge him with breaking and entering, but he didn't break in either, the superintendent of your building admitted him."

"He lied!"

"Ah, I suppose he might be charged with lying to the superintendent of a building. Is that a very serious offense, Inspector? No, you needn't answer. Mr. Kanter, please describe the memorabilia you found in Mr. Kilburn's apartment."

Solly did so.

When he finished, Foxx said, "Thus, a pirate costume with cutlass and pistol, a Revolutionary uniform with rifle, a Roman centurion's outfit with short sword, a French cavalier's costume with what Mr. Kanter so amusingly calls an 'eppy,' and a Robin Hood get-up."

The room was silent.

Foxx emitted a great sigh. "I am appalled. Does no one remember the story of the dog in the night? What was peculiar was not what he did, but that he did nothing. Please, I appeal to your massed intellects, what was missing from Mr. Kanter's inventory? With each costume, a weapon. And Mr. Kilburn was known for applying himself until he was an expert with each weapon he was called upon to use in one of his films."

He spread his hands appealingly.

"Is there still no hope for the wicked?" He shook his head as one bitterly disappointed. "What was missing was Robin Hood's bow and arrow. Mr. Kanter loosed a shaft through the open window of his apartment. It crossed the street unseen by anyone passing below, entered the Hamlin apartment through the open window there, penetrated the light summer curtain, and pierced Miss Jones's temple causing instant death. If you

202

contact the management of Mr. Kilburn's building and have them search the incinerator there, you may expect to find Robin Hood's bow, along with a quiver of arrows, where Mr. Kilburn deposited those items on his way out of the building in response to Miss Hamlin's summons."

Foxx shifted his weight and directed his attention to Solly Kanter. "That was good work, Solly, and good thinking to have the superintendent shut down the incinerator. I believe in most cases incinerators are lighted at night and burn only for a few hours to destroy a day's accumulation of trash. But if by any chance the bow and arrows were destroyed, the hard metal tips of the arrows will be found in the ashes."

Cromwell had turned back to his normal color, but he was still shaking his head. "No bullet, okay, Foxx. She was shot with a bow and arrow. Then where's the arrow? And if Kilburn shot the arrow—from his apartment across Park Avenue, right?"

Foxx made an affirmative grunt.

"How did the arrow get through a closed window, Foxx? And why didn't anybody find it at the murder scene?"

Foxx made a tiny moué. "Miss Hamlin, would you be so kind as to review the events of the terrible morning for us? I know you have done so before, but if I might impose—and please be careful to mention the position of each person at each moment."

The actress in Hamlin made her perform beautifully. "I entered the kitchen and found Miss Jones lying on the floor in a growing pool of blood. I was so horrified, I ran to the sitting room and telephoned Mr. Kilburn. When he arrived at my apartment I showed him the—the body—and left him there and called your office. That was when Mr. Winslow came."

Foxx said, "Thank you, Miss Hamlin. You heard no shot, of course?"

"No."

"I thought not." Foxx raised an eyebrow, then lowered it again.

"And you saw no arrow, of course, protruding from Miss Jones's head? I regret having to describe so gruesome a state of affairs, but it is unavoidable."

"I saw no arrow, no."

Foxx nodded and shifted his attention back to Cromwell. "Obviously, Inspector, the arrow was shot with such force that it left Miss Jones's head, but by then it had exhausted its force and fell to the floor. Miss Hamlin would hardly have noticed it in the horror and shock of discovering Miss Jones's body, and she then left the room and did not return until Mr. Kilburn had done his dirty work."

"What dirty work?" Kilburn demanded angrily.

"My dear sir," Foxx purred. "You first closed the window through which you had shot from across Park Avenue. You then found the arrow, probably snapped its shaft to make it more easily handled, added it to a paper bag of kitchen scraps, and lowered it via the dumb-waiter to the building's cellar. I would venture that it has been incinerated by now. I would also venture that a careful examination of the incinerator ash from Miss Hamlin's building will reveal the pointed metal tip of the arrow, badly charred of course, while the shaft and feathers have been totally consumed."

He turned back. "Inspector Cromwell, please have your men take Mr. Kilburn into custody. This case is closed."

Kilburn was on his feet, raging at Foxx and Solly Kanter until Cromwell's uniformed minions grabbed him by the elbows and wrestled him into submission. They cuffed him and dragged him back to his feet but he didn't want to go. He stood with his feet planted defiantly and shouted at Foxx. "I still say you're crazy. I had no reason to murder Helene Jones. She was a nobody, a nobody!"

Foxx shook his head. "You never intended to murder Miss Jones. You were after Miss Hamlin. From across the street, clad only in pajamas and robe, and seen through the thin, transparent curtains, Miss Jones bore an uncanny resemblance to her employer. In person the differences in their coloring and manner were dramatic. But under these circumstances, the mistake was an easy one for you to make."

"But the voices. The warnings, the voices," Kilburn cried desperately. "There was a whole gang involved."

"A credit to Miss Gluck," Foxx said. "And to your own skills as her student, Mr. Kilburn. In that regard if in no other, I offer you my most sincere congratulations. You do learn well. The voices were all yours, do not attempt to deny that."

Kilburn was about at the end of his rope, that was obvious. He gave it one more shot. "Andrietta Hamlin was my friend. Tell them, Andrietta."

She sat stony-faced.

"I had no reason to want to kill her," Kilburn insisted.

"On the contrary, sir." Foxx's expression was one of disappointment with humankind. "You wanted desperately to resume your motion picture career, and you saw the proposed Dulcie Dixon series as the way to do it. But only if the radio cast were called upon to reprise their performances on the screen. If Christina Gluck was replaced by Andrietta Hamlin, why, the rest of the actors would tumble like dominos. Remove Miss Hamlin from the equation and Gluck stood at least a chance to get the screen role. And if she did so, you might well follow."

Foxx shook his head sadly. "You had the proverbial motive, means, and opportunity, Mr. Kilburn. The physical evidence to convict you will be found in the incinerator of your apartment building. You murdered the wrong person, sir, but you may rest assured that the penalty you pay will be no less than if you had killed the woman you meant to kill."

Kilburn slumped as if the fight had all been taken out of him, which in fact it had. The case was made. Cromwell gestured to his helpers, and they led Kilburn to the doorway and off to the Tombs.

Foxx smiled benignly at Andrietta Hamlin. "I do not mean to appear insensitive, my dear Miss Hamlin, but do you perchance have your checkbook with you?"

Ω

The lonely wail of a steam locomotive echoed across the moonlit prairie. Tall saguaro cactus cast frighteningly human-looking shadows in the bright January moonlight. The train had left Chicago in the midst of a driving snowstorm, the worst that city had experienced in a decade. Now, as it roared across the Arizona desert the light of a full moon and a million stars reflected off the bellowing behemoth.

The war was over and nearly two years had passed. The nation had welcomed its millions of uniformed heroes home, thanked them for their service, and sent them back into the teeming streets of its cities and the lush fields and pastures of its farms.

Time to earn your way as civilians once again, boys. If the jobs just aren't there, if the horrors you lived on the beaches of Normandy and in the caves of Iwo Jima haunt your dreams like bloody phantoms, well, you'll get over it. Just smile and accept the thanks of a grateful nation.

The hour was late, very late. Almost all the passengers had retired for the night, the well-to-do in their private compartments, the middle-class in folding berths, those less fortunate slouching in their seats, hoping to catch a few hours of shut-eye before the desert sun came glaring over the horizon.

By this time the club car should have been darkened, too, but a few neatly folded bills, discreetly passed across the polished hardwood to a receptive bartender, had persuaded him to stay open for a handful of carefully selected customers.

Two of them were perched on tall barstools. Seen from the rear, they could have passed for brothers. Or perhaps for professional colleagues, on their way to a convention of clergymen.

Or undertakers.

Each was dressed in a black suit, elegantly tailored and maintained with care. Each wore a pair of black shoes, polished to a brilliant shine. Perhaps oddly, each also wore a black fedora. Most passengers remove their hats to ride in trains, but who are we to criticize, eh? Leave them to their foibles.

The two men had been drinking separately when the club car manager sent most of his customers on their way for the evening. Some had drunk discreetly. Others were—how shall I put it—let's say they were feeling no pain. But what harm was there in getting a little bit tipsy, maybe more than a little bit tipsy, while heading toward Los Angeles on the Desert Cannonball? Nobody was going to drive into a lamppost, that's for sure.

Finding themselves the only customers left at the bar, the two men struck up a conversation. Well, there's no harm in that. A couple of lonely souls, happy to have someone with whom to while away the hours.

Names were a problem, but only a small one. One man asked the other to call him Whistler.

"As in James McNeill Whistler?" asked his new acquaintance.

"No. It's a nickname I got because of a little habit I picked up a long time ago." He paused and whistled an eerie tune. It wasn't exactly pretty, but the other found that it lodged, somehow, in his brain. A very odd melody, melancholy, haunting, as if it would draw you in and keep you there—somewhere—whether you wanted to stay or not.

"You see?"

The other man said, "Yes."

"That's why they call me—Whistler." He paused to sip his beverage, the ice cubes clinking softly with the swaying of the train. "And you?"

"Traveler."

"Just Traveler?"

"Yes. Some people think there's something mysterious about that, but most simply accept it. I hope you will, Mr. Whistler."

"Just Whistler."

Their conversation was interrupted by a white-jacketed porter clearing away the remnants of the evening's business. Ash trays were emptied, glasses and bottles were removed from tables and carried to the bar to be washed. Abandoned magazines and newspapers were gathered up.

One of the dark-suited men asked the porter to leave a newspaper with him. It was a copy of the Chicago *Tribune*, the self-styled World's Greatest Newspaper. He spread it on the bar and scanned the headlines. Chicago was still reeling from news of the death of Al Capone at his winter home in Florida. Chicagoans who had quailed in terror at the violence of Capone's mobsters two decades earlier now felt a strange nostalgia for the brutal mobster. In international news a Frenchman named Henri Verdoux was suing the producers of the Chaplin film *Monsieur Verdoux* that portrayed its eponymous character as a serial murderer. Closer to home the police promised a prompt arrest in the daring daylight robbery of the Farmers and Cattlemen's Bank on State Street. And on the sports page, fans of both the White Sox and the Cubs were beginning to stir in anticipation of the coming baseball season.

From behind the two men came the sound of a woman's voice. "Hey, up there, can a lonely lady get a nightcap or is this joint closed for business?"

The lighting in the club car was dim, supplemented by the almost daytime glare of a full moon reflected off the sere sands of the southwestern desert.

The bartender, unobtrusively manning his station, rasped his reply. "I'm sorry, Miss, club car is closed for the night."

He winked at his two male customers. "I see you're checking out the headlines," he growled. "What do you think of that bank robbery? Take a gander at that, will ya?"

With a blunt finger he traced the story's subheads. "Looks like the coppers put a couple of slugs into one of them muggs, even if his buddies managed to drag him into their getaway wagon." He shook his head. "Takes all kinds, don't it? That's what I always say, it sure takes all kinds."

The woman's voice cut in again. "I don't see you shutting down those two muggs." She stood up, holding the table-edge to steady herself as the car lurched, jerking a thumb at Whistler and Traveler.

The two men in black exchanged a knowing glance. One of them addressed the woman. "Didn't you get on the train in Chicago, Miss?"

"Yeah. That's home. So what?"

"Oh, nothing. Nothing at all," the second man in black replied. "Chicago is a splendid metropolis. What did that poet call it, 'Hog butcher for the world?' Of course, the winters can be difficult. Are you headed for a warmer locale?"

The car lurched again, and the woman stumbled, caught herself, then made her way forward.

"Here now," a man in black said, "won't you have a seat?" He slid courteously aside and the woman climbed onto a red leather stool between those occupied by the two men.

She looked from side to side. "You two must be brothers or something."

"You might say as much."

"You even drink the same kind of booze." She flicked her deep eyes toward the bartender. "I'll have the same as the brothers here."

The bartender cast a glance at one of the men, caught an almost imperceptible nod in return, lifted a silver-capped bottle and a small glass and poured.

The woman gazed into the glass, not touching it. She turned on her barstool to scan the moonlit desert. Windows had been opened on both sides of the car, and the cool night air of the Southwest provided refreshing relief to the usual stuffy air of railroad cars.

Black shapes flitted through the night outside the car. The woman made an odd gesture, the dark red of her long, pointed fingernails reflecting in the overhead lamps. Something silent and black flittered through the window. It hovered briefly near the ceiling, then flapped its wings, crossed the car and disappeared out the other side of the car.

"Wha—what was that?" the bartender gasped.

"Just a bat." The woman smiled at the red-jacketed server. She was small and slim, her skin pale and her features fine, a marked contrast to her rough speech. In the artificial light of the club car her platinum blonde hair, artfully darkened eyebrows and lashes and vivid lip rouge made a dramatic image. A tiny purse of gold lamé hung from one shoulder by golden chains as fine as angel's hair.

The red-jacketed bartender shook his head. "Pretty weird, but we get 'em now and then on this run. Some women are scared, think they'll get caught in their hair or something." He gave a nervous laugh. "Maybe they're afraid of vampires."

"No," the woman said, "I'm certainly not afraid of bats. I use them in my work. And there are no vampires. No human ones, anyway. My poor uncle back there in the baggage car, he was raised on horror movies, he always believed in vampires. Lot of good it did him, the old fool."

The train's whistle punctuated her words, its shrill wail echoing through the night.

She lifted her glass. "To Chicago." She paused.

"I'll drink to that," one of the men said.

The woman said, "Let me finish. To Chicago, good-bye, you've seen the last of Satin Blaine." She drew the glass to her lips and drained off half its contents. To her newfound companions she said, "How come you two aren't drinking?"

In unison the two men lifted their glasses. A moment later one of them said, "That was quite a trick, Miss Blaine. It is Miss Blaine, isn't it? Yes. Quite a trick getting that bat to fly through the car."

"I've always been good with animals."

"And you're leaving Chicago because of the climate?"

She let out a quick, harsh laugh. "You might say that."

"Too cold for you?"

"Maybe. Or maybe too hot."

She took another sip of her beverage. "Actually, I'm taking my uncle to Los Angeles."

"Oh. I thought you were travelling alone. I didn't see any companion with you."

"He's back in the baggage car."

The lights in the club car flickered, as they often do on trains. In the momentary darkness the bright moonlight pouring through the club car's window settled on the woman's hand. A magnificent Australian opal mounted in a fine gold setting graced her finger; the stone seemed to capture the moonlight and glow with its swirling effulgence.

The electric lights came back on.

"He's dead," Satin Blaine explained.

"It must be difficult, travelling with a casket."

"I can handle a stiff. They never give me any trouble. I've had a lot more grief from live men than from dead ones, you can believe it."

She heaved a sigh, a world-weary gesture for one so young and attractive.

She downed the last of her drink, lowered the glass to the bar and slid from the stool to her feet. "Okay, gents, many thanks for the companionship and the refreshments. I think I'll be on my way now."

"We'll walk you back to your compartment, Miss Blaine." One of the men slapped a bill on the bar. They both joined the woman.

"Well, how nice of you. But call me Satin, then, if we're going to be friends."

They left the club car and started toward the rear of the train only to be stopped by a uniformed conductor. His hair beneath his uniform cap was steel gray. His eyes held the look of one who has seen everything there is to see, or who thought so until now.

"Sorry, folks, passageway's closed for a little while."

"What happened?"

"I'm sorry, you'll just have to stay in your compartments. Everything's all right." The way he said it indicated that everything was not all right.

One of the men in black leaned over and whispered a few words to the conductor. At the same time he pulled back his carefully tailored suit jacket and showed something to the railroad man.

There was a moment of silence. It was broken when the train lurched and the lights flickered.

After a moment the lights blazed again and the conductor nodded. "Okay, follow me."

They made their way through a series of Pullmans and ordinary passenger cars. A seeming eternity later they approached the streamliner's baggage car, only to be halted in their tracks by a frightful sight.

A gray-haired oldster wearing railroad man's overalls staggered toward them, an expression of fright on his face. "It—it—it's a va-vamp . . ." escaped his blue lips. His eyes were open wide. He pitched forward and lay motionless in the corridor.

The conductor bowed over the body, turning it over so that the gaping mouth and frightened eyes stared sightlessly at the ceiling. After a moment the conductor knelt and a uniformed sleeve stretched toward the old man's throat. Experienced fingers felt for a pulse that was not there.

The conductor looked up at the two men in black and the slim, platinum blonde woman. "He's dead," the conductor gasped. And after a moment he added, "and he's cold. As cold as ice."

The woman, Satin Blaine, spoke in her distinctive voice, "He tried to say something. He said, 'Va-vamp.'"

A man in black said, simply, "Yes."

Satin Blaine resumed, "Do you think he was trying to say, *vampire?*"

Briefly, no one spoke.

And what do you think, dear reader? Was the old man talking about a vampire? Perhaps he'd seen one movie too many, or read one tale more than was good for him, about Transylvanian counts with courtly manners and very sharp fangs. Perhaps he was the victim of his own, too-vivid, imagination. Or . . .perhaps not.

We shall see.

One of the men in black asked the conductor, "Who is this?"

"Old Jenkins. Old Ollie Jenkins. He's been with the railroad for forty years. Started as a fireman and worked his way up to brakeman and finally engineer. One of the best. He never married, never had a family or even many friends. Said he loved his locomotives and that was all the love he needed. Management tried to retire him years ago, but he loved the trains so much, he wouldn't let go. Said he wanted to die riding the rails, so they gave him a job as a baggage car attendant, paid him as much salary as his pension would have been. Can you imagine, a top-notch engineer, sitting and watching baggage hour after hour? But Ollie said he'd do anything he had to, just so long as he could keep riding the high iron. Well, I guess he got his way. Poor old-timer."

"Enough sentiment," said a man in black. "Just a moment." He bent and touched the white cheek, then rose. "Cold, all right."

Satin Blaine asked, "What could have killed him?"

The conductor shook his head. "No way to tell, but it looks to me as if he died of shock."

A man in black—the one who called himself Traveler—said, "I need to look in that baggage car." He stepped away from the others and tried the door. "It's locked."

"Baggage car's always locked." The conductor stepped forward. He pulled a huge key ring from his uniform pocket and found the correct key. "Even scared as he was, Ollie slammed the door behind him coming out."

Traveler held up his hand. "Just a minute, then. Don't be so fast to open the door to the baggage car."

He turned and placed the palm of one hand on the metal surface, then snatched his hand away as if he'd placed it on a red-hot stove. At the same moment a trickle of white smoke, or what appeared to be white smoke, crept through the keyhole.

An expression of fear contorted the conductor's features. "Something's burning in there! We'll have to uncouple the baggage car."

"No." Traveler held his hand at shoulder level, rubbing it with the other. "Take a look at Jenkins there." He pointed at the cadaver. "Look at his eyebrows, his moustache. That's frost." He swung around and pointed in the other direction. "Not smoke, not smoke at all. There's something freezing cold in there."

Whistler pressed his fingertips briefly to the door. "You're right, Traveler." Then he addressed himself to the railroad man. "Conductor, what are you carrying in this baggage car?"

The conductor reached inside his uniform jacket. "I've got the manifest right here."

He opened a small, much-battered leather portfolio that resembled an oversized wallet, pulled from it a folded sheet of oversized foolscap and spread it for them all to see. He ran a finger down a column of brief, blue-inked entries.

"You see? Nothing but the usual passengers' luggage, a few trunks being shipped by express service, and—and a coffin holding human remains. We need a special permit to carry human remains. I've got it right here."

A second sheet bore official seals and signatures. It listed the point of origin and destination of one casket, bronze. *Point of origin, Blaine Chemical and Pharmaceuticals Corporation, Chicago, Illinois. Destination, Blaine Works West, Los Angeles, California. Contents of casket, embalmed and preserved remains of Walter Martin Blaine, deceased.*

"You uncle, Miss Blaine?" Whistler frowned at the shapely platinum blonde.

From her gold lamé purse she produced a lace handkerchief and dabbed at her eyes. "Yes. My Uncle Walter. My parents both died when I was a child and Uncle Walter was like a father to me. And now, now he's gone."

The conductor raised his uniform cap and scratched a thatch of salt-and-pepper hair. "I just don't get it. You have my sympathy, Miss Blaine, you truly do. But I don't see how that connects with this icy mystery."

Traveler asked a question. "Could there be any machinery or chemicals in there?"

The conductor shook his head. "Not possible, sir. Anything like that would have to ship on a freight. We don't mix freight with passengers, not policy, sir, no way. Would be against railroad rules and government regulations both. And even if we made an exception, maybe some high-priority defense materials that couldn't wait for the next freight, why, you see . . ." He held the baggage manifest in one hand and slapped the page with the back of his other hand. ". . . you see, it would show on the manifest. It just isn't here, sir. It's impossible."

A pretty puzzle, don't you think? When you have eliminated the impossible, whatever remains, however improbable, must be the truth. *Didn't a great detective once say that? But what happens when you eliminate the impossible—and no other explanation remains? What then, eh? Maybe the impossible is true after all.*

Or is it?

"All right," Traveler hissed. "Whatever killed Oliver Jenkins is inside that baggage car. And whatever it was, we're going to find out. Let me have your key, conductor."

The railroad man had dropped his keys back into his pocket. Now he found them again and handed them to Traveler. "That's the one. Right there. That's the one that opens the baggage car."

Traveler held out his hand.

The conductor laid the collection of keys in Traveler's palm. He pointed to an old-fashioned, oversized blue steel key of a type that had been popular half a century before. "That's the one, sir. That's the one that will open the lock."

Traveler extended his arm, moving the huge key toward the lock that stood between them and the baggage compartment. Even as he did so the cold white mist continued to pour from the keyhole. Once through it crept down the door like a living, malevolent thing and puddled on the compartment floor, forming a lake of white, icy vapor.

As the key made contact with the lock, a woman's voice, angry, authoritative, maybe a little bit desperate, rang out.

"Go ahead, Traveler. Open the door. And when you do, we're all going to take a ride in the baggage compartment."

Traveler and Whistler were calm but the conductor showed his puzzlement. "What do you mean? What—oh." He nodded slowly, his gaze fixed on the tiny pearl-handled .22 that she had pulled from her purse. It was pointing at them now.

Satin Blaine swung the little automatic from one to another, covering Traveler, Whistler, and the conductor in turn.

Traveler inserted the key in the heavy, old-fashioned lock. He turned it and the lock emitted a loud click.

"Go ahead," Satin Blaine ordered. "All three of you, into the baggage car. And don't try any tricks. I suppose you two mystery men are willing to risk your lives but I don't think you'd risk the life of an innocent man. So any tricks and the conductor gets it. A .22 only makes a little hole but if it's through the heart or the brain, it's as deadly as a cannon."

Traveler shoved the door open with a black-clad shoulder. There was a rush of white vapor as the door swung back. The vapor flooded the platform where Satin Blaine and the others stood, then was swept into the Arizona night as the wind caught it.

One black-clad figure, then another stepped across the platform into the baggage car. Hesitantly, the conductor followed. Finally Satin Blaine followed them, her little gold lamé purse swinging from its glittering chain and the pearl-handled automatic steady in her fist.

Whistler looked around the car. Its contents were utterly uninteresting. For the most part they were men's and women's suitcases doubtlessly containing light clothing for wear in the balmy winter weather of Southern California. There were several steamer trunks. Most likely they belonged to wealthy passengers planning to proceed from California to the Hawaiian islands for an interlude of luaus and surfing while their less fortunate neighbors shivered in the Midwestern winter.

Whistler's eyes flicked back to Satin Blaine and caught her glancing involuntarily at a large suitcase. Clearly, it was of high quality but it was obviously well traveled. It bore stickers with scenes of Los Angeles, Honolulu, Singapore and Sydney.

Against one wall of the compartment, resting on a pair of wooden trestles, there lay a casket, its burnished bronze surface reflecting the dim electric lights in the ceiling. A light coating of frost gave its rounded lid the illusion of a graceful, snow-covered hillside. The very air near the casket was frigid.

"You boys are making things hard for me," Satin Blaine hissed. "As for Mr. Jenkins out there on the platform, if he'd just minded his business he would have been all right. That casket was sealed in Chicago and it shouldn't have been opened until we got to Los Angeles. Now I think I'll have to get off before then and leave my poor uncle to his own devices."

The others waited for her to continue.

"What's our next stop, conductor?"

The railroad man went fishing in his vest pocket and came out with a huge old watch. He pressed a button and the engraved metal front of the timepiece popped open.

"Phoenix, Miss. We pass through around eleven tonight. Los Angeles in the morning."

"Okay, bub. Here's what we're going to do. I'm going to lock you in here. You—buster—the keys. That's right. Toss 'em gently."

She caught the heavy collection of keys skillfully.

"I'm sure they'll wonder what happened to you, Mister Railroad Man, but that won't be my problem. And as for you two undertakers, just don't try anything clever and you'll stay alive."

She edged toward the casket.

"All right, all three of you, step back. That's right. Undertakers first, so the railroad man is closest to me. I have a feeling you might try something, even risk getting shot at. You'd figure that I couldn't get both of you. Actually, I might. I'm a good shot. But you wouldn't risk an innocent man getting plugged. So you stay in front of the others, railroad man. Stay between me and them. If they try anything fancy, you get the first bullet, right in the belly. It's a lousy way to go, believe you me!"

What a nice little lady we've got here, don't you think? She looked so appealing up there in the club car, wouldn't any gentleman travelling alone on a streamliner like the Desert Cannonball be happy to buy her a drink, just for the pleasure of her company. I guess the old saying is right. You know the one I mean. The one about appearances being deceiving.

Once the others had followed their instructions, Satin Blaine edged toward the casket. She managed to open her gold lamé purse with one hand and drop the keys into it, holding the gun on the others all the while. Then with her free hand she inserted long fingernails beneath the upper half of the divided coffin lid.

"Looks to me as if poor Mr. Jenkins opened this thing and then dropped the lid back in place when he ran away."

It took a great effort by the slim Miss Blaine, but she managed to pry the lid open, then swing it back on its well balanced hinges. As she did so a cloud of cold, white vapor rose from the casket and pooled around Satin Blaine's feet.

"All right. You—Mister Blackie there—I want you to open my valise." She jerked her head toward the much-traveled suitcase, the one that was all but covered with the stickers from exotic ports of call.

"Dump my clothes out of there. I'll enjoy shopping for a new wardrobe anyhow."

The face of the cadaver Satin Blaine had exposed was white, its eyebrows frosted like those of the late Oliver Jenkins. The body was dressed in a dark blue suit, white shirt and red necktie.

Satin Blaine glanced into the coffin. Still holding the .22 automatic on the others, she reached inside the suit jacket, then stepped back with a packet of large-denomination bills wrapped in a paper label. She tossed it across the car. It landed at the conductor's feet.

"Put that in the valise."

As the railroad man complied she rummaged inside the casket, withdrawing packet after packet of currency and tossing them to the railroad man. As she worked she used them to knock white fuming cakes out of her way. White fuming cakes of dry ice, frozen squares of carbon dioxide, the coldest substance known to Man.

Suddenly she screamed.

The others jerked involuntarily, staring in amazement at the scene before them.

With a single spasmodic motion the cadaver had reached up and clutched the hand that had pulled bundle after bundle of money from the coffin.

"You can't do that—you're dead, dead!"

A horrifying moan rose from the casket.

Satin Blaine's arm was pulled toward the blue suit coat of the cadaver.

"I saw you die. I gave you the *conus purpurascens*, I put it in your shaving soap, I saw you collapse and die. You can't be alive. You can't be alive. You . . ."

The arm clutching her wrist drew her down, down, into the casket. As her face came close to that of the cadaver she screamed again and pulled the trigger of the pearl-handled automatic. It fired again and again, the bullets penetrating the body in the coffin.

Satin Blaine recoiled in a spasm of terror as her warm, lovely face made contact with the cold, white features of the cadaver. She flung herself backwards, her weapon flying from her hand and clattering against the opposite wall of the baggage car.

Traveler stepped forward and retrieved the weapon.

The woman collapsed against the bronze casket, one claw-like hand held in the unbreakable grip of the body in the casket. And it was now indeed a body, a dead body, a corpse. Ever since the poison of the Australian sea-cone had done its work, paralyzing Satin Blaine's Uncle Walter, some spark of life might have flickered faintly in the motionless body.

The .22-caliber rounds had extinguished that tiny, faint spark. And Satin Blaine had absorbed some of the toxin through her pale, delicate, lovely cheek.

The Traveler steadied the trembling, fear-struck conductor.

"It's all right now, old man. There may even be a reward in it for you. You'd better message ahead to Phoenix and tell them to get in touch with the police in Chicago. The Farmers and Cattlemen's Bank loot is found."

Oh, she was a clever one that Satin Blaine. She'd been to Australia, she'd managed to get ahold of the toxin of the Australian cone shell. These snails are among the deadliest creatures in the world. They appear harmless enough, their shells are even attractive looking. But any tourist who picks one up—well, at least it's a painless death. Or so I've heard.

Myself, I wouldn't want to try it. Would you?

As for Uncle Walter—poor, dear Uncle Walter—do you think he really believed in vampires? I mean the human variety of vampires. Maybe he did. Maybe he was trying to become one. What was the famous line from Peter Pan? *Oh yes. Do you believe in fairies? If you believe, clap your hands! Well, dear friends, Do you believe in vampires?*

As for that bat—there are plenty of bats in the desert. They're not really vampires. They live on insects. They're very useful little creatures, don't you know.

Ω

Four o'clock in the damned morning. Pitch-black and freezing out even in Hollywood, and the old Pontiac wouldn't start. Banger ground the starter until the battery started to get weak and the grinding faded to a feeble moan. Then Banger gave up. He leaned his head against the steering wheel.

But only for a minute.

He ran back upstairs, bypassing the elevator. His bifocals were steamed up and he wiped them with his shirt tail. He must be falling apart, couldn't see a damned thing without cheaters. They would have laughed him out of the gym if he'd showed up wearing specs in his prime. But of course in his prime he hadn't needed specs.

At Chim's apartment door he fumbled until he found the key Chim had loaned him and let himself back in. He scurried past the couch that he'd carefully made up after a night's restless tossing and paused outside Chim's bedroom.

Had Chim got lucky? Had some lonesome barfly ex-groupie hung around after the Tiger's Den closed last night, and come home to spend the night with the good-looking bass player?

Banger tapped gently on Chim's door. On the second try he heard Chim moan.

Banger said, "Chim, I gotta talk to you."

Chim mumbled something that Banger couldn't make out. There was a stirring, then Chim opened the door a crack. Banger could make out only a vague grayness behind Chim, maybe the suggestion of a rounded hip under a draped sheet on the bed.

"Jesus, what time is it? What's the matter?"

Banger said, "My car won't start."

Chim opened a bleary eye from quarter- to half-mast. "What the hell time is it?"

"Pushing four-thirty, Chim."

"In the God damned *morning?*"

"Yeah. Chim, my car's dead. I gotta get to the set, Chim, can I borrow the Honda?"

Chim leaned his head on the doorjamb. He was wearing a pair of bikini underpants. His hair was sticking out in all directions and somehow Banger could see how women chased him all the time.

"Can I borrow the Honda, Chim? I wouldn't ask but you know I really . . ."

"Banger, I only been home a couple hours. I got . . ." He looked back over his shoulder, shook his head, stepped out into the narrow hallway. "Man, it's cold. I wanna get back in the sack. I need my rest."

"I know, Chim. I'm sorry. Look, I had a call last night. From the casting director. Katie. I gotta get out to the set, Chim."

"Why'd she call you?" He padded into the living room, pulled a quilted jacket off the back of a chair, shoved his arms into the sleeves. "That's better." He turned the chair around and leaned his arms on its back. "You told me you had the work anyhow. Why'd this Katie call you here?"

"I gave 'em this number. You don't mind, Chim. They have to be able to reach me. You know it's only for a little while."

"You bet it is."

"See, that's what's so great. She called me cause they need me to play Slam Shaughnessy. He's Cole's opponent in the big match. It's a real part, Chim. It's a week's pay at scale. As an actor, not an extra. And billing. I'll get billing."

"That's great, Banger." Chim didn't sound enthusiastic. "I'm going back to bed. Congratulations."

"Wait. Chim." Banger grabbed Chim by the elbow. "My car won't start. There isn't time to do anything about it. I can't afford a cab. Dunno if I could find one now anyhow. Chim, please, let me take the Honda. I have to be ready for makeup at five and they're shooting way out in Pasadena. Please, Chim."

Chim reached for his pocket, discovered that he was wearing only underpants under the quilted jacket. "I need the car tonight, Banger. I'll be around most of the day, maybe walk around the neighborhood, maybe have lunch out. I think, Thai. Yeah. She said she likes Thai. But I need the car tonight. I can't lug a bass on the bus."

He started back toward the bedroom.

"I promise, Chim. The set closes at seven-thirty. I'll head straight back here. It's after rush hour. I'll be here by eight."

"I have to be at the club by eight-thirty." Chim was waking up. Behind him, through the fourth-floor apartment's broad windows, the sky was beginning to lighten. "Eight o'clock, that's cutting it awfully close."

"I'll be on time, Chim. If I'm not, I'll pay for a cab. Don't wait for me. Take a cab. A week at scale, Chim, I'll spring for a cab."

Chim shook his head. "Wayne is pretty uptight about punctuality. Imagine me standing on Hollywood Boulevard in a tux with a double bass and hailing a cab." He disappeared into the bedroom. Shuffling and bumping noises came from the room. Then a feminine sound, half a moan and half a question that drove a knife into Banger's heart. Then the door opened again, just a crack, and Chim handed Banger the keys to the Honda. "I don't wanna take no cab. Be on time."

Ω

Banger pulled into the parking lot. He remembered to turn off the Honda's headlights. The sky was light. The air was still cold. He sprinted across the parking lot and past the trailers. He slapped his pockets until he found his production ID. At least he had that.

An assistant assistant director stood at the square doorway with a clipboard. He looked about eleven years old. Banger waved his pass at the AAD. The pass had a logo of a boxing glove and a stylized atom sign. In block letters it said, *Neutron Kid—Set Pass.*

The AAD ignored the pass. He nodded at Banger and made a mark on his clipboard. He jerked his head. "Better see Katie. She's waiting in Makeup. You're late."

Banger grunted, sprinted across the huge, shadowy room. He could feel the cold concrete floor through his sneakers and heavy socks.

Katie was waiting at Makeup.

She said, "Thanks for coming in, Banger."

"I gotta thank you, Katie. You don't know how—well, what happened to the other guy, whatsizname?"

"Yeah. He got a chance to do a commercial in Maui. A lot more than we were paying him. Saturday morning, I get a phone call. 'I'm on the redeye,' he says, 'I'm calling from a 767. Back in a week. Can you shoot around me?'

"You couldn't." Banger wasn't asking. What happened was obvious. It was a windfall for him. He'd been on line to get extra work, be a face in the ringside crowd for the big Mark Cole-Slam Shaughnessy bout. Now he was Shaughnessy, or he would be as soon as Makeup got through with him.

Katie said, "When I finish talking to that bum's agent he'll think he lost a real prizefight. Okay. You can't wear those glasses for this part. You have a set of contacts?"

Banger shook his head. "I'll be okay. I just wear these to drive."

"All right."

A Makeup tech pushed Banger into a chair. "You better take off your shirt. I want to blend the face pancake into your shoulders. They're just shooting you in the dressing room today, and walking to the ring. Once the fight starts we're going to slime you up a little for sweat. Later on we'll do some nice blood and bruises. Slam cuts up Cole but Cole bleeds all over Slam."

"Yeah. Unnerstand." He took off his shirt. He could feel his skin start to pucker in the cold, but he knew he'd be hot under the lights.

Katie was walking away. Banger had put his glasses in his shirt pocket and Katie looked fuzzy. He yelled after her. "There lines I got to study?"

She turned and walked back into focus. She had a thin face, red hair, pale green eyes. The shadows in the big room were fading. She had a clipboard, too. Seemed like they all had clipboards. She looked at it, said, "No. You'll have a few lines, we'll feed 'em to you. We'll talk to Jerry and Hugh about it. Just so you can hit your mark."

"Hit my mark. Mark Cole?"

Katie laughed and walked away. He must have made a joke.

The technician finished him up and he ran by Wardrobe and got outfitted with a pair of trunks and boots and a robe. The robe was imitation satin. On the back it had his character's name in comic book letters surrounded by sequined stars.

They set up the first scene in his dressing room. It wasn't his picture, he knew that. He hadn't seen the script, only heard scuttlebutt in coffee shops, read about it in the trade papers. That, plus what Katie Healy had told him when she phoned to offer him the part of Shaughnessy. Still, she'd told him that he'd get a scene in his—Shaughnessy's—dressing room, and the walk to the ring, and then the fight itself, and then another scene after the fight. They'd intercut that with Mark Cole's scenes. The loser and the winner.

He didn't know the actors around him. He'd had to leave his glasses in his shirt in his locker. Everybody was a little fuzzy and he could feel his heart racing the way it used to before a bout. He'd never been a headline boxer, either, but he remembered the feeling, the mixture of terror and eagerness to get in the ring and get started. The waiting was always the worst.

His manager was there, wearing a suit, a chippie hanging on his arm, cooing in his ear. She reached over and pushed a long red fingernail into Shaughnessy's biceps. She was wearing a diamond ring with a stone the size of an egg and a bracelet that flashed under the bright lights. She made a little squeal and pulled away.

His trainer was a squatty guy in a gray sweatshirt. He had a fringe of black hair around his bald scalp. A cigar hung from his mouth. He was talking, giving Banger instructions, talking about his opponent. The guy was a pushover, a pansy, a perfessor. He din't know nothing about the fight racket. Just wade in and crunch him up, don't try nothin' fancy.

Banger nodded, made grunting noises, "Yeah, yeah, gotcha, yeah, kill him, I'll kill him."

This was the brightest dressing room Banger had used. Jeez, the lights were strong. Hot, too. There was some kind of machine over there, too. He ignored it.

Jerry Valdez said, "Okay, one more dry run."

His manager's chippie poked him with her red fingernail, squealed, pulled away. The lights flashed on her diamonds.

His trainer started his spiel again. The guy was a pushover, a pansy, didn't know nothing, just wade in and crunch him up. Shaughnessy nodded, grunted. "Yeah, yeah, gotcha."

Valdez was a shadowy figure and a voice from behind the light. He said, "Okay, good. Let's get ready for a take."

Somebody came at Shaughnessy and dabbed at his face. It couldn't be his cut man, he hadn't even been in the ring yet. In fact it was a woman. She dabbed something on his face, nodded, turned away, disappeared behind the lights.

People were hollering. Shaughnessy wondered if they were reporters, cops, hangers-on. He could hear them clearly enough even if the things they said didn't make much sense.

"Sound."

"Speed."

"Rolling."

A man stepped in front of the training table. Slam was sitting on the edge of the table, his robe over his shoulders, his hands bandaged, ready for his trainer to slip the gloves on him. The man had his back to him, some kind of square thing in his hands. He said, "Neutron Kid, scene 238, take one." He did something to it and it made a sound almost like a pistol shot.

His manager's chippie poked his arm, squealed, pulled away.

His trainer started in again.

He nodded, grunted.

How many times did it happen? The shot, the chippie, the trainer.

Jerry Valdez yelled, "Print it. Okay."

An assistant director yelled, "Clear the set." The bright lights went off. The room was darker now. Banger Barnes jumped off the training table. His jump was kind of off, he hit the floor a little harder than he'd meant to and he felt the jolt up to his hips but he was okay.

Somebody from Props pulled his gloves off his hands. An AD said,

"You can take the tape off if you want to. It won't show in the walk scene."

Another AD said, "Take a lunch break. Set up for 239, Slam's walk-to-the-ring, in ninety minutes."

People swirled around. Banger slipped his arms into the sleeves of his robe. He found his locker and got his bifocals out of his shirt. Everything came back into focus.

Katie came over, put her hand on his arm. She still carried her clipboard in her other hand. "Nice job, Banger." She looked up at him and smiled. What a nice smile. She said, "That isn't your actual name, is it? Banger Barnes?"

He said, "Barnes is real. Banger was for fighting. Sounded nice. The sportswriters liked it. I got so used to it, I kept it when I retired."

Katie said, "Catering truck's outside. You sure you want to keep that robe on? Don't spill anything on it. You'll need it for the next scene."

Banger said, "I'll be careful."

He stood in line at the catering truck, behind a couple of technicians who were studying a morning LA *Times*. They were pointing to a photo of a bloody crime scene, handing the paper back and forth, talking about the increase in drive-by shootings, gang wars, strong-arm crime in the metropolitan area.

Banger handed his tray up to the window, got a piece of chicken and some broccoli stalks, filled a cardboard cup with coffee, and looked for a seat at one of the long lunch tables.

All of the extras were sitting at one table. They didn't mix with the actors or the crew. Banger carried his tray past them. Some of them looked away. A couple smiled at him. He could read their minds. Why Barnes? Why not me? What's it take to get out of the crowd scene and get a part, even a bit, even a walk-on? Why Barnes?

An actor gestured him over. He put his tray on the table and pulled out a folding chair. He was sitting with his trainer, his manager, his manager's chippie.

Why Barnes, he asked himself. Because he was a real fighter. There was no substitute for the real thing. He'd been there, he knew the footwork, he knew the moves. He knew the feel of your fist thudding into an opponent's ribs. He knew the feel of hard leather crushing your nose. He knew the joy of dancing around the ring while thousands of people cheered for you. He knew the baffled despair of lying on your back, trying to focus on the referee's fingers, squinting against the glare of the ring lights while the crowd cheered for the other fighter.

His trainer introduced himself, shook Banger's hand. "Nice job this morning. Healy says you used to be a real boxer."

Banger said, "Yeah."

His trainer introduced him to the other actors, to the man who played his manager and the woman who played the chippie. They both shook his hand.

The chippie said, "You really never acted before?"

Banger said, "Only extra work. It isn't much but it sure beats dishwashing or janitor work."

"But you can do better than that. I mean—and all the money you made fighting."

Banger laughed bitterly. He had to take a swallow of coffee before he answered her. The coffee was hot and strong. One thing about movie work, even extra work, they had good coffee on the set. It was a long hard day and if they didn't have coffee to keep them going, they'd use other things. That was more extra scuttlebutt. Who was on pep pills, who was on speed, who was on cocaine.

They didn't do it for fun, they did it to get up as high as they had to, to work, and to work a ten-, twelve-, fourteen-hour day. And then they needed booze to get them unwired at night. Booze or grass or Valium or horse.

It was an occupational hazard.

He put down his cardboard cup.

"You ought to know better than that. Your boyfriend there takes his bite of every purse." He pointed a chicken bone at his trainer, said, "He gets another piece." He glared at the chippie. "I must have paid for those sparklers you like to flash. What did they cost? How many jabs did I have to throw, how many hooks did I have to take to pay for your fancy bracelets?"

She looked puzzled. She said, "Those aren't mine. Look, I had to give them back to Props." She held her hands toward him. The long, polished fingernails were still there but the diamond ring, the diamond bracelet were gone.

His trainer said, "They're only props anyhow, Banger. Paste. You don't think they'd use real jewelry, do you?"

Banger shook his head. "No." He managed a feeble laugh. "No, I just— sorry. I kind of . . ."

His manager said, "It can happen, don't be embarrassed. You get into a role, you kind of stay in character sometimes. The role takes you over. Can happen to anybody."

Banger said, "Yeah."

"Especially since you were a real boxer. Say, I used to follow boxing a little. I remember you. You were ranked, weren't you?"

"Not very high."

"Even so." His manager made a sweeping gesture. "You were somebody. You know, you counted. They wrote about you in the boxing magazines. People knew who you were."

Banger said, "Yeah."

His trainer looked at his watch. He said, "Still a little time. It's nice out. I'm going to have a stroll before we go back to work."

He carried his tray away from the table. The others followed suit. Banger, too. He scraped the chicken bones and the rest of his trash into a barrel and left the tray for the caterers. Then he went looking for the set for the afternoon's shooting.

He felt a hand on his arm and knew without turning around that it was Katie Healy. She said, "Okay, this is a long tracking shot, Banger. You don't have any lines. It's just you walking to the ring with your entourage."

He said, "What entourage?"

She consulted her clipboard. "Your manager, trainer, cut man, bodyguards, boxing groupies."

"All I do is walk to the ring?"

"That's all."

"Okay."

Katie said, "You looked good this morning. Jerry's pleased."

Banger didn't say anything.

Katie said, "You're a member of the guild, aren't you?"

"Since they merged with the extras."

"You never know, you might get some more work."

"I can use it."

The set was like a real arena. The ring was in the middle with a huge light fixture above it. The canvas and ropes looked real, the iron steps leading up to the apron. The timekeeper's table and the press tables were in place, vacant, waiting for officials in fancy dress and reporters in shirtsleeves to take their places.

There were only a few rows of seats on two sides of the ring, and a few seats on either side of the long pathway that led to the ring. On the far side were cameras and lights.

Nobody blew a whistle or sounded a bell or hollered when it was time to work. People appeared, lighting technicians and sound engineers, camera operators and assistant camera operators and focus pullers and assistant directors and property masters and costumers and makeup technicians.

The extras filed in. Each of them had a slip of paper. Each of them found the right seat in the mock auditorium.

Suddenly the timekeeper was in his place and the reporters were in theirs. The referee was in the center of the ring and Slam fidgeted at the head of the runway, surrounded by his entourage.

Still photogs aimed their Leicas and Ektars. One veteran even hefted a massive, ancient Speed Graphic.

A pair of metal guides like railroad tracks ran down the center of the runway. The Paniflex was mounted on a sitting dolly with a cameraman behind the eyepiece. A boom mike hung over the actors.

An AD hit the clapboard.

Slam Shaughnessy and his entourage started forward. His handlers were pawing him, urging advice on him. Women reached for him, wanting to touch the hem of his robe, wanting to feel his glove, his face before he climbed into the ring. His bodyguards shoved them away.

He nodded agreement to everything his handlers told him. He grinned and waved to the crowd. The extras waved back at him. Some of them cheered. More of them booed, hurled angry comments. Clearly, it was Mark Cole's crowd.

Somebody held up a sign and waved it. It read, *Mark Cole—Neutron Kid—New Champ.* Somebody started a chant and in seconds the crowd had taken it up. *New-Tron! New-Tron! New-Tron!*

The dolly was rolling backward along its metal guides. The lights half blinded Banger. He started to reach for his glasses, then remembered they were back in his locker. And he couldn't wear them on-camera anyhow. He tried to remember what Valdez had told him. Valdez himself, the director, not Katie Healy or any other AD.

Hit your marks. They're red tape. Ignore the green tape, that's Hugh Keating's marks. And ignore the black tape. That's for the referee.

Who was Hugh Keating? The crowd was roaring and he hadn't even reached the ring yet. Keating, right, he was the star. The top male star. He was Mark Cole, the Neutron Kid. And Banger Barnes was Slam Shaughnessy, the reigning champ, the bad guy.

He was the champ. That meant that the challenger had to be in the ring already. He tried to see past the lights, past the rolling dolly. He could make out a couple of figures in the ring now. At first when he looked it had been only the referee in his black pants and white shirt and little bow tie. Now he could see the Neutron Kid, too, in his radioactive green robe, bouncing around the ring, waving to the reporters and the crowd, to the bit players and the extras, waiting for the champ to arrive.

Slam arrived at ringside.

Jerry Valdez yelled, "Cut."

Slam started up the iron steps.

Valdez yelled again, "I said, Cut."

Slam felt an AD's hand on his shoulder. "Din' you hear Jerry?" Banger blinked. The AD was pretty close. Slam could see his face. He looked annoyed.

"Sorry. Sorry. I was just into the scene."

"Yeah. Hunnert-fiddy people on the set. You know what that costs per minute? This is *The Neutron Kid*, not *Rocky*."

"I'm sorry."

Banger turned and started back up the runway. He bounced off Jerry Valdez, who was studying a videotape of the scene. Banger said, "I'm sorry."

Valdez huddled with a couple of ADs and the cinematographer. Banger stood with his entourage at the top of the runway. He tried to get a look at the extras lining the runway but they were only a parti-colored blur.

The Valdez group broke up and ADs rearranged Slam's entourage. Now there was a woman in a low-cut red dress on one side and his trainer in his gray sweatshirt on the other. The woman in the red dress wore sparkling gems. A couple of burly bodyguards flanked the trio. A woman from Makeup darted into the group and sprayed glycerin on the bodyguards' bald skulls.

Valdez said, "Okay, we're going to run through it again. On video only."

They repeated the roll. Valdez was happier.

By late afternoon they had a take. By the time they had four takes, Valdez called a coffee-and-relief break. Banger had to get a prop master to take his gloves off for him. He had to go something fierce, and barely made it to the bathroom in time.

The producer had rented a huge building for the shoot, an abandoned computer factory that hadn't found a new permanent tenant, and there were lavatories galore. Slam Shaughnessy's dressing room set was some onetime executive's office. The arena itself had been set up in an area that must have been a main assembly room for the computer plant, and the cafeteria must once have been a shipping dock.

Banger drank a cup of coffee standing at the table in front of the huge urn, then took another cup and a donut and sat down. One of the extras sat with him. There was one set of rules for mealtime, another for breaks. Banger wondered if this was the same extra who'd waved the Neutron Kid sign. Banger didn't have his glasses and he couldn't be sure.

The extra shook his hand and introduced himself. He said, "Everybody envies you."

Banger said, "I was lucky. And I know boxing.'

The extra said, "You know the story line."

Banger said, "I just show up when they call me. This is about boxing, right?"

The extra said, "You ought to stop in the production office and look at the script. Hey, now that you're a real actor, they might even give you a copy."

Banger started to answer but an AD was hollering and shepherding people back onto the arena set.

Jerry Valdez stood near the iron steps outside the ring. He said, "We're doing fine, everyone. We're going to bring this thing in on time and budget. The company and the network will love us for that. But we have to keep pushing. There's time for another scene today. We're going to do this with three cameras, so everybody be on your toes. All right?"

Banger looked around. Everybody was nodding and pledging his all to the success of *The Neutron Kid*.

Valdez said, "Now, Mark Cole, Slam, ring announcer, initial positions please. I can't emphasize the importance of hitting your marks too much. With three cameras, we have to stay in focus and we can't block each other off. No prima donnas here, I know that. We're all professionals, right?"

Everybody agreed.

Banger stood with his hands up while Valdez gave his pep talk. A prop master fitted his gloves back on. Banger dropped to one knee for a second and found his first marks A good broad strip of red tape on the canvas.

He stood back up and looked at the mark. It was fuzzy but he could make it out. He stood with one toe on the mark. A focus puller stuck a measuring tape against his nose and said, "Hold this." Banger managed to grasp the tape between the thumb and body of his glove. The focus puller got back to his camera and said, "Okay, thanks." Banger let go.

The ring announcer took his place and Hugh Keating took his, and they walked through the scene a few times.

Then Valdez ordered a take, studied the video rush with a couple of ADs, then conferred with somebody who might have been the writer. They held a conference with the ring announcer, then tried another dry run. The ring announcer's lines were shorter.

Between takes Banger scanned the ringside seats. He spotted a remembered face in the front row, sitting between a couple of mock celebrities. She had shimmering honey-colored hair and wore a sexy emerald-colored dress. Without his glasses, Banger couldn't see any more detail but he knew she was Helen Silver, the female lead in the film.

Extra scuttlebutt said that her former name was Ellie Silverstein. It took a nose job to get her into the movies. Her habit of powdering her nose from the inside out had got her into a series of legal scrapes and rehab programs and very nearly ended her career. Now she was trying for her umpteenth comeback, making a TV movie-of-the-week and hoping to get back onto the big screen.

By the time they finished the ring announcement shoot it was seven-thirty. Valdez called for a five-thirty start the next day. Technicians started shutting down the set while the cast and extras scattered.

Katie Healy caught up with Banger on his way to the Honda. He'd dressed without showering. He was hustling between the trailers when Katie reached out of the studio trailer and pulled him in by the shoulder.

She was sitting with a gray-haired man in a tweed jacket and button-down shirt and tie. The gray-haired man shook Banger's hand. "Meldrum Cornell," he said.

Banger started to give his own name.

Cornell said, "I know who you are. Just wanted to thank you for stepping in at the last moment. Katie told you what happened with your predecessor in the role. You know we have to run a tight ship here. *Neutron Kid* isn't *Rocky*." He paused. "Or *Heaven's Gate*."

Cornell and Healy laughed. Banger joined in. He'd heard it before. Katie Healy handed him a fat script, multicolored pages held together with brass clips. She said, "You can take this home and study it, Banger. It's a numbered copy. Make sure it gets back here with you. We're shooting 171 through 199 tomorrow. Read those. See you in the morning."

He knew he'd been dismissed. He trotted toward the Honda. It was a square-back model, a funny kind of mini-station wagon. That was why Chim Hughes had bought it. It had room for his string bass in the rear compartment. It was cheap, too. The rusted-out body and the smoking exhaust that would never pass an honest smog check accounted for that.

Banger pushed the Honda as fast as he dared on the freeway, checked the cheap digital clock taped to the dashboard, and saw that it was a quarter after eight by the time he passed Chim's apartment. No way that Chim would still be in Hollywood. Banger headed for Santa Monica.

He pulled into the Tiger's Den parking lot fronting on Olympic. On a Monday night the Tiger's Den was mostly empty and business would be dead. But the Wayne Masters Trio needed every nickel they could earn and the owner of the Den let them play for tips and a tiny cut of the Den's receipts.

A couple of black-and-whites were pulled up in front of the nudie bar across Olympic. Banger took off his glasses and cleaned them, feeling crusty and stale after his day's work. He really needed a long, hot shower, but he'd wanted to get to the Den, let Chim know that he'd brought the Honda, and would make good for Chim's cab fare.

Whatever had happened at the nudie bar must just have happened because there hadn't even been time for a crowd to gather on the sidewalk. Banger could see somebody lying in front of the bar, a cop standing over him with his revolver to the suspect's head. The poor sap on the sidewalk looked like a junior high school student. He wore a baseball cap with the bill turned backward.

Another youngster came running out of the nudie bar waving a gun. He wore the same kind of cap and had a huge scar on one cheek. The cop standing on the sidewalk jerked his arm up to point his weapon at the newcomer.

The prone figure swung a fist awkwardly. It had to be awkward with him lying on his face, but it was good enough to jolt against the cop's wrist. The man running from the bar fired once and the cop fell. The two men sprinted away, disappearing around the corner. More cops came pouring from the bar and jumped into the black-and-whites. They took off in full flashers-and-siren mode.

The door of the Tiger's Den swung open and a couple emerged onto the sidewalk, quarreling. Banger slipped inside and let his eyes adjust from the darkness outside to the deeper darkness inside.

The trio were on their low bandstand playing a schmaltzy version of some standard. Banger recognized "Body and Soul." There were barflies on about half the stools and diners at a third of the tables. Dorothy was holding down the hostess station.

She wore a tawny angora sweater and a gold-and-cloisonné tiger pin. Her glasses hung on her chest by a neck cord.

"Banger, how are you?"

He said, "I'm good, Dorothy. I'm pretty tired but I'm good."

"Chim says you been working."

"Yeah. Playing a boxer."

She laughed. "Chim was pissed."

Banger said, "About the car. I know."

"You owe him."

"I know."

"You want a table?"

Banger shook his head. "I'll get a snack at the bar. I'll leave the keys for Chim. I'll catch a bus back."

Dorothy said, "Better not. Chim wants to see you. Hang around, talk to him at the break. Besides, Wayne's got a new kid trying out for the band. Supposed to sound like Chet Baker. You ought to listen to him."

Banger hoisted himself onto a barstool. On one side a drunk was crying softly between slugs of rye. He had a fedora on the back of his head, like somebody out of a late-night movie. On the other side a sharp-faced woman smoked furiously and scribbled numbers on a yellow pad, not looking up when she reached for a rickey glass between deep drags on her cigarette.

The bartender gave Banger a cup of coffee, straight no chaser. A waitress brought him a T-bone and a baked potato.

Wayne Masters introduced the kid who was supposed to sound like Chet Baker. The kid looked like a high school sophomore. He wore his hair in a pompadour and a sports jacket and a shirt with a rolled collar and a narrow tie. He might have fallen into the Den through a time warp. He was pure 1950.

He signaled to Chim with his trumpet and Chim started a slow walk on his bass that sounded like a heart beating. Wayne Masters sat at the piano and Mike Le Conte sat behind his drum kit and they watched.

The kid put his trumpet to his lips and started playing, so softly at first that Banger couldn't even hear him. Then the kid came on, never rushing, never playing very loud, playing "My Funny Valentine."

The drunk to Banger's right dropped his face onto his arms and started crying seriously. The woman on Banger's left jammed her pad and pencil into her purse and swung around on her stool, watching the kid play.

After the set Banger swiveled through diners' tables and handed Chim the keys to the Honda. "You saved my life, Chim. I owe you one, buddy."

Chim was holding a glass of water. He slipped the keys into his tuxedo trousers and handed another set back to Banger. "You bet. Big time. I figured, if your Pontiac's dead you're just gonna hit me up to use the Honda again tomorrow, so I called my friend Benny Mechanic and had him take a look at it. Your fuel pump was shot. He installed a recon'd unit and put a charge on your battery. You're all set."

Banger held his head. "That's gonna cost. Where's the Pontiac now?"

"In back. I'm surprised you didn't see it when you came into the Den."

"Too much distraction. Some kind of upset across the street."

Chim took a sip of water, then put the glass down on a coaster on top of Wayne's piano. He said, "Did you hear that kid? Too good for us by far. Wayne will hire him for a while, then he'll be gone." He picked up his glass. "I'm going in back, put my feet up for a little. You gonna stay?"

Banger said, "I gotta clean up, get a few hours shuteye. Early call tomorrow."

The temperature had dropped outside the Den, and the nudie bar across the street was closed off with yellow police tape.

The Pontiac ran like a watch.

Ω

Makeup took longer this morning. The technician said, "We have to put on a good base. Jerry wants to get the whole fight in the can today. I don't see how he can do it. This is a twenty-three day shoot. That's four minutes a day for a TV feature. The fight is supposed to run something like twelve minutes. I don't see how he can do it in one day, but I guess that's why Cornell hired him."

Katie Healy came by and asked if Banger had read the script. He said, "I soaked in the tub with it. I didn't have time to read the whole thing, I just read the fight."

Katie said, "That's okay. You don't need to know the rest of it."

"Calls for a pretty tough fight."

"Meldrum insisted. He likes to push the network as far as he can. He strike you as a refined gentleman?"

"I guess so."

"Well he is. He's also bloodthirsty. He gets what he wants. He cultivates that tweedy look. He's a shark. They're all sharks." She narrowed her eyes, gave Banger an odd look. "Me included." The technician took Banger's glasses, handed them to him to put in his pocket. Katie said, "Just remember to hit your marks."

Glasses in his pocket, the Makeup tech working on him, Banger couldn't make out Katie's expression.

Jerry Valdez said, "We don't have time to do all the shots separately on this sequence. We're going with three cameras again. This is a twelve-round bout, two-minute rounds and one minute rests, that would be thirty-five minutes in real time. We're going twelve minutes screen time. We'll shoot silent and add wild sound. We'll have ADs to coach you through this. We'll shoot the corners tomorrow and cut them in between rounds. And keep your mouthpieces in. They change the shape of your face. If you lose 'em, the audience will spot it. Everybody ready? Walk through round one."

It was tougher than half of Banger's real bouts had been. Both fighters started clean and dry. Whenever Valdez yelled "Freeze!" Makeup techs would run out and spray glycerin for sweat. They used water for the referee's shirt. After a couple of rounds the ring lights got so hot that Banger and Hugh Keating were sweating under their own power.

In the third round Slam Shaughnessy was supposed to open a cut in the Neutron Kid's eyebrow. A technician took care of that. A trickle of blood ran into Keating's eye, then down the edge of his nose.

In the fifth round Mark Cole raised a mouse above Shaughnessy's eye. Cole's cut man had closed up his eyebrow with a stapler and put Vaseline on it. In the sixth round, Shaughnessy reopened the cut. It bled heavily. The eye was closing, but the mouse over Shaughnessy's eye was puffing up and Cole opened a cut on the bridge of Shaughnessy's nose and the blood was running into both his eyes.

The referee checked both fighters in their corners after the sixth round, then let them continue.

In the ninth, Shaughnessy staggered Cole with a series of hooks to the body. He nearly had him finished, aimed a hard cross to the jaw but missed. Cole hung on until the bell. Shaughnessy shoved him off and watched him stumble back to his corner.

Shaughnessy slumped into his stool, took a mouthful of water from the ladle, and spit it into a cup. His handlers were all over him, giving instructions, urging him on. He heard the bell for the start of round ten. His trainer slipped Shaughnessy's mouthpiece between his teeth and boosted him toward Cole.

He heard somebody yelling advice to him, squinted through puffy eyes, trying to keep up with the younger Kid. Slam Shaughnessy was the old champ, out to crunch up the young challenger. He should have finished Cole earlier but he hadn't been able to put him away. Now he knew he couldn't but he was ahead on points. If he could look good for a couple of rounds he'd still be the winner, the judges hated to take the crown from a champ on points.

Round eleven. He was almost blind but he thought the Kid wasn't in much better shape. Slam threw a couple of roundhouse rights. The Kid danced away. Slam lost his balance, went to one knee. He looked up. The referee signaled no knockdown, but when Slam struggled to his feet the ref looked into his face, trying to see his eyes.

Slam said, "I'm okay. I slipped." He didn't know if the ref could understand him. He spit out his mouthpiece, said it again.

The ref signaled Slam and the Kid to go at it, but the bell sounded almost before they could move.

Between rounds one of Slam's handlers retrieved his mouthpiece and shoved it between his teeth. Some woman got into the ring and told Slam what to do in the twelfth round. He couldn't remember who she was. He blinked, trying to see the color of her dress through the blood running into his eyes. She looked familiar but he couldn't identify her.

The bell sounded. He started for the center of the ring but his legs were rubbery and his fists each weighed a thousand pounds. The Neutron Kid was a faint blur, moving around him like a wolf circling a lamb. Slam turned, turned, trying to keep the Kid in his sights.

He lost him for a moment. He blinked, trying to clear his head, trying to see his opponent.

Somehow the Kid had circled around, sneaked up and blindsided him. He saw the punch coming but he couldn't move. He felt it connect, felt himself swimming slowly through hot, moist air, heard the thump as he hit the canvas, facedown. He heard the referee counting, heard the crowd cheering. But they were supposed to be shooting MOS—silent—and add the sound later.

Then he was in the first aid room. A nurse was dabbing at him and Katie Healy and Jerry Valdez were there.

The nurse said, "This man isn't injured at all. Look, all of these bruises and injuries are makeup. He's just exhausted. He just needs a little rest."

Valdez said, "Will he be able to work tomorrow? We got the fight. God, Katie, you wouldn't believe it. It's going to make this thing a hit. Cornell is going to love us all. You remember Kirk Douglas in *Champion?* Do you think he'll be able—what's his name?"

Katie said, "Barnes."

"Able to work tomorrow? We can shoot around him, move up 282 through 304. Do the cut-ins end of the week, even Monday if we have to. We don't wrap 'til next Friday."

Banger closed his eyes.

He heard Valdez say, "Take a day off. Take two days off. Get back here Friday, we'll do the cut-ins, Barnes. That'll finish your scenes. You did good, old tiger."

Banger grunted some kind of thank-you.

Ω

He pulled the Pontiac in behind the Tiger's Den, feeling a thousand percent better. A whole day in bed—or on the couch. A few solid meals.

A couple of good hot soaks.

Across Olympic from the Den, the yellow tape was gone from the nudie bar and the establishment was back in business.

The Den was almost full tonight. Dorothy met him at the door wearing a tailored jacket and blouse over a dark skirt. She had transferred the tiger pin from her sweater to the lapel of the jacket. She said, "You're looking good, Banger. I could almost marry you again."

He raised his eyebrows. Even in the dark Den he knew she could see his face by the reflected light of the lamp on the hostess station.

She said, "Just kidding."

He slid into the last vacant barstool in the place. He ordered his usual steak and coffee. It wouldn't keep him up tonight. He felt too good. He would finish his week on *The Neutron Kid*, collect a nice paycheck, look for a place of his own so he could get off Chim's couch and start to have a life again.

He stayed through the first set and into the second. Dorothy came over and put her arm around his shoulders and they listened to the kid play "All the Things You Are."

The Den was almost empty now. The late crowds only came on weekends. Other nights it was an early to mid-evening house.

The door swung open and somebody shouted. Banger swung around on his stool. Two youngsters stood near the doorway, shouting confusing instructions. They both wore baseball caps, their bills turned backward. One had a huge scar on his cheek. They were waving machine pistols. Customers were diving for the floor. The bartender disappeared. The Wayne Masters Trio dropped their instruments, all except for the kid with the trumpet. He stood with his eyes closed, still playing the corny "All the Things You Are."

One gunman ran halfway across the restaurant, pointed his machine pistol at the trumpeter and cut him in half with a short burst of bullets. The second gunman pointed his machine pistol at the bar and raked the back bar mirror and the bottles standing beneath it.

Banger launched himself off his barstool, away from Dorothy, straight at the nearer gunman. He knocked the gunman's weapon aside with his right hand, landed a solid left to the gunman's face. He felt the satisfying crunch of knuckles against jawbone.

The second gunman turned back from the bandstand and cut his partner and Banger in half with the same volley.

Ω

As the great Gene Wolfe has pointed out, there are readers who dislike authors' notes, introductions and other such paraphernalia. They prefer their stories straight, no chaser. Theirs is a logically and aesthetically defensible position. I have no quarrel with them. And if there are any such persons in the room right now, they are hereby excused.

On the other hand, there are readers who enjoy learning the background of their favorite reading matter, the reasons for and circumstances in which the stories were written, the authors' inspiration. In a word: their context. I will admit that I am one such, and for those who share my outlook, I provide the following commentary:

- "The Laddie in the Lake." Nicholas Train—he was originally plain Nick Train—was the first detective I ever invented. His one case was published in a camp newspaper when I was somewhere around nine years old and is apparently lost to posterity. Gordon Van Gelder, my onetime editor first at St. Martin's Press and later at *The Magazine of Fantasy and Science Fiction*, suggested that I bring him back, and this story, set in August of 1946, is the result. (Published as a separate pamphlet by Crippen & Landru, Douglas Greene editor. Copyright © 2008 by Richard A. Lupoff.)

- "What it Means." Once I'd started writing about Nick Train I found myself wondering about his earlier life. I began to explore the subject in this story, set in March of 1946. (Published in *Hardboiled* magazine for January, 2007, Gary Lovisi editor. Copyright © 2007 by Richard A. Lupoff.)

- "Benning's School for Boys." Delving further into Nick Train's background, we meet Nick as an army recruit early in 1942. (Originally published in *The Mammoth Book of Perfect Crimes and Impossible Mysteries*, Mike Ashley editor. Copyright © 2006 by Richard A. Lupoff.)

For what it's worth, I was still not satisfied so I tracked Nick Train back to his days as a young police officer, circa 1938. The result was a novel, *Rookie Blues*, which now resides in my computer, very nearly finished.

- "The Square Root of Dead." Michael Kurland and I spent most of the summer of 1975 working on a collaborative novel which, alas, never found a publisher. But a minor by-product of that exercise was this little story, first written at shorter length by me and then revised and expanded by Michael. The original version seems to be lost, but the revised text did find a home. My recollection is that my share of the proceeds, once all was said and done, was $36 for three months' work. (Originally published in *Mike Shane's Mystery Magazine*, September, 1976, Sam Merwin editor. Copyright © 1976 by Michael Kurland and Richard A. Lupoff.)

- "Triptych." One critic theorized that this story reveals a deep-seated hostility toward women on my part. He may have been right, but I don't really think so. To paraphrase the famous Viennese, "Sometimes a story is just a story." (Originally published in *Detective Story Magazine*, Gary Lovisi editor, copyright © 1990 by Richard A. Lupoff.)

- "Old Folks at Home." After writing seven novels about the detective team of Hobart Lindsey and Marvia Plum, I found them living apart and absent from each other's lives. I had planned an eighth novel to wrap up the series, but I was nervous about bringing them together again. This story was something of a dry run. (Originally published in *One Murder at a Time: The Casebook of Lindsey and Plum*, copyright 2001, Richard A. Lupoff.)

After suffering through a truly monumental writer's block, I finally figured out what I'd been doing wrong and how to do it right, and I did write that eighth novel. It's called *The Emerald Cat Killer* (St. Martin's Press, 2010) and I will be very pleased if you choose to purchase a copy.

- "Dogwalker." Like most of my stories, this one contains elements of autobiography, but the reader is cautioned not to take it too literally. I wrote it for a contest sponsored by a leading mystery magazine. When it failed to win prize money I simply resubmitted it to the same magazine and the editor was quick to accept it at standard rates. (Originally published in *Ellery Queen's Mystery Magazine*, April, 1996, Janet Hutchings editor. Copyright ©1996 by Richard A. Lupoff.)

- "Inga Sigerson Weds." Breathes there a mystery writer who has never attempted a Sherlockian pastiche? Probably so, but I suspect that he or she would find him-or-herself in the minority. My friend Michael

Kurland had asked me for a contribution to an anthology of Sherlock Holmes stories set in the United States. I asked Michael why and how Holmes happened to be in the US. At this point Michael was struck speechless – a rare state for him. I volunteered to write a story answering these questions, and Michael was quick to commission the story. (Originally published in *Sherlock Holmes: The American Years*, Michael Kurland editor. Copyright © 2010 by Richard A. Lupoff.)

- "You Don't Know Me, Charlie." Although I'm fond of hardboiled mysteries—Dashiell Hammett occupies a special place in my literary pantheon—most of my own stories are of a different nature. This one is an exception. (Originally published in *New Orleans Stories*, O'Neil DeNoux editor and in *Hardboiled* magazine for August, 1993, Gary Lovisi editor. Copyright © 1993 by Richard A. Lupoff.)

- "Patterns." Most of my stories are fairly conventional in presentation, but this one seemed to cry out for a different format, and to my delight it landed me for the second time in the world's most prestigious mystery magazine. (Originally published in *Ellery Queen's Mystery Magazine*, December, 2009, Janet Hutchings editor. Copyright © 2009 by Richard A. Lupoff.)

- "Cinquefoil." The first time I read a Nero Wolfe novel I just didn't get it, and thereafter I avoided Rex Stout's great creation for decades. Then my friend Art Scott persuaded me to try another, and this time I did get it—and became a devoted fan of the World's Fattest Detective. "Cinquefoil" is a slightly tongue-in-cheek tribute to Nero and Archie and their world. (Originally published in *One Murder at a Time: The Casebook of Lindsey and Plum*, copyright © 2001 by Richard A. Lupoff.)

- "Streamliner." Historian, scholar, and author *extraordinaire* Jim Harmon has edited several collections of stories designed to capture the thrills and chills that listeners of a certain generation enjoyed while huddled in front of their cathedral-topped radios on many a dark and stormy night. The stories were often over the top, and this one, I won't deny, pushes the limits just a little bit. Or maybe more than a little bit. But I think it's fun. (Originally published in *It's That Time Again 3*, Jim Harmon editor. Copyright © 2008 by Richard A. Lupoff.)

- "Easy Living." It's popular belief that all fiction is to some degree autobiographical. I have grave doubts about that assertion, but I don't want to get into a debate over it. Nevertheless, I will say that this story combines my brief flirtation, as a very young man, with the sweet science of fisticuffs, with my later experiences on a movie set in Hollywood. (Originally published in *Warriors of Blood and Dream*, Roger Zelazny editor. Copyright © 1995 by Richard A. Lupoff.)

- "Introduction." Copyright © 2010 by Ed Gorman.

www.ingramcontent.com/pod-product-compliance
Lightning Source LLC
Chambersburg PA
CBHW050507260626
47157CB00004B/1218